ENCOUNTER

VOICES FROM ASIA

1. *Of Women, Outcastes, Peasants, and Rebels: A Selection of Bengali Short Stories.* Translated and edited by Kalpana Bardhan.
2. *Himalayan Voices: An Introduction to Modern Nepali Literature.* Translated and edited by Michael James Hutt.
3. *Shoshaman: A Tale of Corporate Japan.* By Arai Shinya. Translated by Chieko Mulhern.
4. *Rainbow.* By Mao Dun. Translated by Madeleine Zelin.
5. *Encounter.* By Hahn Moo-Sook. Translated by Ok Young Kim Chang.

ENCOUNTER

BY HAHN MOO-SOOK

A Novel of
Nineteenth-Century Korea

Translated by Ok Young Kim Chang

UNIVERSITY OF CALIFORNIA PRESS
BERKELEY   LOS ANGELES   OXFORD

Encounter is a translation of *Mannam*, published
in Seoul in 1986 by Chongum-sa.

University of California Press
Berkeley and Los Angeles, California

University of California Press, Ltd.
Oxford, England

Library of Congress Cataloging-in-Publication Data

Han, Mu-suk, 1918–
    [Mannam. English]
    Encounter / Hahn Moo-Sook ;
translated by Ok Young Kim Chang.
        p.   cm. — (Voices from Asia ; 5)
    Translation of: Mannam.
    Includes bibliographical references.
    ISBN 0-520-07380-0. — ISBN 0-520-07381-9 (pbk.)
        1. Chŏng, Yak-yong, 1762–1836—Fiction. 2. Chŏng, Ha-sang,
1795–1839—Fiction. I. Title. II. Series.
PL992.26.M8M3613   1992
895.7'34—dc20   91-32825
                                                            CIP

Printed in the United States of America
9 8 7 6 5 4 3 2 1

The paper used in this publication meets the minimum
requirements of American National Standard for
Information Sciences—Permanence of Paper for Printed
Library Materials, ANSI Z39.48–1984. ∞

Contents

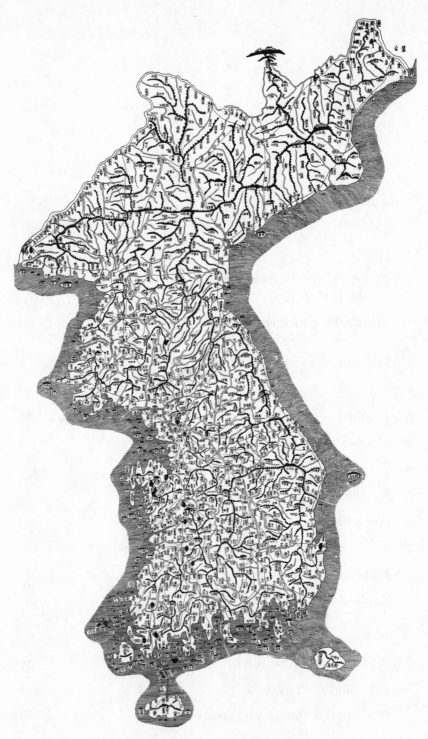

Taedong yojido: A Yi dynasty map of Korea. Drawn in 1861 by
Kim Chong ho.

of extraordinary courage, dedication, and spirituality. They see him as a giant of their faith, a model of virtue and piety they should strive to emulate.

His uncle, Tasan, is widely revered by the Korean public at large, though more for his scholarship than for his religious life. A bronze statue of Tasan stands in the Seoul city park on Namsan; Tasan Road runs through Seoul; and literally hundreds of academic articles on various aspects of Tasan's thought rest on the shelves of Korean university libraries. Just as Ha-sang is considered one of the most important figures in the history of Korean Catholicism, Tasan is regarded as one of the most important thinkers in the history of Korean Confucianism.

To build a realistic novel around such icons, to give the heroes of *Encounter* the conflicting emotions, the moral frailty, and the moments of doubt that would make them fully human and thus enable ordinary readers to believe in them and empathize with them, would contradict the larger-than-life images of Ha-sang and Tasan most Korean readers bring to this novel. Yet a story that focuses solely on the saintly and sagely aspects of its revered protagonists' lives risks becoming lifeless and remote from the everyday concerns of its readers. Hahn escapes the horns of this dilemma by an ingenious borrowing from Korean tradition.

Clearly, Hahn Moo-Sook is capable of creating realistic characters with the insecurities and foibles characteristic of ordinary men and women. In fact, through her earlier writings, she earned a reputation for weaving introspective, psychological tales of egocentric characters suffering from loneliness, melancholy, or alienation brought on by their own mistakes or failings. In stories such as "Taeyŏlsogesŏ" (Among the Marching Columns) and "Ch'ŏnsa" (The Angel), for example, she focuses more on what her characters feel than on what they do. And what they feel is unhappiness, nihilism, and despair. The disillusioned former anti-Japanese nationalist in "The Angel" is emblematic of this early fiction when he states, "I was entirely wrong to believe that there was some meaning and significance in our lives."[2] Hahn paints the mental state of the student revolutionary in "Among the Marching Columns" in equally

2. "The Angel," in *The Running Water Hermitage*, translated by Chung Chong-wha, 19.

dark colors, describing him as "forever tormented by skepticism, a
sense of alienation, remorse, groping, and unjustifiable rebellion."[3]
    No such feelings are attributed to Chŏng Ha-sang or Chŏng
Tasan, nor could they be. Catholic saints are not skeptics. And Confucian sages are not nihilists. Besides, Encounter is more an epic
drama than an emotional portrait. The encounter Hahn writes about
is not a narrow, individual encounter between two lonely people,
but a multifaceted encounter within and between individuals, on
the one hand, and within and between cultures, on the other.
    Encounter is the story of what happened after Roman Catholi-
cism was smuggled onto the Korean peninsula two centuries ago
and the impact that imported religion had on the people who encountered it, the persecutions and the piety it aroused. It is the story
of an encounter between a scholar of Confucianism and the God of
Christianity, and between Tasan's personal moral integrity and his
pragmatic survival instincts. It is the story of an encounter between
the beliefs and the believers of different faiths—Buddhist, shamanistic, Confucian, and Catholic. It is the story of an encounter between two cultures, two competing worldviews, one Eastern and
one Western. It is also, in its literary form, an encounter between
contemporary Korea and its past and, in this English translation, an
encounter between Western readers and the spirits, beliefs, values,
rituals, and history of the Korean people.
    The proper form for such a monumental drama is not a realistic
character study but an operatic theatrical pageant. Larger-than-life
characters in a larger-than-usual situation demand a larger-than-
normal stage. Hahn is familiar with the dramatist's stage: early in
her career she wrote two plays, Maŭm (The Heart) in 1943 and Sŏlig-
got (Winter Flowers) in 1944. For Encounter, however, she reached
beyond the conventions of westernized modern Korean drama. For
an epic tale set in Korea, with Korean heroes, she adapted an older
Korean form. Her novel transforms into a literary format many of the
modes and themes of the Chosŏn dynasty's one-man opera, p'ansori.
    P'ansori is Korea's version of the solo oral drama performed by
wandering storytellers in cultures the world over. In p'ansori, a
single singer, accompanied only by a drummer, alternately sings
and narrates a story of virtue triumphant and evil defeated. The

    3. "Among the Marching Columns," translated by Kim Chong-un, in In the
Depths, 101–102.

singer performs all the roles in the story and also regularly steps
outside these characters momentarily to become a narrator who pro-
vides the audience with asides and descriptions of the settings in
which the characters are appearing. With one person playing all the
roles, it is impossible to develop fully formed realistic characters.
Instead, each major character represents one particular personality
trait, such as filial piety, loyalty, duplicity, or foolhardiness.

In the early twentieth century, Koreans wanting to match the
spectacle of Peking opera and Japanese Kabuki created an enlarged
version of *p'ansori* called *ch'angguk*. *Ch'angguk* today looks like a
cross between Western opera and *p'ansori*, with a large troupe of
actors and actresses, each assigned only one role, filling the stage.
Yet the stories *ch'angguk* tells are *p'ansori* stories rewritten. Ch'un-
hyang, the faithful courtesan, and Simch'ŏng, the filial daughter,
remain perennial favorites, whether in *p'ansori* or in *ch'angguk*.
And both formats utilize an omniscient narrator, providing a narrative bridge between episodes and voicing for the audience the
moral judgment it is expected to make as the tale unfolds.

Such is the format Hahn borrows for *Encounter*. Her major characters, both historical and fictional, are dramatic personifications of
such admirable virtues as piety and chastity or such despicable
vices as treachery and lust. Both Paul Chŏng, drawn from history,
and Maria Kwŏn, drawn from Hahn's imagination, are paragons of
religious faith, never wavering in their commitment to Catholicism
even when it brings great suffering and then death to themselves
and their families. Not for them the questioning that in real life
often leads to a renewed, stronger faith. They quite literally display
the pure and unconditional piety of saints.

Sŭng Nak-chong, on the other hand, embodies the unmitigated
evil of a true villain. An apostate and an informer against the Catholics who reared him, Sŭng is also a thief and a would-be rapist. Sŭng
is clearly a literary creation; few actual individuals would be so
totally lacking in redeeming qualities. Yet Yi Chi-yŏn (1777–1841),
the prosecutor of Catholics in the persecutions of 1839, appears on
Hahn's pages as equally depraved. Few readers of *Encounter* would
recognize the Yi Hahn describes in the rigid Confucian moralist and
scholar depicted in historical records. The actual Yi Chi-yŏn rose to
the third highest post in the Korean bureaucracy, that of third state
councillor, a position roughly equivalent to deputy prime minister

in a Western parliamentary democracy. Yet in *Encounter* he is driven by lust, not by Confucian values. In fact, as one of the villains of Hahn's story, Yi is the only character in *Encounter* allowed to experience any sexual pleasure. More to the point, that pleasure is derived from sadistic homoerotic fantasies, aroused by the purity of Ha-sang's mind and flesh.

Just as Yi Chi-yŏn symbolizes the baneful influence sexual desire can have on human lives, Ha-sang, Maria Kwŏn, and several other of the more admirable characters in the novel symbolize the ennobling effect of the rejection of lust and the embrace of chastity. Teresa Kwŏn (1783–1819) and Peter Cho Suk (?–1819), for example, were forced to marry to conform to the conventions of the day and to avoid detection as Catholics. Yet they remained celibate, living as brother and sister rather than as husband and wife. Though there is historical evidence documenting their mutual forswearing of the normal conjugal benefits of marriage, such unusual behavior makes them appear more iconic than human.

Even Tasan is denied any real sexual feelings, though his biography and progeny make it impossible to attribute lifelong abstinence to him. Although Hahn gives Tasan a mistress to comfort him in his long years in exile, away from his wife, she takes pains to point out that he did not become involved with P'yo-nyŏ "because he lusted after her; the relationship had been consummated spontaneously as a result of their constant proximity." A Confucian philosopher as revered as Tasan could not possibly be subject to the same sensual urges as ordinary men, at least not in any portrayal delineated with such broad strokes as the ones used in *p'ansori* or *ch'anggŭk*—or in *Encounter*.

Hahn employs the same broad strokes to plot the action in which these characters are involved. *Encounter* is filled with dramatic moments that might appear more plausible on the stage than in real life. In one chapter, for example, two women literally drop out of sight without a sound, as though they have disappeared behind a stage curtain. In other chapters, long-separated relatives cross paths without recognizing each other, and Catholics on the run break into prison to free imprisoned believers who reject rescue in order to stay in prison, "bearing witness to their faith and fulfilling the Christian responsibility of loving their neighbors."

Hahn also describes rural markets and shamanistic rituals with such colorful detail that the scenes almost demand to be transferred to the stage or the silver screen. Long before she was an author, Hahn Moo-Sook was a painter, winning a prize at an International Children's Painting Exhibition in Berlin when she was only eight years old. As a novelist, she retains her artist's eyes. From the opening scene of a Buddhist cremation amid autumn colors to Tasan's death amid the winter frost, Hahn recreates nineteenth-century Korea with a vividness a cinematographer would envy.

Colorful staging, iconic characters, and dramatic scenes are all features of *ch'angguk* that Hahn has transplanted into her novel. She has borrowed the device of setting minor characters with common human weaknesses against the ethereal perfection of her major characters. For example, the death throes of the monk Hyejang (1772–1811) contrast sharply with the saintly calm of the martyrs meeting their death. And Charles Cho Sin-ch'ŏl (1795–1839), who ultimately converts to Catholicism, appears first as a simple, good-hearted man with the humorous habit of calling out the Buddha's name at the slightest provocation in a way none of the Catholics in the novel would call upon the Lord's name. Moreover, many of the minor characters Tasan and Ha-sang encounter, such as old man P'yo and the innkeeper Matteo Hong, speak in countrified accents and act in unsophisticated ways. Unfortunately, English translation cannot do justice to their rustic dialect. But even in translation, enough of their language and rural manner survives to add a touch of humor to the story and to cast in relief the dignified bearing and careful diction of the saints and the sage.

Another feature distinguishing the heroes and heroines of this novel from lesser personalities is that, like stage heroes and heroines, the more admirable characters not only have more beautiful souls, they also have more beautiful bodies. The handsome Ha-sang, with his "supple, youthful flesh," and the lovely Maria Kwŏn, with her "alabaster face . . . like a masterpiece portrait by a supreme artist," are typical of the saints. The villains—such as Sŭng Nak-chong, with his "face white as paper, the irises of his eyes entirely eclipsed," and Yi Chi-yŏn, who twice conjures up in his dreams a vision of his own body ugly with blood and open wounds—are just as vividly and physically set apart. Hahn, true to the *p'ansori* and *ch'anggŭk* traditions, allows no ambiguity about who is to be admired and who despised.

Korea's traditional drama shows its influence in what Hahn does not do as well as in what she does. Although many of the short stories that made her famous are first-person narratives in which the narrators dwell on their own emotions, often with a Buddhist slant toward the unhappiness personal changes can bring, she tells the story of *Encounter* from the standpoint of an omniscient, omnipresent observer. There are no stream-of-consciousness meditations, no solitary ruminations on the meaninglessness and absurdity of life, with its inevitable pain and loss. The characters in *Encounter* suffer just as Hahn's earlier characters did, but here the narrator (and the characters) lets us know that suffering has a purpose. Instead of the story ending with the characters beaten down by "the total fatigue of a strenuous life,"[4] as Mrs. Hong is in "A Halo Around the Moon," in *Encounter* they achieve the glorious, and dramatic, reward of martyrdom. Action, not emotion, becomes all-important. Just as in *p'ansori* and *ch'anggŭk*, plot overshadows psychology and the story receives more attention than anyone's mental state.

The very nature of the tale Hahn chooses to tell, and the characters she chooses to populate it, make dramatic narrative more appropriate than psychological exploration. She restricts herself in another way as well. Since she builds her story around well-known historical figures, she has to work within boundaries defined by the historical records that tell what those figures thought and did.

Novelists such as Hahn Moo-Sook have greater flexibility than historians and other academic time travelers. Scholars are constrained by the data available to them; they must remain close enough to their data that the story they weave appears probable. Novelists, however, need only tell a plausible tale. In other words, as a writer of fiction, even historical fiction, Hahn does not have to worry about what probably happened as long as what she says happened possibly happened.

In that, she succeeds. She recreates an eighteenth and a nineteenth century consistent with the eighteenth and nineteenth centuries depicted in the letters and essays of Tasan and his contemporaries. Tasan lived almost seventy-five years. His lifetime spanned

---

4. "A Halo around the Moon," translated by Chu Yo-sup, in *In the Depths*, 92.

the period when the old order was at the height of its glory and when the first inklings of its unraveling and decline began to appear. Tasan, like Charles Dickens, might have spoken of the best of times and the worst of times.

In the eighteenth century the Korean peninsula was able to feed more Koreans than it had ever fed before, yet Koreans were also dying at an ever-increasing rate, turning rapid population growth into rapid population decline. Factional battles over conflicting interpretations of Confucian ethics and ritual, battles that had distracted Korean politics for over a century, were subsiding just at the time when an even more deadly battle over the viability of Confucianism itself was about to start. Neo-Confucian philosophizing in Korea was reaching new heights of sophistication at a time when its arguments and its key concepts were becoming increasingly irrelevant. And beyond Confucian scholarly circles, a new self-confidence among the peasantry was expressing itself in small, tentative forerunners of the popular uprisings that marked the second half of the nineteenth century. These unsettling demographic, philosophical, and political changes were preparing Confucian Korea for a monotheistic revolution.

Before the nineteenth century, most Koreans did not believe in one Supreme Being. Instead, they believed in hundreds of supernatural entities, some of them playful goblins, some of them protective or malevolent spirits, and a few, such as the Buddha and Hanŭnim, wielding great, but not absolute, influence over the affairs of men. Even the Buddha had to admit shrines to local mountain deities within the confines of his mountain temples in recognition of the less-than-universal sway of his powers and authority.

Hanŭnim, "the Lord of Heaven," whose name is now borrowed by Korean Christians for the Supreme Deity, watched over the weather, individual fate, and political fortunes, but he had to share that power and responsibility with other deities. Under the guise of Ch'ŏnsin ("the heavenly spirit") or Okhwang Sangje ("the Yellow Emperor," the chief deity of Taoism), Hanŭnim was the object of some popular devotions, but he did not appear in shamanistic rituals nearly as often as certain long-dead Chinese generals, nor was he depicted in sacred portraits as frequently as the mountain spirit. He was just one powerful deity among many.

Why the change, a change accurately portrayed in *Encounter*?

Why did large numbers of Koreans (over 20 percent of South Koreans today call themselves Christian) begin to believe in one God whom they should serve and obey, to whom they should turn in times of need, and to whom they should be faithful even unto death?

A rising death rate may have been one factor. As Hahn points out, of Tasan's nine children, only three survived the early years of childhood. In the last quarter of the eighteenth century, this apparently was not an unusual survival rate for Korean families. The population of many villages and towns had grown dense enough to provide a fertile environment for the spread of such deadly childhood diseases as smallpox and measles. In addition, the growing use of irrigation reservoirs for rice farming may have bred malaria-infected mosquitoes, like the one that infected Tasan when he first arrived in the land of his exile. On top of that, cholera reached the Korean peninsula for the first time early in the nineteenth century.

Whatever the cause, and historical records speak of increasingly frequent and virulent epidemics, a population that was 7.3 million strong in 1750 (according to official census figures) had grown to only 7.4 million in 1799. An increase of only 100,000 over the course of almost half a century, or an average increase of approximately 1,700 Koreans a year, is an appallingly low rate, even for a preindustrial society. The first half of the nineteenth century was worse. By 1850 census records counted only 6.4 million Koreans, a drop of a million in just half a century. This was well before the advent of modern birth control techniques. There were fewer and fewer Koreans not because fewer Koreans were being born but because more were dying young.

The sight of children, relatives, friends, and neighbors dying before their time at a quickening rate must have frightened many Koreans and shaken their faith in old beliefs and values. Koreans were no exception to the general tendency of humanity to turn to religion in times of physical and mental distress. The shamanistic rituals in *Encounter* are compelling examples of the Korean use of religion as a medical strategy for coping with disease and death. However, the failure of shamanism to halt or even slow the accelerating death rate may have stimulated some Koreans to look beyond the traditional gods of the folk religion for a more powerful deity to rescue them from their misery.

In the second half of the eighteenth century, specifically in 1758 and again in 1787, there were two instances of peasants' claiming to be the Buddhist messiah incarnate, the Maitreya, and temporarily attracting a large, rebellious following. Such Buddhist millenarianism was a new phenomenon on the peninsula; and it could have been the manifestation of an increasing desperation, a growing hunger for a God powerful enough to quell the evil forces bringing suffering and death into Korean homes. By the second half of the nineteenth century, that desperation brought forth Korea's first indigenous organized monotheistic religion, Tonghak ("Eastern Learning," so called to distinguish it from "Western Learning," i.e., Catholicism), founded in 1860.

The educated elite of Korea, represented in *Encounter* by the Chŏng and Kwŏn families, among others, recoiled from a belief in the spirits of Buddhism and shamanism, which they saw as expressions of ignorance and superstition. They preferred the more rational principles and values of Confucianism. However, developments within their Confucian tradition were driving them toward monotheism as well.

Hahn briefly alludes to a metaphysical debate within Korean Confucian circles over the relative priority of Principle and Material Force. Principle refers to the moral realm, to the universal pattern of selfless harmonious interaction which determines what should and should not be and what should and should not be done. Material Force, on the other hand, refers to the physical world, that world of bodies and individuals with their passions and their differences, which can hinder the smooth operation of Principle. For two centuries before Tasan's time, Korean philosophers vigorously debated how best to deal with the selfish impulses that Material Force generated, which often kept men from acting as selflessly and virtuously as Principle required.

This was no abstract academic debate. Confucian scholars believed that disorders in the natural world, such as epidemics, famine, and a rising death rate, were the direct result of moral disorder in the human world. More Koreans were dying and watching their loved ones die, the scholars argued, because the Confucian elite of Korea was insufficiently virtuous. Consequently, there was a growing demand in Tasan's day for a more effective way to enhance ethical power so that Confucian scholars could overcome the obstructions of Material Force and live in accordance with Principle, improving life for themselves and the other people on the peninsula.

This growing frustration with moral frailty, with their own inability to keep selfish desires consistently in check, may have led Confucians such as Tasan to resurrect the Lord-on-High of the ancient Confucian classics. Matteo Ricci's *True Principles of Catholicism* reinforced this tendency toward a theistic reformulation of Confucianism. Fr. Ricci's argument, that belief in a Supreme Being governing the universe would not only be faithful to the original message of the Confucian sages of old but would also give humanity the additional strength necessary to obey that God's commands, struck a responsive chord among morally frustrated Korean Confucians. Some responded by converting to Catholicism. Others less bold merely reinterpreted Confucianism to make room for God.

Both church and government documents from the nineteenth century make clear that Ha-sang was the Catholic martyr Koreans now so proudly claim him to be. Tasan's faith is more problematic. That Tasan believed in a Confucian Lord-on-High is undeniable. That he was an active Catholic for a few years when he was a young man is also indisputable. He admits as much in the epitaph he wrote for himself near the end of his life. However, when Hahn shows Tasan repenting of his youthful apostasy and returning to his Catholic faith shortly before his death, she boldly plunges into a historians' dispute whose final resolution is as yet undecided.

Before writing *Encounter*, Hahn spent years reading and researching both primary and secondary sources on Tasan and on the early years of the Korean Catholic Church. She consulted the foremost authorities in these fields, from priests and nuns to philosophers and historians. The evidence she uncovered for Tasan's religious beliefs during and after the years of exile, which are the years covered in *Encounter*, is ambiguous. She, along with many of the scholars she consulted, is persuaded by nineteenth-century missionary reports that state unequivocally that Tasan was welcomed back into the Catholic Church by Fr. Pacificus Liu Fang-chi, a Chinese priest who had smuggled himself into Korea in 1833. Hahn also assumes that Tasan's frequent references, in his writings late in life, to guilt and regret for past offenses must refer to the guilt he felt for abandoning his faith and the faith of his martyred brother, Yak-chong (1760–1801), for so many years.

Some scholars, more cautious, withhold judgment, noting that the French missionary claim of Tasan's deathbed return to the Catholic fold is not echoed by any contemporary Korean sources. A few also point out that Tasan never says precisely what he feels guilty for, so it is less than certain that he regretted his early retreat from public involvement with the persecuted Korean Catholic community.

Tasan's own copious writings fail to support a strong claim for a lasting commitment to Catholicism. They indicate, rather, that even though he was influenced by some Catholic teachings, he remained first and foremost a Confucian for most of his adult life. On the many occasions he argues for belief in a Confucian God, Tasan never uses the Sino-Korean term for the Catholic God (lit., "Lord of Heaven"); nor does he grant his God the roles of creator, savior, or judge so crucial to the Christian concept of the Supreme Being. In his commentaries on the Confucian classics, Tasan credits the Lord-on-High of Confucian tradition with implanting and managing the principles of selflessness and impartiality, which provide moral order in the universe. Unlike Ha-sang's God, however, Tasan's deity, as he appears in Tasan's extant essays, is a moral force and nothing more. That makes him a Confucian God, not a Christian God.

If Tasan became a Catholic later in life, he does not tell us so in the hundreds of volumes of essays, commentaries, letters, and poems he wrote over the course of his lifetime. He may have feared putting his true beliefs down on paper where his enemies and the enemies of Catholicism could have found them. Nevertheless, as one Korean scholar, required by his professorial position to be more cautious than a novelist needs to be, suggests, "It is better to wait for some more definite proof before we give a final answer to [the] question . . . was he really a Catholic, or was he, after the age of 30, a regenerate keeping his Confucian conviction?"[5]

It is therefore possible, but not certain, that Tasan was as Catholic as Hahn portrays him. It is, however, her novelist's prerogative to portray him so. For Hahn's purposes—and for the purposes of this novel—whether Tasan was truly a Catholic is no more significant than whether the three fictional Kwŏn sisters really existed. The

5. Kum Chang-t'ae, "Tasan on Western Learning and Confucianism," in *Korea Journal*, volume 26, number 2 (February 1986); 4–16 (particularly 15).

actual outcome of Tasan's encounter with Catholicism is less important than the subjective rewards readers gain from their encounter
with the world this novel evokes.

Encounter is an entertaining and stimulating work of fiction, not
a scholarly study of history. Hahn uses the ambiguous evidence of
Tasan's beliefs and values, along with more solid documentation of
the lives of canonized martyrs, supplemented by her own literary
imagination, to bring Tasan, Ha-sang, and their contemporaries
back to life. Her adroit marriage of *p'ansori* and *ch'anggŭk* motifs
with the narrative structure of the modern novel draws her readers
into a resurrected past. With Hahn as a guide, it is a journey well
worth taking.

Don Baker
The University of British Columbia

Principal Characters
in *Encounter*

CHO SIN-CH'ŎL A packhorse driver who befriends Ha-sang during Ha-sang's first trip to Peking. Christian name, Charles. Martyred in 1839 and canonized in 1984.

CHO SUK A nephew of Cho Tong-sŏm, husband of Kwŏn Teresa. Christian name, Peter. Martyred in 1819.

CHO TONG-SŎM An exiled scholar. The teacher of Ha-sang and a friend of Yak-chong. Christian name, Justino.

CHŎNG HAG-YŎN Tasan's eldest son.

CHŎNG HAG-YU Tasan's second son.

CHŎNG HA-SANG 1795–1839. Son of Yak-chong, a nephew of Tasan. Saint Paul Ha-sang Chŏng. Martyred in 1839, canonized in 1984.

CHŎNG YAG-YONG 1762–1836. Tasan. The youngest of the Chŏng brothers. Variously known as Yŏyudang, Mugŭkkwanin, Chahansanin. Christian name, Johann.

CHŎNG YAK-CHŎN 1758–1816. Tasan's second brother.

CHŎNG YAK-CHONG 1760–1801. Tasan's third brother. Ha-sang's father. Christian name, Augustine. Martyred in 1801.

CHŎNG YAK-HYŎN Tasan's eldest brother.

CHOU WEN-MU 1752–1801. A Chinese priest, the first Catholic missionary to arrive in Korea (in 1795). Martyred in 1801.

HONG, MATTEO The innkeeper at the bamboo grove. Also known as Hŏ.

HONG-NIM A daughter of Tasan by P'yo-nyŏ, born during Tasan's exile.

HWANG SA-YŎNG A disciple of Chŏng Yak-chong. The writer of "Silk Letter" in 1801. Martyred in 1801.

HYEJANG 1772–1811. An eminent Buddhist monk, Tasan's friend and disciple during his exile.

KIM CHŎNG-SUN, QUEEN DOWAGER 1745–1805. Queen of King Yŏngjo. As the young King Sunjo's regent, promulgates the Edict of Catholic Eradication; responsible for the Persecution of 1801.

KWŎN HO-SIN Father of Mae-a, Nan-a, and Kug-a.

KWŎN KUG-A The youngest daughter of Kwŏn Ho-sin. Adopted into the household of the Overseer of the Local Agency in Imsil, where she is named Kung-nim. Christian name, Juliette.

KWŎN NAN-A Second daughter of Kwŏn Ho-sin. Adopted by shaman Man-nyŏn, who names her Butterfly. Christian name, Cecilia. Martyred in 1825.

KWŎN MAE-A The eldest daughter of Kwŏn Ho-sin. Christian name, Maria. She goes to live with the former palace lady Myŏng-sim. Martyred in 1825.

KWŎN TERESA Daughter of Kwŏn Il-sin, Francesco Xavier, one of the first Korean Christians. Martyred in 1819.

MAN-NYŎN A hereditary shaman and adoptive mother of Kwŏn Nan-a, Butterfly.

MYŎNG-SIM A daughter of a *chungin* apothecary, recruited to become a palace lady. Christian name, Teresa. Martyred in 1825.

P'YO An old man who befriends Tasan when he first comes to Kangjin and introduces him to Hyejang.

P'YO-NYŎ Daughter of P'yo, a woman Tasan lives with during his exile. Mother of Hong-nim.

SŬNG NAK-CHONG A trusted servant of Kwŏn Ho-sin, who betrays the Kwŏn family and causes the family's tragedy. Christian name, Pius.

YI CHI-YŎN 1777–1841. The deputy envoy during Ha-sang's first trip to Peking; later Ha-sang's prosecutor. Before his death he was the Prime Minister of the Right.

YI KI-GYŎNG Once Tasan's friend, who studied Catholicism with him; later turning Tasan's adversary, pursues him to his banishment.

YI SŬNG-HUN 1756–1801. Husband of Tasan's sister, also known as Manch'ŏn. The first baptized Catholic in Korea (1794). Christian name, Peter. Martyred in 1801.

YU CHIN-GIL A *chungin* translator. Christian name, Augustine. Martyred in 1839 and canonized in 1984.

YUN CHONG-SIM 1793–?. One of Tasan's eighteen disciples during Tasan's exile in Kyuldong.

Chapter One

* * *

"Admonition on the Transitory"

Ha-sang arrived six days after Monk Hyejang had been cremated. Although Tasan was not unaware of this Buddhist practice, actually to witness the ritual for his friend Hyejang from the beginning to the end—first the placing of the body in the coffin, then the incineration, and finally the scattering of the ashes—was unbearably painful. Even for Tasan, a man hardened by the vicissitudes of his ill-fated life and no longer perturbed by ordinary worldly events, the experience was deeply shocking. Ten years younger than Tasan, Hyejang had been thirty-nine, in the prime of life. He had been born into a humble and destitute family, but soon after entering the priesthood he became a renowned scholar-monk. His reputation for extraordinary wisdom and scholarship encompassing both Sŏn Buddhism[1] and the philosophy of divination spread quickly throughout the entire Buddhist domain. He was also so well-versed in the Confucian classics that Tasan had pronounced him a Confucian scholar of great learning and virtue. And yet, Hyejang had been rough in personality, easily aroused to violent temper, eager to accept the offer of a drink and given to wanton drunkenness. He followed the Sŏn Buddhist teaching, "It is not wrong to eat red meat and have women"; however, the realm of sainthood only beckoned him from afar.

Never a common monk, Hyejang had been achingly aware of the

1. Sŏn is the Buddhist sect known largely in the West as Chan Buddhism (in China) or Zen Buddhism (in Japan).

1

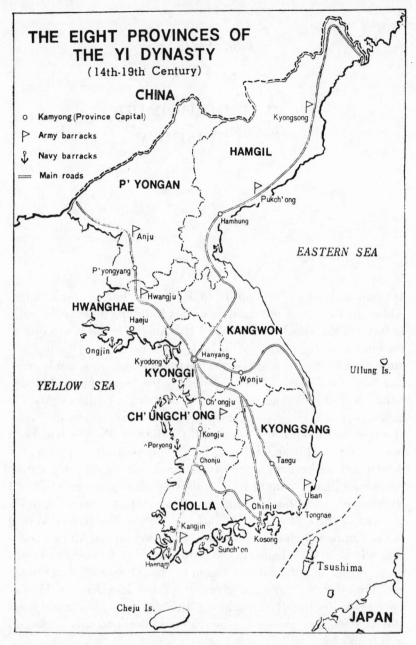

THE EIGHT PROVINCES OF
THE YI DYNASTY
(14th-19th Century)

CHINA

o   Kamyong (Province Capital)

▷   Army barracks

⚓   Navy barracks

═══   Main roads

Kyongsong

HAMGIL

P'YONGAN

Pukch'ong

Anju

Hamhung

EASTERN SEA

P'yongyang

Hwangju

HWANGHAE

Haeju

KANGWON

Ongjin

Kyodong

Hanyang

KYONGGI

Wonju

Ullung Is.

YELLOW SEA

Ch'ongju

CH'UNGCH'ONG

KYONGSANG

Kongju

Poryong

Chonju

Taegu

Ulsan

CHOLLA

Chinju

Tongnae

Kangjin

Kosong

Sunch'on

Haenam

Tsushima

Cheju Is.

JAPAN

Korea in the Yi dynasty. From Han Woo-keun, *History of Korea* (Seoul: Eul-Yoo Publishing Co., 1970). By permission of the publisher.

transitory nature of man's life. Great, therefore, was his worldly anguish. In wine he sought to appease the suffering and remorse of his life, and his body and soul languished in search of a self free from both. For a long time he had been afflicted with an abdominal swelling caused by his uncontrollable drinking, and recently he had been desperately ill for over ten days in the northern hermitage of Taehŭng Temple on Mount Taedun. On the morning of September 15, 1811, Tasan received word from the temple that Hyejang's condition had taken a turn for the worse.[2] Upon receiving the news, he left his thatched abode for the temple, which lay at a distance of some twenty-five miles. Though short, Tasan was powerfully built, but he was aware that his strength had dissipated after ten years in exile. For such a man, the journey was long.

On that day, as he hurried, the sea shimmered like silver sands reflecting an autumn sun, and the heavy fragrance of mellowing citrus filled the air. At the foot of the mountain, reeds swayed, shedding silvery powder as the wind swept over them. Wild chrysanthemums grew in profusion along the road that ran close to the sea, and lovely, too, were the autumn tints of the grasses. Beyond anything else, Tasan loved this dreamlike landscape of his otherwise desolate banishment. However, his glance did not linger upon his surroundings that day. His friend was dying; Tasan ran as though it were his first taste of despair and sorrow. A man of many accomplishments, he had weathered myriad hardships in his life, and yet he was now in a state of total disarray.

"Esteemed teacher, why don't you slow down? Nothing has happened yet. What if you should become ill?" cried Hyejang's disciple, trailing a few steps behind Tasan. The young novice had come from the temple the night before with news of Hyejang's imminent death, and had had no time to rest.

"No. We must get there before sunset."

But Tasan's thoughts outpaced his footsteps. The September full moon hung resplendent in the sky by the time he was on the mountain path leading to the northern hermitage where Hyejang lay dying. His mind, which had been somewhat calmed during the day-

---

2. In this novel, days and months follow the Chinese lunar calendar, which is about thirty-five days ahead of the Gregorian calendar. Thus, September 15 would be August 11 or 12.

long journey, began to race again, causing him to stumble several times despite the brightness of the night.

Beyond the thick forest of camellia, pine, and nutmeg, light flickered from the lone hermitage, and the grave sound of sutras chanted in unison permeated the air, evoking at once feelings of inscrutable solemnity and terror. Deeply perturbed, Tasan climbed the hill, unmindful of hunger and weariness. He found Hyejang panting beneath an ink-black blanket, facing west in the direction of salvation. A circle of monks sat around him, their palms pressed together in the meditation position, chanting "Admonition on the Transitory," a sutra for the dying, to help him cross the bitter sea of life into Nirvana.

Hyejang was now beyond hearing. He fought ferociously against his untimely end, as if his life, though it flickered like a wisp of floating cloud, refused to return to the ultimate beginning—the void. Bereft of consciousness, his flesh, betraying the transcendent soul, obstinately denied death's approach. His was no calm passing into the realm of quiescence. "Gruesome" was the only word to describe the death scene: eyes wide open, teeth grinding, fists striking the air, he clawed at his chest, howling like an animal. Nowhere were there any remnants of the virtue of the exalted self he had attained through his devotion to the classics of Confucianism, Buddhism, the philosophy of divination, and Sŏn.

Tasan wept in his mind as he watched the death throes. Pity and sorrow like a rising tide overwhelmed him, a soundless wail breaking within him. How he wished that this exit from life could have been serene and detached, as befitted the celebrated monk that Hyejang had been.

For two nights Hyejang lay dying. The monks, now weary from chanting, ceaselessly repeated the sutra for the dying as though hastening his demise. In spite of the cruel pain of the death throes, the end itself came with astonishing ease. It was past midnight and the bright moon rode serene in the crystalline sky.

Tasan sank in sorrow, though with an ineffable sense of release. The chants still went on as a few of the monks moved about in noiseless haste. Obeying Buddhist law, however, Hyejang's two beloved disciples did not keen. On the surface of their pale shaven heads, the thick veins that extended from their temples throbbed and wiggled like worms. When a young novice carrying a candle passed them, Tasan saw their contorted faces stained with tears.

The cleansing and clothing of the dead began before dawn, while warmth still lingered in the body. Three monks, the sleeves of their black robes rolled up to the shoulders, began shaving the head in the midst of the Chant for the Shedding of the Hair: "Awake, now, the soul of Hyejang, one who has just entered the Realm of Perfect Quiescence . . ." Soon the body was taken to the bathhouse, and after the washing of the hands and feet and the dressing in an under-garment were completed, a monk's robe was slipped on. While the Chant for the Placement of the Crown went on in unison, a crown was placed on the head.

Tasan, a Confucian scholar well-versed in the classics, had penned many sharp, lucid commentaries on them. He left behind him prodigious volumes of writings, including many on the School of Rites, ranging from a masterwork on major rites called *Designs for Good Government* to lesser ones on household rituals. But his writings on mourning rites numbered the greatest, totalling more than sixty volumes. Thus, although he sharply criticized the cur-rently followed *Family Rites* of Chu Hsi as overly cumbersome, he had a thorough knowledge of the established practice of the time.

Nevertheless, as the Buddhist funeral ceremonies unfolded be-fore him for the first time, Tasan was awestruck. The wonder and the impact intensified as the monks began the ritual of placing the corpse in a meditation position. They sat the body, not yet stiffened, in full lotus position, and draped a monk's robe from the right shoul-der. In a crescendo of chanting, the body was lowered into a rectan-gular coffin, and then carried to the crematorium within the temple grounds. Around a large, flat rock stood flags of five colors—yellow, blue, red, black, and white—each facing the direction which its color symbolized. On the rock were spread thick layers of charcoal, and next to it piled some sacks of charcoal. The coffin was lifted up and placed atop the rock, upon which a monk threw a wet straw mat. In a moment, several monks opened the sacks and piled the charcoal high around the coffin until it was entirely covered. They lit the pine resins and brought them to the charcoal to be ignited, the Chant for the Fire resounding all the while.

In the crystal-clear day, the splendor of autumn foliage, like a spread of embroidered silk, enveloped the mountain; above, the sky hung deep blue in sorrow. The charcoal soon caught fire in the brisk wind and shot up in gigantic flames. Smokeless and odorless—was it because of the wind, or the wet straw mat on the rock?—the lovely fire burned on. One had a sense of witnessing sacred fire. Forgetting his own sorrow, Tasan gazed upon a scene of ultimate pathos. Though this was a time of Buddhist suppression, unconsciously a Buddhist prayer, forbidden to a high-born scholar-official like himself, escaped his mouth: "May his soul rest in peace."

Autumn dusk came swiftly to the mountain temple, but there was still no end in sight to the cremation ceremony, which had begun early in the morning. The cinnabar and yellow flames, even more beautiful and mysterious as the full moon ascended, burned on. At about seven, the flames finally began to subside. At last, a chant announcing the conclusion of the cremation ceremony was sung, while the straw mat, still wet from repeated soaking, was lifted from the rock. In the early evening, the mountain temple was already shrouded with the thickness of the night.

A shock awaited Tasan next morning. After scarcely touching the offering of food, he went out to the crematorium. There was no sign of fire on the rock. In its place was a neat pile of white ashes. A few monks poked the ashes, exposing a scattering of bones, while others, now less numerous than the night before, intoned the Chant for the Gathering of Bones: "Unattainable. Indissoluble." With long wooden chopsticks, they picked up the bones, to the last sliver, and deposited each one in a heavy brass bowl. Still chanting, some of the monks ground the bones to fine powder while others came toward them bearing a large brass bowl full of steaming rice. The powdered bone was mixed with the rice, then scattered over the rock. A dreadful sight followed. Even before the monks left, the birds flocked. In an instant, the snowy white rice was covered with birds. By the time they flew away, nothing remained on the rock. Hyejang had given his worldly flesh in beatitude as the ultimate offering. Overwhelmed by an inexpressible sense of emptiness, Tasan gazed upon the now-vacant rock. It was said that when the flesh had returned to the four elements from which it came—earth, water, fire, and wind—the soul, separated from the flesh like a solitary dewdrop, would return to this world in a form determined by the law of transmigration. Where, then, seeking a new karma, had Hyejang's soul departed? Tasan closed his eyes. He had known of

Hyejang's long suffering and painful path as he sought enlightenment in the philosophy of divination, and he had understood Hyejang's atonement for his heresy. A Buddhist monk, Hyejang had
come to deny the Buddhist doctrine that life is inescapably bound
by the eternal Chain of Causation and had begun to acknowledge
its finality as determined by Providence. In his new insight, life was
not "nothingness," but "fulfillment." Finally, he had grasped the
truth as revealed in the *I Ching*.

In the morning, after a sleepless night full of myriad thoughts
and emotions, Tasan and one of Hyejang's disciples gathered wild
fruits on the mountainside and offered them with some wine at
Hyejang's grave. Asking the disciple to keen, for they were now
alone, Tasan read a eulogy, and he felt sure that Hyejang must be
pleased on his way to Nirvana.

Tormented by the memory of the carnal agonies of Hyejang's
death, Tasan lost himself in wine, and wept day and night trying to
escape from the thought of his departed friend. Thus five days went
by. Finally, becoming aware that he was cold and thirsty, he awoke
from a drunken sleep with a moan.

Someone stirred outside. "Teacher," called a young voice, barely
out of adolescence.

"Oh, it's you, Chong-sim. Have you just returned?"

"Yes. I brought back some nutmeg cake. I'll serve some presently
with the tea." Chong-sim, one of Tasan's eighteen disciples, had
been away on two days' leave. Though modulated with a slight
southern accent, Chong-sim's was correct capital speech. He was
nineteen, and years later he would write an epilogue to *Investigation into Korean Sŏn Buddhism*, which Tasan helped compile. Intelligent and soft-spoken, he served his master with complete devotion.

Nutmeg abounded in Tasan's maternal clan village. It was late
September, and the harvest of the nuts would already be coming to
an end. Knowing how much Tasan loved nutmeg cake, Chong-sim
had taken advantage of his time off to fetch some. Two days would
hardly have been enough time to reach the village, have the cake
made, and return. How he must have hurried; how tired he must
be, despite his youth, to have traveled the distance in such a short
time. Touched by Chong-sim's devotion, Tasan's eyes were filled
with tears as he thanked him.

The responsibility of preparing tea had been Chong-sim's since before anyone could remember. The youth expertly set the tea kettle on a clay brazier. The tea soon began to brew, its mellow aroma filling the air. Tasan trembled unconsciously as the fragrance of the tea seeped into his nostrils. A longing, like pain, pierced him.

Tea, yes, tea. Hyejang, each year on the Day of the Grain Rains, which usually fell in the middle of March, would climb Mount Mandŏk to pick the tea leaves, taking care not to miss the right moment when they were just the size of "sparrows' tongues." He would send Tasan the tea he had so carefully gathered. The loneliness surged in Tasan, missing his friend. In his trouble-ridden life, how many such partings had he experienced, each wound leaving a scar? Tasan could touch neither the tea nor the cake he so enjoyed. Resting his head on a wooden box-pillow, he closed his eyes. He recalled the time when he first met Hyejang, and events of the past ten years surfaced in his mind, rushing before his eyes like the designs in a kaleidoscope.

It was the spring of 1805, four years after Tasan had been sent to Kangjin as the result of the Catholic Persecution of 1801. He spent days in isolation and mournfulness as the people of Kangjin shunned him, afraid of coming into contact with a treasonous heretic. Taking pity on his homelessness, an old woman who kept a tavern at the outskirts of East Gate gave him a tiny room, which barely sheltered him from the harsh elements outside. He named it the Cottage of the Four Principles—peace, ceremony, stability, and activity—and lived there for four years, writing incessantly in that dungeonlike room. Since coming to Kangjin, Tasan had immersed himself in study of the *I Ching*, spending more of his time and energy on it than on any other Confucian classic. Five years of intensive research and refinement culminated in the completion of *The I Ching as Interpreted by Tasan*.

Tasan understood well the people of Kangjin, who feared and avoided him. It was here in this region that his maternal cousin, Yun Chi-ch'ung, had been martyred, and this incident had precipitated the Catholic Persecution of 1801. They knew only too well the severity of the laws and cruelty of the punishment. Indeed, they regarded Tasan as a dangerous heretic who could bring divine wrath upon them. Even the Yun clansmen had mistreated him, one of their own, when he visited them. The Catholics' mortal crime was their faith in Western religion. Their family properties were confiscated, they were executed or died in prison, and their families were forced to disperse. The extreme fear of the townspeople, therefore, was perfectly reasonable.

In the seclusion of his banishment, Tasan was so hungry for human contact that on some rare occasions when a poor man who came to the wretched tavern for a drink happened to exchange a few words with him, it would be enough to cheer him up and sustain him for a few days. In this way a friendship had developed between Tasan and a simple old man called P'yo, the tavern-keeper's brother, who tilled a small lot leased from the Paengnyŏn Temple. The old man regularly came to the market, held six times a month, and then to the tavern. Each time he came, he knelt in front of Tasan's room to pay his respects to him. He was extremely poor, and even on his outings he was always dressed in rags. "How difficult it must be for you," he would say to comfort Tasan, forgetting his own hardships.

The year after Tasan had arrived in Kangjin, the old man had entered the tavern as usual, while the noisy customers were speaking somberly among themselves.

"Did his wound become infected?"

"Such a catastrophe I have never seen before!"

"He must have been driven to it. What a pity, what a pity!"

"Whatever it is, it's really a wicked thing to happen, isn't it?"

Their conversation had suddenly stopped when they noticed the old man, but each had already had his say, and the story was clear to Tasan.

Old P'yo had a nephew who lived in Nojŏn. A son was born to him soon after the funeral of his father. Barely three days old, the infant was registered for military taxation, while the grandfather's name was still on the list. Since the family was practically starving, and unable to pay a tax levied on the three "able-bodied men" in the same family, the family ox was confiscated. The nephew took out a knife and cut off his own penis, wailing, "It's because of this damn thing that my family has to suffer." His wife ran to the officials carrying the severed penis, blood still dripping from it. She begged them in vain for mercy. The guards locked the door, and the woman kept on weeping in front of it.

On market days, Tasan usually closed his door tightly, shutting himself away from the noise. That day, however, he realized what had happened from the exchanges of the crowd outside. He was dumbfounded by the horror and absurdity of the story. Ruefully, he stroked his long beard. Then, taking out a brush, he composed a poem in one sweeping moment. He titled it "Elegy on the Castration":

> Mournful is the young woman's wail in the reed field.
> Echoing against the prison wall, her lament rises to heaven.
> Though many a soldier-husband has failed to return home,
> Since olden times, no story such as this—no tale of castration—
> Has ever been told before.
> She is already clothed in mourning garb for her father-in-law
> And her babe barely out of his mother's womb.
> Why, then, three generations listed on the military registry?

Before reaching the age of twenty, Tasan followed his father, the magistrate of the district, to their native town, and had the opportunity to observe him ruling over the people. For a short time, Tasan himself had served as a magistrate with compassion and fairness. However, it was only in banishment that he had become deeply disturbed by the infinite sufferings of the people under the inconsistencies of the system, the breaches of official discipline, and the corrupt officials.

After the mutilation incident, Tasan became closer to the old man. One balmy autumn day, old P'yo came to see Tasan, though it was not a market day. "How is His Excellency today?" he asked, addressing Tasan in deference to his former official title, Royal Secretary, instead of as the "gentleman from Seoul."

As usual, Tasan was immersed in reading in his room, which was dark even in the middle of the day. The books piled near his desk had been borrowed from the library of his maternal clan, for which he had had to walk more than twenty-five miles and endure the displeasure of his unwelcoming kin. Even the small writing table and the ink-slab were pieces that had been abandoned in their barn, and that he had salvaged and repaired.

Watching the scholar preoccupied with reading in a windowless room—and how could one read in darkness?—P'yo often wondered if Tasan might not indeed be a heretic who practiced magic as they said Catholics did. Out of reverence, he usually refrained from speaking to Tasan, but seeing no one in the tavern and taking advantage of the door that had been left half open to let the warm, springlike air in, he called once again. Tasan, who had not heard him the first time, went on reading aloud in a vigorous and proud voice.

"Your Excellency."

Pushing his spectacles back on his forehead, Tasan looked toward the old man. His face had become pale during his long confinement. P'yo felt himself to be unworthy in the presence of a man who dazzled him with his imposing features—the prominent forehead, noble nose, full cheekbones, large, elongated eyes, and the beautiful, thick black beard. Daunted, P'yo fumbled, "Well . . ."

"What is it?"

"I have a friend who works as a servant in Mandŏk Temple . . ."

"What about him?"

"He tells me that a monk named Hyejang has been living there since this spring."

"Who is Hyejang?"

"He is a young monk of high esteem. Everyone wants to meet him, but they say he refuses. That makes them even more eager."

"Why do they so wish to meet him?"

"Because, being a high priest, he also reads fortunes from one's countenance, and he's good at soothsaying."

"Strange. A Buddhist monk telling fortunes."

"No. It's not what you think," the old man added, shaking both his head and hands vigorously. "He doesn't do it for a fee. Whatever remarks he drops in passing here and there happen to be astonishingly correct."

"A peculiar monk, indeed." Showing no interest, Tasan slid his spectacles back onto his face.

"Your Excellency," continued the old man hastily, "to tell you the truth, the monk Hyejang says he must meet you."

"Meet me? Why?" Tasan's eyes widened.

P'yo lowered his head, avoiding Tasan's eyes as though blinded by them. Looking up, he urged Tasan in earnest, saying, "He wants to meet you very sincerely. Why don't you go see him? He is a very famous monk."

"Who is this monk who anxiously and sincerely wants to meet me, a treasonous heretic, whom everyone else avoids and fears like a demon god?" thought Tasan, and yet he was moved.

The next day after lunch, Tasan, guided by the old man, set out

for Mandŏk Temple. Situated facing the sea on the slope of Mount
Mandŏk, the temple was celebrated throughout the Koryŏ (918–
1392) and the Yi (1392–1910) dynasties for producing famous monks.
Tasan wore an informal outfit consisting of cotton trousers and a
shirt, and a wide-sleeved outercoat tied with a dark blue sash. He
had thought of putting on the more formal long gown left hanging
on its stand, unused in his long confinement, but thinking of his
circumstances, he had changed his mind, and just added a wide-
brimmed horsehair hat. Nonetheless, uncommon dignity and nobility exuded from him. Not for him the swaggering, unsteady steps of
an aristocrat; Tasan's gait was so swift for a short man that, although
accustomed to walking, P'yo was forced to hurry after Tasan breath-
lessly. During the trip, a distance of five miles from town, Tasan did
not pause for a moment to rest and never once stumbled on the
way up the rocky slope to the temple, where fall arrived early. The
temple lay deep in blazing autumn hues. The dizzying splendor of
the foliage, like brilliant colors freshly painted on the sanctuary of
a grand Buddhist temple, struck the visitor with awe. The deathly
calm, in which all sounds seemed crystallized, contrasted with the
grandeur of the colors, simultaneously symbolizing both suffering
and deliverance.

"I wonder where he is. He must have gone further up the mountain to cut wood." Mumbling to himself, the old man disappeared
to look for his friend.

Tasan contemplated a hanging scroll of calligraphy in the style
of the Six Dynasties of China, attributed to Kim Saeng, then his eyes
rested on the sea before him. In the fickle autumn weather, mist
was fast enveloping the sea, and the day soon turned overcast. Only
a portion of the island in front, and the summit of the mountain
behind, were faintly visible. The reeds growing on the slope swayed
in confusion, and fine misty rain like smoke spread from the sea,
filling the temple garden.

"It's raining. Why don't you come in to keep yourself dry?" Tasan
turned around and saw a spry monk of about thirty, wearing an ink-
black shirt and trousers. He did not wear a monk's robe, nor did he
greet Tasan with palms pressed together as was customary for a
Buddhist when meeting all living creatures. Tasan noticed a large
scar on his shaven head. He had a sharp nose, and even sharper
eyes. Instinctively, Tasan knew that this must be Hyejang.

"Thank you," Tasan said gently, following the monk to the entrance, where he took off his shoes. As he was about to enter, he could not hold back a bitter smile. The disorder was just as he imagined it would be, unsuitable for a monk's cell. It was clear that a novice's care had not reached this room, with its uncleared bedding, clothing in a heap pushed into the corner, and bottle of wine lying near the door.

Though stories abounded of the eccentric behavior of many celebrated monks, such disorder was repugnant to Tasan, an orderly and rational man. The waywardness of such monks seemed to him mere pretense, impertinent and even vicious. He mused as he recoiled that he had yet to meet a truly virtuous monk. Pushing away the bedding, he sat down.

"It seems there is no tea left for this poor monk," muttered Hyejang, picking up the empty bottle, and shaking it, his speech slurred as if from drinking.

A faint smile appeared on Tasan's face. He knew that the sharp eyes he had seen outside were not those of a drunk.

"You like to drink, don't you?"

"Like to drink? No, it's only cereal tea."

"Indeed. No doubt, then, it must be fermented cereal."

"No matter. In whatever form one eats cereal, boiled, kneaded, or fermented, monks can eat it, too. Isn't 'Oak in the Garden' also the way of the Buddha, I wonder?"

Tasan tensed slightly. A Confucian scholar, he was unversed in Sŏn Buddhism. However, he had heard of a story told by the Hwadu sect: One day a monk asked a master, Choju, "What is the Buddha's way?" The master answered, "It is in the oak tree in the front garden." Upon hearing this, the monk was said to have attained great enlightenment, realizing that everything contains the Buddha's way.

The paper window squeaked in the wind like a sob as the fine misty rain turned into a heavy downpour.

"I am sorry to be a burden to you. I just wanted to shelter myself from the rain," said Tasan, feeling uncomfortable.

"It must be our karma to meet each other like this. Since everything has its cause and effect, our meeting, too, is the result of five hundred chains of reincarnations. You, my elderly brother, are the old yang, and this humble monk the young yin. This meeting is propitious."

"What do you mean?"

"To tell you the truth, a little while ago, this humble monk had some nutmeg cake. Then a strange thing happened. I dropped a chopstick twice. Yin follows yang, and according to the hexagrams of the *I Ching*, the meeting of the two brings about great attainment."

"Impudence! All phenomena constantly change. How dare you discuss good and evil omens by such superstitious methods?" said Tasan, gathering his coat and standing up to leave. Capriciously, the weather had changed; the rain had stopped and the clouds were now torn, exposing patches of blue sky.

By the time Tasan reached the tavern, the short autumn day had already given way to dusk. He washed his feet, and was about to enter the room when Hyejang, the monk he had so inauspiciously met, dashed in frantically and prostrated himself in front of Tasan's room.

"Illustrious teacher Chŏng,[3] how have you deceived this destitute monk whose only steadfast yearning day and night has been to meet you? I was blind not to have recognized you. I have followed your honorable shadow," Hyejang sobbed, his head still pressed to the ground. Moved by the sincerity of the monk's words, Tasan, in his stockinged feet, came down to the yard and, taking Hyejang's hand, led him to his room. Thus began their relationship, which could not have taken place without the consequential effect of five hundred chains of reincarnations. They spent the night debating the philosophy of divination.

At the time of their meeting, Tasan had just begun to concentrate on studying the *I Ching*, or *Book of Change*, the most difficult of the Confucian classics. Even Confucius himself is said to have struggled; he so loved the book that the leather which bound it wore off three times. If one hundred men pursued the path to the understanding of the *I Ching*, there would be one hundred ways to achieve that understanding; indeed, it was said to be laid out in a labyrinth of darkness. Tasan rejected the idea that the study of divination was a mere practice of magic to determine the principle

3. Tasan's given name was Chŏng Yag-yong. As the story explains, he took the name Tasan as his pen name.

of yin and yang. He argued, instead, that it was a systematic theory developed by the sages of ancient times in an effort to divine the mandate of Heaven.

It was their mutual interest in the study of the *I Ching* that had brought Tasan and Hyejang together, and bound them in deep friendship. Impressive was the picture of the two men huddled together in discourse all through the night under the flickering lamplight, one a somber scholar in banishment, the other a poverty-stricken monk in the time of Buddhist repression. Hyejang's unexpected mastery of the Confucian and Chu Hsi classics prompted Tasan to declare that he was indeed a scholar of great learning and virtue. However, Hyejang, recognizing the superiority of Tasan's commentaries, surrendered himself and became his disciple. Before the end of the year, Hyejang had arranged for his mentor to move into a new residence, called the Mountain Abode of Precious Benevolence, situated on the slope of Mount Ui. Thus, Tasan was finally able to escape from the small, dank room in the tavern. In his new residence, he spent the winter with his son, Hag-yŏn, devoting himself to the boy's education.

Tasan influenced Hyejang in many ways. The disciple discovered in himself a love for poetry, to which he had previously been indifferent. Since his introduction to Tasan's interpretation of the *I Ching*, he had begun to doubt the foundation of his philosophy of life, which caused him to suffer further.

Nor was Hyejang's influence on his teacher's growing interest in Sŏn Buddhism insignificant. Though ordinarily acerbic, rough, and stubborn, Hyejang was gentle and considerate to Tasan. Soon after Tasan moved to his new residence, Hyejang sent the fresh tea-leaf buds that grew on the slope of Mount Mandŏk. It was Tasan's first taste of the beverage, and it converted him into a great lover of tea. His enthusiasm for it was such that he chose for himself the pen name Tasan, meaning "tea-mountain."

In the spring of 1808, Tasan again moved, this time to Kyuldong on Mount Tasan, to a villa owned by his maternal kin, Yun Tan, a retired government official. After settling in his new home, Tasan began accepting disciples to whom he taught the Confucian classics.

He did not waste away his exiled days in idle distraction. With his eighteen disciples, Tasan dug out the area near the thatched cottage which had been built through the kindness of Yun Tan for

Tasan to use as his lecture hall. Bringing large stones from the mountain, Tasan fashioned a square pond modeled after a typical Yi dynasty design. He constructed a miniature island, and diverted water from the mountain stream to make a waterfall that cascaded into the pond. He planted irises and placed camellia bushes around the pond, where their evergreen branches would spread over the water. A celebrated physician, he planted medicinal herbs in the patches along the mountain slope.

Mount Tasan, as the name indicated, was covered with tea plants. Joy filled him as he watched their lustrous leaves and white flowers flutter like pear blossoms, filling the air with fragrance. Plum trees and camellia bushes also bloomed on the mountain, and the age-old trees gave forth their perfumed scent. In autumn, the yellow nutmeg flowers intoxicated the entire village with their sweet aroma. Indeed, Tasan's new home would have been a paradise on earth were it not for the loneliness, and even that Hyejang helped him bear by being both a thoughtful friend and an exceptionally sagacious disciple.

That year on the Day of the Grain Rains, Hyejang came to visit Tasan as usual, though his ailment had reached an advanced stage. The swelling had obviously worsened, and it was clear to Tasan that his friend was suffering from a liver disease. He knew of a rare medicine he believed would certainly help; however, since he was living in banishment, it was out of his reach. Feeling desolate, he had his disciples go out and fish for loaches, which he stuffed into an aged squash and boiled, a humble remedy. Tasan persuaded Hyejang to drink the broth in the hope of reducing the swelling.

Hyejang took out a bunch of newly made fur brushes from his shoulder pack. "I caught some weasels that were making noises near the furnace; I had some spare moments." Known for his dexterity, Hyejang excelled especially in the art of brush making. It must have required all of his last energy to make these. Tasan's eyes filled with tears.

"Because of you it seems weasels will soon be an extinct species in Taehŭng Temple," he bantered, in a rare attempt at humor. "Magnificent work of art! Now I will no longer be able to blame the brush for my poor calligraphy." His face contorted in an effort to smile.

Even as they gathered the tea leaves together, Hyejang had breathed with difficulty. That troubled breathing still rang in Tasan's ears, and the pain of remembrance spread in him. The tea Chong-sim had just brought to him was the same that Hyejang had picked on that last holiday.

"Where are you from?" Tasan heard Chong-sim's voice. Someone must have arrived. A few words were exchanged, then Chong-sim called, "Teacher, someone is here from the capital."

"From the capital? Who?"

"It is I, Ha-sang," came a clear, vigorous, young voice in the capital speech Tasan had been longing to hear.

"Ha-sang?" Tasan could not recall that name at first. He pushed open the door impatiently. Upon seeing Tasan, a fair-complexioned, handsome youth prostrated himself on the spot, and bowed deeply. Suddenly, Tasan felt dizzy, and—supporting himself with one hand on the door—he moved a half step backward.

◆   ◆   ◆

There he stood—a youth with a luminous face, a clear expanse of forehead, full cheekbones, thick eyebrows, a prominent nose, bright, lively eyes—bearing all the characteristic features of the Chŏng clan of Aphae, which is celebrated for producing handsome men.

Ha-sang was taller by a head than Chong-sim, who stood next to him, and his broad shoulders, too, were unmistakably those of the Chŏng clan. However, something about the youth struck Tasan as unfamiliar. For a long time, Tasan stared at his nephew abstractedly. Ha-sang's traveling outfit was that of a true commoner—a shirt and trousers without an outercoat, and the trousers, from just below the knee to the ankle, bound with strings in place of gaiters, and no horsehair hat, but the thick topknot on his head, the size of a young man's fist, was wound tightly with a white kerchief. Seeing his own flesh and blood dressed as a lowly commoner was a great shock to Tasan. A Sirhak scholar,[4] who took the initiative in accepting European learning, Tasan prided himself in attacking the obsolete conventions of the time and in preaching a classless society, so he could not grasp the meaning of the strange agitation he felt when he saw his nephew thus attired.

4. A school of thought which emerged in the eighteenth century and sought a solution to the problems of the day other than the empty formalism and rituals of the Chu Hsi Neo-Confucian school. The Sirhaks advocated an empirical and practical approach to learning as well as to government.

Since his banishment to Kangjin, Tasan had repeatedly used the phrase "ruined family" in his letters to his sons, Hag-yŏn and Hag-yu. In his cavelike room in the tavern, he wrote anxious letters that were carried back home by the family servant. In one, he wrote, "As I try to fathom your thoughts, it seems to me that you are about to abandon your studies. Does this mean that you are to become ignorant commoners? When you come from a family of scholar-officials known for integrity, then there can be no need to worry about military service, provided you are well educated and marry well. But what will become of you if you are both illiterate and come from a ruined family? You may not think it important to study, but a man without knowledge of the requirements of the rituals is no better than a bird or an animal." In another, he asked, "Ruined as we are, what will become of you if you remain without learning and ignorant of the rituals? Only if you study thousands of times harder than others can we hope that a few among us will live like human beings. My days in banishment are very painful indeed, but tidings that you are reading and following upright behavior would lessen my worries."

Tasan took unusual pride in his clan, and in his autobiography he reiterated the accomplishments of his family. A scholar with a wide range of learning and possessing an astounding capacity for hard work, he was nonetheless obsessed with reputation. His nephew's apparel, the clothing of a commoner, was forcing him to recognize the agonizing reality of the downfall of the family.

The youth, unable to surmise what was in his uncle's mind, followed Tasan into his room and knelt down gracefully. The humble outfit, covered with dirt from a long journey, did not rob him of his natural dignity and refinement, and the beauty of his features was only heightened by closer scrutiny.

Not looking directly at his nephew, Tasan spoke. "So you are Ha-sang?"

"Yes."

"What is your adult name?"

"Since childhood, I have been called Ha-sang."

So his nephew had not even had his initiation ceremony; pity and humiliation like a vague pain brushed by his heart. "How old are you?" he asked tenderly.

"Sixteen. When you, my fourth father, left us, I was only six years old."

"It has been ten years since then. Where have you been living all these years?"

"We live in Majae."

"In Majae?" Tasan could not go on. Though his sons and servants came to visit him occasionally, his thoughts had never once dwelt on the family of his martyred third brother, Yak-chong. In his frequent letters to his family, he never neglected to inquire after his eldest brother, Yak-hyŏn and his wife, nor did he fail to express concern for the family of his second brother, Yak-chŏn, banished to Hŭksan. He had repeatedly instructed his sons to be filial to their uncle as if to their own father. However, he had been completely indifferent to the fate of his third brother's family. Tasan felt a numbness in his heart. "And how is your mother? You must have suffered much." A deep silence followed.

"Yes." Ha-sang's answer was brief. In that single word, Tasan read days of sorrow and pain that defied description. Silence again; it was Ha-sang who broke it. "I am a grown man now. I am strong, too. There is no reason why my family of three should starve." Now his words were vigorous and cheerful.

"A family of three, did you say? I remember you had a sister-in-law, and she also had a child. Then?"

A shadow of pain crossed Ha-sang's fine forehead. He spoke feebly. "My mother told me my father was martyred on February 26, 1801, and it was about a month later, on April 2, that my brother Ch'ŏl-sang was murdered. After my brother died, there was no place for us to go but Majae." Ha-sang paused for a moment. "The villagers arranged a hut for us to stay in. The following year, the child died of smallpox. My sister-in-law, though in the flower of her life, lived in a deathly despair."

The villagers! The words of his nephew swirled in Tasan's mind. No one in the family had cared to look after their own pitiful bereaved ones.

"Unable to bear seeing her suffer so much, my mother suggested that she might wish to return to her own family. Although her father, Francesco, had been martyred and her brother, Leo, had also been executed, and the entire clan was about to be wiped out, those who ·

had survived were said to be very close, and did not suffer too much."

Tasan closed his eyes in pain. The memories of the days gone by surfaced in his mind like nightmares. It was now ten years since he had begun his exiled life, first in Changgi, then in Kangjin, and finally here in Kyuldong. Only recently had he freed himself from the sense of mortification, grief, and anger at those who had plotted and snared him into this banishment. If his crime were his Catholic faith, martyrdom would have been the proof of that faith. On the other hand, if he were to insist upon his innocence and continue to feel angry, would he not be guilty of cowardice and betrayal?

But Tasan considered himself different from those who had died defending their faith. He was merely curious about the new learning from Europe and studied writings on Catholicism but did not worship its God. Therefore, he felt no shame in the petition declaring his innocence, which he had presented to King Chŏngjo in 1799. He defended his position and rebutted the memorial calling for his impeachment which his adversaries had presented to the king. In his petition he stated that although it was true that he had been interested in the teachings of Catholicism, he had soon realized that they were merely offshoots of Buddhist teachings, and that what he had taken to be a more advanced system of thought had turned out to be nothing but a stale, obsolete, and contradictory doctrine. His desperate attempt to justify himself had deeply disappointed the Catholic faithful. A great scholar of the day—a renegade!

Tasan saw his action not as a betrayal of faith, but rather as springing from disillusionment with Catholic doctrine. He had begun to have doubts about this religion, which had brought upon his people such terrifying consequences—disrupting traditional morals and manners, causing confusion in society, bringing destruction to families, and leading to the violent deaths of the faithful. He questioned the need for such a religion and thus believed his "confession" to the king was an expression of his beliefs and integrity, not a vindication of self-preserving action. To him, it did not follow that anyone who studied the doctrines was necessarily a heretic. Take, for instance, Yi Ki-gyŏng, who had obsessively pursued Tasan to his downfall. Yi Ki-gyŏng had spent days with Tasan, studying Catholic teachings and copying its writings. Had they not, in their youth, espoused Catholicism with enthusiasm, it would have been impossible for those outstanding disciples of the greatest Sirhak scholar, Yi Ik, to have produced their powerful repudiations of Catholic doctrine.

Thus, Tasan felt helpless rage and mortification at having been falsely accused of mortal crime, and banished as a treasonous heretic; he, the scion of an illustrious family whose members had served as royal secretaries to kings for eight generations. Now the family was on the verge of extinction. He wondered if he could have borne the loneliness and humiliation were it not for his passion for the pursuit of knowledge.

And yet, had it not been for his third brother, Yak-chong, and his disciple, Hwang Sa-yŏng, with his Silk Letter . . . Although he admitted that it was wrong to blame them for the family's downfall, the memory of his brother and his martyrdom filled him with confusion.

Yak-chong had indeed been an unusual man. He alone had remained in Majae, while all the others—his second brother, Yak-chŏn; his brother-in-law, Yi Sŭng-hun; the Kwŏn brothers, Ch'ŏl-sin and Il-sin; a brother of his sister-in-law, Yi Pyŏk—attended a reading society for ten days in the winter of 1779.[5] This meeting was held in Ch'ŏnjinamchuo Temple on Mount Aengja, Kwangju, twenty miles from Seoul.

Yak-chong had not sought fame by serving in public office. Although possessing superior learning and statesmanship, he had preferred to pursue a life of leisure in the countryside, studying Lao-tze's Taoist doctrine, with wandering clouds as his only companions, and instructing the disciples who gathered around him. However, finally persuaded by the eloquence of Yi Pyŏk, and the powerful arguments of Kwŏn Ch'ŏl-sin, a giant among Confucian scholars, he decided to accept Catholicism. His godfather was Kwŏn Ch'ŏl-sin, whose brother, Il-sin, baptized him.

The baptism took place in the spring of 1790, when the Catholics in Korea were in a great turmoil. As a result of a papal ruling in 1742 that deemed ancestor worship incompatible with Christianity, they had received instruction from the Bishop of Peking forbidding them

5. A group of scholars, led by Kwŏn Ch'ŏl-sin and Chŏng Yak-chŏn, retreated to this remote temple to study "Western Learning" intensively. This meeting is significant because it acted as a catalyst for their conversion to Catholicism.

to perform Confucian ancestor-worship rites. Yak-chong had become a Catholic late, unlike many of the other high-born scholar-officials, who had converted to Catholicism earlier but had lately been persuaded by such denouncements to give up the religion. His baptismal name, Augustine, was fitting for one who had so long hesitated to make his decision.

The following year, a death had occurred in the Yun clan, a prominent family in Chinsan, Chŏlla Province. The mother of Yun Chi-ch'ung, a Catholic, had requested in her will that her funeral take place according to Catholic ritual. Yun Chi-ch'ung, or Paul, and his cousin Kwŏn Sang-yŏn, or Jacob, following the wishes of the deceased, gave her a Catholic burial instead of performing the Confucian funeral rite, with its ancestral tablet. This was a capital crime of heresy, for which they were beheaded.

The Yun Chi-ch'ung incident provided an opportune moment for those who had long plotted the destruction of the Catholics. Among them were Hong Nag-an and Yi Ki-gyŏng. Yi Ki-gyŏng, a member of the Southerner faction, was a close friend of Yi Sŭng-hun, the first Korean to be baptized in a Catholic church in Peking. Yi Sŭng-hun had brought many books on Catholicism back from China. Yi Ki-gyŏng, who read them voraciously, was a close acquaintance of Tasan. Who could have foreseen that Yi Ki-gyŏng would later betray them, becoming a leader in the relentless persecution of Catholics? It was difficult to understand precisely how he had come to harbor such evil intentions, but his betrayal might have originated in an incident that took place in Panch'on in 1787.[6] Renting a room there, Tasan and Yi Sŭng-hun were giving lectures on Catholicism to the students of the National Confucian Academy. Yi Ki-gyŏng did not like the idea of Confucian students reading books on Catholicism and neglecting their studies of the Confucian classics. He expressed his feeling to his friend, Hong Nag-an. Hong, an ambitious man, wanted to use the incident for his own advancement by reporting it in a memorial to the king, a not uncommon practice of the period. Yi Ki-gyŏng objected, and the incident was for a time kept from becoming a major issue.

6. Panch'on refers to the area around the National Confucian Academy inhabited by a group of people who supplied sacrificial meat to the academy for ceremonial occasions, such as the festivals in honor of Confucius, which were held twice annually.

But Hong Nag-an persisted. In the following year on January 7, during the National Confucian Academy examination at which the king himself was a judge, he attracted attention by composing a vehement attack on Catholicism as heresy. As a result of this polemic, Hong Nag-an took second place in the examination. With this success, he intensified his unyielding assault on Catholicism.

He sent a long, emotional letter to Prime Minister Ch'ae Che-kong, the leader of the Southerner faction, pointing out in violent language the wrongs of Catholicism and clamoring for the severe punishment of Tasan and Yi Sŭng-hun for their heretical belief. Neither benevolent King Chŏngjo nor gentle Ch'ae Che-kong had any intention of allowing the incident to escalate further. Moreover, Ch'ae, as the leader of the Sip'a clique of the Southerner faction, made up mostly of scholar-officials who had fallen out of power, knew that many of the able members of his faction were Catholics themselves. In addition, Tasan's half-sister was the wife of Ch'ae's illegitimate son.

The king, unable to resist the persistent demands of Hong and his group, gave in and ordered the imprisonment of Tasan and Yi Sŭng-hun. However, the accusers could not produce enough evidence and, furthermore, it became known that they had once been Catholics themselves. The wrath of the king was great. He immediately ordered Yi Ki-gyŏng banished to Kyŏngwŏn. Tasan, freed, took to visiting Yi's household, now without a master, to amuse the young son and give small amounts of money to Yi's aged mother. Tasan did not grudge his concern for them.

In 1795, there was a large-scale amnesty to celebrate a national holiday, but Yi Ki-gyŏng was not among those who were pardoned. Although Yi's intention had been to wrong him, Tasan did not wish to see his adversary impoverished by the lengthy legal process necessary to clear his name. Seeing him caught in his own trap gave Tasan some satisfaction; nevertheless, he feared that Yi might become a source of future trouble. Tasan expressed these thoughts to Yi Ig-un and asked his consent to appeal to the king for his enemy's freedom. The King was moved by their entreaty and granted Yi Ki-gyŏng's release.

After his long banishment, Yi did not have many close friends among those of his rank in the court with whom he could share his thoughts. Tasan alone remained kind to him. Nevertheless, in his heart Yi Ki-gyŏng harbored a deep resentment. With Hong Nag-an, he plotted the capture of the Chinese missionary, Father Chou Wen-mu. His scheme was dark, tenacious, and precise.

Once a Catholic himself, Yi was well-versed in Catholicism. Unlike Hong's outbursts, his cool, well-ordered attacks were fearsome in their lucidity and correctness. To the king's questions, he would begin by saying, "There are many good points in the books; however . . . ," and end by arguing point by point that Catholicism was a heresy.

Among the members of the Westerner faction, a loud voice of condemnation was raised: Catholicism was the way of bestiality; its teachings deluded society and deceived the people; it was licentious and mysterious, undermining the very foundations of Confucian teachings; Catholic dogmas—the existence of God, the virgin birth, the redemptive death and resurrection of Jesus Christ—were totally foreign to them. They were appalled by such an outrageous religion—one that not only prohibited the faithful from performing Confucian rituals, but even forced them to burn their ancestral tablets, a sin beyond salvation. The concepts of Heaven and Hell were absurd to them, incompatible with traditional thoughts and ways. Of the Ten Commandments, two were against adultery; even coveting another man's wife was strictly forbidden. Nevertheless, this religion allowed men and women to worship together—wanton behavior in a society where separation of the sexes was rigidly observed.

Yi Ki-gyŏng's attack went beyond Catholic dogma, extending to protocol and rituals. He wrote: "They have already rejected our ethical principles of loyalty to king and filial piety to parents; instead they engage in magic and sorcery. They are no different from Yellow Turbans, the Taoist zealot, of the Han Dynasty in China."

He continued on the subject of Holy Communion: "They worship their god by offering noodles and wine; eating noodles is like eating the flesh of the god and drinking wine is like drinking the blood of the god. How weird and monstrous; indeed, beyond expression!"

When Catholicism came to Korea during the Yi dynasty it encountered enormous resistance because it challenged existing belief systems as well as the social order, and so caused great internal strife in society. Catholic belief was totally incompatible with the Confucian ideals of the Three Cardinal Bonds (faithful ministers, filial sons, and chaste women) and the Five Ethical Relations (the relationships between sovereign and subject, father and son, husband and wife, elder and younger brother, and senior and junior). It was not through the efforts of missionaries that Catholicism spread in Korea. In the beginning it was studied as an academic interest by scholar-officials of the Southerner faction, who had by then lost political power. Disillusioned with the empty, obsolete, and contradictory metaphysics of the day, they developed a profound interest in the Western books brought into Korea by the annual mission to the Peking court. With an insatiable thirst for new knowledge, they marvelled at the newly introduced learning, more logical, scientific, and practical than any they had known. Scientific advances in mathematics and calendrical computation hitherto unknown to them greatly stimulated and influenced these scholar-officials. They joined forces in a new scholarly trend known as Sirhak, or "practical learning," which used an empirical approach aimed at "institutional reform in government" and "economic enrichment in society." *True Principles of Catholicism*, by Matteo Ricci (a Jesuit missionary working in China), was one of the most frequently read books of the movement. Written in Chinese, it was easily understood by those who were fluent in the language. In it, Ricci publicly announced that he had come to China to supplement Confucian belief, and to attack the absurdity of Buddhism. He argued that the Catholic God and the Confucian Lord-on-High were equivalent, and that the Confucian term Heaven, or Providence, was compatible with the Catholic concept of God the Creator. Citing passages from Confucian classics, he demonstrated that the concepts of the soul's immortality and good and evil in Catholicism were analogous to the fundamental teachings of Confucianism. The scholars found Catholicism, although strange and alien at times, easily accessible for the most part. As their research deepened, many decided to accept it as their religion, among them the Chŏng brothers, Yak-chŏn and Tasan.

Catholicism also spread swiftly among people of the lower classes. At this time, the nation had not fully recovered from the devastation of two wars—the Japanese invasion of 1592 and the Manchu invasion of 1636. The common people suffered under a government rampant with corrupt officials, factional strife, and inconsistencies in the system. The concept of equality, the gospel of love and redemption, the idea of rewarding good and punishing evil gave fresh hope to their otherwise dismal existence; though they suffered interminably in this life, they would enjoy an afterlife in Heaven. They would die gladly for God, believing their deaths God's blessing.

In 1784, those who studied Catholicism under Yi Sŭng-hun, who had just returned from Peking, where he had been baptized, received baptism from him. Tasan's baptismal name was Johann. There were about ten converts altogether. In the winter of the same year, the Korean mission was established. The first Catholic church was born in Seoul in the house of a *chungin* court interpreter, Kim Pŏm-u.[7] Services were conducted each Sunday, and other religious activities took place there as well.

The rumor of strange gatherings spread on the quiet, and came to the attention of the authorities. One day the house was raided. Once inside, the agents of the Board of Punishment were confronted with an amazing sight. A few dozen men wearing blue scarves draped from head to shoulders, their faces powdered white, each holding a book under his arm, sat in front of an image of Jesus Christ. A tall man, Yi Pyŏk, was in the midst of a sermon. The officers dared not touch the aristocrats; instead they detained the owner of the house, a commoner. The high-born scholar-officials demanded the return of the image of Jesus and the release of the man; otherwise they, the aristocrats, would insist on being arrested as well.

The chief of the Board of Punishment became fearful because his actions had not been directly ordered by the king. He attempted to placate the aristocrats but sent Kim Pŏm-u, the *chungin*, into banishment. The man eventually died in exile. In the end, no aristocrat was punished by the law, but the incident remained a matter to be settled within the families directly concerned in the episode, and their pressure on the converts mounted. When Yi Pyŏk's father threatened to hang himself unless his son abandoned the religion, Pyŏk—caught between his faith and his humane ethical obligation—finally succumbed. Yi Sŭng-hun, also reprimanded by his father and brother, burned all his books on Catholicism and wrote a vague defense of Confucianism, at the same time denouncing Ca-

7. *Chungin* was a social stratum in Yi dynasty Korea, immediately below that of *yangban*, or nobles. It was made up primarily of technical specialists in the government; namely, interpreters of foreign languages, medical doctors, transcribers, copyists, and so on.

tholicism. The Chŏng brothers, Yak-chŏn and Tasan, were severely reprimanded by their father.

During the few years preceding the incident, Tasan had been living an exalted life. At the age of twenty-one, in February of 1783, Tasan passed the Augmented Examination in commemoration of the Crown Prince's investiture; in April of the same year, he passed the Classic Licentiate Examination. As a result, he was granted an audience with King Chŏngjo; the occasion marked the beginning of their relationship—the meeting of a brilliant king and a wise subject. In September, Tasan's first son, Hag-yŏn, was born. Felicitous events continued through the following year. In the summer of 1784, he presented to the king his *Lecture on the Doctrine of the Mean*. The book was written in response to the eighty questions the king had asked, while Tasan was a student at High College, on the subject of the Four Virtues and Seven Emotions of Man and Natural Forces. The king was greatly pleased with Tasan, recognizing his scholarly prowess. In September, Tasan passed the First Stage Examination toward Licentiate. At the banquets held on February 25 and 27, the king himself served food to Tasan, an almost unprecedented honor. In the same year, Tasan passed the First Stage Examination toward the Erudite Level. The king, seeing Tasan's examination paper, bestowed his praise on it, saying that he would no doubt be a *changwŏn*—a man who takes first place in a Palace Examination held in the presence of a king—and those who were present thought it certain that Tasan would some day become prime minister.

The king's favor and the affection bestowed upon him prevented Tasan from becoming involved in controversy. Thus, it was not out of cowardice that he failed to display the passion and daring of other converts, but because of his favored position. A short ten-day banishment to Haemi and frequent shuffling between the central and provincial governments resulted from the king's desire to protect Tasan from the venomous hostility and fearsome surveillance of his enemies. Aware of this, Tasan wept in gratitude. How dare he trouble such a king? Herein lay the true reason for his confession, in which he defended himself with every argument available, even claiming that he had never been a Catholic. He forced himself into the delusion that he had merely read books on Catholicism, but had not believed in the religion. Finally he retired from the cabinet. His decision to return to pastoral life, giving up everything before he was forty, stemmed from his weariness at having to endure the attacks of the members of the Westerner faction. More important, however, Tasan could not bear to trouble the king any further.

In the spring of 1800, Tasan returned to his native place with his family. A few days later, upon hearing of Tasan's retreat, the king sent for him with the message of royal intention to recall him to the Crown Prince Tutorial Office. The message read: "It would be only a matter of time. We would not forsake you; therefore, we implore you to await our order to return to the Royal Archive as soon as a suitable residence can be found." On the luminous night of June 12, Tasan was alone viewing the summer moon when someone knocked. It was an official from the Royal Archive, bearing ten books written in Chinese that had been sent by the king. When he told Tasan how the king's august countenance had clouded with deep feeling for him, Tasan wept. But on June 28, the king died, only sixteen days after the night when Tasan had shed the tears of gratitude for the king's benevolence. It was as though the heavens had fallen. Tasan had lost his great protector, and thus it was the end of his day.

The king had been suffering from abscesses since the end of May. They first appeared on his head and then spread to his back, gradually reaching the size of two-inch water-droppers. The copious discharge soaked his clothes and pillows. As the large ones, oozing pus, healed, smaller ones appeared around them, swelling red with venom. The king was unable to sleep or touch the royal meals, and his health steadily declined. In the beginning, the courtiers and palace ladies thought nothing of the abscesses; however, they became alarmed when they realized these were not ordinary ones. The officers of the Royal Pharmacy sucked out the pus from the abscesses, administered acupuncture, and used every means of treatment—disinfection, medicines, ointments—but they failed to halt the spread of the abscesses. Finally, an order was sent throughout the nation calling every medical officer to the court. The doctors prescribed all the rare and esoteric medicines known to them, but all in vain. Unable to bear the pain any longer, on June 28 the king summoned to the palace a few of his closest subjects. He was already incoherent. His trembling finger pointed in the air, but no one could understand the meaning of this gesture. Only by bringing their ears closer to the king's face were the words "Sujŏngjŏn Palace," the residence of the Queen Dowager, finally deciphered. Without any further words, the king expired at about six o'clock in the evening at the age of forty-eight, his reign having lasted for twenty-four years. Why did the king, summoning up his last strength, speak these words?

The Queen Dowager, Chŏng-sun, was of the Kim clan of Kyŏngju and had become a queen at the tender age of fifteen by marrying Yŏngjo, the grandfather of King Chŏngjo, who was then sixty-three years old. Chŏng-sun was the daughter of Kim Han-ku, a destitute scholar-gentleman, and her marriage turned a dream into sudden reality for her family. Overnight, the penniless scholar became a Meritorious Retainer of the First Degree, a title given solely to the king's father-in-law, and the other members of the clan were given high government positions.

The Kim clan belonged to the Old Doctrine clique of the Party of Principle. The queen's brother, Kim Ku-ju, turned his back on his past impoverishment and appointed himself the leader of the party. Two factions had taken shape over the conflict between King Yŏngjo, on the side of Party of Principle, and the opposition party, or Party of Expediency, on the side of Crown Prince Changhŏn and the royal grandson, who would later ascend to the throne as King Chŏngjo. The leader of the Party of Expediency was Hong Pong-han, the maternal grandfather of King Chŏngjo.

Kim Ku-ju was uncomfortable. King Yŏngjo, in advanced age, might pass away at any moment. Kim feared the time when the robust, middle-aged crown prince should become king. Moreover, his adversary, Hong Pong-han, was a man of impeccable virtue, with a depth of learning no one could equal. A man of prudence and upright character, Hong commanded the trust and respect of everyone—from the king to his fellow scholar-officials in the court, to the lowly petty officers and the middle-class citizenry. Kim was determined to eliminate Hong at any cost.

Having been born and raised in poverty, the queen lacked refinement in manner and barely managed to escape being ugly. But she was a blooming girl of fifteen; her freshness was what the king cherished and loved in her. Manipulated by her brother, she played a considerable role in the royal family scandals and in an upheaval of national importance. She spied on the activity of the crown prince and reported to the king his frequent outbursts of madness, thus escalating the ill feeling between father and son. Playing on the unusual dislike the king already had for his heir, she was among those who, in 1762, instigated the murder of the prince.

Kim went further. After the cruel murder of the crown prince, he schemed to eliminate the prince's son as well, declaring that since the royal grandson was the son of a criminal, he could not succeed to the throne. Some Confucian scholars hailed the statement, which resulted in the further isolation of the boy. At the suggestion of his maternal grandfather, Hong Pong-han, the royal grandson was adopted into the household of Prince Hyojang, the elder brother of the murdered crown prince, a move that saved the ten-year-old prince from the evil hands of Kim Ku-ju, and later enabled him to succeed to the throne as King Chŏngjo.

Although benevolent and forgiving, once he ascended to the throne King Chŏngjo banished Kim Ku-ju to Hŭksan Island, where he eventually died years later. At the time of her brother's death the Queen Dowager was a young woman of about twenty; harboring a deep grudge for more than twenty years, she had been living in solitude, hidden deep in the Sujŏngjŏn Palace.

When the Queen Dowager found out that the health of King Chŏngjo showed no sign of improvement, she began frequenting the bedside of her royal grandson by marriage, who was yet her contemporary in age. Her face clouded with concern and anxiety, she would order the courtiers to send messengers to every corner of the country to find medicines secret and sacred for the king, who had become increasingly emaciated after many days without sleep or food. She urged him to take some restorative tonic, remarking, "Your Majesty seems very exhausted. Please take something to protect your noble personage."

The chief physicians of the Royal Pharmacy were members of the Party of Principle, the group responsible for the murder of Crown Prince Changhŏn, the father of the king. So deep was the queen's apparent anxiety over the king's illness that the chief physicians visited her frequently in Sujŏngjŏn Palace to report to her. At her request, a restorative tonic had been prescribed for the king. It was known that a mixture of the root of Japanese monkshood, powdered ginger, and ginseng was most effective in augmenting an enfeebled yang-spirit and restoring exhausted vitality. The physicians no doubt knew of this tonic and must have prescribed it to the king. However, it was midsummer, and the king had been suffering for a long time from the painful abscesses. The tonic, too potent for the king's weakened body, acted like oil on fire. Had the physicians been ignorant of this inevitable reaction? Or knowing what might happen, had they dared to administer the potion to the king? Accident or not, it was regicide.

The king, whose passing was utterly needless, had been a wise sovereign, filial to his parents, lofty and pure in his living, his character humane and generous; above all else, he loved knowledge and able scholars. In an effort to pacify factional strife and maintain equilibrium in society, he had continued the Policy of Impartiality, first adopted by his grandfather King Yŏngjo, which aimed at according equal favor to men of all factions in any appointments to office. Thus, he had appointed Ch'ae Che-kong, a man of the then-declining Southerner faction, as a prime minister, and his trust in him was such that Ch'ae's tenure lasted ten years. The king had greatly favored and held high expectations of such young elites as Chŏng Yak-chong and Yi Sŭng-hun. However, the king himself had been felled, a victim of the very factionalism he had tried to circumvent.

On the day the king died, extraordinary phenomena appeared, causing trepidation in the entire nation. It was reported that the sun's rays collided with each other, sending forth sparks in the air, and that a loud wail came from Mount Samgak. A few days before, the rice plants that had been growing vigorously in many provinces suddenly withered. Watching the sight, people trembled in fear. What catastrophe was about to strike? "It foretells mourning, a sign of some great sorrow soon to occur," whispered wise old folk, frowning with apprehension.

With the passing of the old order, the new king, Sunjo, ascended to the throne at the age of ten. Miraculously, the Queen Dowager emerged out of her retirement deep in the Sujŏngjŏn Palace and, sitting behind the young king's throne, conducted political affairs on his behalf.

On the first of November, King Chŏngjo was buried. After less than twenty days, on the seventeenth of the same month, the nation was swept up in a whirlwind of Catholic arrests. The dagger of revenge, which the Queen Dowager had been hiding deep in her bosom for twenty years, had finally been drawn. On January 9, 1801, the leader of the Korean Mission, Ch'oe Ch'ang-hyŏn, was arrested.

On the eleventh, the Queen Dowager issued a royal decree banning
Catholicism as treasonous heresy. The curtain had finally gone up
on her drama of revenge, which became known as the Persecution
of 1801. It was more a political move than a religious one, intended
to bring down the Party of Expediency, the majority of its leaders
being the Southerner Catholics. The bloody roundup intensified.
One after another, the leaders of the party were arrested. After severe interrogation, some were beheaded, and some sent into banishment. Of the Chŏng brothers, the third, Yak-chong, persisted in his
faith, choosing martyrdom; Yak-chŏn and Tasan declared apostasy,
and were banished to Sinchi Island and to Changgi, respectively.

What caused Tasan to recant, once the king, with his boundless
love for him, had gone, and his own days were numbered? While
the king was still on the throne, Tasan's loyalty and love for him had
led him to declare publicly his innocence of the taint of Catholicism,
using the lame excuse that his interest in it had been purely academic. That was then; what about now? His action was inscrutable
even to himself. Why? To spare his wretched life? Or was his faith
too feeble? Wasn't he a Catholic with the Christian name of Johann?
Wasn't he man enough to uphold his principles to the end?

Remorse tormented Tasan from time to time, but he was also a
man vulnerable to the conditions of man. He could not free himself
from feelings of rage and humiliation when his thoughts dwelt on
Catholicism; how was it possible that he had ever been enticed by
it? His illustrious family had served in the Office of Special Advisers
to the King for seven generations, but it had been out of office during
the reigns of the past three kings because of its membership in the
disfavored Southerner faction. Only since his late father's time had
the family begun a recovery, and with Tasan in the office its fortunes
had slowly improved. Had he never come into contact with Catholicism, he would not have been tempted by it, nor would he have
become a despicable renegade. He could not reconcile the conflicts
within him. How horrible and loathsome was Catholicism! It pursued them relentlessly to the end, driving the clan to extinction.
How to explain the deep silence of God, omnipotent and omniscient, for whom the wretched faithful suffered pain that defied
expression? Where were His saving hands?

As the days of banishment multiplied, however, Tasan's thoughts
gradually withdrew from Catholicism. There were no Catholics

around him to remind him of his religion. His days were filled with activity—lecturing his disciples, pursuing research, enjoying tea with Hyejang, and tending flowers and medicinal herb gardens. During this time he also began reading some Japanese books that reinforced his opposition to the civil service examination system. In a letter to his sons, he mentioned his then-controversial views: "As we look back, we see that the Japanese managed to become literate only through the books the Koreans sent them. Since then, by opening a direct contact with the Chinese, they obtained the finest books from them. Unlike us, however, the Japanese were not guilty of unwisely selecting government bureaucrats through civil service examinations, a waste of scholarship. Because of this, they are far ahead of us in the advancement of knowledge. A great shame indeed."

Tasan had been sitting for a long time with his eyes closed. Ha-sang, watching his uncle, waited in silence. No sign of impatience showed on Ha-sang's face; since childhood, hardship had taught him patience unusual in one so young.

A deep silence settled in the room. An autumn fly appeared out of nowhere and alighted on the paper window, the flutter of its listless wings disturbing the calm.

◆　◆　◆

His reverie shattered by the insect's delicate tremor, Tasan opened his eyes. Ha-sang remained seated with his back against the sliding door. His robust body filling the entire width of a single door, and silhouetted against the light behind him, he looked like a shadow having substance. His lusterless, clumsy topknot protruded as if it were a part of that shadow. He was full of confidence and trust. Staring at the funny-looking topknot, Tasan asked, "When did you get married?"

"I am still a bachelor."

"What? No initiation ceremony, no wedding, and you wear a topknot?"

The shoulders of the shadow shook, and Ha-sang smiled shyly. "It's because I am so tall and large for my age." He touched the back of his head. There was a childish innocence in the movement. In the darkness, Tasan imagined a blush rising on those fresh cheeks. He was smiling in spite of himself. "At the age of sixteen, it's about time you had a wife."

"Getting married? It's out of the question," Ha-sang interrupted abruptly.

"Why not? Are you going to grow old a bachelor?" There was a hint of mischief in Tasan's words. Such light moments seldom occurred to Tasan, who was beginning to take a liking to this youth at the threshold of adulthood.

Separated from his own sons, Tasan had been constantly preoccupied with their proper deportment and decorum. Although both were exceptional youths, they disappointed Tasan, who expected more from them. Even their effort to obtain a pardon for their father seemed to him more an act of degradation and a bending of their principles than a fulfillment of their filial duty. Tasan worried most whether they had begun to display the ignominy of character that was the sign of a ruined family, but the young face in front of him betrayed no such baseness, no trace of gloom; it expressed only strength and integrity. He wondered at the source of that glow, that cheerfulness, which he was unable to see on the faces of his sons, or on those of his disciples.

"I think it's about time you got married and had sons and daughters. It is a filial duty to your mother. Don't you agree with me?"

"I am not to be married," Ha-sang answered quietly.

"Then, you, you . . ." Tasan searched for words.

Ha-sang continued in a still hushed voice, "I have too many things to do. I have no time to have children. Mother gave me her willing consent."

"What is it then that you have to do which is so important, more urgent than having a family?"

His soft, clear face tensed, and then with a lowered voice Ha-sang answered, "I have to travel to Peking."

Tasan almost jumped up from his seat. "What did you say just now? To Peking, did you say, to Peking? Why?"

"We have to bring a Catholic priest here."

Tasan's heart stopped. His low voice now bore added force. "You don't know the enormity of what you are saying. Did you come here just to tell me such a preposterous thing?"

"That's not all for which I have come. I wanted to see you. I have heard so much about you." Ha-sang looked at his uncle's face, dazzled as though looking at something blindingly bright.

True to the stories he had heard, Ha-sang thought his uncle's eyebrows were different from those of any other men. They said such eyebrows were called "three brows." Tasan had recovered almost scarless from smallpox. However, one tiny scar just above his right eyebrow divided it in two, which, together with the left eyebrow, made it look as if he had three brows. Having heard so much about the brows, they gave him a feeling of familiarity as he now looked at his uncle. They looked more distinguished than his uncle's celebrated sideburns and beard. Such an abnormality might well have been considered a deformity on others. On Tasan, however, there was nobility rather than discord in the long, thick brows.

Ha-sang had heard much about his uncle, for Tasan was a man of such esteem that there were numerous stories about him. Since even his relatives shunned Ha-sang like a plague, a son of the beheaded heretic, he played in the servants' quarters, where he felt more comfortable even though it was windowless, dank, filthy, and foul-smelling. In a household where the masters lived in quiet seclusion and sorrow as the families of treasonous brothers, one executed and the other two banished, in the servants' quarters, too, there were no frequent gatherings of neighborhood servants. However, an old servant, Sŏk, who had been with the family for generations, had a few acquaintances, and they came to pay their respects to him as the elder among them. Sŏk alone treated Ha-sang as a young master and cared for him, while even others of the servant class despised him. It was this old man, young Ha-sang's only solace, who told him the family history with pride. Among the many stories he related, the most interesting was about Tasan's wedding day.

Mischievous tricks customarily accompanied weddings. The groom, as he dismounted from his horse, would walk to the "wild geese table," which was covered with a crimson cloth, and make a deep bow in front of it. Then, placing a pair of carved wooden geese, the symbol of conjugal bliss, on the table, he would again make a deep bow and step onto the carpet provided for the groom, which was spread on the path from the table to the ceremonial hall. Before his arrival, playful youths from the bride's family would place rocks, millet stalks, or some such rough objects under the carpet to cause the young groom, in the full formal attire of the ceremony, to stumble. If caught unguarded, he would fall, delighting the anticipant spectators, who burst into laughter.

Even before meeting the young groom, a cousin of the bride, Hong Tae-ho, a prodigy himself, had been scheming to play such a trick on Tasan. Suppressing a gleeful smile, he was waiting for his new in-law, whose reputation as a child genius was well known. Not yet fully grown, an adolescent of fourteen, Tasan was a tiny bridegroom. The bride's family was dumbfounded when he appeared at the nuptial ceremony. He looked too young and too small for his age. It was as if a child actor in full regalia had appeared on stage. But the groom, clever as he was small, anticipated the antic at his first step, and with his head held high walked on, pushing away the rocks with his feet, and finally reached the hall without missing a step. It was Hong who stumbled in front of the terrace stone as he led the bridegroom to the hall, waving his arms right and left in a ceremonious gesture, which caused delighted laughter among the spectators.

Hong loved this precocious young in-law. He thought to himself, "How could a fellow as tiny as a jujube seed have amassed so much knowledge for one so young, and distinguished himself in the composition of poetry? Why don't I test his literary genius?" Hong shouted at Tasan with patronizing admiration, "Look here, groom, since your ability to compose poetry is so celebrated, how about matching my rhymes and ideograms?"

I expected a brother-in-law,
But what I see is a three-foot child—
What is this but a midget's trick?

To this quip, Tasan answered, smiling, with a sonorous voice:

I expected the grandson of a mighty gentleman,
But what I see is a fool's son—
What is this but a devil's farce?

"Everyone present was struck with admiration. I still remember vividly how pleased was the old master of the bride's household." Sŏk's eyes were full of longing. "It's all because they studied so hard. You, too, my young master, must make an effort to study. This old servant watched with his own eyes how hard His Excellency studied. Being so intelligent by nature and studying so diligently was like adorning a beautiful woman with flowers. Even though he suffers hardship now, he is still this generation's greatest man of letters."

Then Sŏk told Ha-sang the way Tasan went about acquiring knowledge.

Tasan was a young boy of barely twelve, with a thick plait of hair swinging behind his back. A scholar on his way to the capital to take the civil service examination happened to pass him on a mountain path, leading a heavily loaded donkey. Struck by the uncommon brightness in the boy's eyes, the scholar asked, "Whose young master are you and where are you heading?"

"I am the fourth son of the Minister Chŏng of Majae. I am on my way home."

"And what are those on the donkey?"

"Books. I borrowed them from my uncle's place," the boy answered, smiling sweetly.

"Who reads all those books?"

"I do. I borrowed them for myself," he replied nonchalantly, still smiling.

They parted, and days later, dejected after failing the examination, the scholar immediately headed for his home. As he was walking on the same path he had taken before, he saw the young lad he had seen on his way to the capital. Just as before, he was leading the donkey with a full load on its back. "Ah! We meet again," the scholar said.

"How are you sir?" the boy greeted him affably. "You are returning home so soon?"

"Yes. I cannot stay in a place not my own for too long. But, what is that on the donkey this time?"

"The books. I am returning the books I borrowed."

"Why? Does the owner want them back so soon?"

"No. I have read them all. I am returning them so I can borrow some more. They have so many more books." Again a smile lit up young Tasan's face; he had read all the books in less than ten days.

"His Excellency worked so hard. Young master, you too must honor his example," the old servant entreated Ha-sang.

Except for his scorned, widowed mother, no one looked after young Ha-sang, and consequently at the age of ten he had not

learned *The Thousand Characters*, a primer of Chinese characters
for children. A woman of wisdom and virtue, his mother worried
about Ha-sang's education day and night.

"Ha-sang, instead of going to the servants' quarters all the time,
why don't you go visit your cousins and study with them?"

"They give me dirty looks."

"Of course. You are still too young for them. You must study even
if it means looking over their shoulders."

"They shout at me to get out."

"You must endure all hardships. You must never forget how your
father died. You have a mission, a holy mission, indeed. For this,
you must study."

"Why did my father die? What was he like?"

"He was a saint of a man. For Jesus Christ he was martyred." Her
face was solemn, and her voice stern.

"But everyone torments me, saying I am a heretic's son."

"They say such things because they are ignorant. Don't blame
them; just uphold your principles. Before it gets too late, let us offer
our evening prayers." The mother took out a rosary from her bosom.

Kneeling on a straw mat on the floor of the shed blackened with
pinewood soot, this family of three, the mother, Ha-sang, and
Chŏng-hye, offered prayers morning and night. The books of religious creeds and prayers having been confiscated, and without fellow believers around them, they were ignorant of Catholic ritual.
They merely repeated what the mother still remembered. In those
moments, when her roughened hands joined together in single-
minded devotion, her eyes were always filled with tears. The
brother and sister recited the prayers devoutly, though the meaning
was unintelligible to them. They forgot for a time the poverty and
persecution they endured daily, for this was the only time that their
hearts were joined together.

They loved their mother most when she was filled with peace,
even though her face was streaked with tears. In offering prayers,
she was meticulous, never shortening or omitting any passages. Reciting the Three Mysteries, her voice was passionate, intoning the
Lord's Prayer, solemn, and her Hail Mary was ardent. Their mother
taught them to believe in the existence of the one who looked over
them in their sufferings, and to praise and offer gratitude for such a
being. Clothed in tatters as they were, the young siblings betrayed

neither poverty of spirit nor servility. On the contrary, their faces were always cheerful and at peace.

Ha-sang was twelve years old when he learned for the first time about his father from someone other than a family member. Taking after his uncle Tasan, he had been slow in growth, and at the age of twelve, he looked no bigger than eight. It was autumn then. The neighborhood urchins gathered together to steal some ripening soybeans from a field ready for harvesting. As the day of the Harvest Moon neared, the soybean plants were heavy, their pods bursting. The children uprooted whole stalks and roasted the beans on a boulder on the hillside, hidden from view. The tender, juicy, fresh beans tasted swooningly delicious for these rascals, but more important, the raids—in early spring of wheat fields and in early autumn of soybeans—were childhood games of unforgettable joy and seasonal pleasure.

Because soybean plants did not grow tall, if a big boy crawled close to the ground among them, he could be seen, but if a child was too young, he might not be strong enough to pull them up by the roots. That task fell on Ha-sang; the raids were the only time these village pranksters included him in their play. Old enough to be strong, yet small and agile, he was perfectly suited for their purpose, and he, in turn, wanted to hear them say how well he had done the job. Since he was so often alone, the pleasure of their company made him forget the commandment that had been sternly instilled in him by his devout mother: Thou shalt not steal. Indeed, it did not seem an act of theft so much as a game of much fun and daring. However, retribution struck him. Suddenly, the owner of the field appeared. The other children fled as they spotted the owner, while Ha-sang alone, unaware of his approach, was caught in the act. The memory of the humiliation and bitterness would remain in his mind the rest of his life. Though it had been a mere child's game, his aunts, who had always ignored him before, became fiercely agitated by the incident, heaping upon him the words "heretic's son."

Ha-sang's mother was summoned. The fourth aunt, Tasan's wife, was the most vicious in her accusation.

"Sister-in-law, whose fault is it that this illustrious household has come to this pass? It's all because of that cursed Catholic faith. If your husband had confessed and repented his wrongs at the time of

the persecution in 1801, as our second brother-in-law and my husband did, we could all have been spared this wretched fate. You
may not realize it, but we all know that in the morning and evening
you chant some kind of incantation. Is it your intention to drive us
into complete ruination? Are you so bitter because we are still holding onto this shred of dignity?" She was hysterical. Because of her
husband's position, she had enjoyed the capital life-style and had
the taste of the fame that accompanied her husband's official position.

Her son's behavior was causing her infinite sorrow, and Ha-sang's
mother was unable to speak.

The second sister-in-law, Yak-chŏn's wife, continued prudently,
"At his age, he should be married soon. Certainly he is too old to
be getting into trouble with low-born children. Even though our
family has become what we are now, how dare he behave like some
commoner?"

Tasan's wife again spoke in consternation. "Sister, you never
seem to come to your senses. You let your son rummage in the
soybean field, mixing with the commoner brats! What next? A still
greater disaster? Either you must go away, or we should move elsewhere. We must come to a decision."

It was now the eldest sister-in-law's turn. The wife of Yak-hyŏn,
she had so far been silent.

"Master Hwang Sa-yŏng, at the age of sixteen, in the presence of
the king, took a first place in the Lower Level Examination, and had
the honor of having his hand stroked by a royal hand. His death,
his unspeakable death—I have been afraid to say this, but I must
now—your husband was responsible for it. He was sure to pass
the Higher Level Examination and after that, his success in the
government would have been assured. And, such a man to meet
such a fate . . ." She could not finish. "That poor, poor woman, my
stepdaughter, was exiled to a remote land as the wife of a treasonous
heretic, and has become, I hear, a slave. The child has been abandoned in Ch'uja Island. Who knows if it is still alive?" She touched
her eyes with the ties of her blouse. She had conveniently forgotten
her cruel treatment of her stepdaughter, the wife of Hwang Sa-yŏng:
she had not even allowed the family into her house when they returned to Majae.

Tasan's wife continued the unyielding attack. "You are so right.

He brought ruination not only upon the Chŏng clan but on his in-law's family as well. He lured Master Hwang, who had been devoting himself to preparation for the civil service examination, into that cursed Catholicism. My heart is seared at the thought of that poor lady, the mother of Master Hwang, widowed young, and her son born after the death of her husband. Her only wish in life was to see her son rise to a high position. I heard she has been exiled to Koje Island. I wonder if she is alive or dead."

Ha-sang's mother stood in silence, her head bowed. In reality, their accusations seemed altogether correct. Because her husband had upheld the Catholic faith, an act of high treason, he and Hwang Sa-yŏng had cruelly met martyrdom, and his two brothers, because of their involvement with the religion, had been banished to remote islands. She understood the reasons for the consternation of her sisters-in-law. Tasan's wife was right when she said that Yak-chong had been responsible for extinguishing the life of young Sa-yŏng, for whom worldly fame was within reach.

Hwang Sa-yŏng was born soon after the death of his father, Sŏk-pŏm. Studying as a disciple of Yak-chong, he was a student of great promise. At the young age of sixteen, when he received first place in the Lower Level Examination, King Chŏngjo, filled with royal pleasure at a scholar of such tender age, commanded Sa-yŏng to come forward, whereupon he stroked his hand, an unprecedented royal act beyond court protocol.

"When you reach the age of nineteen, we wish you to stay with us in our presence," the king told him. Thus heralded by glory and great expectation, his future success seemed firmly assured. Sa-yŏng shed tears of gratitude. For the rest of his life, he kept a red silk brocade scarf wrapped around his left wrist, the one that had been caressed by the royal hand.

Having passed the Lower Level Examination, one could either become a lower grade bureaucrat or be admitted to the National Confucian Academy. The Higher Level Examination was the prerequisite to higher office. Showing no inclination to enter the academy, Sa-yŏng stayed in Majae to prepare for the Higher Level Examination under the tutelage of Yak-chong. At first, Yak-chong advised Sa-yŏng to enter the academy, discreetly declining to tutor him on the pretext that he had nothing further to teach him, but at Sa-yŏng's persistent entreaty he reluctantly consented to keep him.

Good fortune continued in Sa-yŏng's life. A marriage had been arranged between him and Nan-ju, the eldest daughter of the eldest Chŏng brother, Yak-hyŏn. With a beautiful wife at his side and now the son-in-law of an illustrious family, Sa-yŏng worked even harder. As the only son of a widowed mother, he felt obliged to pass the examination at the earliest possible date in order to please her, whose only wish in life had been to see him rise in the world and attain fame. He made great progress in his studies. His innate intelligence and hard work assured his successful passing of the examination.

However, Yak-chong's mind was in turmoil. He was torn with doubt whether his student, untainted by such worldly success, should be thrust into the blind pursuit of fame, as illusory and fleeting as a floating cloud, where lurked the entrapments set by those who harbored jealousy and greed. The path would be strewn with the pitfalls of vicious factional strife. Yak-chong did not want to let this youth of impeccable character throw himself into such a path. Witnessing the sufferings of his two brothers, Yak-chŏn and Tasan, Yak-chong had seen how these men of character had not been able to free themselves from the ambition for power and fame. They had forsaken the scholarly, more primary and higher values only to be mired in the turbid current of mundane affairs. Now what fate would await this unblemished youth? Such a life might well be preserved mounted on a hanging scroll, like priceless writings on pristine paper, but this young man was wasting his youth in pursuit of the rainbow of hollow fame. Pity and regret for Sa-yŏng seized upon him.

On the other hand, Sa-yŏng could not comprehend his teacher's mind. Though he felt a profound admiration for his teacher's encyclopedic erudition, he questioned why Yak-chong was reluctant to take upon himself the responsibility of entering public office to counsel the throne of a benevolent government.

Yak-chong was quite different from the other distinguished Chŏng brothers, less rigid and introspective than Yak-hyŏn and lacking the refinement of Yak-chŏn or the brilliance of Tasan. He was prudent and sincere, a man of sober habit. Always gentle in his countenance and bearing, he treated everyone equally, which made Yak-hyŏn, a man of conservative values, grimace in displeasure. At a time when the line between legitimate and illegitimate offspring was severely drawn, his illegitimate brother felt comfortable enough with Yak-chong to address him as brother, although he could address the rest of his family members only by their official titles. Stories of Yak-chong's egalitarian spirit were circulated among the people. It was said that in his household everyone ate at the same table and that he once carried home on his back a servant's child who had fallen from a tree. The other brothers disliked such behavior. "You must not confuse a clearcut division of hierarchical order. The family reputation must be considered," Yak-hyŏn would chide him.

"As the saying goes, 'a novice thief is unaware of daybreak': it is because he is a recent convert that he really practices what Catholicism teaches." A bitter smile rose to Yak-chŏn's lips, who had become a Catholic before anyone else and had also been the first to renounce it.

"He has no need to go that far." Tasan, too, was uncomfortable; a sharp needle of conscience was pricking him, for he had renounced his faith at the same time as Yak-chŏn.

Until then, Sa-yŏng had not come in contact with Catholicism; he had been too preoccupied in preparing for the civil service examination. But one day Sa-yŏng had to visit his teacher unannounced, having encountered some difficulty in his reading. He made his presence known, but there was no answer from inside. Since the steward had informed him that Yak-chong was in the study alone, he waited awhile on the threshold stone. "Master," he called out, but no stirring came from within. He went into the main hall and opened the paper sliding door ever so gently. He saw Yak-chong's body swaying almost imperceptibly left and right; his lips were quivering. Unaware of Sa-yŏng's presence, Yak-chong was single-mindedly reciting something. The solemnity of his face prevented Sa-yŏng from saying a word; he could neither speak to him nor leave him, but stood transfixed. Still unaware of Sa-yŏng's presence, Yak-chong made the sign of the cross with his right hand over his chest, and finally opened his eyes. Seeing Sa-yŏng, he was perturbed for a moment, but soon composed himself and said serenely, "Sorry to have made you wait so long."

After the incident, there was no change in Yak-chong's attitude. Sa-yŏng made great strides in his studies. However, he often recalled the incident; his teacher certainly must be in the process of acquiring some strange magic, he thought to himself. The face, awe-inspiring in its intensity of purpose, the quivering lips reciting some indecipherable incantation, and the strange symbol he had made across his chest, all caused curiosity, wonder, and apprehension in Sa-yŏng's mind.

Another day soon after, Sa-yŏng again witnessed the same scene. This time, Yak-chong, though aware of his presence, did not stop what he was doing. Everything was just as he had seen it last time, the solemn face, pursed lips, the sign of the cross on his chest; however, this time there was no sign of perturbation in Yak-chong's eyes when he opened them momentarily. "You must have waited for a long time," he said, just as calmly as before.

After having observed the same scene three times, Sa-yŏng could no longer suppress his curiosity. He had to find out. "My esteemed teacher, who are you? What is it that you are doing?" he asked, coming straight to the point.

Yak-chong smiled gently. He closed his eyes again and remained so for a long time. When he opened his eyes, his face was weighed down with an expression of majesty, determination, and beatitude. He opened a chest, took out a book, and handed it to Sa-yŏng. On the oiled-paper cover was written in Chinese, *True Principles of Catholicism*. For the time being, Sa-yŏng put aside the books he had been reading in preparation for the examination. For three days and three nights, without sleep or food, he was totally consumed by a book that he had never known existed. It brought him new, wondrous insight, even though many things in it were unintelligible and unconvincing to him. On the fourth day, Sa-yŏng sought out his teacher. At first glance, Yak-chong understood the turmoil in his mind. During the past few days, Sa-yŏng had become unrecogniz-ably emaciated. In his pale face his bloodshot eyes burned. It was the face of someone who was in the midst of a conflict born of the astonishment and shock of new discovery, a face that spoke of the intertwined emotions of anguish, longing, and joy.

"I have so far lived without being aware of the existence of such a book. What is it that disturbs my whole being like this? Is it be-cause I am so inspired by the discovery of new truth? Or am I merely being sucked into some mire of confusion by the capricious writing? I do not understand the meaning of all this."

Yak-chong shut his eyes, sensing a glow, glorious as sunrise, filling them.

Sa-yŏng advanced his query desperately. "What is God? What is the meaning of the Trinity? The book tells us that God is the Holy Trinity, that is, the Father, the Son, and the Holy Ghost. How is it possible that the three become one, and one three? The idea of the Resurrection of Jesus Christ is absurd. And how about the notion of Immaculate Conception? How is it possible that a virgin can be impregnated without a man's intervention and bring forth a human child, the only son of God?"

Yak-chong's eyes remained closed. In Sa-yŏng's voice, he heard his own echoing down the years from the time when he had first read the book. It was as though he were confronting himself once again, that young man who, struggling to comprehend, had been overwhelmed by the same powerful force. His brothers seemed to have grasped the truth in a flash with the help of the passionate and eloquent persuasion of Yi Pyŏk, the brother-in-law of Yak-chŏn. However, he had been modest and prudent in his acceptance of the teachings. For several years, he had struggled, questioning and meditating in order to understand. He had lost interest in everything but the Catholic dogmas. He had sent away all his disciples. His lonely and painful pursuit continued for several years, but his heart was filled with gladness. Finally, he had come to accept the Catholic religion in its entirety.

Yak-chong corrected his posture, fixed his eyes upon Sa-yŏng, and finally answered his young student. It was the first of many lectures, lucid and rich in allusions, quoting freely from his deep knowledge of the Confucian classics, which facilitated Sa-yŏng's understanding. Yak-chong had written a book entitled *A Summary of Catholic Teaching*, which the Chinese Father Chou Wen-mu had praised as far superior to many books written in China on Catholicism. Sa-yŏng's enthusiasm was so great that he completely abandoned the study of the classics, which he had been reading in preparation for the examination. He renounced gladly, too, the world of wealth and fame that lay before him; instead, by 1801, he had chosen the path to a spiritual life.

At about this time, a rumor began circulating that the Korean Christians were scheming to ask certain Western nations to send naval forces to take over the country. The authorities were unable to determine the source of the rumor. They made a desperate effort to arrest Chou Wen-mu, who had eluded them in the past. The bloody pursuit of the converts spread throughout the nation, accompanied by inhuman atrocities. Many prominent Catholics met with cruel punishment, were forced to denounce their faith, or were banished. Witnessing the intolerable suffering of his flock, Father Chou Wen-mu voluntarily surrendered himself and was beheaded. However, the persecution only grew in intensity.

Finally, in Chinju, Yu Kwan-kŏm was arrested as one of the conspirators, and under severe torture he was forced to make a false confession. Armed with this "confession," the authorities mounted a great manhunt in search of Hwang Sa-yŏng, suspected of being responsible for the plan. He was finally traced to his hiding place in a subterranean potters' cave in Paeron. Hwang Sa-yŏng was in possession of a long letter he had written on silk, addressed to Bishop Alexandre de Gouvéa in Peking, that reported the persecution of the Catholics in Korea and proposed the measures he believed would deliver the faithful from persecution; foremost among them was a plea to the Western nations to dispatch their military forces to compel the Korean government to grant religious freedom. The Silk Letter, as it came to be known, was a missive sixty-two centimeters long by thirty-six wide containing more than thirteen thousand letters. It would never reach its destination. The government, enraged at the enormity of the message contained in the letter, ordered that Sa-yŏng be hacked to pieces, and Yak-chong be executed. In the aftermath, Tasan and Yak-chŏn were imprisoned. Once cleared of involvement in the plot, they were sent into banishment again, Tasan to Kangjin, and Yak-chŏn to Hŭksan Island.

The incident of the soybean field marked a turning point in Hasang's life. Although he could endure the evil castigation and insults of his aunts, the boy of twelve had no way of alleviating the sorrow of his mother. As soon as he was released from the frantic clutches of the women, he ran to the comfort of the old servant, Sŏk. His mother followed him, begging and threatening him to get him out of the servants' quarters, but he stubbornly refused. Giving up the effort and sighing heavily, she returned to her room. Ha-sang buried his head between his knees and sobbed bitterly, until he felt the touch of a rough hand first on his ears and then caressing his hair. Soon, he heard the old man begin to talk in a croaking voice. "Young master, you must not feel sad. You may be young yet, but you are the son of a noble and distinguished man. You must lift your head up high and be proud."

Ha-sang looked up in amazement, "Old man, you are saying that my father was not an evil man?" Many a time young Ha-sang was plunged into confusion. His mother followed devoutly the religion everyone else denounced as heretical. She told him that his father was a truly noble man whom everyone cursed and abused, and that he must honor his father's will. In spite of what his mother told him, he could not understand why his first uncle never let him come near him, condemning him for being the son of the one who had brought ruination upon the family.

The servant shook his head violently. "Of course not. There never lived a man like him, compassionate and gentle, always aware of the suffering of others, even those low-borns. This wretched servant, too, owes much to him."

Ha-sang stopped crying, "Old man, please tell me more about my father. I want to be sure that he was never a wicked man."

"Yes, of course. I will. I certainly will."

After clearing his throat a few times, Sŏk continued the story. "First of all, I must tell you about his honorable countenance. If you want to know how he looked, you are only to behold His Excellency's face. Only two years apart, they looked like twins. He was a tall, truly handsome man, and his earlobes, too, were ample, a sure sign of longevity. But he never lived beyond forty-two . . ." he sighed. "And on his temple there was a black mole which His Excellency does not have. It was just like yours on your temple, in the same spot . . ." With his thick finger, he touched the mole gently. Ha-sang, too, traced it; he could feel it there. For the first time he came to realize its existence, for he had never looked into a mirror. Occasionally he gazed at his distorted reflection on the surface of water, but he had no desire to know how he looked. Now that he knew about the mole, it seemed wonderful and amusing.

The old man coughed, and continued, "Young master, perhaps you may remember men by the names of Han-bin and Il-gwang, who were stewards in your household? Although Han-bin was low-born, the son of a seamstress, he was an upright man. At the time of the persecution, he brought your family back here to Majae from the capital."

"Oh yes. I do remember him."

Han-bin had removed the family, reduced to beggary after Yak-chong was beheaded, to the safety of Majae. He worked tirelessly for the church and was executed at the time of the Silk Letter incident. Ha-sang still remembered the broad back that had carried him. "Your father even took meals with him from the same table. He never discriminated against anyone because of his station in life."

The lamplight flickered. The old man turned up the wick and went on. "That's not all. Il-gwang was the son of a butcher, a man from the most despised class in the world. He was originally from Hongju, but he could not endure the discrimination and moved to Kyŏngsang Province. Even there, they found out who he was, and he was about to leave the place when your father rescued him. He became a convert and was baptized as Alexandre. Your father treated him as an equal even though he was so low-born."

"What happened to him?"

"He was sent back to his hometown, and there he was executed. He was caught on his way to buy some firewood. It was said that he did not show the slightest sign of fear. He shouted at the soldiers, 'I, a magistrate of Namwŏn, was transferred here to Okch'ŏn. Indeed, what a paradise this Okch'ŏn is!' "

Ha-sang's eyes widened; he was unable to catch the joke. Sŏk let out a laugh with his throat full of phlegm, making a sound of gusty wind, and explained, "He was playing the word-game of Chinese and Korean puns. You see, the Chinese ideograms for *Namwŏn* have the same sound as the Korean word for *wood*, and for *Okch'ŏn* the same as *prison*. Having been treated so badly because of his low birth, he was happy to have been treated as an equal since his conversion. In the district office when he was arrested, he shouted with pride, 'I have two paradises; one is the church on earth, and the other the eternal paradise in Heaven!' It's all because he was so deeply touched by your father's benevolence."

Usually a man of few words, Sŏk was talkative that day. Ha-sang wondered if he, too, might not have been a secret convert. The old man continued, still coughing, "Your family was celebrated for producing many scholars of great accomplishment. They were handsome men, too. Your father, though not in public office, was well known for his high learning, no less so than His Excellency. Although he never took the civil service examination himself, do you realize how many of his many disciples passed the Higher Level Examination? So, scholars from all over the country gathered around him."

Ha-sang could not remember anything that the old man told him.

"So, young master, you must now study. How is it possible that a son of such a man cannot read at your age?"

His heart, which had been filled with pride listening to the old man, suddenly sank in shame. He mumbled as though to himself, "I, too, want to be able to read books."

Afterward, his mind was never again clouded or troubled with pain, but the desire for learning increased as each day went by.

Now, facing his uncle, an eminent scholar, Ha-sang was ashamed of his illiteracy. Tasan, too, wondered how it had come about that, though he had tried desperately and obsessively to make sure that his own sons were being well-educated, the thought of Ha-sang's course of life had never entered his mind, even though his nephew shared a kinship no less close than that of his own sons and brothers. He could not suppress the surging sense of guilt, though he vehemently resisted it. Ha-sang's voice, so full of love for his uncle, whipped his conscience. With an infinite longing, Ha-sang looked at Tasan's face, said to be a twin of his father's. Sŏk had told him that if one were to take away the "three brows" from the face of Tasan and put the black mole on the temple, it would be the face of his father. "Father," Ha-sang shouted in his heart—"my father, my great father."

Tasan's face betrayed his fear lest he once again become disturbed, and lose his hard-earned peace of mind. Ironically, he had turned his misfortune into advantage. In prison or in exile, his life constantly in danger, he sent letters to his sons. "Alone between heaven and earth," he wrote, "my fate was so decreed that books and writing brush alone sustain my existence."

Having lost his mother at the age of nine, Tasan had moved often with his father, a district official; he was only fourteen when he went to the capital to study. Looking back, he felt that he had acquired a superficial knowledge in many areas but had accomplished very little of substance. In preparing for the Lower Level Examination and in High College, he had only learned definitions of words or studied belles lettres, the main requirements for passing the Higher Level Examination, but this did not constitute true scholarship.

Moreover, since entering public life during a time of turmoil, Tasan had had no time to spare for the pursuit of learning. It was only in exile that he was able to devote his time and energy to meditation, writing, and reading. The destitution and loneliness of his exiled life finally freed him to question, analyze, and comment upon what he had studied. His tragedy had brought him unexpected opportunity and leisure. Thus, he was later considered as "the one who left more writings behind than any scholar since the introduction of Chinese characters." This passion for learning had been Tasan's fate as well as his mission. No one, nothing must now disturb such a calm. He was absolutely unwilling to let anything once again entangle him in a messy affair. Therefore, now, to this chaste young nephew, toward whom he had begun to feel affection, Tasan acted heartlessly without being aware of it.

Ha-sang was already determined; he was neither saddened nor resentful. He had known since early childhood the meaning of rejection and persecution. He spoke calmly, "At present, the churches are in a pitiful state. Almost everyone with advanced learning and high moral repute has been sacrificed; the only Catholic priest we had has been martyred. Only the weak, women, and children remain. We don't know where to go. It is urgent that we bring a priest here to lead the church, now torn like shreds of paper, to look after our souls."

The church, the priest, martyrdom, soul—Tasan trembled at these words, which he wished he would never again have to hear for the rest of his life. With clenched fists, he sprang to his feet, saying, "I don't wish to hear any more. Go away immediately. When you return to the capital, do not ever again be part of such a throng. I forbid you to bring further ruination upon our family with such a false belief." Tasan's voice was low, fearing someone might overhear him, but each word carried the weight of his strength.

Ha-sang, a shadowy presence, still sitting with his back against the door, went on undaunted. "Soon the annual emissary to Peking will be leaving. Our plan is to send a secret messenger among them, who will deliver a letter to the bishop of Peking explaining the situation of the Korean churches and asking him to send us a priest. My fourth father, I beseech you. There is no one left in our church with learning enough to write that letter. Please write us a letter that will move the bishop. Save our wretched people." Ha-sang was sobbing now, his head pressed to the ground.

The sight did not touch Tasan with pity. Anger only grew in him. "Leave here at once," he said. "I have heard enough of your outrageous talk. I have no more patience. Do you want to see the Chŏng clan driven into total extinction?" Tasan was out of breath with rage. "Why? Who gave you, a mere bachelor not yet twenty, this awesome task?"

"I did not come here alone."

"What? Who else came with you?"

"I came with Francesco, our leader."

"Where is the man now?"

"We had to stop once before arriving here. He did not show up at the place we had agreed to meet. In order to prevent our paths from crossing, he is to stay where he is."

"You must not let it happen again. Go immediately to him. You must not let him come here."

"Fourth father . . ."

"Do what I say right now. You are an outrageous and wicked boy. So, you are going to Peking, a mere stripling like you?"

"I am not going this time. I am not only too young, but also illiterate. I cannot even write my own name. However, I am determined someday to go to Peking; I shall study for that day. Please help us."

An illiterate who cannot even write his own name—an heir to a family with a reputation for scholarly virtue. Stunned, Tasan was speechless. Ha-sang handed his silent uncle a pouch wrapped in white paper.

"Elizabeth made this for you. The old servant, Sŏk, told us that you wore spectacles. She embroidered it with much love and care."

"Elizabeth?"

"Yes. My younger sister. My older sister died a few years ago."

"She shouldn't have gone to the trouble," Tasan said icily.

"Then I shall leave immediately as you command. But I will come again with Francesco."

Tasan, raising his voice, slid open the door behind Ha-sang. "Ha-sang, if you insist upon mentioning such grotesque names to me, I shall never want to see you again! Never come back here." Ha-sang followed his uncle into the inner courtyard. The sky, the tranquil sea, and the silvery tassels of reeds, everything was enveloped in a pinkish hue. A flock of migrating birds was flying through the twilight like a drift of smoke. The scarlet setting sun, quivering in flame, hesitated for a second, and then suddenly sank, leaving no trace. Twilight lingered on for a while after the sunset, but it soon trailed off into a lavender wisp.

The heavy fragrance of citrus hung in the air. Ha-sang was no longer able to appreciate the dreamlike loveliness of the sun setting in the sea. He waited for his uncle, who contemplated the scene before him. When Tasan turned around, Ha-sang bowed deferentially. He stood up and spoke feebly. "I am leaving for today. I will return."

When Ha-sang lifted his face, the twilight's last glow reflected upon it. Tasan had a sudden impulse to shout, "My brother!"—for he saw his brother standing there with all the features he remembered as a young man, even the black mole on his temple.

An icy arrow passed through his spine, an echo of love, a cry of the blood. Without thinking about what he was doing, Tasan grasped his nephew's rough hands. "It's too late now. It's better you leave tomorrow after a good night's rest."

Chapter Two

◆ ◆ ◆

Betrayal

Using the excuse of a sprained ankle, Francesco Kim had spent three days in a corner room of an inn, waiting anxiously for the Kwŏn household servant's arrival from Ŭnjin. Apprehension had parched his lips and sunk his eyes deep into their sockets, making him appear to be suffering from more than a mere sprained ankle. Ha-sang had already left for Kangjin to see Tasan, and still the servant had not come.

Situated at the entrance to the town of Nonsan, the inn was crowded with travelers who filled the tavern room, the rooms adjacent to the kitchen of the L-shaped structure, and a community guest room which could be entered through a gate of woven twigs. Under the tent in the large courtyard, there was not a single empty place among the wooden cots, because the inn stood conveniently at a crossroads that led to Kongju to the north, Puyŏ to the west, Kyŏngsang Province through Magup'yŏng to the east, and Chŏlla Province through Yŏnmu to the south.

From Nonsan to Kangjin was about one hundred miles. It would take more than three days no matter how young Ha-sang hurried. Since Ha-sang had left only two days ago, Francesco must wait several more days for his return. He wondered if he could stay without causing suspicion until Ha-sang rejoined him. The proprietor of the inn, who he had been assured could be trusted, had been away supervising his tenant farms since the morning of Francesco's arrival. It was already nearing the end of September. The Winter Solstice Mission to Peking was to depart on October 27. They must

53

return to the capital at any cost before the end of the month. Francesco was in agony.

From the beginning, this sojourn to the south had been fraught with bad luck. The autumn weather had been fickle; it had started raining intermittently even before they reached Suwŏn, forcing them to stop occasionally under the eaves of a wayside tavern to avoid a heavy downpour. The cone-shaped oil-paper headcover Francesco had been carrying came in handy for his horsehair hat, but his full-length coat was sodden, and his cotton socks and gaiters were coated with mud. Altogether his appearance was that of a weary traveler. In P'yŏngt'aek, he ran a high fever and had to spend two days in an inn. They were almost ten days behind schedule. Because of the delay, something must have gone wrong.

Even in the farthest corner room, Francesco could hear the hubbub of mixed dialects in this crossroads shelter. A question was thrown across the room.

"Kŏm-bong. You are busy again. You are having fun, aren't you?"

"You call it fun? They are like eels. No matter how sneakily we comb the whole town, they all slip away. Unbelievable," a sullen voice answered.

"Of course. They have to save their necks even if they have to leap as high as the sky, or burrow into the ground as soon as they see the shadows of your kind."

"In a matter of minutes the whole town becomes empty of them. Even the womenfolk run to the mountain."

"It seems they fear you petty soldiers more than they do tigers. Still, I hear you are having a good time of it. I saw with my own eyes not long ago a group of men and women Catholics being led away, bound and strung together like dried fish. There were some good-looking wenches among them, too. Tell them instead of throwing away their dear youth to come and do good to this bachelor."

"Please yourself. Those Catholic devils, they'd rather die so that they can go to Heaven and live there forever."

Francesco's whole attention was in his ears, as he sought to glean some useful information from this conversation.

"At any rate, you are famous for your skill in trapping Catholics."

"Well, it's not that difficult."

"You have some kind of trick?"

"Those bastards, because they spend their lives kneeling in

prayer and reciting some incantation, the tips of their upturned cotton socks are flattened, and their knees are callused. You can't see their knees very well, but the flattened socks are easy to spot."

Frightened, Francesco looked down at his socks. Sure enough, as the soldier had said, the tips of his socks were pushed in. He pulled on the pointed tips and they sprang up to their original shape. He listened even more carefully than before, but there was no more conversation; either the men were busy eating, or they had left the place.

Forgetting what he had just heard a moment ago, Francesco knelt down. Although he was still only thirty-eight years old, the deep furrows on his forehead and the sharp line etched across his face from his nose to the chin would arouse pity in any observer. These were not the natural phenomena of aging, but scars left by extreme suffering. The anguish engraved on his face, together with the passionate glow in his eyes and the folded, soft lips that alone remained youthful, gave him a strange air of nobility. Before he knew what he was doing, Francesco began to pray, recalling his nightmarish experience during the Persecution of 1801. He had been a young man of twenty-eight. Looking back, he was ashamed to have survived. Both his parents, his brother, his friends, even the slaves had chosen martyrdom, upholding their faith under the severest tortures: bone crushing that caused bone marrow to ooze out, flesh sawing, and flogging while hanging upside down. Now he alone was left alive. He had not gone into hiding like a coward, nor had he betrayed his fellow faithful by naming them. Most of all, he did not become an apostate, a sin beyond redemption. He had been suffering from tuberculosis, spitting blood. Even the soldiers who had come to arrest him had run from the sight of his face, white as paper, fleshless skin stuck to bare bones, the mouth bloodstained. That was how he had missed the opportunity for martyrdom he had so fervently hoped for. Miraculously, although a living corpse, he had survived the illness—due, his mother-in-law believed without the slightest doubt, to her folk remedy.

After the storm of persecution and martyrdom had subsided somewhat, the Queen Dowager in the dark victory of her revenge became suddenly fearful. Not only had she committed an act of grave consequence without permission from the Peking court,

China being Korea's suzerain, but she had also murdered a Chinese priest, and the realization made her tremble in terror.

Finally, after torturous deliberation, she contrived a plan to send to Peking the "Memorial on the Eradication of Catholics," an obsequious document filled with empty, shameful excuses, justifying her policy of religious persecution. She also sent an emissary with the Silk Letter of Hwang Sa-yŏng, reduced from thirteen thousand characters to a mere eight hundred and sixty, as evidence to support her tenuous position.

To explain the murder of Father Chou Wen-mu, she wrote: "When Chou Wen-mu was captured, he appeared no different from any other criminal in his manner of clothing and speech. Because we assumed him to be the leader of the crafty horde, he was punished by the criminal law of this humble nation. We are still in the dark about the identity of Chou Wen-mu; we do not know whether he was, indeed, of Chinese nationality. However, as protocol dictates, even before we can ascertain its validity, we are forced to inform you of the fact that it was written in the criminal Hwang Sa-yŏng's letter that Chou Wen-mu was a man of your esteemed nation."

This appeal was presented along with enormous bribes. Either the bribery worked or, deceived by the Queen Dowager's scheming international diplomacy, the Chinese court came to an ambiguous conclusion and dismissed the Chou Wen-mu affair without further investigation. They merely sent some vague instructions to the Korean court about keeping under control those Catholics and other delinquents who disturbed the law and order of the nation.

In the same year, on October 21, 1801, the Queen Dowager instructed the young king to hold a ceremony in commemoration of the Conquest of Catholics and to promulgate the Edict of Catholic Eradication. It began by stating that the introduction of the Catholic heresy into Korea, a small satellite of China which had upheld Confucian values since the beginning of the nation, had shaken the beautiful virtue and traditions that had been handed down throughout a long history. The edict went on to assert that the court had no other choice but to persecute the leaders of such a belief. It concluded:

Remove all subject matters of learning other than those of the Six Arts—rites, music, archery, charioteering, books, and arithmetic—or Confucian knowledge. There can be no better way of learning the Way of Heaven and correcting men's behavior than to submit to the sacred teachings of Confucius, and to respect the throne. For just this reason books have been written on the Five Cardinal Principles and on the rituals performed in the district. Great pardons are granted to those who committed noncapital crimes prior to the dawn of October 22, 1801. The benevolence that controls natural phenomena reigns again over the subjects, and the universal felicity that had been eclipsed has reemerged for eternity. In spite of the amnesty extended toward many who caused the calamities that plague us, those Catholics who do not repent their crime must be exterminated by imposing the death penalty of slicing off their noses.

The objective of the edict was to force Catholics to renounce their religion and return to the Confucian path. On the surface, it promised wise government to those who promised to renounce the Catholic faith; but in fact, it forced upon them the Confucian principle that had been firmly established as national policy. This edict was used repeatedly for eighty years in the effort to annihilate Catholics.

Nevertheless, as a result of the edict, a more peaceful mood settled on the nation the following year and Catholics enjoyed a brief respite. Having lost their leader, Father Chou, together with other prominent and influential Catholics, the surviving faithful were lost and in great torment. A flock of sheep without a shepherd—the women and children, the homeless, the hungry, those in rags, and the low-born—did not know where to turn. Their religious books and ritual articles had all been confiscated or burned, except for the few that had been carefully hidden in the ground or in walls. Thus, the cross had been broken and the flock of sheep scattered in all directions, but the church remained alive, stopping just at the threshold of death. In the meantime, after a clandestine power struggle with Kim Cho-sun, the father-in-law of the young King Sunjo, the venomous Queen Dowager was forced to step down as regent in 1804. The next year, on January 12, her life came to an end. She died at the age of sixty. Now, with Kim Cho-sun—a member of the Party of Expediency, sympathetic to Catholics—dominating the throne in royal in-law politics, the persecution ceased, at least in the capital.

Francesco was caught unprepared, therefore, by the ugly conversation he had just heard. However, although the Queen Dowager

was dead, her edict remained in effect, and at the local level persecution was still going on, though not as thoroughly as before. The
nature of the persecution, too, had considerably changed. Handled
as a local matter rather than a national policy, it was now used primarily to settle the personal grudges of local officials, to satisfy petty
functionaries' greed for material gain, or to encourage the many
Judases among Catholics themselves, who betrayed their fellow
converts for money. The central government, however, believing
that they had so well succeeded in obliterating this ephemeral
clique that by now it was lying in its own blood, did not bother
those who were newly converted. Francesco had heard such stories
before, but he tensed anew as he faced the reality of the local Catholics' plight.

"Unbelievable that Mr. Kwŏn, such a learned man and the holder
of the civil service degree, should be a Catholic! What does he lack
in his life that he had to become one? He has plenty of money,
slaves, and heirs. On top of it, we hear his wife's beauty is a slap to
the fairies of the Moon Palace."

Francesco sprang up from his seat as the noisy exchanges once
again reached his room.

"But he is such a gentleman. Take pity on him."

"Indeed. There is no one in this village who does not owe him
something."

"Come to think of it, there was no ancestral tablet hall in his
house."

"He is not an eldest son; it's perfectly understandable." Only
good things about him were being said.

"It must have been that Kŏm-bong again."

"Not this time. I hear it happened in a very strange way; his
servant, Nak-chong, informed the authorities."

"He deserves to be decapitated."

"Hush. You want to be branded as a Catholic, too?"

"That's why the saying goes that one need not save another man's
life."

Francesco paced the small room like a caged animal. It was now
beyond doubt that Kwŏn Ho-sin had been captured. This journey,
its sole objective to see the man who was the pillar of their hope,
had ended in vain. In his mind's eye appeared the disappointed
faces of the fellow Catholics waiting for his return in Seoul.

"Oh Lord, forgive my sins . . ." Kneeling, he prayed. The path to God's truth had been long and hazardous. Each step had been taken in blood, inexorably leading toward a sacred calling. In his desolation he remembered the brothers and sisters of his faith. Their love and trust for each other had been stronger in suffering than at any other time. In the aftermath of the persecution, at least in the capital, those who had been in hiding began to gather again from all directions, and in their communion they confessed their faith; those who had become widows and widowers, orphans, and old people without children comforted each other in their shared miseries. Francesco was among those who had begun to work to rebuild the fallen church.

The new leaders' priority was to improve the livelihood of the converts and to instruct them in the prayers and teachings of the church. Their selfless dedication made it possible for many meetings to take place. Those who had apostatized now returned to their faith, and the gospel spread with reinforced vigor, drawing many new converts. Soon, the vacuum left by the persecution was filled with new members. Now that new steps had been taken, the faithful began to feel an ardent need, stronger than at any other time before, to bring a Catholic priest from Peking. They sought ways to fulfill this extraordinary longing. Despite their astonishing capacity for self-sacrifice, their efforts had resulted in a string of failures, but they never gave up hope. Though ignorant of many Catholic tenets, they had enough insight to believe that they could not become true Christians, and preserve their faith, without the holy sacraments of Jesus Christ. Those who had once received the sacraments remembered the strength and comfort it gave their souls. Aroused by a sacred desire, those who had not experienced the grace of God hoped with all their hearts to be delivered from their sins and to participate in the holy feast. They longed for a leader who could fulfill their hopes, and resolved to send a secret envoy to the Peking diocese with a letter requesting a new priest.

But the plan had encountered much difficulty. A man by the name of Yi Yŏ-jin, or Johann, had volunteered to travel to Peking, fully aware of the perils of the mission. His plan was to join the annual Korean emissary to the Peking court, hiding his noble identity by disguising himself as a servant. The financing of the journey had then become the central issue. Although united in their desire to bring a priest to their country, after the persecution the faithful had no money. The mission therefore had been postponed many times. Finally that year there was a hope for its becoming a reality.

A scholar by the name of Kwŏn Ho-sin, a relative of the martyred Kwŏn Ch'ŏl-sin, lived in Nonsan. Miraculously, he had survived the persecution and remained prosperous, and he volunteered to finance part of the journey. Francesco, accompanied by Ha-sang as his servant, had come to the south to meet him.

Someone coughed outside, trying to make his presence known. Then the door slid open haltingly, and a table bearing a bowl of gruel and a side dish of pickled cabbage and radishes, was pushed into the room.

"Scholar-gentleman, sir, you must take a spoonful of this gruel."

Francesco remembered that he had hardly eaten anything for two days.

A man of about forty who stood behind a humble-looking woman holding a tray bowed his head and said, "I heard that you are not feeling well. I hope in my absence you have not been treated without respect. I am the man called Hong, the owner of this place." His good-naturedness made him seem almost dull-witted.

"Indeed. So you are the proprietor of this inn?" Momentarily losing balance as he tried to stand up, Francesco knocked a chopstick from the table. Shaken, he sat down again, putting the chopstick back on the table.

An expression of tension flashed over Hong's face. The chopstick had fallen on top of the other of the pair, making the sign of the cross. His face now regained its amiable expression. "You look terribly ill. Is your room well heated?" he asked. Anxiously Hong entered the room, and kneeling down, felt the floor for warmth. When Francesco saw the man's hands clasped on his knees, a beatific smile appeared on his face. The thumbs were on top of each other, making them look like a cross.

Hong did not stay for long. He went back out and called to his servant, "Since when has that gentleman been like that?"

"It's been three days."

"How long did he say he would be staying?"

"Because of his sprained ankle, it seems he can't walk for a while."

"Tomorrow is a market day and the man is taking up the whole room; besides, that room is the favorite of Mr. Pak," Hong said fretfully.

"How about moving him to a room in the back wing? It might be better for him because it's much quieter there."

"I don't want him to think I am a heartless person. I wouldn't dare ask him."

"I'll tell him so myself," the young servant declared proudly and strutted toward Francesco's room.

"I have something to tell you, sir."

"Who's there?" Francesco's croaking voice came from within, and the door opened.

"We know your hardship, but ours is a place of business. Please try to understand our situation . . . ," said the boy after some moments of hesitation.

Francesco, his eyes wide open, could not comprehend what the boy was talking about.

"Tomorrow is a market day, and we expect a lot of people."

"I should think so."

"You are not well, and you will feel very uncomfortable with all the noise from the tavern."

"I'll be all right."

"This room is already spoken for on each market day . . ." The boy began to falter.

"You mean that I should give up this room?" Francesco said annoyed. "The room surely must not have been paid for in advance."

Seeing that their exchange was about to become somewhat hostile, Hong came in.

"Please try to forgive this boy; he is country-raised and ignorant," he apologized, bending at his waist repeatedly. On his clasped hands, the thumbs remained crossed.

All of a sudden, Francesco realized that the man was trying to signal him.

"It seems I am not able to move about with ease," he said. "It would be better, after all, if I stayed in a more secluded place. I have to wait until my servant boy returns."

"What is your destination?" Hong asked.

"We were on the way to Naju. I was going there to meet a man who is betrothed to my niece. And look what has happened to me—unexpected misfortune!" Francesco declared, forcing a smile. "At any rate, you must let me stay here until my servant comes back."

Hong kept on bowing. "There is an empty room in the back of the building. It's rather small and dirty, but it can be warmed up. I am so sorry. You can convalesce there as long as you wish."

"To tell you the truth, I was hoping for such a room away from the noise. Please help me walk there. Let's go right now."

Hong shook his hands. "You don't need to rush. The room smells bad and the floor is cold, because it's been left empty for so long. Hurry, boy, start the fire and make the room spotless. Right now!"

It was long past noon, and only a handful of guests were in the tavern, taking a light meal of rice and soup. From the way they used their fingers to shove the pickles into their mouths, they seemed to be regular customers.

"As the saying goes," said one of them, "if you are too good-natured, you will end up having a dozen in-laws in the village. The owner of this place is such a man. Last year I hear he took in a woman about to give birth on her journey and helped her deliver the baby. He let her stay in his storage shed among the soybean cakes being fermented for soy sauce and soybean paste until the baby was a hundred days old. This time, it's a scholar with a sprained ankle."

It appeared they had heard the exchanges between Hong and Francesco.

"He is a veritable example of charitable and virtuous deeds."

"But, you know, he's a businessman all right. He refused to give up the room reserved for his regular customers."

"Indeed, one can spare some soy sauce, but never the jug that contains it."

Obviously, Hong had a reputation as a kind and generous man.

"Boy, is the room spotless? The floor toasty warm?" Making sure, Hong came around the kitchen.

Supported by the boy, Francesco limped after him. The rear of the kitchen was unexpectedly spacious. Outside the kitchen door was a stone well-head, and next to it was a raised kitchen terrace where huge crocks of soy sauce, soybean paste, and pickles were neatly arranged. Beyond it was a good-sized vegetable garden where full heads of cabbages and plump turnips were growing. At the end of the vegetable garden was a shed-like structure with a side entrance and only one window. A flimsy bush-clover fence about a man's height surrounded it, and beyond the fence was a thick bamboo grove where a hill sloped upward.

As soon as they entered the structure and the servant boy had left, Hong's manner and speech changed completely.

"I am Matteo. I have heard of you through Mr. Kwŏn. You must have suffered much on this long journey."

"My Christian name is Francesco. I lead a church in Yakhyŏn. I was delayed on the road unexpectedly and could not arrive on the appointed day. Has something happened to Mr. Kwŏn?"

"A disaster has struck his house. Being such a prudent man, he seldom makes a false move; but unfortunately . . ." Matteo whispered.

"Has someone informed against him?"

"Yes. I sent my men to feel out the situation; there are some suspicious aspects to this incident."

"By any chance does he have some weak spot?"

Matteo shook his head violently, "Absolutely not. He is not such a man. However, we don't know the whereabouts of his wife and daughters. A servant of his household, a Catholic himself, betrayed him. Though this man had been a slave, Mr. Kwŏn made him a free man long ago. Such a beautiful man. That Judas. His name is Sŭng Nak-chong. He, too, has disappeared."

"Doesn't an informer get some kind of material reward?"

"Yes, indeed. Most of them betray for money, bargaining Christians' lives for pitiful sums. The policemen, too, go berserk coveting what little money these Catholics have. Now the situation is different from back in 1791 and 1801. This time people realize that Christians are being persecuted for no reason."

"You mean the man who informed against Mr. Kwŏn disappeared without the money?"

Somber-faced, Matteo answered, "It was said that the man had already gone when the police raided Mr. Kwŏn's house. Usually it is the informer who leads such a raid."

"Perhaps his conscience would not allow him. How dare he betray his own master whom he had served for so long, and he himself a Catholic?"

"I wonder. One way or other, we will soon find out when my man returns. That Judas, Sŭng, knows about the meetings we conduct here. Sooner or later, the police will come here too."

"Then we must hide . . ."

"No need to hurry. All the evidence—books, religious articles—is well hidden. I am known only as Hong, the innkeeper at the bamboo grove, dim-witted but good at business and making money. No one suspects me."

"But that Judas . . ."

"If some can leap, there are always others who can fly. Pretending to be gentle and stupid, I have already taken care of those policemen. And I have been out for a few days on the pretext of inspecting my tenant farms, but in fact I was setting up defenses all over. Today is Saint Luke's Day, and tonight we are supposed to meet here. If Sŭng knows about it, we can expect a raid."

"Tonight . . ."

"You are only to act as if you are terribly ill and complain how wretchedly the innkeeper is treating you, leaving a sick man alone in a storage shed like this; his being base can't be an excuse for his behavior, and so on."

Francesco grew more apprehensive. Remembering that the draft of the two letters, one to Peking and the other to the Pope, had been sewn into Ha-sang's jacket collar, he felt relieved not to have any damning evidence on his person.

"They'll arrive in the middle of the night. They'll cause a riot. No matter how much they search here, they'll find only a scholar with a sprained ankle, and they'll realize they made a slip. Still, I'm afraid sooner or later they might find us out. We must make arrangements before it happens."

"Are there many Christians?"

"About twenty. You may think it dangerous to meet in a place like this, but this place, wide open to everyone's scrutiny, can also be advantageous in that we can observe the movement outside. This is a Christian neighborhood. As you see, the inn is enclosed by a bush-clover fence. At first glance it's an ordinary fence, but there are a few openings. Some come through them, or through my neighbors' doors, who are also Christians. Sŭng does not know about this. When we send messages, it is not one man's task. They are relayed from person to person. Since the persecution, a few whose faith was not firm enough confessed under torture. And there have been some Judases, like this man Sŭng."

"What suffering and hardship you must be enduring."

"Though we can understand those who persecute us from without, what is so utterly sad and unforgivable are the Judases among us. We are so very ashamed of them," Matteo continued gravely. "Anyhow, we may expect some commotion tonight, though I don't anticipate that anything serious will happen."

At about four in the afternoon customers stopped coming. In preparation for the market day, freshly washed white rice glistened, overflowing the huge wicker baskets, and the smell of soup, made of ox intestines and bones, hung heavy in the air. A large ceramic jar of ox's blood, gruesome stains still fresh on the rim, stood next to the water crocks, and on the shelves in the kitchen clean bowls and plates were neatly stacked. A brass bowl was set ready, filled to the brim with seasoned vegetables. In this inn at the bamboo grove, nothing was missing in anticipation of the big day. At about seven, Hong ordered the servant boy to extinguish all the lights except for a paper lantern on the pillar in the hall, and to tend the fire under a big cauldron.

"Tomorrow starts early. Everyone should go to bed right now."

Hong returned to a room next to the hall, which doubled as a guest room during the day and the family's sleeping quarters at night. Through a dimly illuminated paper sliding door, Hong's shadow flickered for a while. He took a kerchief from his head, then removed his jacket. His crouching shadow hovered as he took off his cotton socks. Soon the light went out, and snoring came from the room.

Under the moonless and starless sky, the night deepened in an eerie calm. Except for the hall light, not even a spark from pine kindling penetrated the thickness of the night, yet not a soul in the inn was asleep. Their nerves taut as bow strings, those who had gathered for the service lay in wait for imminent danger. The village, too, was unusually quiet; not even dogs barked that night. It was as if everything had stopped breathing. Slowly, inexorably, chipping away life, time passed. Finally, defeated by tension, when Hong woke from the sleep that had bewitched him, the dawn's first rooster was crowing. Although the police had undoubtedly known of the gathering for the holiday, the raid had not taken place.

◆　◆　◆

Four-year-old Kug-a, usually a sweet-tempered child, kept on crying. Stumbling on an unfamiliar mountain path in the dark of the night, holding the hand of her oldest daughter, Mae-a, Mistress Kim, the wife of Kwŏn Ho-sin, did not know what to do. Carrying Kug-a on her back, the wet nurse was sobbing too.

Sŭng Nak-chong, leading the way with Nan-a on his back, became suddenly furious and shouted at the girl, "If you keep on crying like this, we will all be captured and killed. If you don't stop this instant, I'll shove you into a tiger's mouth. There are many tigers in these mountains, you know."

The girl, however young she might be, was a daughter of his master; he certainly should not treat her in such a manner. Mistress Kim was disturbed.

"Nak-chong, why do you say such a cruel thing to a little child?" she chided him, "How thoughtless of you to speak about a terrible animal here in the depths of the mountains." She squeezed the hand of the girl on the wet nurse's back.

"I'm sorry, but we are being followed. At a time like this, even the hairs on our heads must be hidden," Nak-chong grumbled. He had become insolent. Seized with an evil premonition, Mistress Kim swallowed her words. Everything seemed to her like a nightmare.

It had happened in the early evening of that day. Soon after dinner, the wet nurse had brought in a tray of boiled chestnuts. The girls, Mae-a and Nan-a, were too busy playing a game of cat's cradle to pay attention to the chestnuts.

"Here, I give you a rolling pin," Mae-a, deftly scooping up the string, said indifferently.

Nan-a stared for a while at the string wrapped around her sister's hands, then dexterously hooked her little fingers at each side of the string. In an instant her fingers coaxed out an hourglass-shaped drum.

"Goodness! The drum," said Mae-a, impressed. She knew how difficult it was to make a drum out of a rolling pin. Nan-a was silent; only her eyes glittered.

"Girls, please. Stop playing and eat the chestnuts. If young maidens are too good at the game of cat's cradle, it is said they are sure to be married off to houses with doors to Heaven," Mistress Kim told the girls.

"What is a house with a door to Heaven?"

"Young misses, you are so talented at the game. They say if you are good at the game, you are sure to be skilled in embroidery and sewing too. But for now, please eat some of the chestnuts I have brought. Here, I have already peeled the skins for you."

The wet nurse was pushing the tray toward the girls, when there came the sound of the middle gate being roughly pushed open, and Kwŏn Ho-sin dashed into the room in a state of great agitation.

"Wife, the situation is urgent," he cried.

Without comprehending what was happening, Mistress Kim's face turned pale.

"They say the soldiers are already near the village. Nak-chong found it out and rushed home through the shortcut to inform us. It's fortunate that our son is away with his grandparents. Not a second must be wasted. We all knew sooner or later it would happen. Be strong. Take the children to your parents' place. Nak-chong will lead the way for you. He knows the way. I have instructed him in everything; you can depend on him. He is a faithful servant and would gladly give up his own life to keep you and the children safe. Every second is precious. Please do hurry!"

Decorous woman that she was, Mistress Kim lost her composure. "Lord, what about you . . ."

"I follow the will of Providence. Please take good care of yourself," Kwŏn choked.

"I will remain here, too. Where do you command me to go in a situation like this?"

Pushing away his tremulous wife and crying daughters, Kwŏn went out toward his own quarters. The commotion outside the gate grew in intensity.

That was the end. How long ago was it? An eternity stretched between. While they were escaping through the back gate, a mass of torchlight carried aloft by the roar of the multitude was rushing toward the master's quarters. However, once in the midst of the mountains, the torchlight and their house, hidden by the forest, were no longer visible. Before them in the darkness was an endless stretch of perilous mountain path. Kug-a cried ceaselessly. Nak-chong had become even more ferocious, while Mistress Kim grew more apprehensive. Mae-a, who had barely been able to follow, fell, stumbling against the jagged edge of a rock, and began to cry, the cry she had been holding back all the while. Although the eldest, she was only eight years old and could no longer bear the terror and pain.

"What's the matter with you girls?" Nak-chong shouted.

Mistress Kim was speechless with anger and shock.

"Nak-chong, have you gone crazy?" the wet nurse raged. "It's only natural that the little misses should cry. I feel like crying myself, and they were brought up like precious princesses."

"Damned be those precious births. They are only the bitches of a Catholic. Don't sound so high and mighty, or I'll give you up to the authorities this instant."

"What did you say just now?"

The women were at the limit of their outrage. Mistress Kim trembled like an aspen leaf.

"Please, Pius, what's come over you?" cried the wet nurse. "From the lips of a Christian, such profanity? You don't fear Heaven's punishment?"

"You old bitch. Do you want to be killed, too? You must be out of your mind yourself. I am not a damned Catholic. Where is God anyway? If there is God, why does he abandon those who believe in him? Everything is a lie. I don't want to die for nothing. I have some money now. I'll run far away and live well, wait and see!"

The wet nurse screamed at him, "Pius!"

"Don't call me Pius. I'm not a Catholic devil."

"Then, you bastard, shall I call you Nak-chong? Do you realize where you got that name? Have you heard of another slave whose name is Sŭng? Your mother was violated by a monk, and you are the result of it—the seed of a monk.[1] That's your name: bastard of a slave girl, the seed planted by a monk. The late master took pity on you and allowed you to live. You ungrateful animal! May Heaven punish you!"

"I was born with Heaven's curse anyway. I'm no longer Nak-chong or Pius from now on."

"Then, did you inform on the master? Heaven forbid!"

1. The word "monk" is homonymous with "Sŭng"; the word "seed" is homonymous with "Chong."

Nak-chong let out a wicked snicker. "There are many besides me who would gladly betray him to the authorities. Haven't you heard that bad deeds eventually catch up with you? Everyone has known for a long time that he was up to something. It is only a matter of time that he would have been captured anyway."

"Is this then not the way to Hongju?"

"Wherever we are going, what can you do about it in the midst of these mountains? You must follow me."

"You Satan! You return evil for good. Ingrate! Have you forgotten the mountain of kindness the master bestowed upon you? Infinitely generous, he allowed me to nurse and raise you, but I have raised a Satan. Woe is me!" The old woman ground her teeth.

"Then why don't you run away, and pretend nothing has happened?" Nak-chong said arrogantly.

"What did you say, you worthless scum?" she yelled at him desperately.

"Shut up! Don't you know there might be other people on the mountain, too?"

"Pius," Mistress Kim gasped, "you don't seem to realize the gravity of what you have done, but, since I now know who you are, I cannot go with you any further. I'd prefer you go to the authorities and tell them that two Catholic women and three little girls are lost on the mountain."

She was fighting to keep herself from fainting, and yet the serenity and nobility of her words struck Nak-chong speechless with awe.

"You're an animal with a man's mask! How dare you! What have you done, you immoral, wicked man?" cried the wet nurse, tears pouring out of her eyes.

"Suit yourself. I'm the only one who can take you to Hongju or Naju, or anywhere from here," he answered insolently.

"Magdalene, let's wait here until daybreak. Since we now know the truth, how can we follow this man?"

"Mistress!" The wet nurse let out a heart-wrenching wail.

But Mistress Kim only grew more self-possessed. "Magdalene, haven't we been ready for this for a long time? Now the day has come. This is no time for differences of opinion. We have to be ready for anything." She knelt down. Somewhere, a jackal's ominous howl sounded.

The cloud lifted, exposing the sky resplendent with scintillating stars. It was after midnight, and the late-rising, slender moon was sinking mournfully.

"Mistress, mistress!" cried Magdalene, who could not resign herself. "Mistress, how is it possible, how could it happen? How could he, this animal wearing the mask of a man?"

"This is no time for complaining; this is the time for prayers. We must pray to God to grant my lord the strength to endure," said Mistress Kim, her voice strong and clear. "Pius, what's done is done. Soon it will be daybreak. Let's rest here. When morning comes, we will decide our course of action."

Nak-chong, sulking, put Nan-a down and squatted. In late autumn in the mountains, the morning air was as chilly as that of early winter. The mistress took Kug-a from the wet nurse's back and wrapped her with the hooded cloak she had been wearing. She tucked her long skirt around Mae-a's feet. Magdalene squatted, too, gazing upon the dark, shadowy figure of Nak-chong, her mind torn apart.

Nak-chong's mother had been only fifteen years old when he was born. It had taken her four days to deliver the unusually large baby, and after the difficult birth, the young girl had died. No one knew the father of the infant. Gathering up her last flickering breath, her lips quivering, she whispered to Magdalene, "A monk on the mountain path . . ."

That was how the infant had acquired the name Sŭng. The circumstance of its birth beyond comprehension, the baby cried furiously and incessantly. Noticing that the infant was frantically craving its mother's milk, the late master, the father of Kwŏn Ho-sin, took pity on him. "Now Hyŏn-haeng (Kwŏn's childhood name) is three years old and can take solid food; you may nurse the infant," he said.

In most households of means, the masters forbade the wet nurses to nurse their own children while they were in their service, so his generosity moved everyone. Her own son then was four years old, and because she was not producing enough milk, Hyŏn-haeng had been given solid food and gruel. Soon she had another baby and was completely without milk, so that her child was fed with gruel and was sickly. The master, who had considerable medical knowledge, as did most of the scholar-gentlemen of the time, prescribed various medicines, and the child survived the illness.

Although their stations in life were worlds apart, Hyŏn-haeng, two years older than Nak-chong, loved him like his own brother. Following their Catholic master, Nak-chong and all the servants had been baptized, and had been given Christian names. Since the Bible was read and religious teachings were strictly followed, no one in the Kwŏn household was illiterate. No less intelligent than his master, Nak-chong had come to manage the Kwŏn household affairs. He was also so well-versed in church matters that he served his master as his right-hand man. His faith in Nak-chong was so deep that Kwŏn had entrusted his beloved wife and daughters to his hands. Who could have foreseen that Nak-chong would betray his master, his benefactor, his fellow Christian, for money?

The stern truth confronting her, Magdalene was in great confusion. In the Kwŏn household, she was still addressed as wet nurse. She had nursed the master, who was now the father of four children. To her, he was still a precious little boy in whose service alone she felt fulfilled. On the other hand, just as deep was her affection for Nak-chong, whom by some unfathomable working of fate she had reared to adulthood. Fresh in her mind was the pain of parting with his mother, who had been her sister in the wretched fate of being born as slaves, although they had had a generous master. With what pity had she beheld that baby face darkened with hard work? Fortunately, Nak-chong had been a healthy child, and had earned the master's trust on his way to adulthood. He had been like her own son, and his good fortune had made her rejoice.

Her voice soft, Magdalene called his name tenderly, "Pius. What can we do about spilt water? The only thing you can do to save yourself from your sin is to take the mistress and the young misses safely to her parents' place."

"Magdalene, there is no need for such words," Mistress Kim said calmly. "It is too late for him to repent and go to the authorities to tell them he was mistaken. I know full well my husband's upright nature, and I am sure that he has already declared himself a Catholic. I will never allow myself to become indebted to a man who has driven my lord to such a circumstance. Though we are women and girls, unfamiliar with the world outside, and have no way of directing ourselves, let us somehow find our way ourselves."

Nak-chong, squatting there as before, was silent. The dawn was breaking. The little ones, tears still fresh on their faces, were asleep, huddled together. In the growing light, the two women, without a wink of sleep, were forced to perceive once again the terrifying reality of their circumstances.

Overnight, Mistress Kim's face had grown wasted and pale, her eyes sunken, and her nose more elegantly defined. Although she was fatigued by the sleepless night, her eyes were clear and pure under their delicate lids. Even with their fullness gone, the beauty of the cheeks and the mournful lips, and the exquisite outline from chin to slender neck, remained unmarred. A flash of sensuousness escaped from her slightly disarrayed hair. As if she had seen something dangerous, the wet nurse hurriedly drew the hooded coat over her mistress's head.

"Mistress, oh, mistress," she cried, heartbroken, wiping her eyes with the ties of her blouse. With all her heart she loved this beautiful lady.

"Where are we?" Mistress Kim asked, as if awakened from the depths of sleep.

Suddenly alert, the wet nurse looked around her. In the shadow of the autumn forest, they could discern violet arrowroot flowers blooming in wild profusion, and everywhere clusters of dark-blue mountain grapes hung from vines. It was obvious to them now that they were not heading toward Hongju.

"Pius!" the wet nurse shouted at the dozing Nak-chong.

"What . . ." The whites of his eyes glared as he opened them. Except for his peculiar eyes, he was not a bad-looking man; his forehead was straight, and his well-shaped nose and pleasing mouth would have told no one that he was a person of low birth.

"Where are we now?"

"How do I know?"

"I most certainly heard what the master told us. He said you knew the way. Did you lead us astray on purpose? Anyway, we must go down to the village, have something to eat, and then hire two sedan chairs."

Nak-chong did not answer. Turning his head, he spat. Unmindful of his spitting that came in her way, she drew closer to him and put her hands on his shoulders.

"Pius, you have always been a good boy. The mistress is a person of resolute character. Look at her. How can she walk as far as Hongju? Her beauty would draw too much attention."

Nak-chong stood up lazily and kicked a nearby stone. Her words swirled in his mind. Yes, indeed, it was true. It had been so from the beginning. It was on a spring day thirteen years ago that Nak-chong had first beheld her. A great wedding had taken place in the Kwŏn clan, the most celebrated family in Yanggun, and it was the day of the ceremony marking the bride's arrival to the groom's house.

Nak-chong, then, was an intelligent and good-looking lad with some learning he had acquired over the shoulder of his master. He had been known as a handsome, bachelor manservant, decent in his deportment, with his thick plait of hair pushed back and tied with a kerchief. Even the hairstyle of a low-born man did not remind people of his humble station. At the entrance gate to the village, among the motley crowd of neighbors and other servants, Nak-chong was waiting for the arrival of the bridal procession. Outside the village gate was a wide expanse of plain with a meandering river, and among the hills behind it was a feast of azaleas. Weeping willows swung their jade-green branches. The spring was ripening.

A prosperous clan, the Kwŏn relatives near and distant had gathered days in advance, and the house was filled with festive clamor. Neighborhood women hired to help had brought with them their entire families, even their dogs, and all had been spending days in the house of festivity. Even if a neighbor's daughter familiar to all since childhood had gotten married, the wedding feast was cause for everyone's gathering to gawk at the bride, but on this day, the bride of the only son of a renowned family was entering the groom's house for the first time. It was no wonder, then, that even the busy spring plowing season could not hinder the entire village from gathering.

At that time, the family of the bride was still living in Seoul, not yet retired to the country. The distance from Seoul to Yanggun was about thirty miles. Even if they left at dawn, the magnificent procession—a sedan chair carrying the bride, baggage with an array of gifts to the new in-laws, boxes filled with the bride's trousseau and her personal belongings, men and women servants on foot—would take at least two full days. However, they arrived sooner than expected. The spectators, already intoxicated with excitement, milled about the inner courtyard, which was usually off-limits to outsiders.

They all wanted to catch a glimpse of the bride, whose beauty had been loudly proclaimed to be peerless.

Out of the sedan chair placed close to the main hall entrance, supported by a wet nurse and a bridesmaid, emerged the bride, taking her first step into her in-laws' main hall. Though her back was toward the crowd and her entire body was draped in splendidly colored silk brocade, nonetheless they all agreed that she was indeed a beauty, justly deserving the rumors they had heard.

Even before she had had a chance to rest from the long journey, the bride began the ceremony of presenting gifts and wine and of exchanging obeisance with each member of her husband's household, even with the tiny babies. After the ceremony, she was seated with her back against a wedding screen, and in front of her was spread a large banquet table.

It was then that Nak-chong for the first time had a chance to gaze upon the bride. She sat serenely in front of a table laden with dishes piled high with an assortment of propitious food and sweets of all shades and shapes arranged with artistry—chestnuts, dates, gingko nuts, fruits, fried fish, dried and seasoned meat, and rice cakes.

Only a morsel of food had been fed to the bride before the ceremony, but no matter how hungry she might become after the rigor of repeated kowtows, there was no precedent for the bride to touch any of the beautifully arranged food on display. For a while, the bride would remain seated; then, with infinite care so as not to disturb the shape of the original display, which had been painstakingly executed, the food would be transferred to a large, lidless wicker basket. The basket then would be sent to the bride's household, where judgment would be passed, from the scale and dimension of its contents, as to how well their daughter would be treated in her husband's house. No bride had ever been treated as lavishly as this young bride of the Kwŏn clan that day.

In front of the wedding screen of luxuriously flowering peonies painted in lush primary hues, the child-bride sat with an air of uncommon maturity for one so young. She bore upon her face an expression of a gentle obedience and yet impenetrable dignity. Beholding her, the spectators did not spare words of admiration.

"A fairy has descended."

"The stem of a peony in a vase."

"I fear she is too beautiful for a homebound woman. They say that beautiful women are ill-fated."

Listening to them whisper among themselves, Nak-chong felt a tightness in his throat and a weight in his chest. Ever since then, for more than ten years, instead of abating, the heat of his feeling had intensified every time he faced the lady.

"Her beauty attracts too much attention." Magdalene's words, like a wounded black butterfly's desperate palpitations, fluttered in his head.

Still grumpy, he shook Magdalene's hands from his shoulders and moved a few steps away.

She followed him, and grasping his hands, pleaded, "Pius, are you going to act like this to the end? Please, let us at least get off this mountain."

"It's not me. You have heard what she said; she said she would not follow me."

"Then tell me the direction," she implored, holding onto him. Without realizing that they had reached the edge of a cliff, Nak-chong impatiently tore off the hands that were clinging to him.

"What's the matter with you?" he shouted.

Magdalene, caught off balance, fell and plunged like a leaf down the cliff. And in that short instant, everything ended without even a scream from her.

It happened so absurdly and suddenly that Nak-chong stood there for a while, dazed. Kneeling, he looked down, but he could see only a thick growth of twining arrowroot vines and wild shrubs between the trees. There was no trace of her; not even a piece of her clothing could be seen.

He craned his head upward and looked up at the blue, cloudless sky. All of a sudden, he burst into laughter, which was more like a cry. In the tranquillity of the mountain, it resounded with a sinister echo. It was no longer a human voice.

Mistress Kim heard the cry. A woman whose life had been sheltered from the outside world, she could not comprehend the meaning of that animal-like sound. Drawing her daughters close to her bosom, she strained to listen, but the sound did not come again.

Magdalene did not return. Mistress Kim, speechless with terror and apprehension, remained transfixed. After a while, gathering her

strength, she called out for the wet nurse, "Magdalene, Magdalene."

Suddenly Nak-chong emerged from the wood. "You have not
come to your senses yet, calling her by such a name," he said.

Startled, she gathered her daughters closer to her.

"Don't look for your wet nurse. The old bitch has run away."

"It can't be."

"Wait all day long, if you wish. She told me to come with her,
too."

"You insolent man. What other hideous thing have you done?"

"I only refused that old bitch to save you, my lady."

"Never! Even if I die on this mountain, I will not seek your
helping hand," she cried, clasping her daughters tightly to her
bosom, her stare fixed upon him. Green sparks of anger shot from
her eyes.

Again, Nak-chong felt that burning sensation in his chest, now
stronger than ever before. He grabbed her hands violently and drew
them close to him.

"Don't be a fool, just follow me. I'll show you the way," he
growled.

Trembling in loathing, as though in a serpent's clasp, she
screamed, "No! I will find my own way!"

Nak-chong's hold grew stronger.

"You'd better listen to me." Panting, he was about to drag her
into the wood.

"Mother! Mother!" the girls cried out.

Turning his frightful face toward them, his eyes aglare, he
screamed, "I'll make you suffer if you keep on crying!"

He was a totally changed man now. As he forced her into the
wood, his breath was hot as fire but his face white as paper, the
irises of his eyes entirely eclipsed. Mistress Kim fought off Nak-
chong with astonishing strength, born of a frail woman's desperation, and once or twice even managed to escape from his grasp. Like
a demon in a frenzy, he slapped and kicked her. Her short blouse
was torn to pieces, exposing her translucent flesh of white jade. Just
as he was about to overtake her again, she slipped away from his
grip and hid herself behind a rock. However, she did not realize the
rock was precariously perched at the edge of a cliff. He ran after
her and grabbed her slender arms. She bit into his hands, and he,

stunned, let go of her arms. Losing her balance, she fell into the bottomless abyss.

In the meantime, stealthily, Mae-a and Nan-a had been following their mother. The young sisters had witnessed the last desperate defense of their mother. After the fall, Mae-a raced down the mountain path in crazed confusion toward the place where her mother had plunged. Her only thought was to save her. As she ran crying, her clothes were torn apart by tree branches, and she was covered with scratches and lacerations. But after her frantic search, her mother nowhere to be found, she suddenly found herself before a road where a village came into sight.

"Nan-a! Kug-a!" she cried, looking up toward the mountain, and then was overwhelmed by a sob.

Six-year-old Nan-a saw her mother floating down like a white flower petal in the air. She fancied it was a white butterfly or a firefly's glow in the summer night, or perhaps a shooting star she had seen once from the back of her wet nurse. Leaning against a rock, open-eyed, she remained lost to her senses. A young butterfly flew by, but whose reincarnation it was she had no way of knowing. Though she was the brightest among her siblings, for a long time hence she was not able to form any other words but "butterfly," "firefly," and "shooting stars." Then the memory of her parents, her home, her name, everything, left her.

Soon afterward, a group of travelers was passing along the mountain path: a plump woman, her face covered with a long hooded cloak; a middle-aged slave woman with coarse hair held together in place with a comb; a young manservant with plaited hair tied in a kerchief. At the turn of a narrow, meandering path, they heard a baby's cry, a most improbable sound in the depth of the mountains. At first they dismissed it as the cry of a young beast or a bird's chirping, and kept on walking. At another turn, however, it became more distinct.

"Isn't that the cry of a baby?" asked the hooded woman, listening intently.

"Yes, it is a baby's cry, isn't it?" echoed the slave woman.

"It is a baby. It definitely is," the young man assented with conviction.

"A strange thing, indeed, a baby crying deep in this mountain fastness. While the lady gets some rest, why don't you go look around," the slave woman ordered the young man.

He quickly obeyed the maid, and moved off in the direction of the baby's cry, making his way through the thick undergrowth.

The mistress lifted an edge of her hooded cloak, exposing a pleasing full face.

"It's still warm for this late in September, isn't it?" she said.

"This mountain path is an uncommon one. Even in winter, one perspires while walking on it." The maid fanned her lady's face with her hands. "You didn't have a good night's sleep last night. Indeed, no one comes close to your devoutness."

"No. I am afraid I still lack piety," the mistress replied, sighing deeply.

Mistress Sin was the wife of the Overseer of the Local Agency in Imsil, a wealthy landowner. They lacked nothing in their lives except for the fact that she was already past thirty and they were childless. She had taken every available medicine said to promote pregnancy: bitter ones, sour ones, foul-smelling ones, nauseating earthworms, and even centipedes. She had had a famous shaman conduct rites for her. Without her husband's knowledge, she even secretly carried a bizarre talisman, but nothing had brought any results. On that day, the woman was on her way home after a long-overdue visit with her parents in Yŏnmu.

She was on the mountain path after having offered prayers to the Buddha of the Seven Stars for ten days in the Kwanch'ok Temple, famous for blessing women with sons. She already felt that it might again come to naught, but because she still held onto a slight hope, she had been careful in her conduct. As she walked along the mountain path, ceaselessly reciting a Buddhist prayer, she was careful not to step on any living thing, not even an ant.

The young man was slow to return. The baby's crying had stopped.

"The baby must have stopped crying," the maid said, straining to listen.

"It must have been something else," suggested the mistress.

"It certainly was the cry of a baby. They say that wild cats weep like a human baby, but it couldn't have deceived all three of us," the maid insisted.

At that moment, the young servant emerged from the wood carrying something with both hands, some precious object. His moronic face was full of smiles, his wide-open mouth exposing yellow teeth.

"Mistress, mistress! The Buddha of the Seven Stars has blessed you with a baby. Look, my lady, nobler than Buddha's child, fairer than a babe of the fairest fairy!"

The little one, exhausted from crying, was sound asleep. The tear-stained face was peaceful and beautiful. It breathed with gentle gasps, followed by small spasms.

Compassion and love surged in the mistress's heart like a tide. Taking the child from the young man's hands, she put her cheeks against its face.

"The Buddha of the Seven Stars has heard my prayers, and blessed me with this baby—I, a sinner." Before she knew it she had begun to sob.

Chapter Three

◆ ◆ ◆

Partings

The mineral-water spring was some forty paces away from the thatched cottage where Tasan lectured. A narrow mountain path led farther down to his residence, the eastern apartment. An early riser, each morning he slowly climbed to the spring. With a small gourd he scooped the water from the spring and drank the cold and delicious water, as good as any medicine. After brushing his teeth and washing his hands, he would view the sunrise. Depressed though he was by the loss of some of his teeth and by the discomfort of having to depend on his spectacles, each morning Tasan felt his life being revitalized by this spring-water.

It was early spring, and the chill of late winter still lingered, but in the mountain the camellias flowered all through the year, since some varieties blossomed early and others were late-blooming. That morning, on the branches suspended over the spring hung some fragile, unopened blossoms suffused with a vivid crimson hue. On mornings such as this, Tasan felt a fleeting sense of delight, catching a glimpse of dayflowers scattered like sprinkles of blue sky along the mountain path, or wild strawberries half hidden among the grass suddenly glistening like jewels with morning dew, or solitary clusters of tea blossoms, those late-blooming, sweet-smelling flowers that had missed their season. The crooning of mountain doves, like a long-forgotten memory, reawakened in his heart a tingle of passion which he thought had been extinguished.

A prolific poet, Tasan taught his disciples to model their poems after the styles of the T'ang poets, Tu Fu, Han Yu, and Su Tung-p'o. He told them that Tu Fu's work was the zenith of Chinese poetry

because of his adherence to the principles guiding the three
hundred poems recorded in the *Book of Odes*. These principles
were the true expression of the traditional virtues: loyal subjects,
filial sons, virtuous women, and faithful friends. Tasan believed in
no poems other than those expressing love for one's king, and concern for one's country. Unless they expressed the pain one felt for
the ills of the time, and rage at worldly ways, or distinguished
beauty from ugliness, good from evil, they could not be called poetry. He taught: "Those without firm conviction, with immature
learning, unschooled in the great moral principles that govern life,
or those who have no intention of helping people by supporting
wise statesmen, have no capacity for composing poetry. I implore
you to keep this in mind." At other times he would confuse them
by saying: "It would take the lifetimes of three, myself and my two
sons, to approximate the art of Su Tung-p'o's poetry. But why should
we waste our lives in such a vain pursuit when there is so much in
this world to be explored?" Or: "If poetry did not contain any historical allusions and merely sang about the beauty of nature or described chess games or tales of drinking bouts, it would be nothing
but verses composed by country bumpkins. Henceforth your objective must be to incorporate historical events into your poetry." Indeed, most of his own poetry expressed laments of the time, rage at
the inconsistencies of the system, and the agonies, anger, and sorrow of the poor.

However, in his private moments, he was a sensitive man capable
of being moved by the sight of tea flowers in the midst of snow-
covered mountains, evoking in his mind an elegant crane's snowy
white plumage, and the red flash on its crown. In such moments, he
was tempted into composing a poem on the tea flowers:

> Cold and harsh are the mountain tea leaves,
> Their flowers blossoming in the snow.
> How like the crown of a crane they are!

Years ago, in the late spring of the year when he had first begun
his days of banishment in Changgi, he had spotted a blazing red
flower on a narrow deserted trail. As he approached, he saw it was
a bloom still fresh on a sprig that had been discarded. Taking it
home, he planted it under the window of his hut. Even in his
wretched shanty of a house, cockscombs and balsams bloomed, giving comfort to an exile abandoned by his fellow men.

Around the country kitchen-terrace
Where nothing but cockscombs and balsams bloom
An abandoned stem of flower
As red as blossoms of fire.
On a day in late spring I planted it
Under the window of my temporary abode.

His innate sensibility to the beauty of nature found expression in the construction of a pond with a waterfall, tending flowers, or savoring the aroma of tea. Unaware of it himself, he was leading a life that cultivated his exquisite tastes.

In 1808, when Tasan was forty-eight, his health began to decline. In his letters to his disciples he began referring to himself as "the sick old man of Yŏyudang." This was another of his literary names, meaning "the one who lives in prudence." He suffered from painful arthritis and from a mild case of palsy, and had been bedridden several times during the year. Although in severe pain, he had revised and completed his *Lectures on the Book of Odes*. His passion and obsession for learning had elevated him to a height beyond which no ordinary men aspired, and he produced his greatest works during this time. It was his destiny; he followed the painful path to attain it. But Hyejang was still alive then, sometimes sober, sometimes broad-minded, playful yet harsh in his behavior. Only after Hyejang's death had Tasan come to realize how much those "slanders" of Hyejang's had helped him relax. Missing him, Tasan had not had the strength to go out to the mineral spring for several days since his friend's death.

Tasan scooped up the water with his cupped hands and sprinkled it over his face. As he raised himself after washing his face, a linen towel, made soft and whitened by repeated boiling and pounding, was quietly pushed toward him as if out of nowhere; there was no need for him to turn around. He wiped his face with it and then mindlessly let it drop into the hands of a woman who stood by to serve him. No one could have understood Tasan's needs better than this woman. She could intuit them even before the words could be formed on his lips, such was her devotion to him.

That morning, he had awakened later than usual, so that he missed the grandeur of the sunrise. Deep in reminiscence, he had been wakeful all through the night; only toward morning had he finally fallen into a sleep full of painful dreams. Suppressing a slight pain in his shoulder, he walked toward his thatched cottage. As he was about to turn the corner of the path, an ancient pine tree caught his eye. In that instant, as if a curtain had been lifted, he recalled vividly the dream he had had early that morning. It was not clear whether the tree he had seen in his dream was also a pine tree, but it was a well-developed and lofty tree, beautifully shaped with lustrous leaves of an uncommonly lovely green.

Recently, he had been having strange dreams in which nothing happened. He was always alone and in some strange place. In one dream, four seasons surrounded him. On his left was a ripening spring ablaze with azaleas, forsythia, and plum blossoms. When he turned his head, he saw a thick forest of deep green, the color of summer. Before him spread a deepening autumn enriched with magnificent foliage, and behind him scenes of a white, wintry landscape. In the dream, he felt a certain solace, but, being a physician, he also knew that such dreams were ill omens. He thought to himself, "My spirit must be in decline."

His dream of that morning, unlike his recent dreams, had a plot. It began with a roar of thunder and flashes of lightning. The tree shook violently amid the sparks. Automatically, he closed his eyes. When he opened them again, the thunder had ceased and the lightning subsided; however, a large limb of the tree had fallen, and in an instant changed to a deathly color. Horrified, he turned away and with downcast eyes walked away from it. When he lifted his eyes again, he almost screamed, for the tree was right in front of him, now hideous with its discolored broken limbs, obstructing his path. He retreated a few steps away from it, when before his very eyes, every leaf on it turned into a tongue, and those innumerable tongues began flicking toward him as though sneering at him. Sweating profusely, he woke from sleep and immediately the dream was totally forgotten, his power of reason having prevented so absurd a dream from rising to his conscious mind.

Now, recalling the dream, Tasan tried desperately to avoid looking at the pine tree, and walked briskly toward the cottage. Upon reaching it, he entered through the side door, not wishing his presence to be known since he heard a whispered exchange coming from the back room facing the lotus pond.

"So?" Ha-sang was coaxing the next words.

"Then," Chong-sim continued, "to stop the incessant noise, the teacher used his secret formula."

"A secret formula?"

"He wrote a mysterious charm and threw it into the pond. Since then, those noisy frogs have completely disappeared. Even if they reappeared, they dared not make noise."

"How extraordinary!" Ha-sang marvelled.

Polite and careful in his demeanor, Chong-sim was in high spirits that day, and boasted, "My teacher can communicate with birds, beasts, and even with small creatures. It's true!"

"Really, what a great man he is!"

"He is, indeed!"

One eighteen and the other sixteen, the two youths laughed joyously. Their laughter sounded as if it were coming from one person. Later, one would become a Buddhist convert, and would write with the deepest religious conviction an epilogue to *On Korean Sŏn Buddhism*. The other would become a martyr, just before his execution submitting his "Letter to the Prime Minister," a treatise in defense of Christianity, written in the blood of his tragic belief. Although they worshipped different gods, they were together in the purity and devoutness with which they followed their faiths. It might have been this that made their laughter sound as if it came from one person.

Tasan could not suppress the bitter smile that gathered around his lips. To dispel his annoyance at the incessant croaking of the frogs in the pond, he had written as a joke an outlandish sentence in hieroglyphic script. Written in vermilion, it must have looked like a secret formula. At any rate, since then, strangely enough, the clamor of the frogs had never recommenced. As if he had played a trick on his students, he felt embarrassed.

From outside came the voice of the woman. "Sir, what about your breakfast . . ."; the sentence ended in her mouth.

"I have no thought of it. But if you have some soup . . ."

After a pause, the voice came again, saying, "You have not taken anything for too long. I made some crabs marinated in soy sauce. It may help you regain your appetite . . ."

"Has Ha-sang had his breakfast?" Tasan inquired, suddenly remembering his visitor.

"He said he would eat after you, sir."

"Why, doesn't he realize how late it is already?" Without knowing it, Tasan's voice had become sharp. "Don't fuss. Just bring a
table for two."

"A table for both of you, sir?" asked the woman, perplexed and
unable to leave.

"It is not disgraceful for an uncle to share a table with his
nephew," Tasan snapped, thinking to himself, "In banishment, who
cares about such protocol?"

"One more bowl of rice and another pair of chopsticks will do,"
he said gently.

The breakfast table was soon brought in. The chopsticks were of
humble brass instead of silver, and the bowls were lidless, but Ha-
sang had never eaten a meal like this. The moist, lustrous rice was
mixed with cowpeas. The soybean paste soup of cabbage and
beansprouts with the little clams that the woman had dug from the
inlet was perfectly seasoned. A local cabbage pickle stuffed with
roasted sesame seeds was savory and pleasing in the mouth. There
was also a variety of seafood that had been salted and fermented,
such as agar, fish gills, and crabs, the taste of which would indeed
make a thief of anyone, as they said. The woman, true to the reputation of southern women, was an excellent cook, as well as being
nimble and affectionate. An embarrassingly packed rice bowl for
Ha-sang, not unlike one given to a hungry peasant, betrayed her
warm regard for him. Uncomfortable eating face-to-face with his
revered uncle, Ha-sang was sweating in an effort to hide his young,
vigorous appetite. Tasan, too, felt his appetite return as he touched
the tasty, savory crabs marinated in soy sauce and heavily sprinkled
with spices. The rice that he took for the first time since Hyejang's
death tasted incomparably delicious. No longer at the surface of his
mind was the sight of that snow-white rice he had seen during the
scattering of Hyejang's ashes.

With flavorful rice-water swirling in his mouth, Tasan was thinking of things of quite another nature. The lecture to his sons written
in the letter he had sent a few days ago echoed in his mind. He had
defined in the letter the virtue of diligence and frugality, so that his
sons could apply them in their daily life. To teach the spirit of frugality he emphasized plain diet: "Food is only to support life. No matter how tasty some fish may be, once it passes through your mouth,
it will only become a filthy thing." His own words reverberating,

he could not help a sardonic smile. "My vigor and spirit spent, am I growing old?" He felt uncomfortable. Wasn't it because of the way she cooked that their relationship had begun?

It had come about while he was living in the tavern. Solidly built and then only forty, he had already become sickly. Depression, hard work, unsanitary living conditions, and coarse food had contributed to his declining health. Moreover, he had been consumed with his studies. When he had read every book he had, he would borrow from the library owned by his maternal relations, at a distance of twenty-five miles. One day, he was on his way home after calling on his unwelcoming relatives to borrow books. Accompanied by the old man, P'yo, who carried a load of books in a back-rack, he stopped at a roadside tavern for some food. Suddenly, he felt nauseated, and a chill ran through his body. He hurried on his way in pain. The road began undulating, and he felt as if he were walking upside-down. He made it to the tavern before sunset, but in front of the gate, staggering for a moment, he lost consciousness.

Alarmed, the old proprietress and P'yo carried Tasan, his body as hot as fire, to his room. Next morning the fever finally subsided and he regained consciousness. But the following day he again became feverish and delirious. The fever tormented him every other day. Without a doubt he had contracted malaria. The country folk believed the disease could be cured not by using medicines but by bolstering diminishing energy through exercising willpower to fight back. They advised the patient to be active, even on the fever days. To restore Tasan's strength, the proprietress fed him a brew of the fruits of Chinese juniper and a gruel made of arrowroot starch.

"How terrible," she said. "You must not remain in bed when you suffer from malaria. You have to fight back."

Bedridden in spite of himself, Tasan was frustrated. As a remedy for malaria, the people also fed the patient powder made from the dried skin of ox bladder. P'yo managed to get some ox bladder. He peeled the skin carefully, dried and powdered it, and then gave it to Tasan. However, Tasan did not recover; on the contrary, now he had to endure a fit of shivering every afternoon.

"See," said the disgruntled proprietress, "you have made yourself worse by lying there all the time. Now what can we do about it?"

His eyes closed, Tasan smiled feebly; his heart could not have tolerated such high fever if he had not been lying still in bed, and even that mouth-twisting bitter powder had failed to arouse in him any desire for sweet-tasting food.

Suffering from fever, and unable to eat, Tasan rapidly became emaciated. One day P'yo brought him a bowl of gruel.

"I brought you some gruel," he said. "It's unusual; you might try a bit."

The uncommonly savory aroma seeped into Tasan's nostrils. "You are very kind. Thank you," he answered weakly.

"It's porridge made of pumpkin seeds. Why don't you try a few spoonfuls. You must eat something to get your strength back."

"Pumpkin-seed porridge?" Tasan looked at the old man; he had never heard of such a gruel before.

"Yes. It's really tasty. Here, please eat some." Stirring the porridge in the bowl with a brass spoon, the old man fed Tasan gently.

Never before had Tasan tasted anything like this, simultaneously flavorful and bland, soothing in his mouth. "It has, indeed, an uncommon taste."

The old man, his face crinkled with wrinkles and a toothless grin, said, "My daughter is a good cook. She peeled each seed to make this. She said she wanted to make it for His Excellency. The aroma of seeds being roasted just perfectly was really something."

From that day, Tasan slowly began to eat, and with the food P'yo brought to him daily, soon his appetite was completely restored. Although made of humble ingredients, the food was, without exception, perfectly seasoned and pleasing to his taste: thin pieces of dried seaweed, glued together layer by layer with richly seasoned rice-gruel and dried in the sun once again, then fried in oil or quickly roasted; or pickled leeks with a generous mixture of red pepper and spices thickened with rice-gruel. Without being aware of it, he was cured of the malaria, and the fever and chill that had tormented him every afternoon no longer attacked him.

"See. Proper eating is better than the most precious medicines, like ginseng or slices from the new antler of a deer," the proprietress boasted, as if it were she who had cured him.

After that, Tasan could not eat anything without the pickled side dishes P'yo's daughter made. They made even coarse barley melt in his mouth like honey.

P'yo's daughter, P'yo-nyŏ, was a young widow of twenty-one.

When she was twelve, her destitute parents, unable to manage during the food shortage just before the barley harvest in the early summer, had married her off to an old man who was just as poverty-stricken. After three meager years, she had become a widow at the tender age of fifteen. Since her family was extremely poor, in order to lessen their burden of feeding one more mouth, she had become a maid in the household of a district government clerk.

These petty officials were usually of a corrupt sort, adept in flattery, pledging their undying loyalty to their governor, who, though his comings and goings were heralded by trumpets and six musical instruments, was a temporary fixture in the district government. A governor in name only, in most cases a genteel, ineffective scholar-official from the capital, he would often become a puppet of crafty clerks. Wielding real power as tax collectors, they were cunning, impudent, and cruel, showing no mercy and allowing no exceptions or leniency, even in the case of the dire poverty of starving people. On some rare occasions, however, having heard about the misconduct of certain clerks, the governor might ask the people to come forward and report their complaints, but those poor people would only reply that they had sprained their back by accident, when in reality they had been beaten severely by the clerks. Even if their last, pitifully meager crops and their last ox had been confiscated, they would only claim that these had been in payment of their debt. How could the people of the district behave otherwise? Since their positions were hereditary, the clerks and their progeny would hold their positions for generations, while the governor's sojourn was only temporary. No wonder that even in the severest famine year, when the poor people were suffering from malnutrition, the tax clerks enjoyed abundance.

Quick to learn, P'yo-nyŏ soon mastered the art of fine cooking while working for such a household. Ironically, the cuisine of the southern official households, which were well-known for their extravagant taste in fine food, helped restore Tasan's declining health, despite the fact that more than anything he disliked those functionaries. He had witnessed their corruption and wrongdoing throughout the twenty years of his life in banishment.

Comely P'yo-nyŏ took casually her master's lustful advances, but she could not endure the jealous rage of his wife. She returned reluctantly to her parents' house, which was no longer in utter desti-

tution, thanks to their following Tasan's teachings; the entire family
had turned the wasteland into a fertile farm for buckwheat and millet. They raised chickens and pigs and dug up the ridges of rice
paddies to catch freshwater crabs and snails, supplementing their
diet with fish they angled. P'yo-nyŏ did not have to spend a penny
to please her family at mealtimes. Everything that caught her eye
she turned into food. She never missed picking young soybean
leaves or wild sesame leaves when they were at their tenderest; she
stuck them into the soybean paste, which later would become a
side dish for everyday meals. In her hands, edible weeds and roots
became salted condiments, not to mention the freshwater crabs,
snails from the rice paddies, and clams and oysters from the inlet,
which she turned into mouth-watering salted preserves. Still barely
out of adolescence, she gave up her womanhood, devoting herself
entirely to cooking.

It was about the time Tasan was beginning to regain his strength
that P'yo-nyŏ came to the tavern to work in the kitchen. The proprietress, her aunt, had approached her and spoken her thoughts, which
had been in her mind for a long time. The hard work of running a
tavern was now too much for her in her old age. "Such a dear talent,
why throw it away to the dogs? Come take care of the gentleman
from Seoul and help your aunt as well."

Soon the reputation spread of P'yo-nyŏ's marvelous soup, served
with wine in the tavern. Recuperating from the malaria, to his
amazement Tasan found himself impatiently waiting for each meal
to be served. He enjoyed not only the wine served with dinner,
which he never missed, but also some occasional wine during the
day, because the accompanying tidbits were so incomparably delicious. In spite of his belief in plain food, he was becoming a lover
of exquisite delicacies.

The proprietress of the tavern, having grown old outside the limits of a respectable household, was a worldly-wise and open-minded
woman. One starry night, sitting together on a wooden bench, Tasan
and the old woman engaged in a conversation, and their topic turned
to the difference between a father's and a mother's roles. The argument began by their questioning why, since olden times, the sages
had ruled that by natural law a father's role was higher than that of
a mother, while in fact it had always been the mother who did most
of the bringing-up of their offspring. To this, Tasan replied that

though a mother's love was very deep indeed, the ultimate fact that caused a life was more important. Without a moment's hesitation, the woman disputed his statement.

"Seeds can be compared to a father and soil to a mother," she said. "Once a seed is dropped, the soil nourishes it and makes its growth possible; therefore, it is the quality of the soil that makes the difference. The chestnut seed becomes a chestnut tree, while that of rice, a rice plant. The growth of each seed depends on the strength of the soil, but it is the seed that ultimately determines one or the other. It is, therefore, this principle that the ancient sages thought of as natural law."

Tasan was greatly moved by what she said. He had never met anyone who could express a thought as clearly as this woman. Many took roundabout, vague ways, or engaged in a noisy exhibition of their knowledge, yet were unable to focus on the point, or reverted to biting rebuttal just for the sake of refuting an argument. He could not suppress his amazement at the wisdom of these poor people and their ability to capture the kernel of things. He expressed this feeling in a letter to Yak-chŏn: "Suddenly I came to a clear insight through what these people said, and I stood in awe of them. Who could have known that I would someday learn a most abstruse truth from a lowly tavern-woman. Admirable indeed were her words."

Tasan felt a similar sentiment toward P'yo-nyŏ's cooking. In his letters to his sons, he had taught that a rough and plain diet strengthened character, and provided a way to practice the spirit of frugality and avoid the trappings of vanity. However, after experiencing P'yo-nyŏ's approach to life, a different thought would occasionally flash into his consciousness. Her carefully prepared and flavorful meals had restored his health completely; true to what the old woman had said, a good diet was as good as the finest medicine in the world. His case fitted the saying that "an illness cured implies a celebrated physician, an efficacious potion implies a sacred medicine."

The fine foods P'yo-nyŏ cooked had their beginnings in that very ideal of frugality. Born into utmost poverty, she had acquired the wisdom to survive under such circumstances. Although the tavern was wretched in appearance, it was still a place where food was sold, and the leavings and the waste were plentiful. She was the embodiment of frugality itself. She pickled the discarded fish guts, mixing them with rich spices, which produced a side dish that, once tasted, would never be forgotten. Fins and large bones of fish not fit even for pigs, dried and deep-fried became delectable companions to wine. Every few days, she made a fresh batch of pickled cabbage. She did not waste even a single leaf; one by one, she bound the unusable, outer leaves with straw, and dried them in the shade. They were then used in making the soup served with wine for which the tavern had become so famous. Everything she cooked benefitted from her talent for transforming the useless into the useful, and putting into practice the ideals of frugality and diligence.

P'yo-nyŏ's devotion to Tasan went beyond her cooking. She had two large ceramic water jugs outside the tavern, which were always filled. On top of one was an earthen steamer in which she grew beansprouts; a piece of hemp cloth covered the mouth of the other, which was used to strain water through mulberry wood ashes to make ash-water with which to bleach Tasan's clothes as white as snow.

After she had served Tasan for years in this manner, their relationship was consummated in a most natural way when she was twenty-one, the same age as Tasan's eldest son. The following year, even after Tasan moved his residence to the room in the mountain temple that Hyejang had arranged for him, P'yo-nyŏ remained in the tavern and went on working in the kitchen because she feared that a woman's presence might disturb the sacred atmosphere of a temple. However, she continued to cook for Tasan and attended to his needs as usual. It was only after Tasan settled in Kyuldong that they began living together. They did not, however, occupy the same room. She lived quietly in a room of a small separate house in the backyard, a site that Tasan, who was well-versed in the science of geomancy, had divined to be propitious. The next year, a daughter was born—a daughter of shame, since she was born of a man whose grandson was two years old.

◆   ◆   ◆

Tasan accompanied Ha-sang as far as the reed field, and watched his back disappear around the corner of the road. His four-year-old daughter, Hong-nim, who had followed them unnoticed, paused a few steps behind her father, who stood transfixed as though taken root. Cocking her head gently, she looked toward the distant horizon her father was contemplating, and then at his face. To her, young as

she was, the expression on her father's face was strange. Her al-
mond-shaped eyes widened, their lids as translucent as the inner
skin of gingko nuts. She watched her father blink his large, elongated eyes in an effort to fight off tears. Since she had never seen
him like this, anxiously and gently, she sought his hand. Such a
moment had seldom occurred between them. She had always been
in awe of him and kept her distance, because her mother had warned
her never to trouble him or go near him unless so ordered. Just as
he rarely asked her to come near him or addressed her by her name,
Hong-nim, so she had never called him father. She addressed him
as "sir," "master," or "teacher," just as her mother did. At those
words, his face would become clouded with pity. This was the first
time she had ever touched him. His hands were large, the fingers
hardened with calluses formed by the constant pressure of the writing brush. His forefinger filled her tiny palm.

"Oh, it's you, Hong-nim. How are you?" Tasan picked her up in
his arms.

"Mommy! Mommy!" she shrieked, frightened and ready to burst
out crying. She tried to wiggle out of his embrace, but Tasan held
her tighter. Her little body was fragile yet soft and warm. Pity over-
flowed his heart. Giving up her noisy resistance, she became quiet,
then suddenly she wrapped her arms around his neck with all her
might as if she would never let go again.

Hong-nim did not play with other village children; instead, she
often lurked about her father's residence where she was forbidden
by her mother to go.

One day, Tasan overheard P'yo-nyŏ whispering, "You foolish little girl, why can't you listen to what your Mommy has told you?
Master is an important man. How could you behave in such a way
as to attract others' eyes?"

Tasan felt a pang of pity and guilt listening to what she said to
the child. It was not unusual for an exile to become intimate with a
woman in the land of his banishment. Lonely and lost in a strange
environment, he required the helping hands of a woman. Even
though historically these regions were full of the illegitimate offspring of fallen officials, this woman, to protect Tasan from a blemish on his character, was trying her best to hide her child from the
world, as one did one's private parts. Nonetheless, she groomed her
little girl into incomparable loveliness. Pulling back the fine hair

smoothly from the temples, she plaited it into a checkerboard pattern and tied each end with red string. In her crimson skirt and short jacket with rainbow-colored striped sleeves, the girl took on an almost unearthly loveliness that was incongruous in the remote village setting.

Occasionally, Tasan would inquire after the child. "I haven't seen Hong-nim for some time. What has happened?" he would remark.

At his query, wordlessly, P'yo-nyŏ would only lower her eyes, a blush spreading over her face and down to the nape of her neck.

Once Tasan had come across Hong-nim on a roadside, pretty as a doll. As usual, she had been dressed carefully by her mother, as though for a holiday, and he remembered having seen a young girl such as this a long time ago in his hometown of Majae. Yes, indeed, it had been during a May Festival; his daughter had been about the same age as Hong-nim. She was wearing a short jacket of lime green with elaborately embroidered edging around the border, and a long, pink skirt rustling over the floor as she walked. An iris leaf was stuck in her hair, and from her came the fragrance of iris, for it was the custom on that day for women and young girls to wash their hair with water perfumed with the flower's scent. He remembered that her face had been powdered and rouged, and her hair parted straight in the middle, marking a clear line from her forehead to the crown of her head. His young daughter had been practicing the proper way to make a ceremonial bow. He had marveled as he watched her supple body moving gracefully in accordance with the requirements of etiquette. She had bowed like a dancing butterfly. Now she was married to a member of the Yun family, but her father, an exile, had not been allowed to behold her bridal splendor. He wondered if his being a treasonous criminal might not be affecting her marriage. Becoming conscious that his eyes were filling, he recited a poem about the longing in his heart:

Yesterday:
Young daughter on the day of May Festival
Putting on fresh makeup
Wearing a skirt sewn from red ramie cloth
In her hair a stem of iris.

As she practiced her bow
Elegant were her movements,

As she lifted a wine cup
Her face was full of joy.

Today:
On the evening of May Festival
Who caresses the jewel in his palm?

Suffering from the pangs that shot through his eyes and filled his chest, he closed his eyes. His fate and the world had been cruel to him. Married at fourteen, he had suffered the loss of three sons and a daughter. One of them had died within ten days of birth; the rest had died at three—the most adorable age. Each parting had left a visceral pain that found no expression. The remaining three sons, and the only daughter, had been carefully brought up; however, while in exile he had received word of the death of his youngest son, whom he had seen for the last time at the age of three on the day he had left for the long banishment. It was a bleak, drizzly day at the end of February, with the wind blowing from the mountains, two days after Yak-chong had been beheaded. His own life having been spared after his shameful apostasy, he was on his way to the destination of his banishment. Soon after crossing the Han River on the outskirts of the capital, he saw a group of people following him. Among them were his sons, Hag-yŏn and Hag-yu, who, weeping loudly, kowtowed to him on the wet ground. The women of his family surrounding them let out their unabashed wails. The servants, too, wiped their tears with their fists. Tasan kept his eyes closed.

"Look here. What is this when your husband is leaving? Hurry and show your son to him," came the voice of his sister-in-law.

As he opened his eyes, he saw a lone figure with a baby, separated from the rest of the crowd that encircled him. Though her face was hidden under a hooded cloak, he knew it was his wife. At first the child did not recognize his father, who had changed completely in his appearance, but finally realizing that the strange man was indeed his father, he waved his hands joyously and struggled in his mother's arms, wanting to get down and run toward him. Tasan fought off the flame of pain that pushed up through his throat. Although urged by her sons and coaxed somewhat resentfully by the other women of the family, his wife did not come near him to the end, nor did she weep loudly as the others did. However, she handed their son to Hag-yu so that Tasan could hold him for the last time.

But Tasan clearly saw his wife. She wore the hooded cloak awkwardly, because women of high-ranking officials did not wear them even when they went outside their homes. Her shoulders were visibly shaking under the cloak, and her partially exposed face was covered with sad dark blotches—the marks of suffering and sorrow—but protocol and the requirements of etiquette dictated that women of her station must not weep aloud in mourning for their husbands. Rushing the guards and servants, he hurriedly set out for the long journey to avoid further tormenting his wife.

Only after crossing fields and streams did Tasan allow his tears to fall. The village where the cruel parting had taken place, he was told, was called Sap'yŏng. In tears, he recited a line about the pain of such a parting: "I held my head upright and undaunted, but in my heart the turmoil only grew." That was the end of it. "My poor son," he mused, "who clung to his father, struggling not to be separated, as though he already knew it to be the last parting."

The door of finely woven lattice was carefully slid open. "Here you are. Your Mommy looked all over for you," P'yo-nyŏ murmured, her face lighting up on seeing her daughter. She had been looking for Hong-nim, fearing that she might have gotten lost.

"I am sorry. How careless of me not to keep an eye on the child," she apologized.

"I carried her back home."

"Now, make a deep bow and let us leave," P'yo-nyŏ urged her daughter.

Meekly the girl stood in front of her father, then spreading both hands awkwardly, knelt down and bowed. "Sir, please stay in peace," she said, taking her leave in honorific speech, to which she was not accustomed.

Tasan did not detain them, for it was also the time when he expected his disciples to arrive for their lessons, but for a while he could not erase from his mind the images of the mother's anxious face and his little daughter, groomed to such loveliness, yet her deep bow lacking in refinement. While it had been possible for his legitimate wife, who in his judgment lacked nobility and virtue, to swallow those bloody tears of parting only because of the constraints of protocol, he wondered why P'yo-nyŏ, this ignorant country woman, who was free of such restrictions, must sacrifice herself in his service. Was it because of ignorance or fear, or was it just her nature, or was it love?

He was the man who had written, "Heaven is above and on earth are the people. Heaven does not ask whether one is a scholar-gentleman." In theory, Tasan passionately advocated the equality of men, and opposed discriminating between legitimate and illegitimate offspring; however, he did not make an effort to stop his own daughter—a daughter not born of his legitimate wife—from addressing him as "master."

Because of the prescribed mourning period and his despondency following it, Tasan had suspended lectures for a few days, and this was the first time he had sat at his desk since Hyejang's death. As usual, the desk was in immaculate order. He drew the inkstone toward him and picked up the water-dropper, which as usual was filled. He smiled, touched by Chong-sim's thoughtful attention even to the smallest detail. The slanting autumn sunlight, too high during the summer, now crept in as far as the inkstone. In that sunlight, Tasan noticed an unfamiliar object. Picking it up, he remembered that it was the pouch Ha-sang had left him. It was an embroidered, black satin pouch, sewn at the border with purple thread, and its lining was also of purple fabric. Two plump, macramé cords of the same color were attached to the opening so the pouch could be worn on a belt. Even without the embroidery, it would have been both refined and gorgeous at the same time, but the embroidery caught his attention. Maidens' needlework was usually confined to such domestic needs as the pairs of pads to be attached to either side of pillows, or pouches for spoons or for money, or cushion-covers. The designs often depicted the Four Gracious Plants—plum, orchid, chrysanthemum, and bamboo; or the Ten Symbols of Longevity—sun, clouds, rocks, water, pine, bamboo, fungus of elixir, turtle, deer, and cranes; or peonies with butterflies; or mandarin ducks with their nine ducklings. However, Tasan noted a strange design on the pouch, such as he had never seen before. Commonly, such embroidery was done on a red background, but this was done in black, and the manner of its execution was also different from any he had seen. Clusters of wild roses tangled curiously around the intricate design of T'ang grass. Conventionally, flowers were done in red, yellow, or blue, but the flowers on this piece were predominantly purple with some mixture of grey, and even black, delicate and at the same time flamboyant, expressing an intangible nobility.

"Ha-sang said she is fourteen. Hm . . . Uncommon taste, indeed." Tasan was impressed with her skill, wondering how a mere girl of fourteen could embroider with such sophistication. As he admired it, suddenly he remembered having seen somewhere a design such as this. Where could it have been? Tracing back through his memory, he became alarmed. It was similar to one on the cover of the Latin prayer book from which Father Chou Wen-mu used to read. However, Tasan did not get rid of the pouch; instead, he put his spectacles in it, and tied it to his belt.

She must have been a mere child of four, thought Tasan to himself, at the time of the Persecution of 1801, and too young to comprehend what catastrophe had struck the family. He became ashamed of himself for not being able to recall his own niece's face.

"I have been too indifferent to them," he murmured to himself, fondling the pouch in his hand. In that instant, a thought that hitherto had never visited him suddenly surfaced in his mind. "I have been an unworthy brother." Aghast, he sprang to his feet. The realization had struck him with such force that he was unable to move.

Firmly believing in brotherly love, he had never once doubted the depth of his feeling for his brothers, his oldest brother, Yak-hyŏn, and especially for his second brother, Yak-chŏn. Tasan had great respect and affection for Yak-chŏn, and although uncommonly proud, he was humble enough to defer to his brother and to seek enlightenment from him.

"My virtue and learning trail far behind yours," he had said to him, in humble reference to an occasion when King Chŏngjo had summoned them both to the throne to observe that, "Though the younger may be superior in his intellect to the older, he trails far behind the elder's virtue."

However, Tasan's relationship to his third brother, Yak-chong, had been ambiguous. In addition to the epitaph on his own tombstone, Tasan had written many inscriptions for the tombstones of his friends and members of his clan, from the one he had written for his nephew, who had died at the age of sixteen, to the one for his daughter-in-law, whose unfilial death had preceded those of her parents-in-law. Nevertheless, Tasan had not written a single word for Yak-Chong, let alone an epitaph. What had been the reason? Was it a difference of personality, or did he harbor some need to compete with this brother, or a fear of being associated with a beheaded heretic? Whatever the reason, such behavior contradicted the character of the man who day and night sought tirelessly the means to help poor, defenseless brethren in suffering.

This was what Tasan had come to realize. Again he felt tears welling up in his eyes as he thought of those two; the nobility of Ha-sang, who was filled only with pure love for his heartless uncle, obeying his order to leave without the slightest resentment, and his niece, whose every stitch of embroidery contained her longing for him, neither one of whom had ever once had a word of greeting from him. He collapsed in his seat as he plunged deep into introspection.

Tasan opposed the traditional ideals of the Three Cardinal Bonds and the Five Ethical Relationships on the ground that they were only applicable to vertical hierarchical relationships. Adherence to such ideology suited the purpose of the Confucians in power; in order to maintain their position, they demanded unconditional acceptance from the people. On the other hand, Tasan's ethical principles had their foundation in the concepts of filial piety, fraternal love, and compassion. To Tasan, filial piety and loyalty to the king originated from the same principle. The concept of fraternal love, he advocated, embraced the horizontal ethical principle of equality while binding society together in a harmonious, humane relationship. By compassion, he meant benevolence in governing people.

Tasan had first expounded his ethical theory in Koksan. King Chŏngjo had sent him there to protect him from the schemes of his adversaries. While being a wise magistrate who practiced what he believed, he also taught at the local Confucian Academy. In his lectures, applying pragmatic, empirical logic, he stressed the principles of filial piety and fraternal love. Two years before, in 1795, partly to test his fidelity, and partly to shield him from his tormentors, the king had demoted him to a post in a local government in Kŭmjŏng where many of the inhabitants were said to have been Catholics. Gathering the offspring of the local nobles, he conducted study groups in Sŏgam Temple. There he was successful in persuading many Catholics in the region back to the Confucian path. Tasan had been a Confucian scholar above all, his belief in it deeper than his belief in Catholicism.

Now, more than ten years later, Tasan recalled clearly having written in his *Collected Works of Yŏyudang*: "Brothers are the extension of parents; therefore they are one. The elder comes into the world before the younger, and the facial features and teeth may vary, but if one considers himself apart from his brother and does not love him as he does himself, it only means that he distances himself. What an immature act! Let us consider a tree. Suppose one branch flourishes, bearing plentiful flowers, and some others wither like an old tree. No one would turn away from the sight without a sigh of pain."

Tasan was a proud man. One could detect the voice of conceit in his autobiography. However, alone now in the thatched cottage of his banishment, he suffered self-torment. Indeed, the nightmare of the morning was nothing but the soliloquy of his conscience.

Tasan heard a stirring outside.

"Teacher." Chong-sim had just returned from town, seeing Ha-sang off on the road.

"Well. Is Ha-sang safely on the way?" asked Tasan.

"I am sure by now he must have gone more than ten miles," Chong-sim replied cheerfully.

Standing up, Tasan opened one of the double windows. The gusty wind of the sea gull season swept over his face; the autumn was deepening.

"With his long legs, he walked so fast that I kept running after him," Chong-sim reported, his face flushed and fresh-looking.

"I am sorry to have asked you to show him the way."

"Not at all. I enjoyed it. We have become such good friends. I am very sad to see him go."

It pleased Tasan to hear what his beloved disciple said about Ha-sang, but he could not help wondering what they talked about between them, one an able student on his way to becoming a scholar, and the other illiterate. Tasan tried to convince himself that with his inborn dignity Ha-sang would not have disgraced himself, but he felt somewhat uncomfortable, nonetheless. Even then, however, the thought of calling him back and educating him did not occur to him.

"Thank you. Now, why don't you retire and try to get some rest."

Chong-sim stood there, hesitating. It seemed he wanted to ask his teacher if he intended to skip his lecture again.

"I will begin early this afternoon," Tasan said briefly as he closed the window.

At that time, Ha-sang was walking briskly past the town of Naju. The road stretched on endlessly across the wide open plain of Naju. In the southern provinçes autumn lasted longer. He viewed here and there the satisfying sight of piles of rice sheaves after the harvest, or the fields where the harvest had not yet been completed. In some, fresh green winter vegetables, planted after the rice harvest—scallions, mustard plants, cabbages, and radishes—grew lustily. Ha-sang kept on walking, feeling comfortable in a perfect season of mild weather. His fast steps acted like a magic distance-shortener, but he was in a hurry and wished he could fly. He wondered if Francesco had been able to meet Mr. Kwŏn, if Mr. Kwŏn had kept his promise, and if everything was in order as had been planned.

Ha-sang walked without a pause for rest. Every now and then his hands lingered on the collar of his shirt. It was lined with coarse cotton, but its harshness was comfortable to him, reassuring him of what had been sewn inside. After breakfast that morning, Ha-sang had spoken his words of parting to his uncle with mixed emotions. He was grateful to Tasan who, though he had been cold and stern, could not help betraying the deep concern of a blood relation. Ha-sang had been remorseful that he must leave his uncle without fulfilling the task for which he had come.

He had bowed to Tasan humbly, and as he had lifted his head, Tasan had handed him something wrapped in white paper. "Be careful. Though it is very little, I want you to use this money for your journey. It is a long way back to the capital." After a short pause, Tasan added, "But never for a moment think of using it for the purpose of going to Peking. It is far from that kind of amount."

Blinking away a tear, Ha-sang accepted the money with both hands and, lifting it high above his head, bowed deeply once again. Tasan sat in silence for a long time. Finally, after a few moments of deliberation, he took from inside his jacket some pieces of paper about six centimeters in width, folded many times. Ha-sang felt his face flame. The papers were the draft letters that had been sewn into his collar. After midnight on the night before, Ha-sang had taken apart the stitches very carefully in the dark, and after removing the letters, he had left them at Tasan's bedside.

Catholicism had at first been accepted by the eminent scholars of the time, but the persecutions felled most of them—some were martyred and others banished—leaving only a handful of Christians who could compose a formal letter. Yet now they had to write a letter that could move the mighty pope. Summoning up all the knowledge they possessed, the church leaders succeeded in producing two letters, one to a bishop in Peking and the other to the pope, but after writing them, they lost confidence in what they had written. A long discussion ensued, and finally they agreed to seek assistance from Tasan. They knew Tasan had twice declared his apostasy, but they did not doubt that he was still a fellow Christian, the only surviving scholar who could help them. Tasan was their last hope, but thus far he had been cold to such a request. Ha-sang had come on a doomed mission, hoping for a miracle.

When Ha-sang was on the verge of falling asleep from exhaustion and tension, Tasan got up and lit the lamp. Ha-sang thought that Tasan was about to go to the outhouse, but instead, he saw him pick up the letters and spread them on the desk. In an instant, Ha-sang was wide awake, but he remained motionless, feigning sound sleep. Slowly and deliberately Tasan began grinding the ink in the ink-stone. Soon there came the sound of brisk brush-stroke on paper. Ha-sang's heart was bursting.

Ha-sang had only a few hours of sleep toward morning, but he felt refreshed. Young and healthy, he needed only a short, deep sleep to recover from fatigue. Upon waking, he got up quietly and looked for the letters, but they were nowhere to be seen, neither at Tasan's bedside nor on the desk. He glanced toward Tasan, who was sleeping soundly. Once in a while, a moan escaped from him, as if he were in pain or having a nightmare. Ha-sang noiselessly left the room. Freed though he was from the strain of sleeping in the same room with his uncle, he was still under the spell of the powerful emotion he had experienced last night.

From nowhere, P'yo-nyŏ appeared and motioned him to follow her to the mineral spring. He brushed his teeth, washed his face, and sprinkled water on his hair, combing it with his fingers. His face was once again as fresh and clean as a just-washed, luscious cabbage.

"Is the teacher awake?" Chong-sim, already groomed for the day, emerged from the bush.

Ha-sang told him that Tasan was still asleep.

"He must still be unwell." Chong-sim knitted his brows anxiously, concerned about his teacher, who had been indisposed since Hyejang's death. He sighed lightly, not realizing that Tasan was already up.

The two youths had become dear friends. Usually shy and careful in his conduct, Chong-sim behaved like any other eighteen-year-old. He was exceedingly proud of Tasan, happy and honored to be one of his disciples. In his enthusiasm, he forgot for a moment that Ha-sang was Tasan's nephew. But he knew that his teacher favored him more than he did Ha-sang, his own blood relation, and he was aware of the circumstances of their lives.

Ha-sang followed Chong-sim into the room. First Chong-sim opened the double windows wide and then, with a familiar motion, folded the bedding and began sweeping the room. Watching Chong-sim clean his teacher's room with such devotion, Ha-sang was filled with admiration. Here he was, dressed in a formal coat with a sky-blue tasseled sash neatly tied around his waist and wearing a horse-hair hat, performing menial tasks.

Noticing the water-dropper while dusting the desk, Chong-sim wondered aloud, "Oh, he must have worked late last night . . . That's why he was late this morning . . ."

Ha-sang's heart throbbed loudly. It had not been a dream; what he had seen last night was real. He was bursting with joy. Yes, his uncle had granted his wish.

However, Tasan remained quiet and indifferent to the end, as though nothing had happened. Until the moment when Ha-sang said his last farewells, Tasan did not betray his intention. When Chong-sim left them to prepare to accompany Ha-sang, Tasan finally took the letters out of his jacket and said deliberately, "How dare you leave these abominable documents around carelessly." Then to his amazement, Tasan asked Ha-sang to take off his jacket, and he himself sewed the letters back into the collar.

Ha-sang walked about thirty miles on the first day. He was carrying in his backpack a day's ration of rice packed into small balls and stuffed with radish pickles—P'yo-nyŏ's thoughtfulness. He ate some as he walked.

By late afternoon of the next day, he was near the town of Mu-hyŏn. He wanted to reach Chŏnju before sunset, but it began to rain, and the rain soon turned into a downpour. The night before, he had slept under a sky sprinkled with stars, but he could not spend the night in the open in this rain. He had no other choice but to seek shelter in a shabby inn. Upon entering, he found the inn filled with travelers. His pack still on his back, he leaned against the wall of a room shared by several other travelers. Thirty miles each day had been a bit too rough even for him. He felt his body collapsing with fatigue. He needed sleep more than food. However, a sudden commotion from outside disturbed Ha-sang, and a shriek rose above the clamor. Before he realized it, he was standing up and peering outside.

Chapter Four

♦ ♦ ♦

Shaman's Daughter

The squalid, weather-beaten inn was packed with travelers who filled the grimy tavern-room, the community guest room, and the kitchen; even the storage shed was occupied. But the commotion did not rise among the travelers who had come in from the downpour. It started with the shriek of the innkeeper woman, calling frantically among the unexpected, jostling crowd. "Chŏm-soe! Chŏm-soe! Where are you?"

At her screech, a pigtailed young servant emerged from the shed. "What?" answered the boy blankly only when he approached the tavern-room.

The woman roared in rage, "Taking a nap again, eh? Why did you leave the kitchen door open?"

"I did no such thing."

"Then who did it? A stray cat ate all the appetizers for the guests. There is nothing left to serve with the customers' drinks. I don't understand how it happened. What am I to do?"

In an impoverished inn such as this, even without the stray cat there was not much to serve, but with so many unexpected customers, the woman was frantic at the thought of having to miss this rare chance to make a profit.

"Damn it!" she shouted, "You go tend the fire under the soup kettle, quick! We must serve these drenched travelers with hot soup and rice."

There was no other help at the inn. The dim-witted boy was only good for getting firewood from the mountains and tending the fire at the furnace. From this fortyish woman, her face smeared with powder, her eyebrows plucked, and her upswept hairdo tied with red ribbon, emanated the slovenly bawdiness of a woman who needed a man. As she left the kitchen, the source of her consternation, and went into the backyard, she screamed again, "Heavens, look at this—I caught the cat!"

The boy, who was tending the fire, ran to the backyard, followed by two of the guests.

The woman was shouting, "Look here, you bitch, you devoured everything I had for the customers, ruining my business. Didn't you know the hands of a bitch that steals get broken? A thief-bitch; I'll drag you to the officials and have your mouth seared with a red-hot iron!"

The "stray cat" was a beggar girl of about seven. Her hair, stiffened with mud and rain, stood out like wormwood shoots, and her face was covered with dust. Her clothes were in shreds, exposing her flesh here and there. Leaning against a gatepost outside the kitchen, she had been caught eating like a famished demon the food she had stolen from the kitchen—some boiled eggs and braised, dried whiting. She was a pathetic sight, but the proprietress had no mercy; her business was at stake. She was shoving and dragging the child all over the place, shouting obscenities. Her victim did not resist; her limp, thin, little body was being tossed around mercilessly.

"A mere child; don't be so harsh," said a man at the sight of the violence.

"She must have been so hungry, poor soul," chimed in another.

Provoked by these words, the woman became even more furious. She threw herself into such a maddening assault that the men had to restrain her forcibly.

Drawn by the commotion, Ha-sang came out into the backyard and heard himself saying an astonishing thing, "Why, aren't you Suk-hyŏn? What's the matter, what happened to you?"

He ran toward the girl and shielded her from the woman's blows.

"What did this girl do to you?" he asked. "I don't know what she did, but I beg your forgiveness. She is my sister. I left the capital for business, but she must have followed me. She is so young, she doesn't know what she's doing. Since we lost our mother a year ago, she has never left my side."

"She ruined my business. She stole my food."

"Stole your food? What are you talking about?"

In talking to Ha-sang, the woman regained her composure. She even felt somewhat ashamed for having caused such an uproar over a mere tidbit, yet she managed to get the money for it from Ha-sang anyway.

The rain gave no sign of stopping. From the gutter foul-smelling rainwater, dark as soy sauce, poured down onto the dirt, making small splash-holes. In the backyard enclosed by a bush-clover fence were a kitchen storage terrace and a persimmon tree whose branches drooped with red, ripe fruits. In the gusty wind, all the leaves were blown away, scattering about on the muddy ground. The child crouched under the tree like a piece of rag in a heap of garbage. Ha-sang picked her up.

"Mercy, look at you!" he said. "Didn't I tell you to wait for me in our aunt's house? I told you I wouldn't be gone for long, you stubborn thing."

The girl remained silent, but tears ran down her cheeks.

A strange sensation of love filled his heart, as he murmured, "Poor thing, I made you suffer. But we are lucky. Imagine, if we hadn't met like this!"

At a time when not even a violent rainstorm should detain him, Ha-sang found himself unable to leave the next day. The autumn rain continued, but it was because of the girl that he was immobilized; during the night she had become very sick, burning with fever. Since he had told them that she was his sister, he had no other choice but to stay with her. Looking at the leaden sky, the endless rain, and the panting girl, he could only sigh and shake his head.

"I see you are in trouble, but don't you worry. We have a man here who is a doctor, and his medicine will help her," offered the innkeeper, for she was not without kindness. She brought some millet gruel and a change of clothing for the girl.

After bathing her and putting the clean clothes on her, Ha-sang was struck by her rare beauty, and even the woman exclaimed, "The child is so pretty; in my life I have never seen a girl as lovely. She is like a fairy of the Moon Palace, isn't she?" Although she did not say a word, the child's movement suggested a certain nobility which betrayed her upbringing. "Whose precious daughter could she be? She doesn't seem to belong to an ordinary family," Ha-sang could not help wondering as he watched her through her delirium and her fevered sleep. "Look at the clothes of this beggar girl; they are made of China silk. I know because when I was young, my husband bought me silk such as this," the innkeeper observed.

"They are made from my mother's old clothes," Ha-sang explained, smiling bitterly at the words "beggar girl."

"Maybe your family owns a silk shop," offered the woman, her eyes twinkling shrewdly, but to Ha-sang the child did not seem to belong to a merchant family. She was too graceful; she had the air of having been brought up with the discipline of etiquette. "There must have been some difficult circumstances in her life," said the woman, still curious.

But something more bothered Ha-sang. While they had bathed her dirty body, the girl had fought desperately to keep her undergarment on. He thought that perhaps she was embarrassed by its filth. Once it was off, he found that it had a small pocket on the waistband. No doubt something of great value had been hidden in it. He found out soon enough what the precious object was that she had to guard with all her strength; her left hand was closed tightly as if deformed, and even in her unconsciousness, she did not let it open.

The woman was annoyed. "What a shame! Such a face, pretty as a flower, and a cripple."

As the night deepened, Ha-sang saw under the dim lamplight the girl's hand relax. When her fevered little hand loosened, a small, oval stone of a beautiful shade of green, ornamented with a tassel, fell from her hand and dropped on the floor. Having been raised in poverty, he had never seen anything like it. He brought it closer to the light. It was a gourd-shaped jade bottle with a slender neck. He was ignorant of the fact that it was one of three such jade ornaments strung together with tasseled macramé cords that well-bred women and girls of prosperous families wore at the breasts of their jackets. He was not familiar with such luxuries, but he felt as if he had finally fathomed the source of her nobility.

Seized with the premonition that obstacles loomed in his way, Ha-sang, who could ordinarily sleep anywhere, any time, was unable to fall asleep. Time raced by before his eyes. September was almost gone. He tried to think of a way out of his predicament but could not come up with anything clever; he found himself scratching his head. Anxiously, he looked at the girl. Her left hand was now completely open. He slithered to her side, put the jade bottle in her hand, and folded each finger over it, but soon her fingers relaxed and the bottle fell again. After repeatedly trying without success to replace the bottle, he finally pulled a few stitches from the waistband of her new undergarment, put the bottle inside, and stitched it up again. Only then did he let the sleep take hold of him.

In the room, besides Ha-sang and the girl, there were three men of indistinct station, and a middle-aged man of the servant class. It was already so crowded that they were almost on top of each other; worse, they also had many belongings. Musical instruments—an hourglass-shaped drum, a smaller drum, a flute, gongs, bells—were piled up near them, some wrapped in white cloths and some without covers. There was no way of escaping from this confusion, or from the body odor and the foul breath that suffocated him in the ice-cold room. The wretched inn did not even have enough coverlets to go around.

"Chŏm-soe, where is the fire?" shouted the middle-aged servant as he opened the door noisily. From the way he called the boy by name, he seemed to be a regular customer.

"What do you want?" came Chŏm-soe's insolent voice.

"Put some more wood on the fire."

"I already did, but the mouth of the furnace is full of water; it won't catch fire." With a loud sneeze, the boy wiped his runny nose with his sleeve.

"You stupid good-for-nothing, go get some sleep," the man said, closing the door and burying his head deep into his shoulders.

"Sleep in a heatless room tonight, catch a cold tomorrow, and the day after tomorrow, perform a shaman rite with a sacred bamboo . . ."

"Can't you be quiet?" reprimanded one of the men, with an icy stare and in a low, hoarse voice charged with threat.

"But if you catch a cold, that'll ruin your flute playing."

"None of your business," he answered as he unwrapped the protective covers from the musical instruments and distributed them to his dozing companions. With the one that had been used for the hourglass-shaped drum, he covered himself and lay down. "Here, cover her with this. Doesn't look like an ordinary sickness to me," he mumbled as he handed the coverlet to Ha-sang, who was on the verge of a deep sleep. It was the only coverlet in the room. It was filled with cotton, but flattened with use, weighted heavily with moisture, and smelling as rancid as urine. But the hapless travelers, though horrified by the sight of it, had stuffed their reluctant bodies into it, avoiding contact with their faces. Ha-sang was unwilling to accept the offer; he did not want this monstrous thing to touch her. He would rather take off all his clothes, if he had to, and wrap her with them. The man gave Ha-sang a strange shiver. Ha-sang could not place his station, but he was grateful for his kindness.

"Thank you, but in this weather you need more than that piece of cloth, or you will catch cold," he said.

The man said nothing more.

"Don't you worry. The Seven Stars Spirit, the Jade Emperor Trinity, the Mountain Spirit, the Guardians of the Five Directions, all those gods protect us. We are the ones who are hot even on a sheet of ice," observed the servant with the air of a jester.

Ha-sang's eyes widened; he was unable to comprehend what the servant meant.

Emitting a sinister laugh, the servant added, "That man is a drum-man."

"A drum-man?"

"A shaman's husband, don't you know?"

"Ah yes, ah yes."

Finally understanding, a shudder passed through Ha-sang. He had never seen a shaman or watched a shaman rite. He had been told that shamans were promiscuous, weird people, sorceresses who were possessed by spirits, and who confused ignorant people. Persecuted by the government, they were driven away from the city gates as unfit to live within their borders. Catholics, too, regarded them as phantoms who lived with devils. "Have I come into a dungeon of hell?" thought Ha-sang, tense with fear. "Is it the devil's trick that this child is so ill?" The thought suddenly made him brave. Though the son of a martyr and a devout mother, he was as ignorant of Catholic tenets as he was passionate in his belief. As he had gradually been drawn into the group who worked for the rebirth of the church in the capital, he had grown more impatient with his ignorance, and his longing for learning had increased. Now, his mind in trepidation, he remembered the prayers his mother had taught him.

"In time of distress, recite these prayers. Engrave them on your heart and ask for the Lord's grace," she had said as they parted on the day he left the capital. As always, a warm feeling spread in him whenever he thought of her. He began his prayer, "Hail Mary, full of grace! . . ."

The man again spoke to Ha-sang, "From your speech, I figure you are from the capital. Since you are here in Chŏlla Province, why don't you stay and watch a shaman rite? I tell you, they are the best; and tomorrow's is the biggest one of them all, something you don't want to miss. The shaman staying in the inner room with the proprietress is the most famous in the province. But how is the child? Why don't you pray to the Great Spirit Grandmother to exorcise her sickness tomorrow?"

As the man's voice grew louder, Ha-sang made the sign of the cross in his heart. His eyes tightly closed, he prayed even more ardently, trying to shut off the persistent voice. "Lord, have mercy on us. Christ, have mercy on us. Jesus, graciously hear us." In his prayer, he became calm once again.

"I can't sleep in a place I'm not used to," mumbled the man and lay down with his arm for a pillow, curling his body like a shrimp. "Too cold to sleep." However, soon he dropped off, grinding his teeth.

Even after the man fell asleep, Ha-sang could not lie down. The room was too small for him to stretch, and the horrid sound of his teeth grinding, his snore, and the smacking of his lips kept Ha-sang awake. Above all, this unexpected turn of events made him sleepless with anxiety. Nevertheless, he was no longer tormented by the presence of his strange bedfellows, for he believed without a shadow of doubt that his prayers had been heard. His mind thus comforted, he finally went to sleep sitting up.

In the meantime, the light from the inner room did not go out. The room was connected to the tavern-room across the hall so that not an inch of space was wasted. Every corner of the inn could accommodate people: the inner room, the room next to it, and the hall. In the hall in front of the inner room, the proprietress served the customers, spreading out jugs and bottles of wine, dishes and bowls, and tidbits to accompany the wine. Near the hall, wooden cots were set up for travelers in a hurry or for those who came in to

banter with the woman. There they drank wine or ate a simple meal
of rice and soup.

In the middle of the night, the proprietress went into the kitchen.
There came the splashing sound of water being scooped up from
the water crock, and she emerged with a bowl of water. In the room
were two women, one not in her prime but still retaining a volup-
tuous beauty and the other, her kitchen-maid, aged about thirty.
Between them a girl-child lay asleep.

The proprietress handed the bowl to the woman, saying, "Here,
make her drink this water, or she'll die, lying all day long like this.
It's been four days, did you say?"

"The one in a possession-sickness does not eat or drink," the
woman answered calmly.

"You are not the one who is possessed by the spirit; it's this
girl." Shaking her head disapprovingly, the proprietress went on,
"Tomorrow you are to perform a big rite. You'd better come to your
senses."

"What did I do wrong? I did not get this spirit-daughter for nothing. I intend to raise her to be a real shaman, the best there is."

"Aren't you a real shaman yourself then? You have never been
someone's spirit-daughter. Why all of a sudden this talk about a
spirit-daughter? Such a pity, such a pity!" the proprietress clucked
in despair.

"That's why I'm telling you. I learned the incantations from my
shaman mother, I married into a shaman household, I apprenticed
under my mother-in-law, and I learned to perform the rite with her,
yet in all that time I have never experienced divine inspiration. The
rite performed by such a shaman is no rite at all; it's only games,
mere tricks."

"This woman—something has gone wrong with her today. At
any rate, it's none of my business," muttered the proprietress. "I'm
going to get some sleep now. Tomorrow is a busy day from breakfast
time." Taking a folded quilt from the top of the iron-bound blanket
chest, she spread it on the floor and threw herself on it and went on.
"You and this bitch, both of us are cursed with our sins. They say
when you reach forty, it's time to cool off. Let a daughter-in-law
take over the burden of household chores and you enjoy the easy
life. But look at us; your voice is hoarse from shouting incantations
and your joints ache from dancing, jumping, flying, and all that, and

I am growing old in the service of others, from early morning on serving those who are not even my own husband or children. I must adopt a daughter or I'll be dead soon, someone to help me and support me in my old age. I can't go on like this . . ." She fell asleep even before her rambling came to an end. The kitchen-maid, too, dozed off, and the two did not wake until dawn.

Gazing into the face of the little girl who lay wasted, with her eyes tightly closed, the shaman, Man-nyŏn, was deep in thought. Man-nyŏn came from a hereditary shaman household where she was taught shaman chants from early childhood. By custom, hereditary shamans begin teaching their daughters the chants at the age of nine; Man-nyŏn began her lessons three years earlier. The mother, a celebrated shaman, had a large repertoire of shaman songs, which she wanted to transmit to her daughter, so when she was six, she began to teach them to her. Unusually bright, the girl learned her lessons well, though she did not understand their meaning. The process of apprenticeship was a rigorous one. Since both mother and daughter were illiterate, they had to depend on their memory, and the lessons were taught orally. The parents, who presided over a large territory, performed the rites daily, but they never took their daughter with them. Instead, before leaving for the day's work, the mother would give Man-nyŏn a few tunes to memorize, and when she returned she would test the child's recitation. When she failed, she was beaten. For a child, it was an arduous task, for she sometimes misunderstood what her mother had recited to her, or even repeated her mother's own errors, thus further distorting the original. However, when she recited in her still innocent, childish voice, her narration so touched her listeners with sadness and wonderment that even before she reached the age of ten, her reputation had spread in the shaman domain. She had become so well-versed in ritual procedure that it was within her capability to perform the first step of a family rite.

This ritual was usually held in the inner room where the woman of the house resided, or in a main hall, to invoke the spirits of the supreme household gods—ancestral gods and trinitarian gods, who consisted of the ground spirit of the house, the god of children, and the god of health and peace. The chants might sound simple enough, but the sophisticated ritual had to be followed with humility and the reason for the rite clearly stated in the incantation:

O, our heavenly king,
We offer this prayer in a temple
Whose native soil is in Namsan.
The spirit, Se-gyŏng, is from Seoul
Of a nation called Korea.
We offer this rite in Chŏlla Province
On behalf of Tae-mok
In the year 1785.
The month is July
The day is the ninth of the month.
This is no ancestor rite
Nor an ordinary supplication,
But for the offspring of this household
Who has taken ill.
Hear our prayer . . .

As though possessed by the spirit, Man-nyŏn's recitation was flawless.

"No doubt, she will be a great shaman."

"Indeed, her rites are divinely inspired," the spectators exclaimed as they watched her.

The shamans of the south differed from those of the north-central region in the way they became shamans, as well as in the structure and nature of their trade. Southern shamans were hereditary practitioners, while north-central shamans were charismatic. Charismatic shamans first experienced possession-sickness. When such sickness occurred, a rite was performed by an established shaman to officially invite the spirit to descend and enter the possessed. The spirit who possessed her then became her guardian god and the source of divine inspiration in the performance of her rites. An altar for the spirit was placed in her room. The shaman who performed the initiation rite became her spirit-mother and guided her as she gained experience. Once the novice became familiar with the ritual procedure, she would establish herself as a full-fledged shaman and go her way independently. Possession-sickness could strike anyone in society, regardless of station. Since charismatic shamans were not bound by professional rules, the competition among them depended upon individual skill in performing the rituals, and the ability to communicate with the spirits.

Hereditary shamans, on the other hand, did not experience the painful possession-sickness or the ecstasies or trances that accompa-

nied the rites of divinely inspired shamans. Therefore, such a shaman had no definite view on the gods she served. She had neither
a spirit-mother to guide her, nor a shrine for her guardian spirit.
However, each shaman had authority over the territory where she
resided, and within it she enjoyed an intimate relationship with the
people, serving them as family shaman. The succession of the trade
was bilateral; the territorial right was hereditary through the male
line, and the necessary technique through the female line, from
mother-in-law to daughter-in-law. Not endowed with the charismatic power to communicate directly with the gods, these shamans
had a different function: to officiate at rituals offered to various gods.
Lacking divine inspiration, the southern shamans had to cultivate
technique to perfection, and the emphasis was on rigid formality
and artistic expression.

Although the people regarded shamans with contempt, they depended on them for emotional well-being and personal enrichment.
Thus, no one grudged the crops offered in spring and autumn to the
shaman of the district. The shaman offered rites to various gods to
pray for her clients' welfare and to dispel myriad demons from their
homes. The people sought shamans for all the misfortunes they
endured in their lives, such as illness in the family, wayward husbands, or childlessness. Shamans were also invited to pray when
people built a new house or moved to another residence. In the
spring and fall, the Village God, the Mountain God, and the Dragon
God were worshipped in community festivities. Everyone in the
village gathered together, and in the communal dancing and singing
they resolved the worry and suffering of their lives. The clamor of
the instruments—drums, flutes, gongs, and cymbals—intoxicated
them, and after the frantic dancing they felt their hearts' burden
lightened. The feeling of benevolence extended to their neighbors,
and relationships among them improved. Nevertheless, although
shamans had the power to bring the villagers together, no one
wanted to give his daughter to a shaman household, nor was anyone
willing to receive a shaman's daughter as his daughter-in-law. Thus,
they had to intermarry among themselves.

When Man-nyŏn, the daughter of a hereditary shaman, reached
thirteen, a husband was found for her in a shaman family named
Myŏng, whose members presided over the Imsil territory. Male
shamans played musical instruments, accompanying the rites per-

formed by female shamans. Man-nyŏn's husband excelled in flute playing. The skill with which Man-nyŏn performed the rites, together with her good looks, made her famous even before the age of twenty. Because she was regarded as exceptional, she performed both inside and outside her own territory, even though the territorial right was usually inviolable and, if transgressed, could bring severe sanctions against the violator. Busy and absorbed in her work, she never once regretted the fate that had consigned her to the life of a shaman. For her, time passed by like a dream.

One day, when Man-nyŏn returned home from her work, there was a boy of about five eating a rice cake in the hall. In shaman households, fresh rice cakes were made daily to distribute to the spectators of the rite, and afterward there were always some left over for the neighborhood children; therefore, she paid no attention to the visitor. However, he was there even after nightfall. On the next morning, he appeared at the breakfast table. "Whose young master is he?" she asked her mother-in-law.

But instead of answering, the mother-in-law remarked, "Isn't your husband over thirty now?"

Man-nyŏn did not speak again. As she was about to dress for the daily rite, her gaze fell upon her breasts. They were not those of a woman who had nursed a child; the dazzling expanse of the translucent mounds was without blemish. A faint dizziness swept over her. "I am a barren woman," she muttered to herself.

That day a cleansing rite was being performed, an important ritual to cleanse the souls of the dead, to pray for their safe passage to the other world, and to relieve them of the grievances of this world. It was also performed in the case of grave illness, when the illness was attributed to the spirit of an ancestor who had not been ritually prepared for death. The rite was then offered to appease such a spirit.

The wealthy owner of an inn had hired Man-nyŏn to perform the rite, with no expense spared, for his only son, who was dying of kidney disease. This rite, which was conducted in the kitchen and consisted of a series of twelve steps, began with an offering to the family gods. The rice was cooked in an iron kettle; the lid was removed, and a ladle was stuck into it. Vegetables, fruits of three colors, broth, slices of seasoned dried meat, and wine were displayed on top of the cooking-fireplace. Sitting gracefully on a straw mat in front of the mouth of the fireplace, Man-nyŏn, clad in a white costume, recited a narrative chant. Her recitation was serious, ardent, and solicitous all at once. Some wept, though there were no sad passages in it. After the recitation, she burned the sacrificial paper for the dead, offered prayers, and began the rite of the Seven Stars Spirit. Her rite reached the state of the divine that day; there was not a dry eye in the audience.

However, unknown to the spectators, she had become aware that some change was taking place within her. The table for the dead was moved from the room to the middle of the courtyard. Man-nyŏn placed a straw effigy of the dead at the edge of the hall and spread two lengths of cotton cloth on the floor, tying seven knots in each. She then draped them on a fresh bamboo stick about three meters tall, with leaves still on it, which had been stuck into a straw-sack filled with rice. Dancing and leaping, she proceeded to untie each knot. In the courtyard stood another bamboo pole, called the Divine Pole, much taller than the one draped with the knotted cloth, through which the spirit would descend. Lack of concentration must not mar the rite, but as Man-nyŏn untied the knots her eyes wandered toward the Divine Bamboo Pole and noted that the leaves on the freshly hewn plant were already withered. It was only a split second, and no one noticed. But in that instant, suddenly everything became starkly clear to her. The bamboo pole, the medium of the spirit's descent, was nothing but a shabby stick. She realized that she had been misled for a long time. However, without betraying her inner turmoil, she went on with consummate skill and grace. Dancing and leaping as before, she continued to untie each of the fourteen knots. She washed the lid of the kettle containing the spirit of the deceased first with clear water, then with wormwood-water, and finally with incense-water, bringing the ritual to an end.

It had been an elaborate rite; the noisy entourage consisted of four male shamans, two assistants, and the laborers to carry their equipment. Afterward, some of them got drunk as usual, but that day, for some unknown reason, Man-nyŏn was repelled by them. She was in need of a deeper inspiration; her soul was in search of an answer.

In addition to the emptiness she already felt after the rigors of performance, she was burdened with disquiet. "For a woman who serves the gods, I haven't even been possessed by the spirits. I

am no different from a song-and-dance girl," she mused, feeling
nauseated. "A shaman dance must be different from those of dancing girls. Of course it must. How can I ever hope to be a real shaman
when I have never had a divine encounter?" The process of becoming a shaman had been extremely difficult, and the songs and incantations she had learned as a child were flawless, but she felt something was lacking because they were not of divine inspiration.
Depending on the nature of the rite and the messages carried in the
incantations, her recitation was pious and humble, piteous and sad,
fast and slow, delivered in an angry or a dignified voice. During the
rites, impersonating the deceased, she would ramble on about his
unfulfilled wishes in life or his words of instruction from the other
world to the living. At such a time, her face would be streaked with
tears, and her monologue would tear the hearts of the spectators,
not to mention those of the family members, causing them to weep
loudly. Then the people, moved to tears by her performance, would
utter words of admiration, saying, "Astounding. It moves my heart
in a strange way." But, even though she could move others, she
herself had never been inspired by her own performance.

Now Man-nyŏn was gripped in the turmoil of a new insight. She
had come to realize that her performances were nothing but crafty
theatrics, that she had lost in herself the sanctification of the gods
because she had been contaminated by the adoration of her acts. She
began to question whether the rites performed by secular shamans
merely to earn their livelihood might not be a blasphemy to a Supreme God in whose existence she had come to believe. For herself,
born into a shaman household and knowing no other life, she had
never doubted the presence of all the gods. Now, for the first time,
she was beginning to look into herself. She wanted to become a
truly great shaman of whom all the gods would approve.

Man-nyŏn had visited the capital only once, thanks to the invitation of the wife of the former governor. In March and October each
year, Man-nyŏn had regularly gone to the governor's official residence to pray to the tutelary spirit of the building. After two years,
the governor was promoted and sent back to the capital. The grateful
wife, sure that the happy event was all due to Man-nyŏn's blessing,
invited her to come to the capital for a visit. Once there, Man-nyŏn
had no other thought but of her calling. She wanted to observe the
charismatic shamans and the initiation rites which were absent in

her region. Such a rite happened to be taking place in a shaman village outside the city gate, and Man-nyŏn, accompanied by the wife's personal maid, went to see the famous practitioner who was officiating. Her dance and song did not much impress Man-nyŏn, but the initiation rite greatly moved her. She was seized with a strange sensation when the initiate, dumb until she received her spirit, opened her mouth and delivered its message with a loud wail.

"It was a very difficult sickness," confided the maid, her face flushed with excitement. The initiate was her distant cousin.

"Is possession-sickness such a painful thing?" Man-nyŏn asked her.

"Yes, indeed. They say it is as bad as death itself. No one knew she was suffering from it. She was given all the medicine in the world in vain, and her family did not know what to do about the damned ...''; here, remembering whom she was talking to, she corrected her speech and continued, "Well, she now has no other choice but to become a shaman. After such a rite, if she did not go into the shaman business, the sickness would again possess her."

"Where I come from there is nothing like this. It is strange indeed."

"But I heard from a peddler who went to Peking with the annual mission that there are shamans in the countries beyond China. He told me that their sickness is far worse than ours. It is said that they open up a living human body, cut up the flesh, break the bones inside, and later put them back together again—it might be only the images they see in their trance." After a pause, she continued, "It must be so difficult to be a shaman. How could it be otherwise, being possessed by spirits?"

The woman's words left an indelible impression in Man-nyŏn's mind; she recalled them often in the years to come. After the arrival of her husband's concubine, her skill mellowed into perfection. However, she was not freed from a sense of remorse; her mind was in a misty confusion. "I have become a shaman too easily, while others become one only after a painful process." She recalled once again the face of that capital shaman who, as she had received her god with loud weeping, was overwhelmed by the intensity of the experience.

Now, her eyes fixed upon the face of the girl in delirium, her meditation coming to an end, Man-nyŏn recalled the events of the past few days. It was four days ago when the kitchen-maid ran into the room in perturbation.

"Ma'am, a strange thing is lying near the kitchen terrace," she cried.

"A strange thing?"

"Yes. A little girl. She is dead."

"Are you sure she is dead?"

"Yes. She is surely dead."

However, the girl, about six years old, was still alive, but in such disarray that they wondered where she had been. Man-nyŏn carried the freezing girl into the room. Her dirty face and her eyes captured Man-nyŏn's heart. Her crystalline eyes glistened and, fixing them upon Man-nyŏn's face, for no reason she smiled faintly. "Butterfly," Man-nyŏn heard her say distinctly. Instantly, a shiver passed through Man-nyŏn. The girl closed her eyes and did not utter another word. Seized with a strange love for the creature, Man-nyŏn could not leave her side. After being bathed, the girl proved to be uncommonly beautiful.

"She is too beautiful for a human child. I have never seen a child so noble and lovely," the kitchen-maid said, running in and out of the room to look at her.

Man-nyŏn began to believe that the girl was suffering from possession-sickness. The sudden, mysterious appearance, the incredible beauty, that imperceptible smile around her lips, and above all the word "butterfly," all caused Man-nyŏn to indulge in this fantasy. From that day, she could not free herself from a constant state of excitement. Her preoccupation with the girl embarrassed everyone around her. She carried the child, not yet recovered, in her bosom, and took her to work. Thus, on this day, they had been caught in the downpour, and sought shelter in the inn.

"Come to your senses, or you might lose the girl. But I can understand how you feel," said the proprietress, shaking her head and sighing.

◆   ◆   ◆

A narrow street meandered through the Changt'ongbang district in the capital. Imposing tile-roofed houses lined the canal, but this was not an aristocratic neighborhood. The burgeoning *chungin* people, mostly money-lenders, lived in the large, handsome houses. Although they did not wear the nobleman's horsehair hat, they nonetheless enjoyed a life of abundance, unlike some of the genteel, poverty-stricken aristocrats who lived in the southern section of the capital. Their opulent lifestyle exuded wealth. Their knowledge of etiquette, too, exceeded that of some of the nobles; as the saying goes, "one must be well-clothed and well-fed before one can be well-bred." A few among them even had access to the royal chambers, because the palace ladies were recruited from *chungin* households. They cultivated extravagant tastes for fine clothing and cuisine, and indulged in elegant pastimes. Recently, many among them had begun to acquire learning as well, for thanks to their commercial dealings with China, they could obtain many Western books. They lived in the middle of the capital, in a neighborhood commanding a view of the canal, albeit a turbid section of it, where they could afford to take time to appreciate the changing seasons, and to enjoy the best view of the festival of Trotting on the Bridge.[1]

However, these houses were not numerous. The narrow street soon found its way into a dingy enclave of grass-roofed houses, where it was necessary to tread carefully in order to avoid stepping into the feces scattered about. On the roofs, left unrepaired for many years, hovered stinking centipedes which from time to time would drop on the heads of passersby. At the end of this mazelike alley, a shabby house stood half hidden, pushed back from the street. This oddly built house had no discernible front gate. Directly through the door was a front room adjacent to the hall, and a kitchen with an uneven dirt floor which emitted the stench of poverty. Behind the kitchen were two more rooms and a door to the back street. In a long, narrow, back room, various pouches containing medicinal ingredients hung from the ceiling; against the wall stood a medicine chest with many drawers.

The wretchedness of the apothecary shop suited the neighborhood. The customers came through the back door, inquiring, "Is anyone home?" When such a call came, a single sliding door would

---

1. On January 14, the citizenry congregated around Bell Pavilion to listen to the ringing of the bell, then milled toward the bridge. In this annual folk ritual, the people walked back and forth over the bridge all night long to the accompaniment of drums and flutes. This, they believed, would strengthen their legs for the rest of the year (the word for "bridge" is a pun on the one for "leg").

open and the patient would enter through it. The windowless room next to the kitchen was divided from the shop by a low, sliding paper door, which one could enter only by bending halfway to the ground. Several men were gathered in this room. They had closed the sliding door and lit the lamp. From outside, no light could be seen.

Since the Persecution of 1801, Christians had met in constant fear, and had contrived various ways to evade police surveillance. Many had abandoned their homes and belongings and fled into the mountains, working slash-and-burn farms; some formed Christian villages, eking out a living by making and selling pottery.

After the death of the Queen Dowager, persecution gradually died out, and some measure of peace returned. There was still sporadic persecution by local governments, but a few brave souls came forward to work for the church's new beginning, including those who had gathered in the back room of the shabby apothecary: Yi Yŏ-jin; Francesco Kim; Hong Wu-song, the son of the martyr, Hong Nang-min; Kwŏn Ki-in, the nephew of the martyr Kwŏn Ch'ŏl-sin; and Chang Su-hyŏn, the owner of the shop. They huddled together over two letters in the small, suffocating room.

"After all, he hasn't given up his faith," said one of them.

"What sort of a man do you think he is? Certainly he is incapable of committing such a shameful sin," Kwŏn Ki-in whispered, since only a thin wall separated the room from the outside.

"At any rate, it would have been a disaster if we had sent them as we wrote them. We have much to learn," said Yi Yŏ-jin in a barely audible voice.

They were talking about the two epistles that had been sewn into Ha-sang's jacket, one to the bishop of the Peking diocese, and the other to the pope.

Tasan had not made any changes in the contents of the letters. Out of mere curiosity he had begun reading them, the hideous reminders of his predicament that Ha-sang had left at his bedside. The agitation caused by Ha-sang's visit and the memory of his brother, which once again aroused in him a sense of guilt and remorse, had made him pick up the letters. They were written in small characters on the paper used for making sliding doors. The style and writing were crude, there were many misspellings, and some ideograms were incorrectly used. As he read them, he could not keep himself from being deeply captivated just the same. These new church leaders' lack of learning no longer mattered to him. What they had tried to say in the letters was clearly conveyed with passionate simplicity. Each word contained a sincere longing that filled the reader with overwhelming sympathy. As he read on, Tasan found himself correcting the misspelled words and misused ideograms. Although much needed to be done to improve them, in the end he left the sentences untouched—not out of unwillingness, but because he believed the letters had the strength and sincerity of their simplicity. With a bit of malice, one might, on the other hand, have assumed that by not touching the contents he had given himself the comfort of not having had any part in such an awesome undertaking. His attitude harked back to the time when, under one of his literary names, Chahansanin ("man of the violet mist mountain") he had—with several eminent monks of the Taedunsa Temple—helped compile *On Korean Sŏn Buddhism*. At that time, he had requested that his name be removed from the list of six virtuous monks, Hyejang among them, who jointly compiled the book. The consequence of his having become interested in Western books had been his downfall. Once again, in a time of Buddhist suppression, he feared that his part in the compilation of the Buddhist text might bring yet another calamity upon him.

Not much had changed since then. He no longer desired involvement with anything other than Chinese studies and research into the administration of government and the wise governing of the people. He now wished only to devote himself to the perfection of his ideal: "Cultivate the self and govern the people." Even after more than ten years in exile, he had yet to free himself from worldly affairs.

Now, those who gathered were greatly encouraged by Tasan's edition of the letters. Having confirmed once again that he had not forsaken his faith, they felt as if a powerful ally had come to their aid.

After purifying himself in the bath, Kwŏn Ki-in, the best calligrapher among them, copied the letters on silk in minute characters so that they could be easily hidden on the person of Yi Yŏ-jin, who, disguised as a groom, secretly joined the emissary to the Peking court. The letters finally reached their destination.

The situation in Peking had changed greatly. In 1805, a French priest carrying a map of Shantung province intended for Rome had been captured by the Chinese authorities; he was subsequently sent into banishment along with thirteen Chinese converts. This incident marked the beginning of Catholic persecution in China. The persecution continued throughout the reign of Emperor Chia-ch'ing (1796–1820), who had proscribed Christianity as heterodoxy, until his death. The missionaries had gone into hiding and had been forbidden any contact with the people except for the rendering of academic services.

Bishop de Gouvéa, with whom the Korean Catholics had been in close contact, had died in 1808. Bishop Joachim de Souza Saraiva had been appointed by the pope to succeed Gouvéa as the titular bishop of the Peking diocese, but he had been unable to obtain permission to enter Peking, and eventually died in Macao in 1818. In the meantime, before his death Bishop de Gouvéa had designated a Portuguese Lazarist missionary named Pirés to be the bishop of Nanking, but Pirés was forbidden to leave Peking. After Gouvéa's death, the Peking diocese had fallen under the leadership of a Lazarist Father named José Nunes Ribeiro, who held the post until his death in 1826. A year after Father Ribeiro's death, Father Pirés had been appointed by the pope to succeed Ribeiro as the bishop of Peking diocese.

The letters were received first by Father Ribeiro, and forwarded in turn by the Peking mission to Bishop Souza Saraiva, who remained in Macao. After translating them into Portuguese with the help of two Chinese interpreters, Bishop Souza Saraiva sent the letters to the pope. The letters arrived in Lisbon in August 1814, and eventually reached the Office of Propaganda. In its rare book archive, one of them, the one addressed to the Bishop of Peking, remains to this day, although the original is missing. It was later translated into Italian and French.

The letter's impact on the papacy was great, since it made real the existence of a remote, small nation, whose name was yet unknown, where countless converts had died defending the sacred teaching they had acquired without the leadership of a single missionary. Beyond any doubt, the pope believed that the courage with which the Korean Christians had directed their petition to him, the living representative of Jesus Christ on earth, could only be attributed to the very miracle of the Cross of Jesus Christ. Even today, the letter, written in the blood of suffering imposed by constant persecution, conveyed the converts' pure and unwavering faith so sincerely as to cause readers' eyes to fill with tears, and to make them sit up and take notice of the message.

This astounding document of faith had finally reached Pope Pius VII just before the Catholic revival that followed the Napoleonic War, at a time when he and the French were engaged in a bitter dispute. Napoleon had annexed the papal state, and the pope, unyielding, had been taken prisoner and sent to Fontainebleau. The church survived in spite of guillotines, imprisonments, and banishments, but almost everywhere in the world religious orders were on the brink of destruction. Moreover, Christendom was still feeling the shattering impact of the French Revolution, which threatened its very existence. Confronting the reality of the sufferings expressed in the letter, the captive pope suffered agonies of helplessness. He could only pray, invoking the miracle of the Cross of Jesus Christ for these scorned, persecuted, and oppressed.

The pope was struck by the fact that the Korean converts, without the guidance of missionaries, had acquired a considerable grasp of Catholicism even though its tenets were incompatible with the traditional belief system of their society. The letter detailed the brief history of the Korean church, the religious persecution, and the bloody, painful path to their faith. Devoid of superfluous display, the simplicity of the petition was even more persuasive. He began to read:

Francesco, with other Korean Christians, beating our breasts, humbly prostrating ourselves, hereby send this petition to the one on the supreme heights and possessing supreme greatness. Your Holiness, have mercy upon your wretched flock. Appealing to your boundless compassion, we beseech you to grace us at once with your blessing, which could lead us to the path of redemption.

In the beginning, we of this small nation learned the teachings from the books, and ten years later we had the happiness of participating in the Seven Sacraments and thereby learning the Holy Tenets. The persecution ensued seven years later, and our only leader, Father Chou Wen-mu, together with many of our faithful, was martyred. Those who survived the persecution are now scattered, living in fear and pain. We are unable to gather together, or to perform religious exercises. Now we have no other means than to appeal to the infinite mercy of our Lord and to Your Holiness, whose benevolence and compassion have no bounds.

We pray for your swift hand to save us without delay; only this we ask of you in the outcry of our faith. For ten years, we have been oppressed by adversities of all kinds, and as the result of such hardships, we cannot count the number of the sick and dying. Those of us left alive do not know when we will again be enlightened by the holy teachings. We await the time when we may have the happiness of receiving a leader, as desperately as those who thirst for water, as those who pray for rain in drought.

However, Heaven is too high, the ocean without a bridge. We read in the holy book that the Christian faith has now spread to every corner of the world; however, our country, a small nation in a corner of the East, is without a missionary and has had to learn the faith from books. In spite of this, many hundreds among us have sacrificed their lives for the glory of God, and the number of the faithful exceeds tens of thousands . . .

Therefore, now, beating our breasts in deepest fear and sincerity, we humbly beseech you in the name of Jesus Christ, who came to the world and died on the Cross for our sins, for he loves the sinners even more than he does the righteous, and we appeal to you, Your Holiness, a minister of God, who on his behalf looks after us and saves us from sin. We have come out of darkness and are thus redeemed. However, worldly pains still torment our flesh, and sin and evil still oppress our soul . . . Soul rules the flesh, and flesh gives assistance to the soul in a most natural relationship.

As he finished reading, the pope found himself truly moved by the correct understanding of these simple people, and the purity of their faith.

Chapter Five

◆ ◆ ◆

True Principles
of Catholicism

As Ha-sang sat apart in a corner of the room and watched the elders respectfully hovering over the epistles, reading them with the deepest emotion, he found himself feeling ashamed and forsaken. Even while he was carrying the letters, he was unable to comprehend a single word of them; then as now, his ignorance pained him. Remembering that his cousin's husband, Hwang Sa-yŏng, had passed the Lower Level Examination with first place honors at the age of fifteen, he felt unworthy of membership in a clan celebrated for its learning. He resolved that the first thing he must do now was to acquire learning at any cost. Above all, as befitting the son of his eminent father, he wished to study Catholicism. He bit his lip in determination, his youthful eyes glistening in the lamplight. Thus began Ha-sang's lifelong mission dedicated to the rebuilding of the church and the fulfillment of the Korean faithful's longing to bring a Catholic priest to lead it.

However, another problem required Ha-sang's immediate attention: the beggar girl with whom he had inadvertently become involved in the inn near Muhyŏn. She had recovered from her high fever of that night, and the next day she had even been able to take some rice and soup. Since he had told them she was his sister, Ha-sang had left the inn carrying the girl on his back. As weightless as a sheet of paper, she stuck like a cicada on the back of his tall frame. Carrying her presented no difficulty; however, at the first sight of a village, he put her down. "I'm in a hurry," he told her, "I can't take you with me. Here is some money. Buy some rice cakes and candies on your way back to your home, eh?"

Fixing her eyes upon Ha-sang, the girl neither spoke a word nor cried. Something in that gaze stung his heart, but he began to walk away from her. After a while—he did not remember for how long—he turned around on an impulse. He paused, transfixed. The road stretched straight in a wide-open plain, nothing obstructing his view. On that road he saw a speck of a figure rolling toward him. He closed his eyes tightly as if he had seen a forbidden object. "Francesco is waiting for me!" Like a thunderbolt, his mission flashed in his consciousness; he must be firm in his decision. But as he started to move again, he saw the girl collapse. She did not get up again. There was nothing else for him to do but to rush back to where she lay, her breathing barely audible, but her chest heaving. He feared she was dying. Almost in tears, he carried her toward the village. Before he reached it, she became conscious again. As she became aware that she was being carried on his back, she began to cry so pitifully that he could no longer think of abandoning her.

The girl was not a mute as he had believed. Soon after they passed the town of Chŏnju, she began to talk to him. He paused for a rest on the mountain path.

"Where do you live?" he asked, letting her down.

"We live in Ongjin."

"Ongjin? This is Chŏlla Province. How did you manage to come this far all by yourself?"

"Chŏlla Province? I am heading toward Hongju."

"Hongju?"

"Yes."

"You are going the wrong way. Hongju is in Ch'ungch'ŏng Province. You are now heading toward the south. Ch'ungch'ŏng Province is toward the north."

Her gaze dropped. Ha-sang had never seen a face so full of despair.

"But why do you have to go such a long way all by yourself?" he asked.

She did not answer, but large tears skimmed her cheeks.

"There must be some reason. Whose daughter are you? What is your father's name?"

"I am a daughter of the Kwŏn household. My father's honorable name is written in the ideograms of Ho and Sin," she answered after a long silence, as if she had made up her mind.

Wide-eyed with amazement, Ha-sang was speechless. In his ignorance, he had used the speech pattern of the uneducated, and the little one had answered his questions in flawless honorific style, referring to her father and his name with the reverence required by the protocol of the upper class. But it was more than embarrassment at his crass speech in contrast to her decorous manner that struck him.

"Then, you are the daughter of Mr. Kwŏn Ho-sin?" he repeated the question in a rising voice.

"Yes. My elder brother, do you know my father?" She did not hesitate to address him, a young man in the guise of a commoner, with the appellation "elder brother."

"I was in Ongjin to see your father."

"To see my father?"

"How long do you think I waited in the inn there? But no one came from your father with instructions. From your appearance, I see something grave must have happened. What was it?"

Mae-a could not answer him. She had matured in the short span of a few days and was aware of what had happened to her family, as well as the reason for the calamity, but she also knew that she must not relate them casually. She began sobbing, throwing herself on the withering mountain grass. For the time being, Ha-sang forgot his own anxiety and confusion at being detained on the road. Looking at the weeping girl, her body trembling, grasping a fistful of grass with her thin fingers, his eyes became hot with tears. She did not stop crying for a long time. Suddenly he thought of something.

"Child, I am a Christian too. My name is Paul. Do speak to me," he pleaded.

Mae-a lifted her head. Eyes brimming with tears, she looked at him intensely, then began weeping again. As Ha-sang held her, she went on sobbing in his bosom.

"Why? Did the soldiers raid your house? Your parents have been captured?"

She shook her head sideways.

"Then, are you the only one in your family lost like this?"

Again, she shook her head.

"Now, take time and try to tell me. I must know the truth."

After a pause, she said between sobs, "My father was taken and my mother . . ." but she could not finish.

"Didn't I tell you I am in a terrible hurry? If you keep on crying, I'll leave you here by yourself," said Ha-sang, clucking his tongue impatiently.

Mae-a buried herself deeper in his chest and went on incoherently.

"My mother fell from the cliff and I could not find her anywhere, and I could not find my sisters, either."

"Let's talk while we walk. Here, hop on my back."

Ha-sang could not linger any longer. They were again on their way. Mae-a, fearful of being abandoned, stopped crying and began answering his questions. She told him everything she had witnessed with her young eyes.

"I must look for my sisters," she insisted. "First I must go to my uncle's place. Please, I beg you, do you mind taking me as far as Hongju?"

"I can't do that. I am in a great rush." He was flabbergasted.

"Then please let me down; I must go there without you."

"You are driving me crazy. Where in Hongju?"

"Just Hongju."

"Hongju is a big place. Is it in the town or on the outskirts?"

"I don't know. They are the Kims of Hongju . . ."

"What is your uncle's name?"

"I don't know. An uncle in Hongju . . ."

"Hopeless! Not knowing the names or the place, how can we find them?"

"And my sisters . . ."

"It's a wild goose chase. How can we find them without knowing where they are?"

"But we each have a token. When we escaped from our home, Mother put an identical gourd-shaped jade bottle into each of our undergarments, telling us that in case we were separated, we were to keep them to identify ourselves to each other."

"How old are your sisters?"

"I am the eldest, eight; the next is six, and the youngest is four. We were named after the Four Gracious Plants. I am Mae-a (plum);

the next is Nan-a (orchid); and the last one Kug-a (chrysanthemum). Oh, Nan-a, Kug-a . . ." She wept noiselessly on Ha-sang's shoulders.

His perturbation grew as he became more and more involved with the girl, and he himself wanted to cry. Now that he knew she was a daughter of Kwŏn Ho-sin and, moreover, that she had been orphaned, he could not abandon her. What would Francesco say? In tears, he decided to take her as far as the capital and ask the advice of the elders. Sulking, Ha-sang ran so fast that the girl on his back became dizzy. Dejected, she fell into silence, but in time she disclosed that their Christian names were Maria, Cecilia, and Ju-liette. As they neared the inn where Francesco was waiting, he told her, "Maria. Pray to the Holy Mother, your patron saint."

Francesco and Ha-sang decided to bring Mae-a to the capital with them, for leaving her in an inn of such dubious repute was unthinkable. Upon their arrival, Ha-sang left the girl with Magda-lene, a maid to the wife of a high-ranking government official, be-cause Francesco, a recent widower, could not keep Maria. In the capital the Persecution had left the faithful wretchedly poor, and everyone was hungry. Fortunately, Magdalene, though a lowly maid, was able to keep Maria in the servants' quarters, thanks to her mistress's trust in her. Magdalene, moreover, frequented the house where the Christian widows and unmarried women lived, and she suggested that Ha-sang and Francesco entrust Maria to them.

Ha-sang had heard about these women and wondered if they would agree to accept Maria, for there must be many children or-phaned as the result of persecution. What if they should refuse? However, he was firm in his determination to convince them to take Maria, who had become as close to him as if she were his own sister, so that he would be free to begin his studies. If he could only find a scholar willing to teach him, he would gladly become his servant and sleep in a storage-shed. Ha-sang's fists, clenched on his knees, shook with resolution.

Two days later, Ha-sang and Maria followed Magdalene to the Christian women's house. Maria was uncommonly beautiful that day. Her side locks were braided and pulled behind her ears to join at the nape; the rest of her hair formed a long thick braid that reached below her waist. Magdalene had adorned its end with a swallow-shaped crimson ribbon. "Nowhere have I seen such beau-tiful hair," she marvelled.

While she stayed for two nights in the servants' quarters of the official's household, everyone treated Maria with unexpected affection. She was introduced to them as Magdalene's distant relative, who was left orphaned after her widower father, a commoner but not a slave, died suddenly of food poisoning on the Harvest Moon Festival. These servants of a powerful household were as gallant as they were audacious, reckless, and cunning. They had been told that Maria was to be adopted into the household of a childless couple. Garrulous but warm-hearted, they treated her well, doing their best to comfort her in her dire circumstances. The seamstress took apart her mistress's old coverlet lining, dyed it crimson, carefully trimming out the unworn parts, and then sewed them together to make a skirt for Maria. From the small remnants she had been saving, she made a patchwork jacket. The lining of the China silk coverlet was also silk, so the dye took most beautifully, and since the remnants were silk of the highest quality as befitting a grand household, the jacket looked as exquisite as if it had been made from new material. Mae-a was a picture-perfect image of her mother's beauty; even her tiny feet in tight cotton socks, resembling cucumber seeds, were lovely to look at. Gazing at her, Ha-sang could not conceal a smile of pride and wonderment.

The house was situated near Taegunbang district beneath Mount Nak. Opening a trim little gate, Ha-sang was struck with the orderliness of the house. In the good-sized yard there was no separate servants' wing; around the large garden were leafless shrubs and tree peonies, and in the central area, where spent flowering plants had been pulled out, the freshly upturned soil was neatly raked. Under a tall jujube tree was a kitchen storage terrace where dark brown ceramic crocks of all sizes glistened as if polished with oil. Following a middle-aged woman who opened the gate, the visitors entered the room at the end of the L-shaped house and were again surprised by its graciousness. In the corner was a three-storied chest of persimmon wood trimmed with heavy brass ornaments, and next to it was an iron-hinged blanket chest, a patchwork blanket-cover of uncommon beauty and intricacy spread over the folded coverlets. Next to the small sliding door was a document chest with drawers, and a maroon mattress with a royal blue border was placed under a wall closet decorated with paintings of the Four Gracious Plants. Altogether the room, though simple, revealed refinement and character. No one was in the room. No sooner had they seated themselves in the place of lesser importance, than a woman barely over thirty entered. Following Magdalene, who stood up abruptly, Hasang and Maria also rose. The woman was delighted.

"It's been so long, Magdalene, but what brought you here today?" she greeted Magdalene, looking puzzled at her companions.

"My dear Mistress Teresa. We come here to ask you a great favor."

"A favor?"

"Yes. It's this child . . ." Glancing at Maria, Magdalene urged, "Maria, child, pay your respects to the lady."

Maria stood up and made a ceremonial bow, kneeling gracefully.

"What a lovely child! Whose daughter is she?" Teresa asked, impressed.

Maria maintained her graceful dignity as she related the tragedy that had struck her, her decorous posture never faltering until she had finished her story.

"Such things still do go on, I hear. And sooner or later the same fate may befall us. But we are so far safe here; you may stay with us," Teresa remarked after listening to Maria.

In her new home, too, Maria was treated with affection. Her rare beauty and graceful manner astonished everyone, but she had another exceptional accomplishment for one so young. It was discovered on an early morning three days after Maria arrived in the house. It was the first frost of the season, and the air in the room was cold. Reared in the south, Maria woke from hazy sleep with a slight cough. In her blurred vision, the room took shape. It was light, though the dawn was still far off. The light came from the writing table where Teresa sat deeply occupied in her work. Maria's eyes were now wide open; she blinked them hard. The sleep completely gone from her, she was able to discern the figure of Teresa more distinctly. Not a hair on her head was out of place, and silhouetted against the lamp, her serious face bore a solemnity tinged with mystery. Before she realized it, Maria was sitting up. Deeply preoccupied, Teresa was not aware of Maria's intense gaze fixed upon her. Her posture straight and elegant, she held in her left hand a narrow scroll of paper; her right hand guided the brush, the strokes coursing on the paper like the flow of water. Once in a while, her hand would pause for a moment and she would look down at the table, then she would continue again.

She was copying something. The task of copying must have begun quite some time ago, because part of the scroll on which the writing had been transcribed in a beautiful palace-style calligraphy was spread thickly on the floor. Teresa paused and put down the brush; the ink had run out. She stretched out her arm to reach for the water-dropper and tipped it over the inkstone, but there was not a drop left in it. At that moment, Maria, who had been silently observing, stood up ever so gently. Without speaking a word, she knelt in front of the desk and picked it up. As if accustomed to doing it all her life, she went out and came back with the water-dropper filled. She poured the water onto the inkstone and began grinding. Teresa was silent in amazement at such an unexpected turn of events. When Maria finished grinding the ink and put down the inkstick, Teresa abruptly embraced her, her clear eyes filled with tears. "Oh, Maria, Maria!" she could only repeat her name, holding her tightly.

From the next day, Maria got up with Teresa at the stroke of midnight. She brushed her teeth and washed her face in icy cold water. The two would light the lamp and sit before the desk. Maria's task was to grind the inkstick and wash the brushes, fold the scroll of paper into equal parts, and draw the lines on the folds for Teresa to follow as she wrote. When the paper was filled with writing, Maria would cut it off along the lines she had drawn and bind the sheets together. Finally, Teresa would write the titles on the covers with utmost care; on some she wrote, *True Principles of Catholicism*, and on others, *Prayers*, all in the Korean vernacular alphabet.

One unusually chilly night, Teresa had difficulty falling asleep; she had been affected by a discomfort in her body since early evening. When she opened her eyes, it was far past midnight. Feeling slightly dizzy as she tried to get up, she noticed Maria sitting primly at the desk. On the desk, the lined scroll of paper, the inkstone filled with freshly ground ink, the inkstick, and the brushes were precisely arranged. In one corner of the room lay a brass basin filled with water, and next to it were bowls of water, and a dish of salt for brushing teeth; Maria's nightly chores for Teresa had been accomplished impeccably. Having fulfilled her responsibilities, Maria was now writing on the scraps of paper. Noticing that Teresa was awake,

Maria hastily stood up, grabbing the piece of paper on which she had been writing.

"Ah, you are practicing? Then soon you will be able to help me. Let me take a look at what you did." Teresa extended her hands smiling adoringly at Maria's gesture, but Maria withdrew a few steps and shook her head.

"It's all right. No one is full with the first mouthful. The beginning is always unsteady."

Even then, Maria did not give up the paper. Teresa looked at the brush on the table.

"My goodness! Even Wang Hŭi-ji [Wang Hsi-chih], the famous Chinese calligrapher, couldn't do anything with that!" she exclaimed. Light laughter escaped Teresa's lips. The brush, worn out, was one she had meant to throw away. The ache she had felt earlier was disappearing, and Teresa became cheerful again. "Anyway, I am so glad that you want to learn. I am going to make you a model, so that you can practice copying from it. Let me look at what you did; I must know where to begin," she coaxed Maria.

Only then, ashamedly, did Maria put the wrinkled paper on the desk, a sheet made by gluing together small scraps. When she cast her first glance on it, a cold shiver passed through Teresa's spine. She read:

Many are the creatures and troubles under heaven; therefore, how may we verify the handiwork of our Heavenly Father? Nothing comes into being by itself but everything is caused to exist. If towers and houses come into being through their builders, how much more is it obvious that the universe's limitless boundary is not mere chance? The sun and moon in their rotation divide the day from the night. The Holy Spirit causes the four seasons to return unerringly, so that plants and flowers flourish in the mountains, and fish and dragons inhabit the waters, and nature's energy causes birds and beasts to thrive. In the midst of all creatures, alone endowed with intelligence, man soars above and reigns over them. Therefore, all this is not accident. How can we doubt the omnipotence of our Heavenly Father?

It was the first passage from the Korean translation of Matteo Ricci's *True Principles of Catholicism*. Her intelligence in forming not a single misspelled letter was astonishing indeed, but even more extraordinary was the beauty of her calligraphic hand. Teresa had never come across a style such as this. The vernacular palace-style calligraphy used by eunuchs and palace ladies had two distinctly differing styles, a "male brush" for eunuchs, and a "female brush" for palace ladies. Palace ladies who were exceptionally talented scribed for the royal women in their correspondence and diaries—queen dowagers, queens, royal secondary wives and concubines, crown princesses, princesses, or daughters of the royal secondary wives—and recorded the events that took place in the palace. Therefore, palace-style usually referred to this "female brush," done in a running grass-hand script. However, what was written with the worn brush on the patched-up paper was not in a cursive style, nor was it in a well-balanced square script, but somewhere in between. It was not as bold and rigid as the official script, but not as free and wayward as grass-hand. It possessed the strength of both—a combination of the trim elegance of the square style and the fluid expressive freedom of the grass-hand style. Indeed, Maria's writing was a model of elegance and clarity, which would come to be known as the Princess Tŏgon style, because the princess, a daughter of King Sunjo and a celebrated calligrapher, later adopted it. But she was then only a child, barely out of swaddling clothes; no one in the palace was yet aware of the existence of such a writing style.

"Who, who taught you this?" Only after a long silence, having recovered from her astonishment, could Teresa speak.

"My mother taught me . . ." Maria faltered, her eyes full of fear, as though expecting a scolding.

"Your mother must have been a lady of supreme refinement." Teresa's words were like a deep sigh.

Years later, Teresa had the chance to view some examples of Princess Tŏgon's calligraphy, which had been kept by her friend, a lady-in-waiting, and she was astounded to note the striking similarity to Maria's hand. Although each was unaware of the other's existence by even so much as a whispered rumor, these two women wrote in the same calligraphic style, one a noble princess deep in the royal chamber, and the other, Maria's mother, the wife of a member of the Southerner faction far removed from the official path.

From that day, each night at the stroke of midnight, Maria would cleanse herself, and together with Teresa, would begin the task of copying books of Catholic tenets, prayers, and lives of the saints in her clear, legible hand, cultivated since the age of five, and now already in its maturity. Without realizing it, she had become an indispensable person in the household. In the Persecution of 1801, most Catholic writings had been either confiscated or burned by the Christians themselves. As the persecution gradually subsided, the need for religious books once again became urgent. Now they hand-copied from the small books some of the Catholic women had managed to hide. With no hope of having the books printed from wood-blocks, those with good calligraphic hands copied the texts written in the vernacular for the uneducated faithful, as the women in this house were doing.

Maria enjoyed her sacred assignment. She felt it providential that she had been fond of calligraphy since early childhood. While she moved her brush, she was released for a time from the sorrow of her woeful fate, and the fear of never being able to find her sisters. Copying the books, she also came to understand more deeply the teachings and the gospel. As she repeatedly transcribed *True Principles of Catholicism*, its meanings, which had been totally unintelligible in the beginning, became vaguely fathomable. She also came to realize that although the book was written in the Korean vernacular, it had been first written in Chinese by an Italian Jesuit priest, Matteo Ricci, and had been translated. The Chinese original would have been too difficult for a young girl like Maria or for the ordinary folk, who were unable to pursue rigorous training in Chinese; its philosophical and theological content were beyond their comprehension. Also beyond her knowledge was the fact that the book, published two hundred years earlier, had been brought into Korea by the annual emissary to the Chinese court, and together with other books on Catholicism had been studied exhaustively by the intellectuals of the Southerner faction as an academic interest. Prominent Confucian scholars had also shown intense interest in it, which had resulted in numerous publications, each with sharp and pertinent commentaries upon it from the Confucian point of view. Thus, since its introduction, *True Principles of Catholicism* had been instrumental in the spread of the religion throughout Korea. The birth of the Catholic church in Korea had been miraculously accomplished not through proselytizing, but autonomously, as a result of these scholars' insatiable desire for learning. Translated into the vernacular, copied repeatedly, and read widely in secrecy by the common people, it had paved the way for the salvation of many lives. She had no way of knowing the history of Catholicism in

Korea, but, as she copied the book, Maria gained a deeper knowledge of the teachings, which strengthened her faith.

She also copied *A Summary of Catholic Teaching*, edited by the martyr Chŏng Yak-chong. Its two volumes, written in the vernacular and quoting extensively from Ricci's book, were intended to help ignorant converts understand the true meaning of Catholicism. Its main thrust was the defense of the faith and the theory of redemption, which Yak-chong had organized and systematized from the vast knowledge he had acquired through research on the treatises of Catholicism. Maria found this book easy to follow, but it seized her with a strange agitation when she realized that its author was Ha-sang's father.

◆ ◆ ◆

"I'm on my way now. The rice for lunch is in the big cauldron in the kitchen. Serve it after the midday prayer. Lucia and Agatha are busy getting ready to deliver the court dresses to Judge Kim's household, and I promised the mistress that I'd get her the face-powder she is looking for. So, please, you have to help us today." Having thus instructed Maria, Barbara, a middle-aged woman, left in a hurry, a cloth-wrapped basket tucked under her arm. Martha had already left in the same manner a while earlier, and the house was suddenly empty. Teresa was praying with a rosary in the inner room; in the room across from it, Lucia and Agatha were busy sewing. Although still young, they were excellent seamstresses, so that there was always more work than they could handle; moreover, the neighborhood maidens came to them for sewing lessons. In this household of women, even without men to serve, daily life was often hectic; so from time to time, Maria had to help in the kitchen. But not much had to be done there, because the usual meal was simply rice mixed with rough millet and served with a few pieces of pickled radish and bean paste. In the backyard vegetable garden, lettuce, crown daisy leaves, green squash, and peppers were plentiful; however, these women cultivated the habit of eating only coarse food and were uncompromising in their observation of fasting. Sometimes Teresa sprinkled ashes over the millet-rice mixture. They followed this strict regimen based on the ideal of "deny the body and overcome the self."

Altogether there were seven women in the house. All except Barbara and Martha were unmarried. Past thirty, Teresa had once been a palace lady; and now, even though she was clad in ungainly cotton clothes and subsisted on coarse food, her youthful loveliness had not left her. One could conjure up the image of the beauty of bygone days resplendent in the magnificent court dress of a palace lady. Her hands, smooth as white wax, bespoke her past. She looked no older than twenty and had been ignorant of worldly ways outside the palace, where her hands had known no other toil than that of brushwork.

When she was six years old, Myŏng-sim, for that was Teresa's given name, was recruited to be raised as a palace lady. As they grew older, the young girls who had been recruited into the palace were taught the art of calligraphy along with their other training, and those with superior skill were assigned to the royal chambers. Recognized as one with an exceptional calligraphic hand, Myŏng-sim was selected to scribe for King Sunjo's mother, the royal secondary wife, Princess Pak. Because of her gentle nature, intelligence, and strict observation of decorum, and because she had given birth to a crown prince for whose arrival the whole nation had been praying, Princess Pak's esteem equaled that of the queen herself, and she required more palace ladies than did the childless queen. Basking in King Chŏngjo's special affection, an air of gentle harmony always surrounded the princess's residence. As some would appease the pain of growing old by indulging in nostalgia in springtime and meditation on autumnal days, so for Myŏng-sim and the other palace ladies, nature offered solace in the anticipation of spring's flowering and autumn's elegiac musing.

Fifteen years after entering the palace, Myŏng-sim marked her formal acceptance as a palace lady in the ceremony prescribed by court convention. It was very much like a wedding, but without a groom. Her hair was put up in a chignon befitting her new station, and Myŏng-sim—her position assured by her intimacy with the royal personage—at twenty already possessed an air of dignity uncommon in other palace ladies. With her hair oiled and slicked down from either side of her artfully shaven forehead, her loveliness, too, outshone that of the other ladies. After the rite, according to court protocol, she was treated like other ranking court ladies, and was permitted to go about without bowing to anyone in the palace.

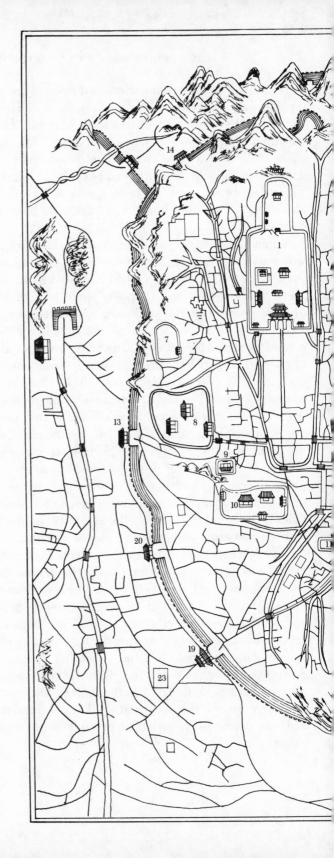

Seoul in the nineteenth century. Adapted from a map edited by Harold F. Cook for the Korea Branch of the Royal Asiatic Society, January 1973. By permission of the publisher.

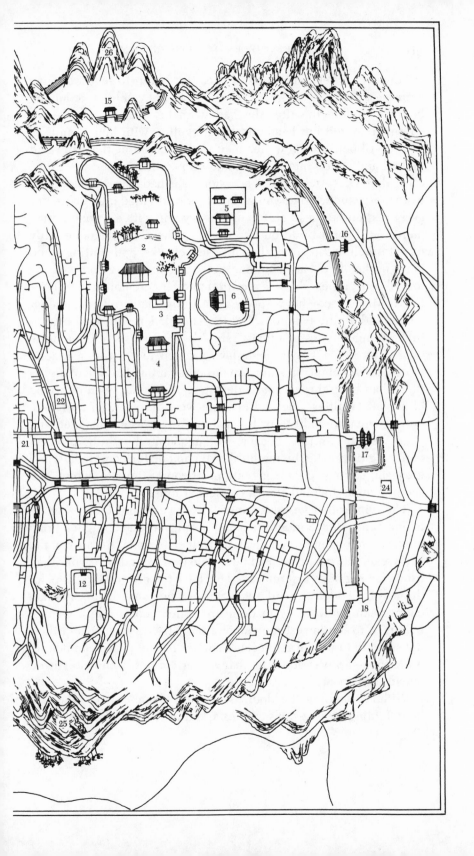

However, after her initiation rite, she began to feel a strange emptiness that she could not shake off as she would an annoying blemish. Before the rite, she had worn her hair in two tresses wrapped around her head and held together with four strands of maroon ribbon, but now her hair was gathered at the nape and plaited and coiled into a large knot with an ornamental pin thrust through it. On certain official occasions, she had to do her hair in an even more cumbersome and elaborate way, divided into ten tresses and piled on her head on top of a heavy wig with a wooden ornament. As if for a bride on her wedding day, her elaborate daily toilette included painting her lips and cheeks, and putting a red mark on her forehead. Donning her outrageous wig and wearing formal court robes, she was required to offer ceremonial obeisance to His Majesty, pay her respects to each royal lady in her chamber, and attend all the banquets. But the table laden with food beautifully arranged with the utmost care, like the one served to a bride adored by her new parents-in-law, seemed to her like a funeral table. All was empty gesture, devoid of meaning. She felt alone, as if she had been thrown into a desert, as if she had been deprived of all her faculties. She had become weary of such meaningless, empty, ritual formality. In this manner, the seasons changed and years went by, and she became well acquainted with the protocol of distinguishing the hierarchical order among the court ladies, and grew impervious to the conventions of court etiquette, which had seemed unnatural and almost comical at times.

The winter that year was unusually severe, and the spring remained unsettled. Suddenly a balmy spring day that brought myriad flowers into bloom turned bleak with sleet and rain. Because of the bad weather, Myŏng-sim had been released from duty earlier than usual, having been first reminded to check the fire and the doors for the night. Though she did not yet have a personal maid-servant, a charwoman had already made a fire in her room. These women belonged to the lowest rank among the palace servants, and their duty was to build a fire in each chamber in the palace compound. As Myŏng-sim was about to change her clothes, someone stirred outside her room.

Without opening the door, the young chambermaid who had been folding Myŏng-sim's clothes asked in her still childish voice, "Who is there?"

The door shook from outside.

"Ma'am. Ma'am," came a muffled, urgent voice.

It was Ch'oe, one of the charwomen in charge of carrying water for the palace ladies' toilette. Myŏng-sim motioned the chambermaid to open the door. Ch'oe let out a loud sneeze, her face flushed with cold. The rain had stopped and the moon shone through the violent wind. "What is it?" Myŏng-sim inquired.

"The lady is in grave condition. The palanquin and the carriers are here already," she answered, hugging herself to keep warm.

"What? The old lady?" Myŏng-sim dropped the tie that bound her skirt.

Unaware that her long skirt had slid to the floor, in a dire haste she squeezed her feet into the tight cotton stockings. "Child, I have to hurry," she was about to dash out.

"Ma'am, your skirt . . . ," the chambermaid reminded her, handing the skirt to Myŏng-sim.

"Yes, oh, yes." In a fluster, Myŏng-sim draped it around her, saying, "Hurry, where is the foot-lamp?"

"The moon is bright as daylight." Ch'oe led the way.

In the clear, moonlit night, the gusty wind howled through the trees, threatening to blow the branches off them. Myŏng-sim ran faster than the wind.

The old lady was still alive in a tiny room next to the laundry room. The panting of her last breathing was audible from outside. She was almost lifeless; her lusterless, thick white hair hung loose upon her skeletal face like a soiled cotton skein, and her sallow, brown skin stuck to her face like a flabby rag on a skull.

Collecting her breath after the dash, once inside, Myŏng-sim stood dumfounded as she heard the grumble of the palanquin-carriers.

"Why are you procrastinating? We must hurry or she will die right here in the palace grounds. Then you will see who is to be punished. Let's stuff her into the palanquin first," one of the carriers grumbled.

As they grabbed the fleshless arms of the old woman in her death throes, one of them exclaimed in disgust, clucking his tongue, "What is this? A brocade scarf on her wrist? Does a skeleton still bask in the royal favor? I'm dying of shock."

Myŏng-sim could not control herself any longer. She threw herself over the body, and touched her cheeks against the red silk scarf wrapped around the woman's wrist. Overcome with wailing, she could only utter the old woman's name repeatedly; she had lost all other words.

"Control yourself, Ma'am. Don't you realize you are within the royal compound? You must obey the palace regulations. If we delay longer, we commit a grave crime. If you interfere, a calamity might befall you," said one of the men.

They shoved Myŏng-sim roughly into the corner, dragged the body of the dying woman to the palanquin, and stuffed her into it. They closed the door of the filthy, worn-out palanquin, which had no ornaments adorning it.

"Why is she so heavy? She's all bones," lifting it, the one in the rear complained.

"Do you think she is already dead?" asked the one in front.

"Corpses weigh heavier, as they say," his companion observed, sneezing loudly. "Anyhow, we can't stay here all night. Let's get going. As soon as we get outside the palace gate, it's none of our business if she's dying or gone to the other world already. Damn it, why so cold tonight!"

A gusty wind roared by again. As if swept by the wind, the men disappeared through the gate. Collapsing to the floor, burying her face in her knees, Myŏng-sim sobbed. The charwoman, Ch'oe, put her hands gently on her shoulders. Even in the cold of the night, they were warm.

"Forgive me. It's so cold, and they must have been hungry. I couldn't even offer them a cup of wine. I am sorry. The thought of the old lady breaks my heart, but what could we do? The palace regulations are absolute," she said in her soft voice.

"But how dare they treat her like rubbish? We all share the same fate, and no one came to send her off . . ." Unmindful, Myŏng-sim kept on weeping and lamenting.

"That's not true. In the early evening many ladies came to see her. But they are all so busy in their duties, and this horrendous weather . . . Though they could not stay for her last moment in this world, they left in tears and with heavy hearts."

"But don't we deserve to be treated like human beings? Why are we palace women forbidden to die within the palace gates, not even on the heaps of garbage? They bring us here before we are old enough to know what's going on, and we must work locked up like caged birds. And when we are about to die, they throw us away. Even bandits and demons would be ashamed to do such a cruel thing!"

"Our life on earth is but a journey and this world is only a temporary inn. The lady has now returned to her eternal home."

In amazement, Myŏng-sim forgot her sorrow. "Who is this woman? Who is she who could speak such words?" Myŏng-sim looked up at the charwoman, who stood bathed in moonlight.

The woman's face was broad with small eyes, flat nose, and thick lips. She was one of the lowest of the palace servants, assigned to do heavy work such as carrying water and tending the fires. She was wearing the uniform of her station—a long jacket like those worn by menservants, over a long skirt with a wide sash tied around her waist—all in a jarring mixture of green and blue. In addition, as she did her chores she was required to wear a tag of identification on her belt, which allowed her to pass through the palace gates.

"Who are you? Are you really a maid who carries water and tends the fire?" asked Myŏng-sim, looking at the woman who was strangely unfamiliar now.

"Of course I am. Sometimes I go outside the palace for errands, as well."

"No. You must be hiding something. Come to think of it, the lady, though her life was wretched, never seemed to suffer or feel sad. She used to tell me how grateful she was for your care, and she seemed always to be at peace. How did you manage to give her such peace of mind?"

"She was a good-hearted lady."

"No one knows her better than I do, because I was her chambermaid. She taught me everything, a mere child of six, and raised me like her own daughter. She tutored me in palace etiquette, proper deportment and behavior; she even taught me to read and write."

"And you have been kind to her to the end."

"She used to confide in me the sad circumstances of her life."

"She was only a mortal . . ."

Dozing nearby, the chambermaid sneezed.

"Poor thing, she doesn't know what lies ahead . . ." Myŏng-sim, suddenly alert, held the child's cold body.

"The wind is so cold. Please hurry back to your room. I'll carry

the girl." Lifting the sleeping child onto her back, the maid reminded her once again, "As soon as you get back to your room, you
must make yourself warm, or you'll catch cold."

Myŏng-sim stood up feebly. Suddenly, feeling the chill seeping
through her bones, she shivered. Outside, the blustery wind had
blown away the clouds, and in the blue-gray sky an almost full moon
rode in plaintive luminosity. The women walked on in silence.
Within the palace grounds, all lights had been extinguished; reflecting the moonbeams, the tiles on the roofs shimmered like
waves. As they passed one of the buildings, a gust of wind swept
by, scattering the pear-blossom petals like snowflakes in a blizzard.

"They call it 'Pear-blossom Rain,' the rain of the flowering season. But I wonder if it means the petals, not the rain," Myŏng-sim
mused.

"Yes, indeed."

"So lovely and evanescent, like the life of our lady."

"She was a beautiful lady," Ch'oe remarked pensively.

They had now reached the pear tree. The flowers that had been
in full bloom were now falling in the sudden cold and rain, and they
lay scattered beneath the tree like snow. As they fell on the muddy
ground, their pristine loveliness was no more than a heap of rubbish.
Increasingly sorrowful, Myŏng-sim stumbled on the root of a tree.

"Be careful." Ch'oe supported Myŏng-sim with her hand. Leaning on that hand, Myŏng-sim suddenly felt guilty; it was as large as
the iron lid of a kettle, and with hard work, it had become as rough
as a grater.

Myŏng-sim spent the night sleepless with anguish. For a spring
night, it was cold and raw. Thinking of the old lady, who must surely
have died being stuffed into that drab palanquin, Myŏng-sim was
overcome with dry-eyed grief. The old one had been her teacher,
much as her own mother had been. Now twenty-one, Myŏng-sim
was deep in the remembrance of her past, as if it had happened
long, long ago.

It was on a spring day. Myŏng-sim was playing house with a
neighborhood girl when a manservant came looking for her. "Little
miss, your mother wants you. There are some guests in the house,"
he said.

The guests were two women. Myŏng-sim had never beheld in

her life such shiny hair and fashionable clothes. Urged by her mother, she made a deep bow to the women.

"Did you say she is six?" asked the elder of the two, scrutinizing her.

"Yes," her mother's answer was strangely feeble, "and she is but a baby. She is very immature."

"You don't say. How well she made the bow and how intelligent she looks!" The visitor smiled for the first time, as if fully satisfied.

"Indeed, she stands out among the other girls we have seen," chimed in the other.

Despite their praise, her mother's face remained clouded.

Two days later, accompanied by a palace slave, the younger woman returned; she presented a bolt of silk, saying, "We have consulted the horoscope, and the last day of the month is divined to be propitious. We will send a palanquin in the early afternoon of that day."

Her head bowed, after they left, her mother held Myŏng-sim tightly to her bosom and wept. Only many years later did Myŏng-sim come to realize that their visitors had been a palace lady in charge of letter carrying and a privy lady-in-waiting.

Myŏng-sim's family owned a thriving pharmacy, and was well-to-do. The palace ladies were usually chosen from *chungin* families like Myŏng-sim's, although in some cases they were selected through the recommendations of other palace ladies, or their relatives. They were recruited at the age of six or seven, and once having entered the palace, they were never allowed to return to their homes. The little girls lived under the supervision of older court ladies, looked up to them as their teachers, and served their needs. The court ladies, in turn, reared them like their own daughters.

On the appointed day, in accordance with the regulations, wearing a yellow jacket and a royal-blue skirt over a white silk underskirt and pantaloons, Myŏng-sim mounted the palanquin sent by the palace. The court lady whom Myŏng-sim was assigned to serve was the Lady Pak, the same old woman she had just seen being carried away to die outside the royal compound.

Lady Pak had been just past forty when Myŏng-sim entered the palace. Wearing a blue skirt, and a pale silver jacket with maroon borders on the sleeves, she had been a beautiful woman whose deportment was as gentle and unobtrusive as if she had been clad in white; perhaps it was because she would have preferred in her heart to dress in white, but was prevented from doing so by the strict regulation that prohibited palace women from wearing the color designated solely for national mourning.

It usually took fifteen years for a palace woman to reach the rank of senior privy lady-in-waiting after she had her initiation rite, which occurred about fifteen years after she had entered the palace. Thus, most of the women were over thirty-five when they finally attained their rank. If the king favored a young palace lady by taking her to the royal bedchamber, and if the union resulted in the birth of a prince or princess, she would be elevated to the nobility, and a title bestowed on her. If, as happened in some rare, fortunate cases, her son became the crown prince, she would enjoy the life of splendor that befitted the mother of a king. However, most of these women grew old as virgins. Furthermore, they were strictly prohibited by law to die within the palace grounds, a privilege reserved only for members of the royal family. Such was their fate.

Once in her youth, the palace lady Pak had been honored by the royal favor. Fair and in her flowering youth, she had caught the roving eyes of King Yŏngjo, well known for his sensual pursuit. One night she was chosen to accompany the king to his bed. In her jealous rage, Lady Mun Sug-ŭi, the king's then-current favorite, stopped just short of murdering her. She removed her from the royal chamber to the embroidery quarters to instruct the palace ladies. Lady Pak remained there until she became ill. She so excelled in drawing the patterns for embroidery that the needlework done on a pattern she had drawn was said to look as if the dragon and phoenix came alive on it. Even though she was expelled from the royal chamber, the sewing and embroidery quarters were next only to the royal chamber in prestige; therefore she continued to be treated with the deference accorded to those close to the royal chamber, and to wear her skirts wrapped around to the left side as did the women of highborn scholar-official households. It was at this time that Myŏng-sim had entered the palace and had been assigned to Lady Pak, who instructed her in proper deportment and etiquette, as well as in the art of calligraphy and painting.

Until the previous winter, at sixty-three, Lady Pak had been elegant and beautiful in her approaching old age. However, one day late in the winter, after taking a spoonful of red bean porridge, she began to vomit. After that, she had been unable to eat anything. A physician felt her pulse and diagnosed the illness as intestinal tumor. The vomiting persisted and she wasted away to skin and bones within a month. It was a strict palace regulation that once a palace lady became gravely ill, she was to be sent back to her home. However, Lady Pak had left her home some fifty years before, and had had no contact since then with her family. She had nowhere to go. Since she was not permitted to stay in the embroidery quarters, she was moved to a tiny room next to the laundry room until the night she was carried away. In the beginning, the women from the embroidery quarters took turns visiting and nursing her, but as her illness lingered on, the visits became infrequent. As the saying goes, "In a long illness, no son is filial." Though tormented by anxiety, Myŏng-sim was not free to nurse Lady Pak.

She had grown exceedingly emaciated, but for some strange reason, Lady Pak looked serene, and bore well the cruel pain of her illness. She appeared to be well taken care of, and the bedding and linens were always clean. Puzzled, Myŏng-sim mentioned this to the lady. She replied that the charwoman, Ch'oe, had been nursing her and taking care of her needs. As she spoke, she appeared to be full of joy.

A month went by, but Myŏng-sim could not free herself from the pain she suffered in her heart. In her mind's eye hovered the image of the red silk on the old woman's fleshless wrist, the mark of royal favor in her youth, which she wore to the end of her days, and the mop of thick gray hair covering her face. Sometimes the image was juxtaposed with the soft baby face of her young chambermaid, causing a chill to pass up Myŏng-sim's spine.

Myŏng-sim spent days in melancholy.

One night, Ch'oe came to see her unexpectedly. The weather, which had been alternately balmy and chilly, had suddenly become warm for a few days. Even in the heat, the maid did not seem to mind wearing her heavy, drab, olive-green uniform.

"My lady, I respectfully inquire after you. Your complexion does not look right. Are you taken ill by any chance?" she asked.

"It's been so long since I saw you last time. How have you been? I have been troubled since that night. I don't seem to be able to digest anything I eat," Myŏng-sim replied, happy to see her.

"It must be because of the lady, I'm sure."

"My heart aches as I think of her, driven away in the cold of the night. She must surely have died during the night. And those cruel, ignorant men—I was afraid that they would abandon the corpse on the roadside . . ." Myŏng-sim's eyes filled with tears.

"She did not pass away that night. I have many brothers. I asked them to bring the lady to their house. She stayed with them and died the night before last."

"Then she lived for a month longer?"

"She did not recover," she said apologetically.

"She was no better than a corpse when she left here, and her life lingered on in that condition for a month . . ."

"But she was peaceful at the end. She died gracefully as if in her sleep."

Myŏng-sim grasped Ch'oe's rough hands in gratitude. "Thank you. I am so grateful. You have been so good to the poor, lonely lady."

"Not at all. She was a good-hearted lady all along and bore her pain and suffering well. I couldn't help her much."

Once again, Myŏng-sim looked at the woman closely. Her face, though ugly, was full of goodness and affection. Hesitating for a moment, Ch'oe took a book the size of her palm from her bosom. "The lady asked me to give you this book."

The hand-copied book was small but thick, written in a good calligraphy, though Myŏng-sim noted that the lines of the script wavered unevenly. On the oil-paper cover were written the words *True Principles of Catholicism.*

"What is this?" asked Myŏng-sim.

"You'll know when you read it."

"Did the lady read this book also?"

"Of course. Since her eyesight had gone, I read it to her; so did my niece. She is twelve and can now read Korean vernacular writing."

"Then you too can read, I see."

"Me? Mine is only a cricket's feeler. I only stammer. She must have been very impatient with my faltering, but she was so very happy when I read it to her," the maid paused for a moment and went on. "The Lady Mun, who left the palace a few years ago, she came to see her, too."

"Lady Mun? The one who left because of that strange, horrible disease?"

"Yes, the one who served in the royal chamber."

Lady Mun, a senior privy lady-in-waiting, had been a woman of exceptional beauty, but having contracted a strange disease, foaming at the mouth and seized by convulsions, she had become a total cripple. She had returned to civilian life, and had severed her ties with the palace.

"But how? How could she in her condition?"

"She is quite all right now. She is no longer frail as before."

"Then have you been in contact with her all this time?"

"Yes, indeed. We are all of one mind."

"One mind?"

Ch'oe did not answer. That night, Myŏng-sim began reading the book. The new world that had been beyond her imagination suddenly unfolded. Mesmerized by the book, she spent the nights reading it. At the persistent urgings of the chambermaid, who was puzzled by the change in her mistress, Myŏng-sim reluctantly went through the motions of dressing herself and applying her toilette, but she could not slip out of the world she had just begun to discover. The lack of sleep made her face look bloated and her complexion sallow, but her mind was clear and at peace. The book gave direction to the soul wandering in agony, taught the existence of the One who ruled all creatures under the heavens and on earth, and showed the ethical path for man to follow. For the first time, as she looked at the gilt ornament in the shape of a frog that her mistress, Princess Pak, wore proudly on her crown, Myŏng-sim felt an aversion, although the lady always treated her with affection. A new awareness took root in her. Overnight, she had become a different person. She began to gain insight into the meaning of the discrepancy between vanity without and integrity within, pride and piety, the rich and poor. Life within the palace became repugnant to her.

However, many things in the book were incomprehensible to Myŏng-sim, such as the Immaculate Conception, the Resurrection of Jesus Christ, the Redemption, and so on. Each time she had questions, she would send her chambermaid to look for Ch'oe. Because these charwomen lived outside with their own families and daily commuted to the palace grounds, it was not easy to locate them while they worked. This did not discourage Myŏng-sim; it only increased her desire to find Ch'oe. Until then, Ch'oe had been only a low-born charwoman to Myŏng-sim, but now Myŏng-sim knew this woman was the only person who could free her from her suffering and enable her to satisfy her longing.

Ch'oe was always deferential and apologetic.

"I am only an ignorant woman. I regret not being able to answer what you ask me," she would say. Then she would add in a whisper, "but, after all, one cannot follow the holy teachings within the palace grounds."

Myŏng-sim's weariness with life in the palace only increasing, she went on in a strange confusion of joy, pain, and anxiety. Unusually humid days continued. Although the rainfall had been adequate, in the severe heat the rice plants that had been growing lustily in the provinces suddenly withered, and a rumor began to circulate that this "Rice of Mourning" was an omen of a national mourning to come.

The rumor reached even to the palace. Even without it, the palace had been shrouded with an oppressive cloud of unrest and apprehension, more uncomfortable than the sultry weather. Although the royal age was only forty-eight, King Chŏngjo's strange illness from abscesses was growing worse, and it ultimately caused his death in the prime of his life.

A young king ascended to the throne, and the Queen Dowager, the incarnation of enmity itself, reemerged after more than twenty years hidden in the depths of her palace. Sitting behind the dragon throne of the boy-king, she conducted the affairs of the nation, engaging in a "regency behind the blind." Soon the bloodshed of the Catholic persecution, unprecedented in history, had begun.

Tales of the persecution, and the strange behavior of the martyrs, reached even the palace women shut off from the outside world, and became the topic of whispered conversation among them. They exchanged gossip in muffled flurry.

"These Catholics are said to have some magical power. They don't suffer, even under the most severe torture. They don't even change their expressions when they are seared with red-hot iron."

"Wretched souls!"

"It seems that their god protects them from such pain."

"But, oh my dear, how cruel!"

"Do you think that's all? Even when their heads are being

chopped off, they only rejoice, saying that they are joining the sacred banquet table."

"Stupid people! Whatever it is, they are hopelessly possessed."

"I heard that Lady Mun was also a base Catholic," whispered one.

"What? That beautiful lady who attended the royal chamber?"

"So I hear."

"But wasn't she a cripple?"

"They say it's all because of the magic. Remember how beautiful she was? So they tried to save her life, but she insisted that she be killed. They cut off her head."

"Mercy! How horrible!"

"Then, I'm telling you, instead of blood milk gushed out of her neck."

"A lie!"

"It's true!"

"But I heard that a long time ago in a Western country, when a certain Catholic woman was beheaded, milk poured out of her severed neck, just like Lady Mun's."

"Why do they kill Catholics?"

"They say it's because Catholics don't believe in the principles of loyalty to one's king, or filial piety to one's parents. They are but beasts."

"Then they surely deserve to die."

Myŏng-sim found out about the martyrdom of Lady Mun a few days later through Ch'oe. The charwoman had changed unrecognizably in a short time. Loss of weight had turned her sallow complexion even darker, making her lips appear even thicker than before. As soon as she entered Myŏng-sim's room, she knelt down and bowed her head.

"Ma'am, this may be my last visit," she announced.

"What are you talking about?"

"Though I am only a lowly, sinful woman, I wish with all my heart to have the honor of martyrdom." To the perturbed Myŏng-sim, Ch'oe tearfully related in detail the tragic circumstances of the persecution.

The martyrdom of Lady Mun had greatly moved Myŏng-sim, as had the wisdom, courage, and integrity of a woman called Colomba, with whom Lady Mun had lived until her death. For the first time,

Myŏng-sim spoke the thoughts she had been pondering for the past few months.

"I want you to know that I, too, believe in the Heavenly Father. I hear any Christian can baptize others. Please baptize me," she pleaded.

"Though I am humble, in a situation such as this, I might be presumptuous enough to give you a baptism, but it would be better to wait for a priest who can truly baptize you someday, while you prepare yourself for that day." Ch'oe stood up to leave.

"Then at least be my godmother."

"I am too unworthy."

"I must find a way to get out of the palace and lead a celibate life."

"It's hard to follow the holy teachings in the palace," the maid replied, repeating the words she had spoken before.

A smile surfaced on her face, which had now recovered some of its brightness. Myŏng-sim's words "celibate life" surprised her. In the traditional value system, the concept of celibacy was unacceptable; it was to be avoided and must be obliterated from consciousness. Only in the most dire circumstances would a man remain unmarried, and when such a man died, he would become a bachelor-demon. A virgin who could not be married off would become a restless ghost, sure to bring calamity upon the family. Thus Ch'oe rejoiced to hear Myŏng-sim say the forbidden word that showed she believed in the celibate life as a supreme virtue. She felt that Myŏng-sim, though not yet baptized, had now become a true believer. At the time when many had chosen martyrdom, and just as many had declared their apostasy, Myŏng-sim became a Catholic, taking the Christian name, Teresa.

Chapter Six

◆ ◆ ◆

Sowing

"Please, have mercy. You can't take that, too. Without it, the children can't survive the winter." Old Sin's entreaty was mixed with sobs.

"Christians never get hungry. They have magic, I hear. We Koreans can't live without grain. Why? Do you prefer the taste of flogging just to save a handful of millet and potatoes?"

"Catholics?" Coming out from behind a mud hut just at that moment, Ha-sang stood still, as if he had seen a serpent.

"You didn't know, did you? But we knew all along that you are Catholics. Reporting you to the authorities is as easy as turning over one's palm."

"That's a groundless accusation," the old man quavered, his voice shaking with fear.

"The rumor began when you started the slash-and-burn farm. We, the people of Kangwŏn Province, are kindly; we have been lenient so far. But we know you sold some tobacco yesterday, so you'd better give us that money too."

"That money is to pay the debt," panted old Sin in fright.

"Shut up. Give it to me, or else . . ."

Ha-sang heard the old man fall with a thud.

"Father!" shrieked a young woman. A baby cried sharply.

"A Catholic like you, how dare you lie to me?"

"That's not a lie. I am here to collect the debt," Ha-sang said, emerging out of the mud house.

"Eh?"

The shouting aggressor turned, wide-eyed with disbelief as he

155

confronted stout, broad-shouldered Ha-sang, almost six feet tall, on whose still adolescent face a thick beard had begun to grow. "I am here from Ch'ŏlwŏn on my father's errand to collect the money," Ha-sang declared.

"From Ch'ŏlwŏn?"

"Brother, he is lying. I saw the bastard with this old fellow's son selling tobacco in the marketplace yesterday," the man's companion warned.

"Then do I have to carry the tobacco back to Ch'ŏlwŏn?"

Ha-sang's menacing glare made his adversary withdraw a few steps. "Go away, don't steal the money from this man. It is not enough even to pay back the debt. I was wondering why he couldn't pay us back. Now I know: it's because of evil people like you."

"What did you say?" blustered the intruder.

"Why, did I say something wrong?"

Pushing his broad chest forward, his hands behind his back, Ha-sang stood rock-solid. At that moment, Sin's son was coming down the mountain with a load of firewood on his back. An imposing presence in spite of his unkempt hair, he stood there in confusion, unable to grasp what was happening.

"Sin, just listen to this. These men want to steal the money your father owes me," Ha-sang explained.

"What?" asked the younger Sin, putting down the load and brushing the twigs from his clothes. Shorter than Ha-sang, he was also stoutly built. The strangers were taken aback by the presence of these two powerful young men.

"Just you wait and see, you Catholic bastards," the intruders threatened, retreating down the mountain.

The elder Sin remained blankly on the ground where he had been pushed down, but he finally lifted his face toward Ha-sang. "Thank you, thank you, young man. But you must leave here at once. They are sure to return soon, and next time they will come with a group, or with soldiers."

The younger Sin nodded in agreement.

"This is not the first time," the old man said, letting out a deep sigh. "We find a barren mountain, slash and burn the weeds growing there, and after unspeakably hard toil, as soon as we have managed to make things grow, we are forced to leave."

Between sighs, the old man called to his daughter-in-law, who
stood beside her husband.

"Listen to me carefully, mother of my grandsons. What do I have
to hide from you now? What they said was true. We are Catholics.
We have caused you much hardship—you, who knew nothing about
it. We'll raise the children well no matter what happens to us, so
you must leave here at once. Forget about us, meet a good man, and
lead a better life from now on. You served us well; we shall never
forget you wherever we go from here. Thank you, thank you."

The young daughter-in-law, with her baby on her back, began to
sob, covering her face with her hands. Her thin shoulders shook
inside the tatters that clothed her flowering youth. Her little son, a
child of about three clinging to his mother's skirt, his stomach swollen with malnutrition, began to whimper upon seeing his mother's
tears.

"Come here, Myŏng-sik, come to your grandpa. You are a big
boy, a general. A general must never cry."

The elder Sin, though really only a little past forty, looked older
than sixty, with his hair already turned completely white and his
face lined with minute wrinkles.

Turning to Ha-sang, he cautioned, "Young man, you must leave
here immediately, or you will be implicated, too."

Before he realized what he was doing, Ha-sang found himself
kneeling down in front of the old man. "Grandfather of Myŏng-sik,
my name is Paul. I have heard about the suffering of Christians, but
this is too much for you to bear."

"Did you say Paul? My son's name is Paul, too. Oh, merciful
Lord, you do not give us a trial we cannot bear. I thank you for this
joy and comfort you have sent to us."

The elder Sin knelt down, his son, Paul, joining him. "It's almost
midday prayer time; when the shadow of the tree over there shrinks
back to its roots it means noon. I have sinned and am not always
able to fulfill my Christian duties, but today I feel my sins are for-
given," the old man declared, joining his gnarled, work-roughened
hands together in prayer.

The three Christians made the sign of the cross, and as they were
about to rise, they noticed that the young woman had been kneeling
beside them. In her hands was a rosary.

"Oh—you, too . . ." Tears flowed from the old man's eyes.

"Yes. My Christian name is Catherine."

"We did not know."

"Neither did I."

"Not knowing you were one of us, we prayed and observed the Christian duty in secret . . ."

"I had a hard time hiding my rosary."

The two young Pauls laughed heartily.

"Glory . . ." The old man began the prayer.

All three joined him, their hearts filled with thanksgiving, "to the Father, to the Son, and to the Holy Spirit, as it was in the beginning, is now, and ever shall be, forever and ever. Amen."

However, they could not remain for too long engrossed in joy and thanksgiving. The experience of their misfortune made them alert to the dangers ahead; they knew only too well the ruthless persecution, the betrayals by many Judases, the greed and cruelty of the soldiers. There could be no end in sight to the suffering of Christians so long as the Edict of the Catholic Eradication remained in effect. Their property confiscated, the families of the martyrs had become totally destitute, and others, too, after selling all their family belongings, were forced to retreat deep into the mountains to survive in the most primitive conditions. The weather in the mountains was always unsettled; the rain and snow fell unexpectedly. The fugitives had built mud huts for themselves as protection from the harsh environment. They wore nothing but tatters, having no other resources even to clothe themselves. They eked out a meager existence through slash-and-burn farming, growing millet, potatoes, and tobacco. As the number of the Christians growing tobacco increased, the price fell drastically. The day before, the loads of tobacco that Ha-sang and Paul had carried to market, their backs bent with the weight, had yielded a ridiculously small sum of money. Moreover, as soon as the fields began to grow fertile and they could look forward to the next year's harvest, the merciless claws of persecution lay in wait to ravage once again their short-lived peace.

The people of Kangwŏn Province were known, because of their gentle dispositions, as "old sitting buddhas under the rock." In their dealings with Catholics, however, they turned cruel and savage. They believed that Christians were fugitives from the law of the nation, heretic creatures worse than beasts who deserved only to die. They entered Christian homes at will, and stole their crops right in front of the owners' eyes. The soldiers, too, had learned the fun of taking the property of these converts; they had even come to derive a morbid pleasure from the sight of the converts' blood as they tortured them. As for the Judases, the easy gain to be had by selling their erstwhile brethren-in-faith enticed them; Christians feared most these Judases, who were intimately acquainted with the religious behavior of their victims. Never missing the telltale signs in a Christian's every move and word, which non-Christians might overlook, they mercilessly informed the authorities. For this reason, even in the depths of the mountains, the faithful could not openly perform their religious duties.

When their offspring reached marriageable age, parents were faced with the problem of matching them with the right spouses. Since matches with Christian families were not always possible, they often tolerated marriage outside their faith. After the marriage, they struggled to hide their religion from the new member of the family, even though the newcomer might also be a secret Christian. In many cases, the newlyweds were both Christians and lived together in mutual deceit, unaware of each other's faith. Even as their worldly love grew stronger with the birth of children, they worshipped in secrecy, lamenting the fate of having married a non-Christian.

The daughter-in-law of the elder Sin was from a Catholic family. Betrayed by a Judas one Easter Sunday at a prayer gathering, her parents had been captured and had died in prison. She had been reared by her aunt and uncle, who had also fled from the persecution into the mountains of Kangwŏn Province. The devout but destitute couple brought her up with care and did not neglect her religious education even though their own had become somewhat hazy during their long period of fugitive life. When the girl reached thirteen, the couple began searching for a suitable husband, as was the practice at the time. All their Christian acquaintances had been dispersed, and as they were unwilling to match her with a non-Christian, they were unable to marry her off. As they grew older, the couple finally reached the sad conclusion that after their death, the young girl of nineteen must not be left alone in the wilderness far away from home; they must marry her even into a non-Christian family.

One day, her uncle sprained his ankle when he fell from a cliff

while digging for medicinal herbs. The younger Sin, who was passing by to cut firewood, rescued the unconscious old man. Sin carried
the old man on his back to his home. Eighteen years old, vigorous
in body and spirit, he was as gentle-natured as a maiden.

"Although not a Christian, he is perfect for my niece," thought
the uncle. The old couple took a special liking to him. The elder
Sin had the same idea when he saw the girl. Thus, though each
family harbored sadness at not being able to marry the children in
a Christian ritual, they nonetheless rejoiced in the young couple's
happiness.

Having survived the Persecution of 1801, the elder Sin had come
to this mud hut from his native town of Nonsan in Ch'ungch'ŏng
Province. A young man at the time, he had been away to attend his
father-in-law's sixtieth birthday celebration when his village was
raided. It had been a long time since they had last paid a visit to his
wife's family, and the children had never met their grandparents.
On their way home after a five-day visit, in the mountain path overlooking the village, they met an acquaintance who told them about
the catastrophe. Having lost his parents when he was young, Sin
was not among the newly bereaved, but his uncles and cousins and
their Christian neighbors had all suffered recent losses. After the
villagers had buried the dead with care and devotion, Sin gathered
the surviving families of the martyrs and led them to the mountains.
Sin established a Christian village with five families, about thirty
people altogether, and it was not until they had endured hardships
that defy description that they finally settled down. Not yet forty at
the time of the persecution, he had gone through more than twenty
times what others suffered in their entire lifetime. Each hardship
engraved a new furrow on his face like a scar.

The persecution left them all in deep fear. Nevertheless, they
had managed to save a few small books of tenets and prayer books,
and though trembling in terror, they did not neglect their religious
observations. After they had managed to escape starvation by sub-
sisting on wild fruits and the roots of trees, and the poor mountain
land had begun to yield some meager crops, yet another trial would
devastate them: betrayal by an informer would force them to leave
the land they had suffered to till. This pattern was repeated many
times until at last only the Sin family remained, while all the rest
had dispersed.

Two years earlier, after a scanty harvest, the uncle of Sin's daughter-in-law died. When Sin, together with his son and daughter-in-law and their children, returned from the funeral, once again he had to witness the devastation of his home, a devastation rendered more severe by the death of his wife and daughter. The remaining family members had to seek a new refuge in a more remote area, where they began yet another slash-and-burn farm. The bloody claws of persecution tenaciously pursued them. Unknown to them, both the persecutors and the persecuted played roles in the propagation of the gospel. Catholicism had entered the capital region first, reaching next to Ch'ungch'ŏng and Chŏlla provinces, but the gospel spread as oppression mounted and Christians fled in all directions. Indeed, men err and God is omniscient.

Now old Sin was in a state of extreme agitation. Since he had lost his wife and daughter two years before, he had been quietly resigned, as if there were nothing left in the world to pain him, but watching his young grandsons, he was again seized with maddening anxiety. A few days earlier in the marketplace, he had seen the man he most feared. Slash-and-burn farmers like him ventured to the market only to sell the tobacco they grew and the medicinal herbs they dug, and to buy salt, cotton cloth, and needles and thread. Since no peddlers came to the mountains, they had to put by these necessities for the winter before the snow came. It was in a tavern in the marketplace that old Sin saw the man, sitting on a wooden bench. It was not the first time he had seen him in this province; he had spotted him in another marketplace a few days before the tragedy of two years ago. Seeing him then, the old man had been overjoyed to meet Sŭng Nak-chong, a Catholic with the name of Pius who was from a village near his own. He knew that Pius had been a servant at the household of Kwŏn Ho-sin who, following the example of his master, had been a devout Catholic. Believing that Pius, too, had come to this province in flight from the persecution, he related to him the hardship he had gone through and invited him to come to his mud hut if it were not too much trouble; he even showed him a shortcut. Since he was away at the time of the tragedy, he had no proof of his suspicion that Nak-chong had been an informer. However, later recalling his behavior when he saw him soon after the tragedy, he had no doubt that the Judas was indeed Nak-chong. As he remembered, it was the horsehair hat Nak-chong was wearing that had aroused his suspicions. It was not a nobleman's hat, but one with a narrow rim of the kind worn by lower local government officials. In addition, his drinking companions had been those disgusting petty soldiers. His suspicion proved right. Nak-chong had become a professional informer, traveling throughout the country looking for Christians and their villages to report to the authorities.

It was only Nak-chong's back that he spotted, but he could not be certain that the traitor had not seen him first. In haste, Sin and his family began packing their pitiful belongings. In the mountains that night, tigers' eyes gleamed unusually bright, glowing like lamp-flames, and between these glares came the repulsive howls of jackals. As they packed, although they thought they owned nothing, they were surprised by the things they had collected: potatoes, as precious as life; a burlap-sack of millet; soy sauce and soybean paste; leftover salt; and two ragged piles of bedding. The young daughter-in-law did not want to part with her chipped kettle and pots, nor did she wish to leave behind the radish-and-cabbage pickles she had made only a few days before. Ha-sang and the younger Sin carried these wretched belongings, piled high on the frames on their backs. Before daybreak, after a meal of millet with potatoes, the family set out without a destination, in search of a new place to settle. The young mother carried the baby on her back, balancing a bundle of clothes on her head, and in her hands she held the chipped pots and pans, bowls, and dishes. The grandfather walked with the elder of the two children perched on the bundle on his back. Ha-sang's head was bent not from the weight of the load he carried but by the strange, dreamlike events in which he had become entangled.

As they proceeded, the leafless, dead branches scratched their faces and hands. September was not yet gone, but in the mountains it was as cold as winter. The fallen leaves rustled in the dried grasses as their eyes followed the long tail of a wolf scurrying by. Everywhere mountain birds twittered. The path was strewn with rocks and half-obscured by fallen leaves, and the young woman stumbled repeatedly, desperately holding onto her paltry belongings, her shins under her ragged skirt already bloody.

They never once questioned the cause that had driven them into this unutterable suffering. It would suffice for them if they could only find a place where they could freely worship their Heavenly Father. Hungry and naked, a sword at their necks, they thanked the Lord for his infinite mercy. Their death in the service of God was their everlasting life, their martyrdom the ultimate grace. The single word that would put an end to their interminable suffering, that awesome, sinful word, they did not dare utter: Apostasy! They trembled in fear, believing that even the mere thought of the word would be like committing a sin from which there is no salvation.

It was an unusually lovely day; there was no wind and the sun began to warm them. They did not know where they had been walking and how far they had come, but the old man knew by his sundial that it was noon. They had come to a small spring that flowed between the cracks of rocks.

"A spring!" Ha-sang shouted.

"Yes!" the younger Sin clapped his hands in joy, as they dropped their loads beside it.

More good luck awaited them. While they were gathering the wild fruits that grew along the rocky cliff near the spring, they discovered a cave. The old man's eyes filled with tears of thanksgiving, for he had been worried about a place to live during the approaching winter.

"God looks after even a bird in the sky . . . ," he breathed.

"It's dry and warm inside the cave," the young men said to each other as they came out of the cave.

"You never know; it may be a tiger's den."

"Never mind, the two of us could kill it."

"And then we could use the skin for our cover when we sleep."

They decided to spend the night there to see if the place was suitable for a permanent settlement. Strangely, the fear and anxiety disappeared from their hearts. Even as night fell, no tiger returned. They built a bonfire outside the cave and roasted the potatoes, eating them piping hot with salted radish. A crescent moon hung in the blue-grey sky drenched with twinkling stars. The red tobacco fire at the tip of the old man's long pipe glowed like pomegranate seeds. In the calm and peace, the night deepened.

The elder Sin emptied the ashes from his pipe beside the bonfire and soon began to recite: "As I look upon the sky each night, I am awestruck with the omniscience and infinite goodness of the Lord. Behold the orderliness of the sky; the sun and moon, day and night, and the position of the numerous stars. Without our Lord-on-High, how is it possible that they should keep unerringly their solemn principle? I am powerless to find adequate words in praise of our Lord."

As he watched the old man uttering these words, Ha-sang's head bent in reverence. He had never before listened to a confession of faith as solemn and sincere as that which came from this old man, bathed in the starry glow, driven by persecution that had reduced him to the destitution of a beggar. Although he was in a hurry, Ha-sang spent two more nights with the family, fearing that the tiger might return to reclaim its lair. Each night they could see the animal's eyes glowing in the dark and hear its roar, but it did not come near the cave.

On the morning of the fourth day, Ha-sang left them. After a rough passage down from the mountains, stumbling on rocks and tearing his clothes on the branches, Ha-sang finally reached a clearing, and a village came into sight. He turned and looked up toward the mountains from which he had just emerged. In the clear sky, thin smoke spread; they had begun to burn the mountains in preparation for the spring planting. Hot tears filling his eyes, Ha-sang recited the prayers: "Lord, have mercy on us. Christ, have mercy on us. Lord . . ." For those he had just left, whom he might never meet again in this life, he prayed with the utmost strength of his faith.

Ha-sang resumed his walk. His destination, Musan, lay far away. September was almost gone and he was still wandering in the mountains of Kangwŏn Province. Knowing nothing about the place and with only a vague direction in mind, he was heading toward Musan. He was not even certain whether the man he wanted to meet there would welcome him. He only knew that ever since he had heard that Cho Tong-sŏm was a man of profound virtue and learning, he had wanted to go where he was said to live.

Ha-sang was determined to seek him out and become his disciple, in both traditional learning and Catholicism. Since childhood, his mother had incessantly instilled in him the importance of an education. However, it was only after he had come back from seeing Tasan in Kangjin that he had felt ashamed and guilty for his lack of learning. Moreover, since he had decided to dedicate his life to rebuilding the fallen church, his thirst for knowledge had become more intense. The persecution had driven most of the scholars from the capital, and no one remaining there dared to teach Catholicism.

Reduced to extreme poverty, Ha-sang managed to survive by working as a servant, but his work merely fed him. He was staying with his maternal cousin, Barbara, who herself lived with a distant relative. The family, devout Christians, set a beautiful example for Barbara and Ha-sang. However, they were also in such extreme poverty that Ha-sang felt a twinge of pain each time he was given a bowl of rice. As for Barbara, her situation was just as pitiful. When she was fifteen, she was married into the Nam family, who were among the earliest converts. Two years after her marriage, her father-in-law and her husband were banished; her father-in-law died in banishment. Her husband, twenty years old at the time of his exile, was not a devout Christian; he was only barely able to offer evening prayers. Using his wife's childlessness as a pretext, he took a concubine in the land of his banishment. (Many years later, after being baptized at the age of forty with the Christian name of Sebastian, he—together with Barbara—became a martyr during the Persecution of 1839.)

Separated from her husband, Barbara led a solitary life. She was not a barren woman: soon after she married she had given birth to a son, who had died immediately. Believing that it was her inability to bear a living child that drove her husband to live in sin, she was always sad.

Left alone, her family driven to the brink of extinction, she had no other place to go but to her brother. But he mistreated her so badly that he had become the talk of the neighbors. Finally, she decided to come to the capital to live with her distant relatives.

A gentle-natured woman, she was always protective of Ha-sang. "How wonderful it would be if that gentleman lived near us," she would often say, ever since Ha-sang told her of his determination to learn. "That gentleman" was the very Cho Tong-sŏm, or Justino, of whom Ha-sang had frequently heard the older Christians speak as a renowned scholar of both Catholicism and traditional learnings. Cho Tong-sŏm was as devout in his faith as he was compassionate in human relationships; his love encompassed all humanity, regardless of their faith. Arrested at the time of the Persecution of 1801, he was the first one to confess his Christian faith during the interrogation; however, owing to his age, sixty, and his impeccable character, he was spared the death penalty and sent into banishment to Musan. As Ha-sang listened to the other Christians speak of him with reverence, his affection and respect grew for this man whom he had never met. Ha-sang was firm in his determination to seek out this venerable scholar and become his disciple.

Barbara soon found out Ha-sang's thought and warned, "You don't know where Musan is and I'm just as ignorant. But I heard them say it's a desolate place in the northernmost part of our country near the big, big river called Tuman'gang. Beyond it they say the Chinese live. It's so very cold that your breath freezes in the air. They say the area is surrounded by mountains with large deposits of iron ore and the wind is full of iron dust." But she was also encouraging. "But even at his age, he went there. You're a strong young man. It would take you only a month to get there. Take care of yourself. Serve him well as you learn under him. I'll send word to your mother about your decision as soon as I can."

In the middle of April, at the age of eighteen, Ha-sang left the capital. He had only six taels of silver which Barbara had earned from her sewing, five taels that Maria had given him from the money she had earned copying the Bible, and two sets of jackets and pants Barbara had made for him with much care. They figured that though Hamgyŏng Province was at the northern end of the country, Ha-sang, a vigorous youth, would reach his destination within a month. The money was inadequate to cover the long journey's expenses, but he would not starve if he hired himself out as a farmhand as he went along. But there was an unexpected drought in rice transplanting season; from the parched rice paddies only dust rose. Even the live-in farmhands idled their days away with nothing to do. No one needed an extra hand. Forced to buy his meals, Ha-sang was becoming desperate as the money dwindled.

Ha-sang's education began even during the journey. The lot of peasants in the countryside was one of abject poverty. The children had no one to look after them. Their stomachs were swollen from malnutrition, and their thin arms and legs hung from their bodies like threads. In the balmy weather, the children roamed naked except for sleeveless vests, a custom that was a blessing to the families who could hardly make ends meet, but one that could also bring calamity. Ha-sang happened to come upon one such disaster. While playing, a boy of about two, everyone's favorite, was stung by a bee on his little penis. He let out a scream as if a knife had been stuck into his throat. When the frightened adults reached the boy, it was too late. "For god's sake, why there, of all places . . ."

"It's a vital spot . . ."

There was much consternation among them.

On another occasion, Ha-sang walked into a house for a drink of water, but there was no sign of anyone inside. "Anyone home?" he called out repeatedly. A single-hinged door opened hesitantly from inside, and a voice called, "No one is here," followed by a chorus of children's laughter. When he looked into the room, he saw a cluster of children's faces peering out from a rag of a coverlet, boys and girls together, all naked. When they saw Ha-sang, in an instant all the faces disappeared into the coverlet. He found out that their mother had taken off the only garments they had on them and had gone to the stream to wash; the children had to remain under the covers until the wash was done.

Another time, he passed a roadside house where the light was still burning in the deep of night. Inside, a few men huddled together. In the decaying thatched roof foul insects swarmed. A man with sunken eyes stood there, his face devoid of any expression. An old man among those who stood around him was saying, "Think it over very carefully. This document will make you a slave. With only this piece of paper, you will have to toil like a beast of burden. I'm telling you, you will work until your bones break, and you'll never see a penny. Do you realize how difficult it would be to free yourself again from service?"

The man answered feebly, as if talking to himself, "Why should I be free? What's the use of being a free man? Military and household taxes and forced labor; that's the lot of a free man. I'm sick to death of being a freeborn commoner. Being a slave is much more tolerable. Life is short. Why suffer? We'll be dead soon enough."

Ha-sang's wisdom deepened as his journey continued.

The rainy season came as Ha-sang entered Kangwŏn Province. For a traveler, it was a deadly inconvenience. In good weather, young Ha-sang had no trouble sleeping under a tree or on top of a rock, anywhere. But in a downpour, he had to seek out an inn, grudgingly using his precious money.

As he traveled, he hired himself out for all kinds of services: a funeral bier-bearer, the carrier of a silk-covered lantern as he ushered a groom in a wedding procession, a cutter of weeds around graves, a slaughterer who wrung the necks of chickens and pigs for banquets, a laborer who moved twenty rice sacks a day in a brewery. All these brought him some cash, but he gained more than money. He observed the people who found themselves at the bottom of society in circumstances of unspeakable poverty and pain, oppressed by tyranny and corrupt government, and above all, their souls in a darkness from which there was no salvation. Ha-sang was so moved to thanksgiving for his religion's creed of equality, love, and salvation that his resolve to dedicate his life to the church only grew stronger.

Although he was most anxious to resume his journey, Ha-sang could move on only after the Harvest Moon Festival in mid-September, for during the harvest season farmhands were needed everywhere. It had been a temporary employment for Ha-sang while he avoided the rainy season, but he had become indispensable on the farm. Grateful for the kindness they extended to him in his need, he felt he owed it to them to stay until the harvest was over. The people of the household for whom Ha-sang worked were loathe to see him go.

Ha-sang had been told that once he came out of the rough passage through the mountain ranges of Kangwŏn Province, the eastern seaboard would not be far away and the road would be smooth going. He had figured he would be out of the mountains in a few days, but he got lost in their depths for a month. Some men gathering wild honey had given him incorrect directions, or else Ha-sang had misunderstood their heavy, unfamiliar dialect as they spoke, pointing at a mountain ridge. It was only after losing his way repeatedly that he finally reached the mud hut belonging to a group of natural-ginseng diggers. They told him that he had been heading in the wrong direction, south instead of north. Every night, the strange sounds of wild beasts surrounded him, and once in broad daylight he even came face-to-face with a tiger which, for some inscrutable reason, did not even cast a glance at Ha-sang, but moved away from him. When he remembered the confrontation, his armpits would sweat. Then, as he continued on his way north, he had an even more nerve-wracking narrow escape from mountain bandits, and the hair-raising experience made him remember what people said: it was more frightening to meet a man in the mountains than a wild beast.

For a few days he subsisted on fruits and plants that grew in the valleys, until he met young Sin cutting firewood. He followed Sin to his mud hut and spent the night with his family. Enjoying their simple hospitality, Ha-sang forgot for a moment the hardship he had endured during his journey. The next day, he helped young Sin carry the heavy loads of tobacco to the marketplace.

The fact that these good people were fugitive Christians surprised him. Driven by persecution, they upheld their faith and courage even in the face of hardships that defied description. Ha-sang's encounter with old Sin and his people only made his wisdom grow. Moreover, since they had lived in the mountains for so long, they were familiar with the directions Ha-sang needed, and with clear instructions from them, he was on his way once again. Before the end of September, he passed Wŏnsan and was hurrying along the road that ran alongside the sea toward the north.

It was the middle of October when Ha-sang finally reached Musan. In the north country winter arrived early; the wind and snow blasted mercilessly. The snow melted as it fell on the iron-rich, dark soil that had not yet frozen deeply. A scattering of flat homes crouched here and there, imparting an air of desolation to this land of banishment. It was not difficult to find the residence of an exiled Catholic scholar from the capital, a house situated on top of a small hill. As he climbed the hill and stood in front of a bush-clover fence, Ha-sang saw—through the bare branches of oak trees below—the river of clear blue-green, its serene current moving with slow majesty. The gate was locked, but there were no guards. Only after Ha-sang had cleared his throat a few times to make his presence known did a boy of about thirteen emerge, covering his bare arms with his sleeves.

"Where are you from?" asked the boy in a northern dialect as he opened the gate.

"I am from the capital. Is the teacher home?" Without waiting for the reply Ha-sang went inside the courtyard and knelt down.

"Teacher, someone is here from the capital," the boy shouted, which prompted a few young men to come out of the room.

"What brought you here?" one of them asked.

"I am here to see the master, Cho."

Hearing capital speech, a sound he had missed, an old man came into the yard even before the announcement of the guest's arrival.

"You came here looking for me? Who are you?" He must have been over seventy, but his voice was as vigorous as that of a young man.

Ha-sang prostrated himself on the ground and bowed. "I am a son of the Chŏng clan of Majae."

"The Chŏng clan of Majae?" As he spoke, his voice as intense as a scream, the old man's eyes pierced Ha-sang's. "A son of Master Chŏng Yak-chong?"

"Yes, he is my father."

The old man hastened toward Ha-sang, grabbed his hands, and raised him. "Oh, oh, how is it possible, the son of illustrious Master Yak-chong is here!" he stammered through his tears.

"I am here to become your disciple." Ha-sang, too, became aware that his eyes were growing hot.

The old man was not listening to what Ha-sang had said. "A son of Master Yak-chong, a son of Master Yak-chong!" he only repeated.

Thus began their life together: an old scholar of seventy-four and his young disciple of eighteen. Cho Tong-sŏm gave his utmost in the effort to teach the son of his departed friend, with whom he had shared everything—hometown, political faction, traditional learning, and, above all, Catholic faith. Perfect harmony existed between the student's burning desire for learning and the scholar's deep dedication to share it, and Ha-sang's progress was nothing less than astounding.

The teacher, who was well-versed in all aspects of Catholicism, paid special attention to Ha-sang's religious education. The theological foundation of Ha-sang's later "Letter to the Prime Minister"—the document of heartwrenching honesty and conviction in defense of his faith that he, Saint Paul, would present to the prime minister just before his martyrdom—had its beginning in this desolate, windswept northern land of banishment.

Justino spoke of the martyred friends who had preceded him. For the first time, Ha-sang learned the circumstances surrounding his father's arrest and martyrdom. Reading extensively all the books on Catholicism that had found their way into Korea from China, Yak-chong interpreted the main ideas of the books written in Chinese, translating them into vernacular Korean so that everyone—including women and the ignorant—could understand. It was the theory of "Three Enemies," which Yak-chong emphasized in his book, A Summary of Catholic Teaching, that the authorities found lawfully condemnable as heretical teaching. Yak-chong asserted that the Three Enemies—worldly ways, flesh, and demons—were the cause of man's fall. Bent on murdering him on any pretext, the authorities lost no time in identifying the idea as heresy and ordering his arrest. They argued first that what Yak-chong meant by worldly ways was the nation, the society, and the family, and determined that what he preached was a beastly way, incompatible with the unassailable Confucian dogma of king over nation and parents over family. Second, they argued that if by flesh was meant one's body, which was given by one's parents, Yak-chong's theory of flesh as enemy was no less an offense than the first. Last, if Yak-chong taught that celibacy was a more perfect state than marriage, that certainly would lead mankind to extinction. They concluded that Yak-chong was a leader of the heretic Catholics who believed in neither loyalty to king nor filial piety to parents, and thus dwelt in a state lower than birds and beasts. Yak-chong, a treasonous criminal, was to be beheaded and his property confiscated. He had already known his fate: the sympathetic King Chŏngjo had died and when King Sunjo had ascended to the throne, the Queen Dowager began to exercise her political power as regent to further her personal vengeance. He moved all his religious books, articles, and letters from Father Chou Wen-mu to a safer place and left the capital for Majae. Cho Tong-sŏm, twenty years his senior and an ardent admirer of his learning and character, followed Yak-chong to Majae and met him at the house of Yak-hyŏn. Although they both knew tragedy was imminent, they indulged in a relaxed conversation, scholarly as well as affectionate, during which Cho imparted his deepest thoughts to Yak-chong.

Cho stood up to leave. Yak-chong also rose, and Cho was stunned as he stood before his friend, bathed in the setting sun's glow and draped in a strange garment Cho had never seen before. His eyes were blinded by the innumerable small crosses twinkling like stars on it. "Go in peace, go in peace." Cho grasped Yak-chong's hands and wept.

Three days later Cho heard that Yak-chong had been arrested. He was told that on January 11, the very day that the Queen Dowager sent out the edict proscribing Catholicism as heresy, Yak-chong had seen an arresting officer on his way to Majae. As he passed the officer, he realized that he must be looking for him. He sent his

servant to inquire, and, if it were indeed so, to tell the officer he
need not go far. "I am the man," Yak-chong said to the officer, who
was open-eyed with amazement.

At the news of Yak-chong's arrest, Justino sank deep into meditation, remembering with pain that though his own life was as precarious as a lamp-flame in a wind, Yak-chong, resigned to his fate, had
gone to his hometown to bid his final farewells to family and friends
and to make arrangements for his family in anticipation of his capture and execution. He also remembered that Yak-hyŏn had been
an indifferent, heartless brother, even though he granted that Yak-
hyŏn had suffered much because of his brothers' religious activities.

The final blow came on January 19. It was the first thaw, the
weather was mild, and people were still in a festive mood after the
full moon holiday. On the other hand, they were strangely agitated
by the ongoing arrests of Catholics, and the court was in deep turmoil. On that day, a warehouse guard on his rounds in search of
illegally slaughtered meat had discovered a suspicious-looking box
hidden under some pine firewood. Instead of illegal meat, he found
strange objects and books inside the box. He immediately arrested
the man carrying the box. A great commotion arose as they examined
its contents: religious books, sacred pictures, a rosary and other
ritual objects, and letters in a strange language written from left to
right. The shocked authorities interrogated the man, and the box
was traced back to Yak-chong. The man confessed that he was a
Christian by the name of Thomas Yim; he told the interrogators that,
having become suspicious of the box, he was on his way to Yak-
chong's house to return it. Occurring only eight days after the edict
had been promulgated, the incident was of the gravest consequence
to the church as well as to the court. After ten days of eerie calm, a
massive manhunt began, and Catholics were rounded up from all
over the nation. Among them was Cho Tong-sŏm.

The old teacher's reminiscences moved not only Ha-sang but all
the young disciples of the land of his banishment, separated by five
hundred miles from the scene where the holy rite of blood had taken
place. They listened with avid ears to their teacher, shedding tears
of righteous indignation.

Justino had many disciples. In this outlying border at the northern tip of the country, people with sons eager for learning sought
out this eminent scholar. A benevolent man, he was touched by

their earnest desire for education and was only too willing to teach them. At first the authorities tried to forbid the "criminal" from accepting students, and the gate was locked, but these youths in their eagerness climbed the fence and came into the house. After trying repeatedly to stop them, the authorities gave up their efforts and overlooked the activities within the gate. Justino taught them traditional learning as well as Catholic doctrine. In this manner, in the remote land, the exile had become an apostle, and the gospel, rooted and nourished, spread in all directions. None could have foreseen that in this forsaken place the unfathomable will of providence would be at work.

Time passed swiftly for Ha-sang. It had been a year since he had left the capital and over half a year since he had arrived in Musan. Spring was almost at an end. Spring in the north was as splendid and short-lived as a dream. Yesterday's barren fields and mountains were suddenly imbued with the vivid pink of azalea and the fences around the houses burst forth with yellow forsythia. The flowers fought with each other in their haste to bloom; unlike the south, where one followed another, here everything bloomed all at once in a tumultuous burst of color, and then suddenly it was all over. Now everything was dark green, and Ha-sang thought that the time had come for him to leave. Thanks to his eminent teacher's pertinacious tutelage and his own assiduousness, he had become a changed man. The foundation for further learning had been solidly laid, and he was now well equipped to pursue higher learning on his own.

"No doubt it must be in his blood," Justino repeatedly told himself, teary-eyed with the love he felt for the youth. His long imprisonment had enabled him to attain the enlightenment that overcame bodily attachment, but he had yet to overcome the attachment of the heart. Knowing Ha-sang's decision to leave, he was pained at how much he would miss him. Justino, who had been leading an ascetic's life, denouncing worldly comfort for paradise in Heaven, had begun accepting honorariums from his disciples since the arrival of Ha-sang. He had known all along the difficulties Ha-sang had endured during the long journey that had begun in early spring and only ended in early winter. Now he wanted to help Ha-sang on his way back to the capital; he wanted to save enough money for his beloved disciple to make his journey in comfort.

Justino's house was situated on top of a hill perched at the edge of a cliff. A zelkova tree stood with its branches spread over the courtyard. Justino loved this spot for the shade the branches gave and for the view of the Tuman River it afforded. One day he was standing under the zelkova tree, tinted with light green leaf-buds, as Ha-sang came by carrying water. Justino beckoned to him, pointing to the river.

"Paul, that river over there is Tuman'gang. Along the river westward is Mount Paektu and further is the Yalu River; some day you will cross it to go to China, you with your magnificent body." Caressing Ha-sang's stout shoulders, he continued, "You must know the way of Providence, know God's reason for endowing you with such extraordinary vigor of body and spirit." He paused for a moment, and looked at Ha-sang with eyes filled with compassion. "When Father Chou Wen-mu died, he prophesied that this nation would be without a shepherd for the next thirty years. Now half of that time has elapsed. We must not remain inactive merely waiting for a miracle. Remember: 'Do your human best and wait for Providence.' You are that harbinger."

"I shall inscribe your words in my heart," came the answer.

"It is urgent that Catholic clergy come to this country and lead our forsaken flocks. They alone can administer the holy sacraments, so that our souls will be given comfort and courage." Wordless for a moment, hesitating at first, then abruptly rushing on, the old man said in one breath, "Leave here immediately."

"Teacher . . ."

"Do not linger, but hurry."

The teacher led Ha-sang briskly into the room. He opened a closet and took out a set of new clothes and a bundle. "Change into these. You are to carry only this bundle. This money is not much but enough to last till you return to the capital. And when you return look for a man called Cho Suk, who lives in Okdong Street at the foot of Mount Pugak. He is a son of my cousin, and his wife is a daughter of the martyr, Kwŏn Il-sin, or Xavier. They are also long-standing friends of your family. They will most certainly welcome you."

The old teacher's deep concern for him filled Ha-sang with gratitude. "Teacher, oh teacher . . ." Weeping, Ha-sang could utter no other words.

With the agility of a young man, the old man set out to prepare for Ha-sang's journey back to the capital, and finally he took off his own horsehair hat from the wall and put it on Ha-sang's head. "That's all. Leave at once."

From nowhere, other disciples had gathered around Ha-sang, expressing their sadness at seeing him go. Everyone presented him with parting gifts, so that Ha-sang had to untie his bundle repeatedly. To the end, Justino did not shed a tear. As Ha-sang rose after making a deep bow, unable to contain the turmoil in his heart, the teacher grasped his hands firmly.

"Goodbye, go in peace, Thomas," he said in a voice trembling with a suppressed sob.

"Thomas?"

Looking at the surprised faces around him, Justino corrected himself in a fluster. "No, no. I meant Paul. Go and do great deeds!"

After Ha-sang left, Justino entered his room and locked the door. Only then did he let the tears flow unchecked.

"Thomas, oh my son, my magnificent son!" he shouted silently. In his mind surfaced vividly the scene of their tragic parting more than ten years ago. A filial son, from the time of his father's arrest and subsequent banishment to Musan, Thomas had been constantly with him, nursing him back from near death caused by torture and the long journey. Such devotion touched the hearts of all the people in the land of exile, and they looked upon the father and son with respect and love. When the old man's health improved and they had become somewhat accustomed to the difficult life in exile, soldiers came from their hometown, Yanggun. The district magistrate, a corrupt bureaucrat who harbored a personal grudge against Justino for some unknown reason, had been displeased with the fact he had been spared the death penalty. He was determined to use any means within his power to punish Justino further. All earlier attempts having failed, the target became Thomas. The soldiers arrested Thomas and brought him to the magistrate.

After subjecting him to torture of the most extreme cruelty, the magistrate asked him, "Do you realize your father's crime?"

Silent until then, Thomas lifted his head and reprimanded the magistrate in a rising voice. "How dare you ask me such a question? Are you blind to man's ethical principle? My father is innocent. It is I, an unfilial son, who have caused what my father is enduring."

Unable to answer this, the magistrate ordered even more severe punishment. Succumbing to the repeated torture, Thomas died early in October of the same year.

Hearing the news of his son's death, Justino closed his eyes and cried out in his heart, "We shall meet again in the Paradise of Eternal Blessings."

Now Justino in his mind's eye saw his son once again. As Thomas was led away, Justino then, as now, silently removed the horsehair hat from the wall and tried to put it on his son's head, but on the "criminal's" head the topknot was already undone, and the unkempt hair fell over his face.

From the day Ha-sang left, Justino was unable to eat anything. His mind overwhelmed, he could not accept any food.

In the meantime, Ha-sang walked with a light heart, his steps effortless. He traveled as swiftly as if a magic spell had been cast on his feet. As he passed through the same mountains of Kangwŏn where he had wandered a year ago, he paused for a moment to turn and gaze upon the mountain ridges. He could not recall the places he had roamed, nor could he see once again the smoke of the slash-and-burn farmers. He turned around and strode ahead even more swiftly than before.

Chapter Seven

◆ ◆ ◆

Pondering

As the nutmeg forest on the slope of the mountains began to come into sight, Tasan could hear the tumultuous music of folk instruments. Even from this distance, he could already feel the village air thick with an eerie intoxication. Although he was still too far away to distinguish the incantation, he knew a shaman rite must be in progress. Tasan grimaced with annoyance. A Sirhak scholar, he considered shamans to be priestesses of a promiscuous cult, who agitated ignorant people. Their audacity in disturbing the gravesite of the noble and distinguished Yun clan made him even more indignant. His brows knitting in displeasure, he walked on at a brisk pace, while the unyielding clamor of the music grew in intensity.

"I hear the shaman is from another territory, and that her incantation and her dancing are matchless. And they say her daughter, though she is so young, is just as good at performing rites."

"Yes, I heard it, too. She is frightfully pretty, they say, too beautiful for a human child."

"Anyhow, such a rite has never been performed in this village before."

"But, just imagine, the family of a great scholar driven to this, to have a shaman rite performed!"

"You are so right. Isn't it their fourth loss? At this rate, the family will soon die out, so I suppose they're willing to do anything, even a shaman rite, if it will help."

Behind him, women exchanged gossip, not daring to overtake a gentleman wearing a horsehair hat and a formal coat. Their chatter continued.

"We are already late. I'm sure they must have finished with the first few steps already."

"They say it's a full twelve-step rite. Are you going to stay to the end?"

"That pretty child-shaman is going to do the 'Princess Piri.' I must stay for it."

"You mean she has not yet put up her hair?"

"Did I hear she is ten or twelve?"

"How can a young girl who has not yet had her coming-of-age ceremony perform a rite?"

"That's what they tell me."

"Strange, indeed, eh?"

Even more deeply annoyed, Tasan slowed his pace. He remembered that when he was a child people would say: "Why have a shaman rite performed in your house when you know you'll have to watch your eldest daughter-in-law make a fool of herself by dancing and enjoying herself in public?"

"Wicked ones, driving those ignorant people into wantonness," Tasan mumbled to himself.

However indignant he was, he could not avoid the place where the rite was being performed, because the person he was coming to see was the very one having the rite performed in his house. Yun Chi-mok, a distant cousin to Tasan on his mother's side, had five outstanding sons. Spread two years apart, they were all equally intelligent and promising. Eight years ago in the autumn, the first tragedy struck the family; the youngest son, nine years old at the time, died suddenly in an absurd accident. He was a handsome boy with a joyous disposition, whose positive nature and studious habits made his parents love him exceedingly. In his mischievous playfulness he had bitten into an unripe persimmon, and bitter though it was, had eaten it. A piece of the fruit had stuck in his throat. In the men's absence, the frantic women gave him sesame oil, thinking it would make the morsel slip down his throat. They did not realize that in such a case salt had to be given, which would have caused the hard fruit to soften; instead, the oil only hardened it and the boy choked to death. Two years later, again in the autumn, the third son had died at fifteen in equally absurd circumstances. He squeezed a pimple which had appeared at the center of his upper lip, causing a high fever; three days later he died. Two more years elapsed, and then the fourth son suddenly began barking like a dog in delirium, and died. The cause of his death was certainly rabies, but he was not known to have gone out of the village, and within it no rabid dog could be found—until after the end of the mourning period, when it was discovered that his puppy had been rabid.

After the loss of three sons, the parents took to their bed as if all their faculties had left them. The father lost interest in everything. The light had gone out of the house and it turned into a dark, dreary place. It was painful to see the white mourning garb of the young daughter-in-law, who had become a widow less than a year after her marriage.

"That poor little thing." The mother-in-law, a white band tightly wound around her head, sobbed in dry-eyed agony.

Time healed the wound, but again, as soon as they were able to swallow a few spoonfuls of food, yet another calamity struck the family. It had happened twelve days before Tasan's arrival. As required of the eldest grandson of the branch family, the father, accompanied by his two remaining sons and bearing sacrificial offerings, visited the ancestral graves near his house. It was a lovely, cloudless day. The sons, wearing their long white coats with azure tasseled sashes around their waists, were tall and handsome. Overcome with a sense of gratitude, the father felt warm tears welling in his eyes. "Yes, I still have two more sons," he thought. Coming down the slope of a mountain path, he was filled with a happiness that he had not experienced for a long time. Slightly intoxicated with the offering wine, his chest swelling with pride, he looked up toward the sky.

Suddenly he became dizzy and stumbled. The eldest son hastily came to his aid and helped him steady himself, saying, "Father, be careful."

That was all. However, that same evening the son developed a high fever and became delirious, and the doctor could not fathom the meaning of his irregular, violent pulses. In her determination to save him, as a last resort, his mother cut off her finger so that she could feed him her own blood. Even that failed, and two days later he expired without ever regaining consciousness. Only when they washed and dressed the body for burial did they discover that his right heel was swollen. No one could have foreseen that a slight cut, too superficial even to bleed, would have been the cause of his death. As the son had come to the aid of his father, he himself had lost his balance and had held onto a rock that harbored the fatal, poisonous germs. He had died of tetanus.

The father again took to his bed, trembling, speechless, beside himself with grief; the mother went into the storage shed and tried to hang herself. A servant who was passing by became suspicious of the half-open door, discovered his mistress, who was barely breathing, and managed to save her life.

Because the calamity had struck so soon after the visit to the graves, all sorts of rumors began spreading. People agreed that they must have angered the spirits of the ancestors and would have to move the gravesite to a more propitious place. The talk among the people went on until everyone concluded that the spirits of their sons, who had died of evil causes, must be comforted by offering prayers to Buddha, the Heavenly King, the God of the Seven Stars, so that the strength of these prayers would enable them to enter paradise. The family must offer the service to myriad household gods; they must propitiate the Ground Spirit of the House, the God of Fertility and Longevity, the God of Health and Spirit, the Trinitarian Spirit, and the God of Smallpox, a guest spirit. In addition, the spirits of bachelor ghosts, and the restless spirits of virgin ghosts—all these demons must be placated so that they would never again come near the house to bring calamity upon the family. For all these, a shaman rite must be performed, and such a rite must not be an ordinary one; they must bring in a famous shaman with miraculous power and hire plenty of male shamans, too. They must let the music stir up the hearts of the people, and not grudge the money or worry about their reputation at a time like this.

Around the father, who was still shaking, and the mother, who had stopped eating and lay like a corpse, gathered the womenfolk of the clan and a sister-in-law of the wife, their faces dark with anxiety. Concerned about the fate of their natal household, the father's aunts, sisters, and married daughters argued with him.

"Listen, nephew. You mustn't stay in bed like this. Come to your senses and try to figure out a way to prevent such a thing from ever happening again," the elderly aunt, wiping her tears away with the tie of her jacket, implored.

Yet he remained wordless.

"Brother, what has come over you?" the sisters chimed in. In spite of their weeping inquiries, he kept a firm silence.

"Oh, father, father!" His married daughter, still childish-looking though her hair was in a chignon, wept.

The newly widowed daughter-in-law came into the room with a bowl of rice gruel for her father-in-law, her mourning clothes paining the onlookers. On her back she carried a baby not yet a year old.

As she put down the tray, the child, stretching out his arms and struggling to get out of his sling, called out, "Grandpa, grandpa . . ."

Suddenly light flashed in the grandfather's vacant eyes, as if the departed soul had returned in him. He snatched the baby from the back of his mother and ran to the inner room where his wife lay like a corpse. He thrust the baby into her arms and embraced the two of them. For the first time since the death of his eldest son, he allowed his cries to burst out unchecked. The house was once again submerged in an ocean of weeping.

Persuaded by three generations of women, he agreed to have the Cleansing Rite, to exorcise evil and to send the souls of the dead to the other world, performed on a grand scale.

For this rite, the shaman Man-nyŏn was invited. Her reputation as the possessor of miraculous powers had spread far and wide, as had the renown of her daughter, Butterfly, who was beginning to stir up the people with her performances. With them all the male shamans of her district were also summoned. The shamans of the district were generous in granting Man-nyŏn permission to perform, even though she lived in a different shaman territory, because of the illustrious reputation of the family and the gravity of their catastrophe.

Scion of a great scholar, Yun Sŏn-do, who had served King Hyo-jong as his tutor, Yun Chi-mok had never had any reason to be ashamed of himself as a scholar-gentleman. However, since the day he had wept with his wife and his fatherless grandson in his arms, he had made up his mind that he would undertake any shameful thing for the sake of his grandson, even a shaman rite of extravagant scale.

Tasan received word late of his unfilial kin's death, a death preceding those of his parents, and he was thus on his way to pay his respects to the bereaved family. Noticing Chi-mok sitting among the womenfolk, Tasan's face became distorted with displeasure. As he had overheard in the women's gossip behind him on his way, the rite was already in the midst of the fourth step, and the "Messenger Ballad" was resounding.

In the inner courtyard under the tent were two sacrificial tables, one for the deceased and the ancestral spirits, and the other for the Messenger Spirit who would take the soul of the dead one to the underworld. Man-nyŏn wore a white outfit set off by a sleeveless vest-like coat of deep blue. A wide, sky-blue sash around her waist was tied in back in the shape of a swallow, and her hair was beautifully wound with a white hair-band. Sitting before the tables, she was singing the "Heavenly King Epic" while sounding the hourglass-shaped drum to the accompaniment of the instruments played by the male shamans.

> Gathering around him a hundred million
> Demons of hell
> Summoning twelve dead souls,
> The Heavenly King asks the deceased:
> "What charitable deeds have you done in your life?
> Have you given water to the thirsty?
> Have you given food to the hungry?
> Have you given clothes to the naked?
> Have you given medicine to the sick?
> Have you built a bridge for the people to cross?"

Man-nyŏn's icy voice reverberated with dignity and menace. Abruptly changing her role to that of the deceased, she went on, trembling in pathos:

> The deceased one in reply says:
> "I was growing in age.
> Springs and autumns had I many.
> I would have lived longer,
> I would have eaten more.
> Many were my wants,
> Few were my possessions,
> Limitless my difficulties,
> Fathomless my destitution.
> I have come without virtue;
> I vow to be virtuous."

Feigned theatrics though they were, her recitations could not help conveying the working of man's mind and fate.

Flesh decays and becomes water,
Bones rot and become loam.
Leaving behind my honorable parents,
Leaving behind my wife and son,
I lie alone on Mount Pungmang
Only cuckoos as my companions.
Wretched is my parents' lot,
Who spend their nights weeping.
Have pity on my parents.
How many days without food?
How can I go, how can I go?
This unfilial son, how can I go?
Forgive me, o, forgive me
My poor little son—
Helter-skelter, immature—
I pity my little son;
If I go now
I shall never see him again.
Don't you fret, wild roses,
When your flowers fall.
Next year in the month of March
You will flower again,
But our lives, once gone,
Are without renewal.

Now Man-nyŏn's chanting was like a sob. Here and there among the listeners rose sounds of sobbing. Weeping herself, she rambled on about the regrets of the departed during his lifetime and his sorrow at his own death. As the father knelt in front of the table for his dead son, his emaciated shoulders trembled.

As Tasan's eyes became hot with tears, he no longer felt contemptuous of Chi-mok. The womenfolk wept and an old woman wailed loudly. Chi-mok's dignified face bore a solemn expression. Feeling stupid for being overcome by the atmosphere, Tasan could not help a peevish smile when Man-nyŏn finished her recitation. He wondered if he had been swept away by such a preposterous emotional stirring because of his fifteen years of banishment, which had rendered him weak in his five faculties, or if he had indeed become a country bumpkin, living buried in a barren land, out of touch with the realm of higher values.

He shook his head. Silently he pondered: "Where did this simple, pure empathy come from? Birth and death are the only absolute bonds men share with each other; did I come to accept another's death as my own? Or do I believe in our foundation myth that the son of the Heavenly King, Hwanung, was united with a she-bear who bore him a son, Tan'gun, the first ruler of Korea? After that time, these primitive people were ruled by the shamanistic tradition of religion and state integration; the collective unconscious of the people nurtured in the womb of a shamanistic myth had now become the national soul. Hwanung, Ch'ach'aung, Chayun, the names of the rulers of our forefathers in our early history, strongly connote shaman origins. Does this mean that in the beginning, the one who officiated at the rites to Heaven also ruled the people?"

Although Tasan dismissed these thoughts as improbable, he could not deny the myth surrounding his country's nationhood. Seized with a strange sensation, he followed Chi-mok and the shaman into the inner room whence the rite was now being moved.

The arrangement of the inner room caused Tasan a peculiar shiver. In the corner of the room reserved for the place of honor was a rolled straw mat, tied in three places, containing the clothes worn by the deceased in his life. On top of it lay a white paper cutout in the form of a man. White paper tassels hung from it, symbolizing the soul of the deceased. In front of it were three ritual tables—the middle one for the deceased, the left one for the ancestors, and the right one for the Guardian God. In front of the table for the dead one was a small wicker box containing a complete outfit for him and his "soul," a large wooden bowl of rice, a roll of rice-paper, incense, and sacrificial burning paper. On the table were two bowls of sacrificial rice, a dish of steamed rice cakes, a bowl of clear water flanked by wine cups, and a pile of rice spread over white paper in which lighted candles were stuck. Beside these stood a selection of sacrificial foods—persimmons, pears, jujubes, chestnuts, and fish. The other two tables were smaller in scale but similarly arranged. In the hall outside the inner room was yet another table, laid to feed the myriad minor demons. Here, the air was thick with uncanny terror, as if the demons swarmed around it.

Man-nyŏn placed an outfit of the dead one in front of the tables in the inner room, exactly the way it had been worn in his lifetime; even the socks and shoes were in their exact places. On the front panel of the jacket and around the waist as well as inside the tie of the jacket, Man-nyŏn placed coins for the traveler on his journey to the netherworld. Over the clothes, she put a wicker box containing a bolt of cotton; she threw some more coins on the box and placed two swords on top of it. Finally, she placed on the very top the rolled straw mat that contained the "soul." Man-nyŏn then ordered the family members to make three ceremonial bows and to sit in front of the tables.

Tasan was once again irritated at having to witness such a weird and absurd scene. As if bewitched, the man of the house, a renowned person, sat down as ordered by the shaman. The sight of him standing up, kneeling down, and bowing at the behest of the shaman was so repugnant to Tasan that he wanted to leave the room, but he did not dare cut through the crowd. He had no choice but to remain, his brows tightly knitted.

Now the most important step of the rite was unfolding. Accompanied by the incantation to Princess Piri, who in mythology was said to be the ancestor of all shamans, the soul of the deceased was about to be sent off to the other world. Many shaman incantations were retellings of familiar legends and myths. While listening to them, the family members and spectators, moved by the stories, became one with the shaman and prayed for the soul of the dead to enter the paradise of Nirvana. "Princess Piri" was one of the most representative of such shaman incantations.

Sitting in front of the sacrificial tables, Man-nyŏn held a spoon in her left hand and a drumstick in her right. Age had not diminished her beauty. At thirty-eight, Man-nyŏn still had the capacity to dazzle; the white headband on her lacquer-black hair set off her intelligent eyes, and the white and blue of her costume complemented her still flawless complexion. Lifting her right hand, she struck the drum once. In that instant, flashes of vibrant colors rushed into the room and settled in front of her like a rare, gorgeous butterfly floating down from midair.

"Look, look! It's Butterfly, Butterfly!" A commotion rose among the spectators, but soon complete silence reigned.

Again Man-nyŏn struck the drum just once. With the sound of bells came a voice of otherworldly loveliness. Shaking small bells, Butterfly began the Princess Piri song. It was like the song of beautiful birds, or the mellifluous, soft breeze. A voice that defied all description flowed on like running water:

Time is like the flow of a river;
In its heartless passage,
We are blown away in raging wind.
Now His Majesty's auspicious marriage
Is in its third year
New indications appear in Her Majesty.
She has lost her taste for her royal meals
Heavenly fragrances become
No better than the smell of common grass.
Even the soft breezes of the west window
And the east window displease her.

The child-shaman, Butterfly, wore the full regalia of a shaman: a rainbow-colored skirt, a long robe of fine silk over it, and a headdress on her upswept hair. As she chanted this epic song, designed for a memorial service dedicated to the soul of an unmarried son or daughter, the uncanny beauty of her exquisitely made-up face, unlike anything of this world, caused icy tremors to pass through the spectators' spines. Kneeling behind Man-nyŏn, they were spellbound.

The "Princess Piri," an epic describing a legendary princess, was long and difficult, taking more than an hour to perform and requiring an especially sharp memory. Butterfly presented it flawlessly with not a word left out; her intelligence as well as her art touched the spectators.

"Indeed, indeed! She must be the reincarnation of Princess Piri herself."

"Surely the dead one must already be in the paradise of Nirvana."

"Well, didn't the Princess herself send him off to the other world?"

Princess Piri, whose name means "one who was abandoned," was the child of Prince Ubi. Her father had married against the advice of a shaman, and begot six girls. Angered at having only daughters, he had abandoned the seventh, Princess Piri, when she was born. As a punishment, the parents were made critically ill. They sought a shaman for divination, who advised them to look for Princess Piri and have her go out to find the sacred water of eternal life. The princess, in the meantime, had been reared by the Mountain God. The parents, learning of their daughter's whereabouts, sent messengers who brought her home. Reunited with her parents, she set out on a seven-hundred-fifty mile journey to the netherworld to find the sacred water. Once there, she married Monk Mujang and bore him three sons; afterward, she returned with the sacred water. The parents were restored to health, and Princess Piri became the Goddess of Mansin Sinju, the Goddess of Ten Thousand Gods.

Butterfly sang this legend particularly well. Accompanying her along with the male shamans, Man-nyŏn, as always, became tearful. When Butterfly stopped to catch her breath, the musicians with their various instruments solemnly gave her their thoughtful accompaniment. Their eyes fixed on the forlorn beauty of the child, they wondered if her own fate might have been not so very different from that of the princess. Everyone knew the tragic circumstances of her life. Knowing neither her parents nor who she was, Butterfly was totally without memory. She could not even remember her name, her age, or where she came from; she had only remembered one word, "butterfly." The princess of the legend found her parents, but such a thing was not possible for Butterfly.

She had become the only light in Man-nyŏn's desolate life since the day five years ago when the arrival of her husband's concubine had reminded her that she was barren, and so useless as a woman. Man-nyŏn was in the grip of torment, above all questioning her ability to communicate with the gods. Although her reputation as a shaman, her skill and beauty, had made her the provider of the people's emotional well-being, she had been unable to free herself from feelings of despair and vacillation. The appearance of Butterfly had been a miracle and a deliverance for Man-nyŏn. A child from nowhere and utterly without memory, with a dreamlike loveliness and the sad circumstances shrouding her arrival, could only be of divine origin. Man-nyŏn did not doubt that the child was a gift from the Goddess of Ten Thousand Lights, her spirit-daughter, a true shaman. She needed to believe this.

Soon after her appearance, Butterfly began to talk in the lovely tones of standard, capital speech, but she was still completely without memory. As the years went by, she began to show unusual intelligence. Man-nyŏn loved Butterfly with an intensity that exceeded the limits of common sense. With an equal ardor, Man-nyŏn trained her in the techniques of shaman ritual, and in this manner Butterfly, even before she was old enough to wear a white headband, began

to perform shaman songs. Only married shamans were allowed to
wear headbands, and only after their marriage could they perform.
Marriage was more than a convention for them; it signified their
initiation as a shaman. Butterfly's performing the rite without her
headband was therefore a breach of shaman laws. However, no one
blamed Man-nyŏn for letting Butterfly perform, for they believed
that her appearance was miraculous, and the virgin-shaman's reputation spread as one whose rite was divinely inspired. She was often
invited to perform in other territories as a full-fledged shaman.

Listening to Butterfly's chant, Tasan gave up the thought of leaving; the young shaman touched him with the pathos of her beauty
and with her unfathomable intelligence. "A person of low class;
wherefore such nobility?" he mused.

Among the spectators was the aunt of the dead boy, Mistress Sin,
the wife of the Overseer of the Local Agency in Imsil, who had
come as soon as she heard that the boy's mother had attempted to
hang herself. Although deeply disturbed by the behavior of her only
sister-in-law, at the first glimpse of the virgin-shaman, Butterfly, she
was frozen with astonishment. Butterfly's resemblance to her own
daughter was too extraordinary. Her daughter, Kung-nim, had been
given to her by the Seven Stars Buddha as the result of her prayer
at Kwanch'ok Temple five years ago. The memory of the experience
was still clearly engraved on her heart. She had found the crying
child on the mountain path as she returned home after ten days of
prayer in the temple. For a few days, the child did not stop crying;
then she disclosed that she was four years old. Mistress Sin was
reluctant to learn the name of the little one, but she was told that
the child's family name was Kwŏn and her given name Kug-a. The
only consolation was that the child could not tell where she had
lived.

"Kug-a, Kug-a? What a curious and rare name!" To this the child
added, "They also called me Juliette."

"Juliette? What kind of a name is that?" The mother said in a firm
voice, "From now on, your name is Kung-nim. It's a good name,
isn't it?"

The youngest of three sisters, she had been a docile, sweet-tempered child since infancy, but she did not fail to keep deeply hidden
in her bosom the fact that her real name was Kug-a, not Kung-nim.
After her arrival, the household was filled with harmony and peace.

"Blessed child. It's her karma." The mother's love only increased as the time went by.

The following year, Kung-nim was taught vernacular writing, but more than studying she liked to mimic her mother as she cut and mended clothes.

"She is a little woman all right. For those of us in the inner room, real happiness is in having many children, keeping the family love going, and being a good cook and seamstress."

The mother did not bring Kung-nim to the shaman rite that day, for she did not want to bring her daughter, as precious as a jewel in her palm, to a house of mourning, even a close relative's. When she saw the gourd-shaped jade bottle fastened to Butterfly's sash, the woman once again felt that her decision not to bring her daughter had been absolutely right. Her heart began pounding so loudly that she feared others might have heard it. The tremor did not stop until she reached home and saw her daughter's face.

The rite was to go on all through the night. Each step of the twelve that composed the whole rite had its climax, preventing the long rite from becoming tedious or boring for the spectators. However, Tasan was close to sixty and tired from the long journey from Kangjin; the rite had exhausted him. He slipped away from the still-festive clamor and headed toward his maternal cousin's house, situated on the foot of Mount Togŭm. In the daylight, the magnificent nutmeg forest was visible behind the house, but the night was lacquer-black. A scythe-shaped sliver of a moon hung in a sky saturated with resplendent stars. The incessant chirping of insects in the grass made Tasan aware of the nearness of autumn.

The light was still on in the servants' quarters. The house was quiet, as most of them had gone to watch the rite. Tasan shook the gate-knob a few times, and finally the bent figure of an old slave came out and welcomed him.

"How did you find your way on such a dark night as this? The master is already asleep, so you must wait until tomorrow to see him. Please, come this way. I have already warmed the room."

Because of the mourning in the branch-family, for two weeks almost every household in this village of the Yun clan had several house guests. The slave led him to separate guest quarters. The property had been given by King Hyojong to Yun Sŏn-do, the king's teacher, one hundred years ago. The house had been built on ninety-nine *kan*,[1] one *kan* less than the hundred allowed for those other than royalty. An imposing structure, the property contained an ancestor-tablet hall, an inner wing, an outer wing, servants' quarters, a storage shed, a separate house in the rear, and a mill. In the outer wing were main and auxiliary guest rooms, a library, a medicine room, a storage room, and a hall. In the garden in autumn, from the old gingko tree whose trunk's circumference exceeded an armspan, would fall a shower of leaves like streaks of rain; for this reason the house was named the Pavilion of Green Rain.

Ever since Tasan had first arrived here in banishment, he had frequented his cousin's house, even though no one welcomed him, fearing him as a treasonous heretic. The temptation of the ancient paintings handed down from generation to generation, and the great collections of rare books and old documents, was more powerful than the humiliation he suffered, and Tasan could not help visiting the house often.

Tasan lay on the bedding the old slave had arranged for him and closed his eyes. As weary as he was, sleep did not come soon. Everything was pitch dark, even the interior of his mind, with only the sound of insects disturbing the calm. Eventually, in his mind's eye rose a vivid image of the shaman rite he had just seen, and once again he could hear the shaman song. The images of elegant Man-nyŏn and the ethereal beauty of the virgin-shaman swept into his vision, fluttered there for a while, and disappeared. Then he saw the fresh-hewn bamboo reaching to the roof, with two lengths of cotton cloth hanging from it and seven knots tied in each, but on the cloth he evoked in his mind there were many more knots. Once again, he heard the lovely, haunting singsong voice of the child-shaman. Dancing and floating like a butterfly, she sang while loosening each knot, but the knots in his heart remained tied tightly, unresolved. His closed eyes filled with tears, a soundless cry breaking in him, "Brother!"

Of all his brothers, Tasan had been closest to Yak-chŏn since childhood. After passing his civil service examination, Yak-chŏn had become a high-ranking bureaucrat with a promising future, a holder of fifth degree rank in the Ministry of Military Affairs. However, implicated in the Hwang Sa-yŏng Silk Letter incident, he had been

1. A *kan* is approximately eighteen square meters.

exiled to Hŭksan Island for fifteen years, where he eventually died without ever having seen freedom again. Tasan revered this brother as his teacher and corresponded with him on scholarly matters. Instead of lamenting their fate, they stimulated each other's research and continued to support one another even in their banishment; they were not only brothers but respected colleagues in their scholarly pursuits.

The news of Yak-chŏn's death had reached Tasan while he was visiting Taehŭng Temple. At the time, Tasan had been with his friend Monk Ch'ŏui in Ch'ŏui's cottage, nestled in the ravine below Mount Turyun some distance away from the temple. Ch'ŏui was thirty, fifteen years younger than Tasan. Unlike Hyejang, he was graceful and neat in his manner, and for one so young he was already an enlightened monk. He had worked hard to revive the tradition and art of tea, which had disappeared from Korea long ago. Behind his cottage was a thick bamboo forest, and in his garden he grew vegetables, fruits, and flowering trees. Drawing water from the stream, he would brew his tea.

Enjoying the refined pursuit of tea-drinking, Ch'ŏui spent his days in serene diversions. In his book *In Praise of Korean Tea*, he wrote:

> Bright moon as my candle and companion
> White cloud as my cushion and screen
> Clear in mind and in body
> I welcome them both as my precious guests.
> No enchanted abode of a Taoist monk
> Could ever compare with this.

He studied the Confucian classics and poetry under Tasan, who loved his gentle disposition and his desire for learning. Above all, Tasan cherished Ch'ŏui's elegant pastime, the Way of Tea. Ch'ŏui served Tasan as teacher with as deep a devotion as Hyejang had in his lifetime. Ch'ŏui wrote: "Tea in general tastes best when brewed with tea-leaf buds harvested exactly on the "Day of the Grain Rains"; within three days, it tastes second best, and three days before, it is the least satisfactory. However, Korean tea in particular is at its best three days after the holiday."

Each spring exactly three days after the "Day of the Grain Rains," Ch'ŏui picked the tea-leaf buds and sent the fragrant tea to Tasan with an invitation to attend the tea ceremony in his cottage. Tasan could not have wished for anything more than this invitation. A man who so loved tea could not miss the opportunity to share the joy of tea-drinking with Ch'oŭi, a master enlightened in the Way of Tea. In the sweet breeze of early summer, drinking to wash away his worldly soil was indeed a visit to the realm of the immortals, a luxury beyond his circumstances. However, that year Tasan had missed the season because of arthritic pain in his knees, which prevented him from visiting Ch'oŭi. It was only in the summer that he could once again visit his friend. At the unexpected pleasure, Ch'oŭi was overwhelmed with joy. He offered a meal prepared only with the wild vegetables that grew abundantly on Mount Turyun, which were as good as any medicinal herbs; local seaweed, which was celebrated for its flavor; and tea to accompany the meal. Indeed, it was a repast fit for immortals. Ch'oŭi wrote extensively on all matters concerning tea, especially Korean tea: how to make a good brew and to appraise its quality, how to judge the temperature of the fire when brewing it, how to boil the water for tea, and how to put the leaves in the kettle. He also described the secret way of preserving the true values of tea: sweetness, flavor, and energy. Tea served by such a man, Tasan felt, could overcome all his illnesses.

The news of his brother's death reached him at just such a moment. It pained him unbearably, devastating him as if the heavens had fallen. For a long while, he remained totally numb, then burst into uncontrollable, unashamed wailing. Knowing well that Buddhists never keen, he continued to weep loudly in the presence of Ch'oŭi; nothing mattered now—not the dignity of his advanced age, or his renown, or his circumstances. Exhausted from such powerful emotion and weeping, he plunged himself into indiscriminate wine drinking, and when he awoke from the stupor of violent drunkenness, he continued to weep. Only after a few days of repeating this routine did he finally become sober again.

"How were the formalities of my brother's mourning handled?" Tasan asked the youth who had come from Hŭksan Island with the news, and who still remained with him.

"Everyone on the island took turns carrying the funeral bier. As he had been such a good person, there was no lack of keening; everyone cried loudly. We buried him on the sunny side of the

mountain slope." The gentle, simple youth described bit by bit the
scenes of his brother's funeral.

"Woe is this wretched brother of yours! I could not even arrange
your funeral service. I am a sinner; yes I have sinned." Beating the
bare floor, once again Tasan succumbed to a fit of weeping.

When Tasan heard that the people of the island had buried his
brother with respect, he was somewhat comforted. "Yes, indeed, he
was such a man. I heard that when he was transferred to another
island, people there wept to see him go." The image of his generous
and benevolent brother surfaced in his mind as he tearfully remembered. "In prison, too, the jailers who had beaten him mercilessly
wept when he left. Of whom else could one hear such a story? That
is the kind of man my brother was."

He rambled on to this simple, ignorant boy who had come from
the remote island of banishment, as forsaken as those places where
Buddhist monks retreated when they renounced the one hundred
eight torments of this world.

"King Chŏngjo, when he was alive, told us, 'Although they share
intelligence, the virtue of the elder is far superior to the younger.'
He was a sage king, and his insight was just as deep. My brother
was indeed a vessel of unparalleled virtue, and his scholarship and
knowledge were just as extensive." Tasan went on, "He was never
like me—I am a driven man. Although he did not leave many writings behind him, I could never come near his virtue. The world will
never again see a man like him."

Yak-chŏn, though not as prolific as Tasan, left behind him a monumental book entitled *Registry of Hŭksan Fish*, an encyclopedic document that recorded each species of fish found in the sea around
the island. He wrote the book, a task in which no one had ever
become interested, in the loneliness of his banished life. The nobility and pain of this undertaking touched Tasan. The book could
have never been written had it not been for Yak-chŏn's love for the
poor people of the fishing village and his determination that, though
forsaken by the world, he must do what he could even under the
most trying circumstances. It must have been a toil of supreme willpower and brutal hard work. In his deep sadness, Tasan bowed his
head in reverence.

The rainy season had just begun, and after the youth left, Tasan—suffering from a high fever and the pain of arthritis—had to

remain for a few more days in Ch'oŭi's cottage while his host nursed him.

Now, in his cousin's house, listening to the stirring of the insects outside, Tasan found himself plunged into sorrow anew. In his mind's eye, he still saw the shaman bamboo pole with its innumerable knots, each signifying an ordeal one encountered in life. The pain he endured—the loss of his brother, loneliness, regrets—all those knots in his heart still remained tightly tied. No famous shaman with her dancing and singing could untie them.

He spent a sleepless night, and early in the morning he rushed to prepare for his leave-taking. Although the breakfast table was brought in adorned with his favorite nutmeg cake, he touched neither the breakfast nor the cake he so loved. Tasan was on his journey back home.

◆　◆　◆

"All things are the product of the elements of darkness and light, the yin-yang forces, which are named in accordance with physical phenomena. The principle that causes the clouds to shade the sun is called yin, and that which causes the sun to shine is called yang. These forces, which we consider to be the parents of all creatures, are vague and amorphous, without substance or form; they are metaphysical forces."

Tasan's voice as he lectured was always tinged with hoarseness, as rich, grave voices when suppressed tend to become. His sonorous voice could reach the islands beyond the sea if he so wished, but he preferred to lower it as he imparted his knowledge to the mere eighteen disciples. The topic of the lecture that day was his interpretation of the yin-yang theory, which he had perfected in his book, *On the Doctrine of the Mean*.

Tasan spoke in a soft, easy manner. However, the theory he was advancing was revolutionary in a society that had been dominated for the past three hundred years by the Neo-Confucian School of Nature and Principle. He was critical of the then-current philosophical reasoning advanced by the school, which maintained that all principles are contained in the Great Ultimate. Tasan insisted on the need to base theory on practical experiment instead of merely following an abstract argument that, separated from practical reality, tended to become abstruse and unintelligible. He suggested that

the basic concepts of the School of Nature and Principle, such as
Principle, Material Forces, or the Great Ultimate, were all ill-de-
fined. Further, he was deeply troubled by the fact that the semantic
debate spurred by this school of thought was deteriorating because
of its exploitation by factions struggling in the political arena. Tasan
did not subscribe to the Neo-Confucian belief that Principle could
be found in the phenomena of the material world of yin-yang, nor
did he believe that there was a principle that linked the material
and spiritual world. To him, Principle was an attribute of the material world; therefore, even the Great Ultimate was an expression of
material phenomena. He believed that above the Great Ultimate
was a personified god, Lord-on-High, who transcended impersonal
Material Forces. Tasan based his theory on the Confucian concept
of the Lord-on-High and on the Mandate of Heaven as revealed in
the classics, namely, *The Book of Odes* and *The Book of History*.

Though in agreement with the yin-yang theory that sought to
explain the origin of all things in the universe as happening not by
accident or mystery but through the operation of strict law, Tasan
attempted to explain the phenomena of the universe not by referring
to the interaction of the Principle and Material Forces but by observing concrete phenomena in the visible world. Rejecting the Chu
Hsi ontology based on the yin-yang theory, Tasan followed the eminent Korean Neo-Confucian scholar Yulgok, who believed in the
priority of Material Forces over Principle. Tasan believed that
everything in the universe was simply a matter of natural phenomena.

Tasan continued his lecture: "*The Book of Odes* is a collection
of some three hundred poems from various feudal states of early
Chou times, used by the aristocracy in their sacrificial ceremonies,
or at banquets, or in praise of the virtue of the mandate of Heaven.
It records that 'Heaven gave birth to the multitude of people; they
have bodies, they have moral rules. The people hold onto these
norms through the love of that beautiful virtue. Heaven looked
down upon the domain of Chou and brightly approached the world
below; it protected this Son of Heaven.' *The Book of History* shows
us that the sage King Yao became ruler through the mandate of
Heaven for his virtue, wisdom, and humility. The Lord-on-High,
who as the creator of all things not only presides over good and evil
and rules over the universe but also gives the mandate to rule. The

one so chosen is called the Son of Heaven. True Confucianism must look back to Confucius and Mencius in their original state, which teaches us that man's ultimate objective in life is enlightenment based on the Will of Heaven.

"In *The Analects*, Confucius said, 'He who sins against Heaven has none to whom he can pray.' He also said 'I wish I could do without speaking.' 'If you did not speak, Sir,' said Tzu Kung, 'what should we disciples pass on to others?' 'What speech has Heaven? The four seasons run their courses and all things flourish, yet what speech has Heaven?' said the Master. When his most worthy disciple, Yen Hui, died, the Master exclaimed, 'Alas, Heaven has destroyed me! Heaven has destroyed me!' Confucius meant that over what Heaven wills man has no power. He repeatedly mentioned the sage-emperors Yao and Shun and Duke Chou, because he looked to antiquity for models of morally superior men."

Interrupting himself, Tasan sighed. He had developed this habit after the death of Yak-chŏn. Now he had little urge or strength to continue writing. By the previous spring, he had finished twelve volumes on the rites of music; now he was barely able to write an inscription for Yak-chŏn's tombstone. This was Tasan's first lecture in the two months since the mourning in the Yun clan in June. His cottage was hardly large enough to accommodate eighteen students. These sons of provincial district officials listened to Tasan's lectures without their own desks, because the room was so small. Also new were the frequent dry coughs that interrupted Tasan's discourse.

After the coughing subsided, he continued: "Confucius said that he understood the will of Heaven at the age of fifty. What could he have meant by it? Perhaps we can divide his life into two phases, before and after fifty. He devoted himself to self-cultivation and learning the Way until he reached fifty. After that, he devoted himself to governing the people and practicing the Way. To Confucius, Heaven is purposeful and is the master of all things. He repeatedly referred to the mandate, will, or order of Heaven. I interpret it to mean that the Supreme Being not only reigns but also operates moral law, the Way according to which civilization should develop and men should behave. Are you with me?"

Tasan paused, and looked at his followers. Their faces taut with seriousness, all were silent, not daring to make any comment. Tasan felt a slight disappointment. He had chosen his nephew, Hak-ch'o, a son of Yak-chŏn, to be his intellectual and spiritual heir, but the young man had died prematurely. Tasan wondered who would inherit the knowledge he had so painstakingly acquired, who would propagate it in later generations. Because Tasan hoped for "sons superior to their father" and "disciples greater than their teacher," he could not help feeling a certain disillusionment in his sons as well as in his disciples, even though they were scholars of considerable accomplishment and among his eighteen disciples were some who were able to help him in his many writings on the *I Ching*. Yun Chong-sim, for instance, helped him to compile his book, *The Records of Taedun Temple*. His love for his disciples was as great as his expectations of them. Was it because of his fifteen years of secluded life away from the mainstream of scholarship, with only himself as the standard? He often wondered. The disciples were mostly his maternal relatives of the Yun clan; three others were from the Chŏng clan, and five from the Yi. Among them was a son of the martyr, Yun Chi-ch'ung, who, as the son of a treasonous criminal, had nowhere to go. Even in his family genealogical document, Yun Chi-ch'ung's name was written in vermilion, indicating that he was regarded as a criminal. In spite of his own adverse circumstances, Tasan pitied this son and looked after him.

"Confucius believed in a moral order and in the perfectibility of man's virtue," Tasan continued. "Acting in accordance with the will of Heaven is equal to love of mankind. Man's innate goodness is the energy that moves mankind."

Tasan was seized with another coughing fit. As he was about to continue, he noticed the anxious expressions on the faces of his disciples.

"I rambled on for too long," he added haltingly, shutting his book.

Deeply concerned about his teacher's health, Chong-sim mused, "He is beginning to resemble the portrait of my ancestor Yun Tu-sŏ."

Twice a year in the spring and fall, the library of the Yun clan was aired and inventoried. It contained more than ten thousand volumes, old documents, and heirloom paintings. Since childhood, Chong-sim had always helped in the project, and as he handled each diary, letter, document, or poem of his forefathers, he was filled with pride and curiosity. What interested him most were the paintings of Kongje—a pen name for Yun Tu-sŏ—who was considered one of three artistic giants of the Yi dynasty. At a time when artistic expression was regarded as the lowest skill, this artist, a high-born man, painted portraits and animals; it was not literati landscape paintings that fascinated him. Chong-sim enjoyed scrutinizing Kongje's self-portrait. He knew that the convention of the time was for a portrait to be a perfectly faithful reproduction, even to the last detail, so he had no doubt that it was indeed a true representation of the artist's appearance. The broad expanse of his face, the large, deep-set eyes, the prominent nose, the small, gently closed lips surrounded by a thick beard, all gave an impression strikingly similar to the features of Tasan.

"Amazing! His likeness appears on the face of his maternal descendant more than one hundred years later," Chong-sim overheard people say in awe, looking at the portrait. He felt a thrill of joy and pride at the thought that he shared the same blood with the teacher he adored and respected.

"I am closing the lecture for the day. Tomorrow, I begin the commentaries on *The Analects*. Be well prepared," Tasan said softly, and leaned on his desk.

The disciples left him, each bowing deferentially before leaving the hall. As the sliding door opened, the fragrance of tea blossoms seeped gently into the room. The perfumed scent of autumn flowers enveloped the mountains, and spread toward the cloudless blue sky.

"Ah, someone is here," said the first student to leave in a surprised voice. "Where are you from?"

Looking at the stranger, Chong-sim too stood puzzled for a while, then with sudden recognition he shouted.

"It's you! When did you get here?" He ran out in his stockinged feet and grabbed Ha-sang's hands.

"I was listening to the lecture all the time," Ha-sang said, smiling softly. He was no longer in the guise of a commoner, but wore a wide-brimmed horsehair hat and a formal coat. Tall and muscular, his gaitered legs were like small pillars.

Impressed by Ha-sang's gentlemanly appearance, Chong-sim called to his teacher, "Your nephew is here from the capital!"

As Tasan emerged from the room, Ha-sang knelt on the ground and bowed. As he raised his head, Tasan let out a moan.

"Ah . . . so you are here."

Instead of leading Ha-sang inside, Tasan himself came into the courtyard. The late afternoon September sun was soft and clear, the gentle breeze enhancing the fragrance of the tea blossoms, as if the scent came from both the flowers and the freshness of the youth.

"You have grown." Tasan's words were like a caress. "When did you get here?"

"I was listening to your lecture from the beginning."

"My lecture? Hm . . ." Recalling Ha-sang's words five years ago—"an illiterate"—a smile escaped his lips.

"But listening to you," Ha-sang went on, "I felt as if I were listening to a lecture on Catholicism. The only differences are that the Confucian idea of Heaven is from man's standpoint, and that although Confucius recognized the Lord-on-High as the creator of all things, he limited his view to this world and failed to visualize the afterlife in eternity."

Tasan was speechless with amazement. "You?" he finally uttered, looking at Ha-sang.

"I am presumptuous enough to ask this of you—from now on I want to seek learning from you."

The more he looked at Ha-sang, the stronger grew the affection he felt for his nephew. For the first time since the death of Yak-chŏn, he was released from pain.

"It has been a long time since I saw you last. Is it five years? What have you been doing all these years?" His query was genuinely warm and full of concern.

"I lived mainly in the capital, but I also traveled all through the provinces. And I stayed in Musan for a while."

"You mean Musan in Hamgyŏng Province?"

"Yes."

"Why there? The place is as far as China."

"Yes, it's on the border separating Korea from China. Master Justino lives there in exile."

"Justino?"

"Master Cho Tong-sŏm from Yanggun."

"Ah, him."

"Do you remember? I heard our family is his close acquaintance."

"Of course, we share the same political faction, and . . . ," Tasan swallowed the rest of the words, "the same faith." It had been a long time since he had let the word "faith" surface in his consciousness, let alone utter it. Since the Persecution of 1801, he had obliterated the word from his vocabulary. "Is he in good health? He must be close to eighty."

"He just turned seventy-seven."

"How is he faring?"

"He strives to be a good Christian, first of all. In the land of his banishment he is unafraid of the authorities. Though he is advanced in age, his discipline in the ideal of 'deny the body and overcome the self' is complete. He never misses morning and evening prayers, in addition to his strict observances of fasting and abstinence. He teaches traditional learning as well as Catholicism to his disciples."

"Disciples?"

"Even in the land of exile, people want to learn."

"They let him teach, then?"

"In the beginning, I heard, they made trouble. They locked the gate to his house, but the students climbed over the fence. Now they overlook what he does in the house."

"You, too, are his disciple, I presume." Tasan sighed softly.

"Yes. For a long time, I heard others talk about him. Until I was almost nineteen, my circumstances did not allow me to pursue learning; I was barely able to write my own name. But as I told you when I came last time, I felt a calling, though it may sound preposterous, to go to Peking and bring back a Catholic clergyman. I am determined to bring the fallen church back to its original path."

On Tasan's forehead appeared an imperceptible frown and he turned his head sideways. He let his listless gaze rest upon a tea plant. In the soft breeze the flowers trembled, diffusing their fragrance into the air. Tasan avoided looking at those pristine flowers, for their purity affected him in a strange way.

Ha-sang continued. "How could I hope to follow the urging I felt in me, if I remained ignorant? Providence endowed me with health, and Holy Mary and all the saints looked after me on my journey to Musan, a long and arduous one which I undertook with few resources."

These expressions of the faith, which Tasan had not heard for a long time, slashed at his ears. Frowning even more deeply, Tasan was seized with a strange sensation: he did not know whether it was anger, fear, or shame.

To his silent uncle, Ha-sang went on. "I was with Master Justino for almost a year. He opened my eyes, which had been blind. His teaching awakened this clumsy, ignorant mind to enlightenment."

There was nothing Tasan could say.

"He told me about my father's martyrdom, his love for his God as well as for his fellow men. Though I wanted to stay with him forever, serving him as my own father, the Church needs me, unworthy as I am. I am so strong, and with these legs, powerful as those of base laborers, I'm perfectly suited for messenger service. I run errands better than anyone else can. I am willing to do anything that the Holy Church asks of me. I would gladly undertake any labor, no matter how lowly, how difficult or dangerous, no matter what distance it might take me." Ha-sang paused, embarrassed at his own enthusiasm.

A silence fell. From the forest behind the cottage came a raven's long, ominous croak, and in the aftermath of the shrill sound, the calm felt even deeper.

"How much did you accomplish in reading?" Only after a lingering silence did Tasan speak to Ha-sang.

"I could not go too far. In that isolated place, it is difficult to get books on Catholicism. Of classics, I read *The Analects, Mencius, The Book of Odes, The Book of History*, and so on. On Catholicism, I read some of the writings of the missionaries in China, such as Matteo Ricci's *True Principles of Catholicism*, and *Seven Mortifications* by Diace de Pantoja. In addition I read Francis Sambiasi, Julius Aleni, and Mailla. Master Justino taught me how to begin my study. The real task is what I do from now on."

"But there were some books on Catholicism left after the persecution . . ."

"They are all those small pocket-books."

"Master Tong-sŏm must have been saddened to see you go, a disciple like you."

"He was a strong-willed person. He told me, 'Paul, Buddhism teaches us that those who meet must part, but we Christians shall meet once again in the Paradise of Eternal Blessings.' He also spoke about you."

"About me?"

"Yes. He said, 'Paul, though it appears as if your honorable uncle has left the Church, I don't believe he has given up the faith entirely. Some day you will be able to understand your uncle's *Lecture on the Doctrine of the Mean*, which he presented to the late King Chŏngjo. Unless he denounced it or rewrote it, I don't believe that he has apostatized. Even though he wrote a memorial to the king exonerating himself from the treason of being a Christian, the message in his *Lecture* has basic similarities to Catholic thought.'"

Again on Tasan's face a shadow of displeasure appeared. Unwilling to show the uncertainty in his own mind, he looked down, keeping an uncomfortable silence. In the chilly breeze, he coughed lightly.

"It's getting cold. Let's go inside." Ha-sang wrapped an arm around his uncle's shoulders and led him into the thatched cottage.

Tasan meekly followed Ha-sang inside and sat down in front of the desk. His coughing continued.

"Where are you staying now?" asked Tasan.

"I am staying with a man called Cho Suk."

"Cho Suk?"

"He is the nephew of Master Justino. I think you know his wife."

"I do?"

"Her father is Francesco Xavier Kwŏn."

"Could you call him by his other name?" Tasan asked irritably.

"I was told his name is Mr. Kwŏn Il-sin of Yanggun."

"What? Kwŏn Il-sin?" Tasan straightened himself, holding onto the desk. As the shock subsided, he mumbled to himself, "He was a good person."

"His daughter is also a fine lady. She looks after me as though I were her own brother. I live in comfort now."

"But what brought you here this time?" Tasan queried, as if the thought had just occurred to him.

Ha-sang's face tightened.

"To tell you the truth," he said, lowering his voice, "next winter I am planning to go to Peking with the annual Winter Solstice Mission."

"What? To Peking?" Tasan was not as perturbed as he had been five years ago, but he blurted out nonetheless, "Preposterous idea!"

"I plan to go disguised as a groom for an official translator. I had to pay a bribe to get the position."

"Instead of paying you for the service, they sell it to you? How absurd!"

"Some amass a fortune during the annual mission to Peking."

"Impertinent people!" Tasan raged. "And you allow it?"

Instead of answering his uncle, Ha-sang smiled softly. His boyish innocent expression invited Tasan to smile back.

"You must be careful," Tasan said, no longer objecting to the idea. "Aren't you going to need a lot of money?"

"Yes."

"I don't even know how much it would cost. Where do you get the money?"

"Teresa is mostly responsible, but Barbara and Maria are also contributing. This trip is financed by the Christians in Ch'ungju. I went there to pick up the money, and since I was in the vicinity, I came to see you."

Ha-sang mentioned openly the Christian names of all these people of whom Tasan knew nothing; however, it did not annoy him any longer.

"It seems there are many Christians now," Tasan mused.

"Yes. I hear there are still some incidents of persecution in the countryside, but the capital nowadays is relatively quiet. The number of Christians, too, has increased to as many as there were at the time of the Persecution of 1801."

"Hm . . ."

"It's obvious that God's truth can never be vanquished," Ha-sang declared.

That night, uncle and nephew lay side by side in the same room, just as they had done five years ago, but both were unable to fall asleep. Although fatigued by the long journey, Ha-sang kept turning and tossing in his bed, careful not to disturb his uncle, while the incidents that had happened on his way kept appearing in his mind. It had been a beautiful day, and his mood was peaceful and carefree, so different from the day of his arrival five years ago. When he reached Ch'ungju, it occurred to him to look for Maria's maternal uncle, but he abandoned the idea. Without knowing anything about him, it appeared to be a hopeless task. Moreover, he could not openly inquire about the man whose brother-in-law was a treasonous heretic. Ha-sang obtained the money from the church in Ch'ungju, and on his way from there met a man he had never expected to see again. Only after his legs had suffered from trekking the rough passages of the Ch'ungch'ŏng mountain range did he realize that he had made a miscalculation in starting the journey so late in the day. He had been overconfident of his powerful limbs, and the journey had taken longer than he had planned. It was past ten at night when he finally came to an inn. Sorry for awakening the innkeeper woman from her sleep, Ha-sang went to sleep without asking for food, though he was hungry. But when he was on the verge of sleep, the door suddenly slid open and someone rushed in. Ha-sang was about to scream when a man's hand reached out and covered his mouth.

"I am being chased. Please save my life," the man whispered.

Ha-sang snatched a filthy blanket from the blanket-chest, made the man lie down in the corner, and covered him. Even before Ha-sang had time to lie down himself, a commotion rose outside the room, followed by a shriek from the innkeeper woman.

"Sir! Sir!" she called, flashing a torch.

"Boy, get up, someone is asking for us," Ha-sang spoke deliberately. Then he feigned exasperation and muttered, "For heaven's sake, snoring in this noise! Being tired from the long journey can't be an excuse."

Clicking his tongue, he angrily shouted toward the outside, "What do you want?"

"Sir, the honorable policemen here want to open the door for inspection." The woman's voice was shaking with terror, even though she must have endured this sort of trial countless times.

"How dare you, so late at night?" Ha-sang gently chided her, but added, "Tell them to open it."

No sooner had he finished speaking than the door was pushed violently open from outside. Framed by flashing torchlight, ferocious faces peered into the room. Confronting Ha-sang's imposing presence, which exuded dignity and authority, they bowed obsequiously.

"Forgive us. We are looking for a man who raided the prison," they apologized.

Only long after the policemen had gone did the intruder get up in the darkness and kneel to Ha-sang. "Thank you. You saved my life." He knocked his forehead repeatedly on the floor.

"You are safe here, but I am sure they are keeping watch outside. You don't seem like a criminal," Ha-sang observed.

"Of course they are watching. For the next few days they will keep a close surveillance on this neighborhood."

"I am leaving at daybreak. I can't leave you here like this. You may come with me as my servant, if you wish."

"You are too kind. I'll never be able to repay your generosity." The man kept thanking Ha-sang, but Ha-sang needed to sleep.

In the morning light, when Ha-sang saw the man's face, he almost screamed. This was Hong, the proprietor of the inn at the bamboo grove of Nonsan whom he had met five years ago. Without recognizing Ha-sang, who now dressed and acted like a scholar-gentleman, the fellow was doing servant's chores, rolling the bedding and bringing water for Ha-sang to wash his face. After an early breakfast, they left for the road. As they expected, two soldiers were posted at the entrance to the street, but they did not stop to question a gentleman with a servant in attendance.

However, Ha-sang did not know the true identity of Hong. He knew him only as the proprietor of the inn where Francesco and he had stayed when they came to see Kwŏn Ho-sin. Neither did Hong recognize Ha-sang as the servant who had accompanied Francesco. When the village was no longer visible, Ha-sang told Hong, "They will not follow this far. You are safe now, but if you are returning to your home, I might come with you and have lunch in your inn at the bamboo grove."

"Then, then, you know me . . ." Hong paused and stammered, his eyes wide open.

"You must have forgotten. You do remember the scholar-gentleman with a sprained ankle who stayed in your inn five years ago? I am the servant boy who attended him."

"Ah, that young man Francesco was waiting for."

"Did you say Francesco?"

"You don't have to hide anything from me," said Hong. "I am Matteo. I know everything. Francesco has told me."

"How do you know?"

"I was in close contact with Mr. Kwŏn. On the night when he met with tragedy, we expected that the same fate would befall us, but that traitor Sŭng had already disappeared and we escaped disaster."

"I see."

"We thought Mr. Kwŏn had been clubbed to death, but soon we found out he was alive in a prison in Kongju."

"So you tried to rescue him."

"Yes. He is too weak to move; moreover, he insists on remaining there."

"Why?"

"He implores that he be allowed to stay there. He came to realize his mission in that hell of a place. We don't know the situation in the capital, but here in the provincial government, persecution still goes on in a most crude and cruel manner. It would be far better if they just put the faithful to a swift death—beheaded, or hanged, or clubbed to death; it's worse to let them live in that purgatory indefinitely. Many have been there for more than ten years. Those who suffer from the hunger and the cold and the vermin that plague them are vulnerable to temptation. That's the weapon of those Satans. They laugh with pleasure at their own despicable cleverness in making the faithful apostatize."

Matteo's eyes gleamed in fury. "Mr. Kwŏn remains there in order to enable them to face martyrdom with courage and gratitude."

Tears ran down his cheeks as he continued, "We don't know what happened to his family—his virtuous wife and their three daughters. Only his son is safe with his maternal grandparents."

"I had the unexpected good fortune of looking after their eldest daughter." Now it was Ha-sang's turn to relate his story. "Maria now lives in peace with Christian women, following strict Christian teachings. She has an exceptional calligraphic hand, and the books she copies are very much valued."

"I didn't realize that she is old enough to be engaged in such an important task."

"She began when she was eight years old, I was told."

"For Heaven's sake!"

"Her mother must have been an extraordinary lady."

"Her beauty blinded the eyes of the beholder, the servants used to say."

"So does Maria's," Ha-sang thought. A strange shyness taking hold of him, he could not utter these words, which took shape only in his heart. Even those Christians who believed only in inner beauty could not help noticing thirteen-year-old Maria's loveliness.

Having vowed a life of celibacy, Ha-sang felt disquieted by her beauty. He changed the subject.

"Are you still operating the inn?"

"To tell you the truth, I am planning to leave the place soon. I heard a rumor that the traitor, Sŭng, who caused the tragedy in the Kwŏn household, is now a professional informer, ferreting out Christians all over the nation. Did you hear about the disaster that struck last Easter Sunday? It was caused by a Judas called Chŏn Chi-su, whose betrayal of his fellow Christians throughout the Kyŏngsang Province is now notorious. Here in this province, we had a severe famine following last year's disastrous flood. In the beginning, the Satan had lived only through the charity of Christians, but becoming greedier, he soon began selling those who helped him. Since he was well acquainted with Christian activities, he informed the authorities that there would be a prayer meeting on Easter Sunday. Since then, we can't even count the evil deeds of this devil. We hear Sŭng has become just like him."

"What wicked men!"

"If only I weren't a Christian! Look at them; these fists could kill a tiger, let alone a man!" His fists shook in anger. "I must sell the inn as soon as possible, and move to a safer place far away from the authorities, where we can follow a true Christian life in peace."

The inn by the bamboo grove was peaceful and quiet. Matteo's trusted servant, a Christian, had returned unharmed. (When Matteo realized that he had failed in his attempt to rescue Kwŏn Ho-sin from jail, he had instructed the servant to run. Drawing the attention of the soldiers to the opposite direction, he himself had narrowly managed to escape.) After the hospitality of lunch, Ha-sang left Matteo, making sure that Matteo would convey the news of Maria's safety and whereabouts to her father, if he ever had a chance to visit him in prison. This unexpected detour delayed him, but he felt that the grace of God was with him because he had learned of Kwŏn Ho-sin's safety; that alone was worth the trip to the south. His steps were lightened by the realization. He expected to reach Somni before sunset and stay there overnight, and then he would arrive at Kyuldong within two days. But as he hurried, he was again detained when a shoelace of his hemp-cord sandal broke. He had to pause to change it under a tree with luxuriant limbs shaped like the roof of a pavilion, where several travelers were resting. His back to them, he unpacked his bundle to take out a spare shoelace, but he could not find one. He was so desperate that he was ready to use anything to repair the broken sandal, but he was now a man very much conscious of his appearance. He continued to dig into his bundle, knowing too well that it was a hopeless search. Suddenly, he felt a tiny, soft, velvety hand holding out a hemp-cord. Taken by surprise, he stood up. From nowhere had appeared a girl of about eleven, holding a shoelace, who looked up at him. She had a strange look about her. Nothing was unusual about her scarlet skirt and lime-green jacket bordered with maroon, but it was her hairdo that caught his eye. Her hair was not in a long plait with a swallow-shaped ribbon at the end, as most girls her age wore. Instead, her plaits were coiled around her ears like loops and tied at each end with ribbons. What was so startling to Ha-sang, however, was not her unusual hairdo but the resemblance her face bore to someone he could not quite place. In that instant, although the face was so familiar, he could not connect the two images; he was only struck by the clarity of the resemblance.

The girl could not remain there long, for a loud voice began to call, "Butterfly! Butterfly! What are you doing? We must hurry."

She handed the hemp-cord to Ha-sang and disappeared in a flash. "Who could it be?" he wondered, evoking in his mind the child's face, which had an enchanting and almost sensuous beauty for one so young. The touch of her soft hands was still fresh in his hand. Suddenly, the face of Maria surfaced in his mind and superimposed itself on that of the girl; then they became one. Now Ha-sang knew that it was Maria he saw in the girl's face. He trembled in a shock of recognition. Was it the girl's hair that had prevented him from recognizing her? Or was it her strange air? Deliberately, he bit his lips.

In the meantime, next to Ha-sang, Tasan lay just as sleeplessly. No less intense was his sense of shame as he basked in the joy of seeing his nephew, whom he had never desired to look after and educate, a young man as rough as a wild horse when last he had seen him, now appearing before him a noble stallion. In his ears still rang the words of Ha-sang: "Master Justino, in spite of his advanced age, is undaunted by the watchful eyes of the authorities and upright in his observation of Christian duty . . . If he has not abandoned or rewritten his *Lecture*, then your honorable uncle has not given up his Christian faith." The words Justino had spoken cut through his heart like a dagger's edge.

In 1784, when he was twenty-two, after having passed the Preliminary Stage Examination, Tasan was a student at High College. That year, the late King Chŏngjo had asked the students eighty questions on the Doctrine of the Mean. Tasan had sought advice from a renowned Confucian scholar, Yi Pyŏk. Although he had never taken the civil service examination and had never held a government position, Yi Pyŏk was a scholar of profound learning, whose opinions Tasan accepted in their entirety. However, only on the interpretation of the Doctrine of the Mean did they disagree: Yi Pyŏk followed T'oegye's stance that Material Forces preceded Principle, while Tasan pursued Yulgok's priority of Principle over Material Forces.

The Doctrine of the Mean had traditionally been attributed to Tzu Ssu, the grandson of Confucius. On the Way of Heaven and human nature he wrote: "Human nature, endowed by Heaven, is revealed through the states of equilibrium and harmony, which are themselves the 'condition of the world' and the 'universal path.' The Way of Heaven transcends time, space, substance, and motion, and is at the same time unceasing, eternal, and self-evident. Man and Nature form a unity, and the quality that brings them together is ch'eng, sincerity. Sincerity is not just a state of mind, but an active force that is always transforming and completing things, drawing man and Heaven together in the same current." Tzu Ssu said: "That which is bestowed by Heaven is called man's nature; the fulfillment of this nature is called the Way; the cultivation of the Way is called culture."

It was Tasan's interpretation of the Mean that the late king had praised and favored. A few days after the examination, the question had passed among the Royal Secretariat: "Who is this young man called Yag-yong? What is the extent of his scholarship? Today, when around the throne is nothing but a wasteland, the commentaries of this man alone stood out among all the students of the Confucian Academy. He must be a scholar of extraordinary stature." The remark left such an indelible impression on Tasan's young mind that later he recorded it in his autobiography. Thirty years later, refining his old manuscript, he wrote *On the Doctrine of the Mean* in two volumes. But he did not change the main thrust of his thesis, only deleting the passages that were not relevant to his main argument, and supplementing the king's previous questions with a new chapter.

This year, Tasan had finally been cleared of culpability, but the Letter of Pardon had been detained on the road and had not yet arrived. Appeasing his pain, he plunged into his writing, while waiting for the document to arrive. Remembering a past filled with exultation, he added an epilogue to the newly revised *On the Doctrine of the Mean*: "Now that the sage king is no longer, and his royal voice has no path, I have no one to whom I can address my queries. It has been thirty years since I had discussions with Yi Pyŏk, with whose advanced virtue and erudition I dare not compare myself. He would have clear opinions on my old and new works, but alas, he is gone and I alone live. I can only shed tears over my books."

The full September moon drenched the paper window with a silvery luminosity, and the tumultuous chirping of insects vivified the calm of the night. The memory of loved ones and the pondering of the events of long ago kept him from his sleep.

Chapter Eight

◆   ◆   ◆

The Winter
Solstice Mission

Journey to Peking

More than a month after they had left Seoul on October 24, the day
of the river crossing finally arrived. The mission had been staying
in Ŭiju for about ten days, busying themselves with many necessary
details before they began the journey for entering Peking. They
carefully examined the royal tribute to the Chinese court, gifts of
articles indigenous to Korea, which they sealed in wooden crates.
They inspected numerous attendants, completed provisions for the
horses, and replaced and supplemented servants and grooms. The
military officers had been kept busy thoroughly searching the bun-
dles and packages of the peddlers who accompanied the mission,
as well as the shipments sent by merchants who specialized in trade
between China and Korea. All the while, the members of the mission had been tormented by the snow that had begun after they
arrived in Ŭiju. The howling wind made the northern winter even
more unbearable.

During the Yi dynasty, the Korean government had regularly dispatched envoys to the Chinese court. There were embassies to mark
the passing of the winter solstice, to offer congratulations during
national celebrations, to report on the affairs of the nation, to offer
condolences, incense, and written addresses to the deceased when
a member of the royal family died, or to report the death of a Korean
ruler and receive permission from the Chinese emperor for a new

ruler's accession to the throne. In the later Yi dynasty, the annual winter mission, called the Winter Solstice Mission, had been combined to present New Year's felicitations and to honor the Chinese emperor's birthday. The main delegation consisted of a chief envoy, a deputy envoy selected from the six ministries, and a recording secretary appointed temporarily by the government from a slightly lower bureaucratic echelon to accompany the mission.

This year, 1816, the chief envoy was Yi Cho-wŏn, the deputy envoy was Yi Chi-yŏn, and the recording secretary was Pak Ki-su. Below them were three interpreters and twenty-four military officers who were responsible for managing and guarding the tributary articles as well as the merchandise exchanged by the traders of both nations. Altogether, the main delegation consisted of thirty men. With the inclusion of physicians, herb doctors, translators, scribes, servants, employees of each post station, military police, cooks, and grooms for the horses belonging to both the local government and the post stations, the total number of the procession reached more than two hundred and fifty. Around them flocked the retinues of the merchants who represented the trading houses of P'yŏngyang, Songdo, and Ŭiju.

The gifts to be presented to the emperor and empress of China included ginseng, tiger and otter fur, straw mats with floral designs, Korean paper of superior quality, and bolts of ramie cloth and unpatterned raw silk. These articles had been strictly inspected by the various cabinet members in the state council, each article carefully checked against documents. They were then presented to the king for his review. After the king's review, they were stamped with the official seal, and finally handed to the bureaucrats selected by the central government to pack and guard the tribute.

The articles brought by private merchants were another matter. Ha-sang, who had come as a servant to a lower-grade translator, felt overwhelmed by the mountains of crates and packages piled up on the grounds of the provincial government office. Positioned high in the hall, the Ŭiju governor and the recording secretary were receiving the packages for inspection. From their perch they were unable personally to inspect the contents of each package, for their number was truly staggering. Their assistants and the translators, including Ha-sang's master, were performing the actual examination, weighing each package with stern accuracy while the merchants protested. The packages included silver, dried seaweed, dried sea cucumbers, skins of cattle and wild animals, paper, tobacco, and cotton cloth. For days the inspection continued from dawn to dusk, and still the end was nowhere in sight.

After this meticulous preliminary inspection, the reexamination at the time of the river crossing was executed with even more severity, taking a long time and confusing a massive crowd. Amnok River was about nine miles west of Ŭiju. The procession had left immediately after a hasty early-morning breakfast. The snow had stopped falling, but the leaden sky was oppressive and the cold chilled their bones. As they reached the river, the only sight was an endless stretch of frozen snow. In this desolate landscape, a tent was pitched near two tall trees, a rope tied around each trunk, marking the entrance. Military officers from Ŭiju stood at either side of the tent, inspecting each man and horse before passing them through. Nearby stood a smaller tent, where the assistants of the recording secretary thoroughly checked the contents of each package. Except for the translators and assistants, everyone carried wooden identification tablets, which had been branded a few days earlier with the recording secretary's signature. The packages, which had been so carefully inspected only days ago, were once again ransacked. Bedding and clothing were scattered about in confusion in the snow, and leather boxes and paper crates rolled here and there. Those who had passed inspection were busy repacking their possessions. Names, addresses, ages, and physical characteristics, such as beards, scars, and height, were also recorded. The servants were made to undress; their topknots were undone, and the insides of their pants searched. Even the horses did not escape scrutiny: the color, the length of their legs, the shape of their shins, tails, and manes were carefully recorded.

In the bitter cold, the tents shook with the northern wind. The three envoys inside the tents were served tea and cakes, but they had lost their appetites and sent the food back untouched. Outside on the frozen river, the mission's cooks, together with the families of the merchants and the food-peddlers from Ŭiju, built bonfires to prepare meals. Since they had not had an adequate breakfast, everyone gathered around the fire, waiting for the food to be served. From the cauldrons and the mouths of people around them rose white steam, which instantly turned to frost. The crowd jostled among the horses and the piles of goods littering the snow-covered wilderness. It was impossible to distinguish the river from the hill, and still the caravan of men and horses from Ŭiju flowed ceaselessly like a streak of spilt ink.

The inspection continued. As it progressed, the officials became weary and careless in their search. In fact, some native merchants managed to slip through undetected and cross the river. At this time of year, when everything was frozen solid, it was impossible to catch everyone who illegally crossed the river. Yet for anyone who was caught, the punishment was extremely severe. If illegal articles were found at the first inspection, not only were they confiscated, but those who carried the goods were flogged; at the second stop, the criminals were banished; and finally at the last gate, the smugglers were decapitated and the severed heads put on display for everyone to see. Contraband included gold, pearls, and packets of ginseng over seventy-five kilograms in weight, otter skins, and silver weighing more than seventy-five kilograms.

The inspectors were not unmindful of their duty, but they became fretful and ill-tempered as they endlessly repeated the same task. Just when they were in such a mood, Ha-sang stood in line before them, towering conspicuously over those who surrounded him, who happened to be unusually small.

"Name?"

"I'm called Chu Ŭi-jong," he answered in the unmistakable speech pattern of a servant.

"Age?"

"I'm twenty-two."

Though he gave his real age, Ha-sang used the alias Chu Ŭijong, homonyms for "servant of the Lord," indulging himself with a surreptitious pleasure. The official sharply scrutinized Ha-sang from head to toe and recorded: "Height: eight feet." Ha-sang swallowed a bitter smile. Although over six feet tall, he was not as tall as that! From the corner of his eye, he noticed the officer recording the fact that he had a black mole on the temple. The officer, solidly built himself, came only to Ha-sang's ears. Looking up at him, he shouted, "Take off your earmuffs."

The blue cotton-filled cloth earmuffs were a gift from Maria. First he took off the kerchief that bound his hair, then removed the earmuffs and handed them to the officer. After carefully fingering the cloth, the officer approached Ha-sang and grabbed hold of his plump topknot for inspection. This was followed by the shout, "Untie your pants and socks!"

Nothing was to be found inside his cotton socks or his pants. Finally, the officer began searching his body, beginning with his shoulders and examining armpits, waist, and even groin. At that moment, the unexpected happened. The rough handling of his body caused Ha-sang's pants to slide down for a split second, leaving him no time to grab them. In that blink of time, the beauty of his young naked abdomen and thighs were exposed in the midst of the snow-covered, windswept wilderness. The severe cold did not diminish the gleam of the supple, youthful flesh, which was made even more dazzling by the cruelty of the surroundings. Ha-sang deliberately pulled up his pants and tied his belt while the officers gazed at him, speechless.

Among those who had witnessed the little sideshow from beginning to end was a noble personage, the deputy envoy, Yi Chi-yŏn. He had been inside the tent shielding himself from the cold; feeling an urge to relieve himself, he had bent over to come out of the tent-flap while a valet held it. As he raised himself, he witnessed the scene. A nameless shudder passed through his spine, a strange sensation akin to fear or anger. Without realizing it, he found himself asking, "Who is that lowly man?"

"Sir, he is the servant of a translator," the valet answered.

"A peculiar and outlandish one. I think he ought to be flogged."

"Yes?" the valet stood perplexed, not understanding what the master had just said.

"Nothing. But he is a wicked one indeed," the deputy envoy corrected himself, coming to his senses. Calming down a feeling inscrutable even to himself, he moved away.

That same night, Yi had a dream. For no reason at all, the husky, blooming young servant he had seen that day stood naked in front of him. The same thrill he had felt earlier again ran through his spine. With the horsewhip he was holding, he whipped the youth's naked flesh. In an instant, blood spurted from the wound. He was seized with a pleasure so powerful and clear that he trembled. He struck the youth again, this time harder. From the larger wound the blood flowed more profusely. In a frenzy, he repeated the whipping. The pain and pleasure sliced through his flesh, the pain more intense than that endured by his victim. It seemed as if the youth was smiling, unaware of the pain being inflicted upon him. Exhausted, he threw away his whip. Then, as he mindlessly looked down at his body, he let out a scream: he found himself stark naked and his body covered with wounds and blood such as he had just inflicted on the youth.

After making Ha-sang suffer these indignities, the inspecting officers became gentler in their searches, and finally between one and two in the afternoon finished inspecting everyone, including the merchants, a total of more than three hundred men and two hundred fifty horses.

Before the crossing, the party changed clothes. The three envoys wore their everyday clothes. The attending servants, military guards, and supply officers in charge of dried rations all wore long, sleeveless, vestlike uniforms slit at the back; helmets decorated with silver flowers, peacock feathers, clouds and moons; and blue money-belts around their waists, from which swung medicine sacks, kerchiefs, and pouches for eyeglasses and tobacco. All the rest—the grooms, the paymaster from Ŭiju, and the other officials—wore long outercoats with narrow sleeves and helmets. The translators wore horsehair hats and iron epaulets. Ha-sang, like the other lowly pack-horse drivers, wore a short outfit and a helmet. He served his master with the utmost diligence. Although one of the lowliest in the party, he was liked by everyone for his strength, diligence, and cheerful disposition. Accustomed to hardship, nothing was too difficult for him to bear. Without complaint, he performed all tasks with selfless devotion even before he was asked. The aged master loved him as if Ha-sang was his own youngest son. And, although he had become famous in the mission because of the incident that had occurred before the river crossing, the filthy mouthed servants dared not talk obscenely about it among themselves, almost as if they sensed the inviolably chaste and pure air that emanated from him.

Nor did it take long for Ha-sang to become friendly with the prison guards. These petty soldiers, usually recruited from among the oldest families in Ŭiju and Anju, one from each family, had almost the status of slaves. Given the roughest food and the most work, they were responsible for guarding the three main envoys as well as the prisoners. Impudent and lazy, they turned deaf ears to repeated orders from various quarters, answering tardily with loud, insolent voices, as if hearing the calls for the first time. Once dismounted from their horses, they walked slothfully like pigs or cows. They had small blue flags stuck on their shoulders; each carried in one hand a wooden board with military orders printed on it, and in the other brush and ink. All of the horses were used to carry the loads, so these soldiers perched without saddles on whatever small part they could squeeze onto. They had trumpets to blow and from under their seats protruded a dozen or so clubs painted in red. The long line of the party wound behind them on the frozen river.

At the river's edge the local governor, the official entertaining girls, and their servants, all of whom had followed the party from Ŭiju and Anju, turned back. There remained some prison guards and a pair of military officers in front of a carriage drawn by two horses; these carriages were used only by the chief and deputy envoys during their foreign missions. A groom stood to the right of the carriage while another, on the left, held the ceremonial noseband; clerks, guides, and a sun umbrella followed behind. From time to time, travel-weary grooms let out short cries to urge the horses onward. It was also their duty to announce place names every nine miles to Peking, a task which after many such trips they accomplished with seasoned accuracy.

The river was named Amnok because of its clear water—water as blue as the feathers on a duck's neck—but its true shade was hidden under the frozen surface. The river was divided into three channels, all frozen so solid that the travelers found it hard to believe that they and their horses were trekking on water. Along the bank was an endless stretch of reed fields. The going became rough. Making a path barely wide enough for a wagon to go through the thick undergrowth, slipping and pricked by dry reeds, the men and horses pushed their way over the lumpy, glacial ground.

As they came out of the reed field, they saw an ancient pine tree at the edge of the road. A groom slipped out of the procession and, producing a piece of paper, draped it on a branch; then, dropping to his knees, he bowed twice, gathered his hands across his chest, and prayed there for a long time. Following his example, other grooms and servants began to pray. Soon the tree was covered with white paper, like bursting flowers. Holding the reins, Ha-sang stood gazing at them.

"Why, don't you have any wishes? Go and pray," someone urged him.

Ha-sang turned around and saw a simple-mannered man of about thirty.

"I see this is your first trip. They say if you pray to that tree, you will come out of this journey safe, and more than that, all your wishes will come true. Here, take this and let's go together," the man said, handing him a piece of paper.

"Thank you very much but . . ."

"Don't be shy. We are all in the same boat."

"What do I pray?"

"If you have nothing to pray for, why don't you just pray for a safe journey?"

"I'm grateful, but I have never prayed to a tree before."

He declined politely, but he was repeating within himself, "Our father, who art in Heaven . . ."

"You stubborn fellow. We all need someone or something to believe in, something to lean on," said the man, but without annoyance. He took back the piece of paper that Ha-sang was returning. "Good. Then I'll pray for you." As he walked toward the tree, he added, "My name is Cho Sin-ch'ŏl. Let us be friends."

The procession, which had been interrupted by the encounter with the pine tree, started up again as the guards began shouting the order to move on. The distance from the river to Kuryŏnsŏng, where they would spend the night camping in the open field, was a mere half mile. By the time the whole procession finally arrived, however, the winter day was ending. The bitter cold had become even more intense, and everyone on this alien soil was seized with thoughts of home.

Three tents about ten feet apart had already been set up for the three envoys by the advance team of local government officers, who commanded the labor of a few dozen petty soldiers. The collapsible tents of cloth could be folded and opened like umbrellas. Under the floor, the earth was hollowed out for charcoal fires, and fur blankets and thick cushions were spread over the floor. Each tent had a plank door in front and was surrounded by a canopy. These tents, in the style of the Mongol *yurt*, could accommodate five or six people, and when screens were set up and lamps lit, they were as cozy as any house. Heated tents had also been set up for the translators, but the merciless wind seeped in through their flimsy cloth. The servants gathered around the bonfire within an area enclosed by nets, which barely protected them, fighting off the bitter cold by rubbing their hands together and stamping their feet. Each night they were given a piece of dried meat and a few sweets, and in the morning hot soup with rice dumplings, but many of the servants had become ill, and Ha-sang finally realized why not a single soul had missed the chance to offer a prayer to the ancient pine tree.

The old master allowed Ha-sang to come inside the tent, but Ha-sang could not bear going inside while his companions remained shivering outside in the net enclosure. He often spent the night standing around the bonfire, suffering from the cold and the stench of the unwashed men who had walked and driven the horses from Seoul, a distance of two hundred and seventy-two miles. They still had six hundred and twenty-five miles more to go to reach Peking—and they must yet walk the same distance to return home. Now that they were across the river, having left their home and country far behind, these bone-weary souls grumbled and lamented in the merciless cold.

"I wonder if we will reach the border gate before sundown tomorrow?" someone mumbled.

"Goddamn it. We will soon be seeing the sight of those Manchu barbarians."

"It's the price we pay for the sin of having been born Koreans."

"They weren't born the citizens of a powerful nation, either. They stole others' lands," the man spat in disgust.

"Damn!" the other man rejoined. "What were we doing while others stole our land? They have it easy, hunting and harvesting millet. I'll bet all this land once belonged to us Koreans. I heard my master say that the Su [Sui] emperors who invaded Korea could not steal from us; each time they tried, we drove them away. During the Tang [T'ang] dynasty, Emperor T'aejong [T'ai Tsung] invaded us, but he was defeated and had to return as a one-eyed cripple. Our brave general shot an arrow right into his eye."

"There you go with your tall tales again. But they sure cheer us up."

"I'm not telling you lies! I even know the name of the general," the man protested vigorously.

"It must have been Chang Kŏn-bok," they teased, using the name of the man telling the story.

"You stupid ignoramuses. It's no good telling you anything; it's like a monk reading a sutra to a cow. I tell you, his name was Yang Man-ch'un and the battle took place in Ansong City."

"A royal academician you are. You're wearing off your tongue."

Everyone joined in the hearty laughter, but soon someone began complaining, "What is this anyway? I don't understand why each year we must go to China bearing gifts to their court."

"It's a shame, indeed. But we all know that what they give back to the Korean court in return is far superior in quantity and quality. This isn't a bad business. But how nauseating it is to watch them groveling to the barbarians, thrice kneeling and nine times knocking their heads on the floor."

"It's called the Winter Solstice Mission now, but it used to be called *Choch'ŏnsa* during the Ming dynasty. They were the ones who helped us fight back the Japanese. We ought to be grateful."

"Why on earth, for all the warm days we have, must they choose to go north in the coldest of winters? I'm afraid we will all become ice-devils who wander forever looking for graves in which to be buried," the man grumbled, letting out a deep sigh.

"Were you dragged here on an iron chain? Why complain? You came of your own free will," another man retorted.

"That's true. No one can forget the journey once he has had a taste of it. Just think of it. Though we suffer loathsomely, once we step out of the border gate, we are in a different world. We earn good money and we see astonishing sights as well."

"Have you ever seen a camel or an elephant or a peacock in Korea? They say we have many tigers in Korea, too; and I hear many stories about the calamities they cause, but I saw one for the first time in a tiger park in Peking."

Suddenly from the tents of the envoys came the sound of trumpets and the roar of people shouting in unison. The clamor was made by the military officers guarding the tents, commanding the spear-bearing soldiers to prevent the wild animals from coming near the tents.

"Ha! Speak of the devil, and he is sure to appear. Tigers and leopards are said to prowl around here."

"They tell me that the masters' tents are as comfortable and warm as the inner rooms of their own houses, but how can they sleep with all that noise?"

"They take naps in their sedan chairs. It's we who need sleep. We are the ones who must walk on the slippery ice."

The bonfire shot out a few sparks like flowers of fire and then began to die out. Ha-sang silently fed a few more logs into it.

A man crouching with his head on his knees spoke to Ha-sang. "This is the first time for you, I hear. I bet you'll keep coming again and again. As for me, once I skipped a couple of years, weary of all this suffering. Do you know what happened? I began to miss this ice field and bonfire. The warm, heated floor at home became boring." When he paused, he laughed scornfully at his own words.

"It's all because we were born under bad auspices," the man went on. "Wouldn't it be a pity, though, if we never had a chance to get outside the boundaries of Korea? We would be big frogs in a little pond. I'm only a lowly, illiterate groom, but I must say I've become more open-minded about trifles, because I've seen larger sights during this journey. They may say I'm a man who's been around and a worldly slob, but I can laugh at almost anything."

He fumbled about his waist, took out a pipe, stuffed tobacco into it without even looking at it, and lit it from the bonfire. After a few puffs, he pushed the pipe to the corner of his mouth and continued, "We stay in Peking for a month. Try to see as many sights as you can. You may not be able to see the emperor's palace, but you'll see the resplendent Glass Factory Market, the Elephant House, the Horticultural Garden, the Garden of Exotic Birds, the magnificent Buddhist temples, and you'll see magic shows you can hardly believe. And you must not miss the grand spectacle of the towering Catholic temple that soars toward the sky without even a crossbeam. Since the Persecution of 1801, we Koreans are afraid to go near it, but before then, it used to be at the top of the list of the ten sights to see in Peking."

Jolted out of his drowsiness at the mention of the Catholic church, Ha-sang felt his heart jump.

Puffing on his pipe, the speaker went on; in the dark, the tobacco glowed like a ruby suspended in midair. "I don't understand it. Just looking at a Catholic temple can't make you a Catholic devil. We let the Chinese intimidate us, and we worship everything Chinese," he went on. "Yet when it comes to the Catholics, while the Chinese allow their people to hold services and even build those magnificent temples for them, what happens in Korea? We try to wipe them off the face of the earth, even to the last member of the family."

A man who had been dozing off with his head buried between his knees suddenly looked up.

"Brother, how many heads have you got on you? There are those besides rats who listen in the dark. To prove it, I myself heard what you just said," he warned.

"Damn you! I'm only giving him an idea. He might regret it if he went back home without ever laying his eyes on the magnificent structure. It's a once-in-a-lifetime sight, after all the trouble he's going through to get to Peking."

"A good-natured village wife has a dozen fathers-in-law. Don't you know that saying? It's your karma to be too kind." Picking up a stick and giving the fire a poke, the man continued, "This land of ours now belongs to those Manchu barbarians. After having roamed in their vast country, I became confused; the good and the bad have become all mixed up. The things we worshipped at home as if they were gods have suddenly become things to laugh at. The principles we insisted were right became wrong. I'm lost. Things have different values in a different country, I think."

"When did you turn into such a sage?"

"Are you praising me, brother?"

"Let's just say I am."

"I don't know. But I was told that the master in the tent is a scholar of great learning, though they say he is quite different from other high-born gentlemen. He is bored with books of old learning. He came here because he does not want to be confined within Korea; he wants to see the world outside. Instead of calling them the Manchu barbarians, he wants to see the new things that are happening in China."

"Where did you gather such a smattering of knowledge?"

"Brother, I've been around. I haven't traveled to Peking twenty-five times for nothing. I've heard and seen plenty."

From the tents trumpets and voices sounded loudly again. "With all those bonfires everywhere, damn animals!" the first man groused, pulling the pipe from his mouth and tapping it on the ground.

"Are you hearing the noise for the first time? You are awfully cross tonight; you must have indigestion from the cold rice you had for supper. But I agree with you. What an insane thing to do. Are they trying to chase away the wild animals or our sleep?" the other retorted.

"Did you say chase our sleep? If they shot cannon under our ears, do you think they would wake up from their sleep?"

He was right. Everyone around them was sound asleep, snoring loudly.

"Poor devils. Of all the callings in the world, why did they choose to sleep on a sheet of ice in this godforsaken barbarian land? They must be dead tired, or how could they sleep so soundly in this atrocious wind? We must not let anyone freeze to death. Let's look after the fire."

The black coverlets stuffed with cotton and bordered with red had been carried by thirty horses and distributed to each person, but they did not keep the travelers from feeling the cruel cold of the open field penetrating into their bones. They took turns caring for the fire so that it would not die out or set the clothing or coverlets on fire. Their day had begun early, for they were driving the horses on the icy road before sunrise; now they lay asleep like corpses in a slumber so deep nothing could wake them.

Though it was not his turn, Ha-sang found himself tending the fire that night. The wailing wind swept over the plain, flogging the bodies under the coverlets. Following another ululation of wild animals, the trumpets and clamor of soldiers once again shook the night, but none stirred around him. As the animals were silenced, the roar of the wind sounded even more fierce. Ha-sang realized the necessity, after all, of all those guards and night-watch soldiers. The wind blew away the clouds, and suddenly the full moon appeared. He heard a noise from inside the enclosure and saw a few men emerging, carrying something heavy. In the moonlight, he saw that they were struggling, without a stretcher, with the weight of a body. The leaden face, which had become visible under the moon, belonged to a man of about thirty. He had not been dead for very long, and the corpse, not yet stiff, yielded to the movement of the men carrying it. Ha-sang supported the dead man's head, replacing the man who had been struggling with it. He then lifted the whole weight of the corpse and almost carried it by himself, leaving the others merely holding onto the legs.

"Thanks. Sorry to bother you." Everyone was grateful.

"How about behind that hill over there? It's enough just to cover him so that no one will see," someone said with a loud sneeze.

"Good. There's even a tree there," another agreed.

It was not far to the hill, which provided a good place to dispose of the body, well hidden from the tent area and bonfires.

"Hell, it's cold. We leave early tomorrow. We've got to get some sleep."

"Are we leaving him here like this?" As they were about to leave, Ha-sang heard a somewhat familiar voice.

"What then?"

"We can't leave him here like this."

"You mean we have to dig this frozen earth?"

"It won't take long."

"You must be out of your wits. Do you have a magic spell or something to move the earth? It's frozen solid as a rock! They say the barbarians throw the bodies of those who die young into an open field."

"Are we Manchu men?"

"You do what pleases you, but I don't want to become a corpse myself. I'm going. I need sleep."

The men left, and only Ha-sang and the latecomer remained. Ha-sang recognized Cho Sin-ch'ŏl, who had earlier urged him to pray to the pine tree. Ha-sang shouted to the disappearing men, "Please look after the fire for me!" and returned to the corpse. "What shall we do?" asked Ha-sang.

"Let's cover him with snow. In the spring when the snow melts, he will be exposed anyway, but how can we leave a still-warm body in the open?"

Silently Ha-sang gathered snow around the corpse with the hoe Cho handed to him.

"Go in peace, leaving regrets and pain behind, poor soul. Save us, merciful Buddha," Cho prayed, rubbing his palms together.

They began walking back toward the fire. With downcast eyes, Cho broke the silence. "He was so excited about raking in a fortune, and look what happened to him—abandoned in a barbarian field."

"Do you make lots of money by going with the mission?"

"Usually, if you have no shame and you're deceitful."

"What do you mean?"

"If you steal and deal in illegal articles."

Bathed in moonlight, Ha-sang pondered his own mission. He was no different from the others: he was also dealing in illegal articles. Worse still, he came hoping to bring a Catholic clergyman into Korea, one whom the law denounced as a heinous criminal, and he would return home with religious objects—Bibles, prayer books, books of catechism and of lives of saints, holy pictures—all contraband.

When sleep was about to take gentle hold of him, Ha-sang heard a trumpet sounding once again, one quite different from the noise made to frighten away wild animals during the night. It was the first trumpet, a long, smooth blare before daybreak, which signaled the travelers to awake. They straightened their clothes, smoothed their hair with their fingers, placed earmuffs carefully over their ears, and tightened the kerchiefs around their heads. After relieving themselves, they covered their feet again and wrapped their trousers tightly around their legs. They loaded the folded coverlets back on the horses, and finally, and most important, fed them. With the second trumpet, sounding sharply, it was time for breakfast. Inspection of men and horses followed, and all stood ready to move again. Everything in order, the procession began to move with the third trumpet. They had now become accustomed to this daily routine, a routine which without exception continued until they reached Peking.

From Kuryŏnsŏng to Onjŏngp'yŏng was about twelve miles, and there they had their lunch. Immediately after lunch, they began the twelve-mile journey to Ch'aengmun (Stakes Gate) near the Manchu city of Feng-huang Ch'eng. The trip took all day even at a brisk pace. The Chinese government had kept this area as a no-man's-land for a long time as a precaution against invasion from either side. However, since the reign of K'ang-hsi (1662–1772), as the population around Feng-huang Ch'eng had increased, farming and cattle-raising were allowed to spread to the area. Mount Feng-huang sloped toward the north, and toward the south the peaks of a mountain range lined the sea. In between, in a space of about one and a half miles, a stockade was set up marking the border between China and Korea. About eleven feet high, it had been carelessly erected so that any small person could easily slip through. A gate about ten feet high stood in the middle of the stockade. Its plank door was barely wide enough for a cart to pass through. From one of the rafters hung a board carved with the inscription, Korean Tributary Mission.

A general was posted in Feng-huang Ch'eng to oversee the opening and closing of the gate. However, that day the general did not show up, although the translators had already been dispatched from Ŭiju to prepare the Chinese customs officials for the arrival of the mission. The general had gone to Shenyang, they were told, on sudden official business. They had no way of knowing if indeed he had an urgent mission that had taken him away, or if they were being slighted by the Chinese. The entire party, unable to pass, had to wait. Even the private merchants who had come ahead of the mission and were already within the city, staying at native households, had to come outside of the gate after dinner, where they warmed themselves over charcoal braziers while waiting for the general to appear. The cooks busied themselves preparing the meal. The party had no choice but to prepare for yet another night in the open. Because of this unexpected turn of events, the suffering of the poor servants was even worse than the night before.

The general arrived next morning, and finally the border crossing began. After an early breakfast, the same tedious process of inspection was repeated, a procedure as confusing as it had been at the river crossing. Beyond the stockade, the Chinese, a few lines deep, waved their hands and shouted at them in their tongue; they all seemed to be welcoming them. No doubt, in this border town, the livelihood of the citizens must depend on the mission's comings and goings.

Finally the gate was opened and the chief and deputy envoys, dismounting from their carriage, passed through the gate. Then followed the recording secretary and the entire retinue, one after another, forming an endless line.

A new world unfolded before their eyes. The architecture, the manner of dress, the streets all were foreign. Houses were built with bricks in a straight line, all the people wore black, and their jackets overlapped from left to right. The shirts had no ties, and the Koreans found strange the sight of all those buttons hanging from the jackets. The Chinese wore trousers with such narrow legs that the Koreans wondered how they could bend at all. Men and women freely mixed as they watched the procession. Since everyone wore long outer coats, men and women would have been indistinguishable had it not been for their hairstyles. Men shaved their heads, all except the top, and grew their hair in a long pigtail that swung behind their backs. It was an ugly sight. In Korea, only an old, unmarried servant looked like that.

The women piled their hair in a chignon, like a man's topknot, which they kept in place on the top of their heads with a large hairpin thrust through it. Contrary to what they had heard, they saw no women with bound feet; Manchu women did not bind their feet. And, regardless of her age, every woman wore a flower in her hair and heavy makeup on her face. The sight of those white powdered faces and blood-red lips was repugnant to the Koreans. But the wine and noodle shops were decorated with pretty paper lanterns, and the shops were so full of interesting and unusual goods that it was difficult to believe they were in a small, isolated border town.

They stayed in Ch'aengmun for a few more days, occupied with various activities. Gifts had to be presented to the general, his deputy, the customs officials, even to petty officials. The tributary articles had to be reloaded. The town had inns with heated floors, but the servants could not afford to stay there.

After so long a journey in the middle of winter, the appearance of the mission grew more wretched as each day passed by. Everyone began to take on an air of shabbiness. The servants looked especially battered; their cotton-stuffed clothing had become stiff with dirt, their hands rough with sores, and their faces covered with grotesque beards. And they had no more changes of socks and straw sandals.

The towns and the stopping stations bustled with activity during the mission's sojourn. The journey continued, and at each stopover they received different responses from the townspeople. In some, they became fast friends with the residents, exchanging reluctant partings even after a short stay, but in most, they were not welcome guests, since many of the servants, ignorant and crude, thought nothing of stealing from the townspeople.

As they reached Kao-li Pao, where they began to sense the nearness of Peking, the city was almost devoid of people, and all the shop doors had been locked. Ha-sang was told that the citizens deliberately closed the shops when the Korean mission passed by.

"Who are the inhabitants of this town?" Ha-sang asked Cho Sin-ch'ŏl.

"During the Manchu Invasion of 1636, many Koreans were taken as prisoners and eventually settled here. These people are their descendants. Kao-li means Korea."

"Then they share our blood."

"Yes, indeed. That's not all. You may not have noticed, because it's winter now and the harvest is over, but all around town are rice fields just like ours in Korea. When I first saw them after crossing the river, I was beside myself with joy."

"Why then do our own people refuse to come out of their locked doors to welcome us?"

Becoming pensive, Cho continued after a long silence, "It's all our fault. In olden times, when the mission passed through here, everyone used to come out to welcome them. The townspeople refused to take payment for the wine and food they served to the servants and grooms, and the women didn't run away from them. They shed tears of homesickness, hearing the Korean words. Save us, merciful Buddha . . ."

"Then, why? What has happened now?"

"Are these lowly servants gentlefolk? They took advantage of their hosts' generosity and behaved shamelessly, devouring everything in sight, even stealing the utensils. No wonder the townspeople refused to welcome them. Then they resorted to wholesale stealing. That's the reason why they've begun to avoid us. Save us, merciful Buddha."

"What a shame!"

"Shame, indeed."

Cho's account went on. The townspeople refused to open their shops; only after repeated entreaties did they reluctantly consent to sell anything, but only at inflated prices and after being paid in advance. But the cunning servants somehow outwitted the townspeople, got even with them by deceit, and finally succeeded in making them enemies. "So when the mission passes the town now," Cho continued, "they never fail to shout rebukes: 'You, the descendants of the Korean people, we are your grandfathers. Why don't you come out and pay your respects?' Then the angry voices of the townspeople retort, 'There are only Korean grandfathers here, no descendants of yours.' " Cho paused with a sigh. "How sad! Save us, merciful Buddha," he said, and took out his pipe from his belt.

Since the night Ha-sang helped him bury the corpse on the road, he and Cho had become close friends. The more intimately Ha-sang had come to know him, the more he realized the goodness and purity of Cho's nature. Though Cho's habitual Buddhist prayer was somewhat disturbing, Ha-sang found his sincerity and his expertise in dealing with the problems of the journey helpful to him.

One night while staying in Kao-li Pao, Ha-sang saw Cho, who had been sleeping next to him, get up from among his snoring companions and go out carrying a bundle under his arm. Ha-sang followed him silently.

"Where are you going?" he asked.

"I'm going for a visit. Would you like to come with me?"

"If you'll let me."

Both men left the enclosure.

"Stop! Who goes there?" the night guard shouted, intercepting them.

"We're going out to relieve ourselves," Cho answered, as if in a hurry.

"Both of you want to take a shit at the same time?"

"Yes, yes, we do."

"You sons of bitches. Do you share a bowel, then?" The guard did not question them any further.

Although the servants still had to endure sleeping in the open, their lot had become somewhat easier now that they were at a way-station and more able to move about undetected.

Once inside the town, Cho and Ha-sang made for a lighted house, and Cho knocked at the gate. No one answered, but they sensed someone observing them through a crack in the door. Soon the door was slowly opened, and a man whose face was invisible, silhouetted against the lamplight, made a welcoming gesture, grasping Cho's hands. They exchanged brief words in a tongue foreign to Ha-sang. The only word he understood was "Master Ki," and he realized that Cho was inquiring after the man called Ki.

With reverence, the man led them inside the house, where they came into an empty, corridor-like space. The man pushed open the back gate and led them through a garden and through several wings of the house, one layer after another, all exactly the same. Each wing had a door at the same place in the middle, so that when the doors were open, all the separate structures could be clearly seen through them. From the size of the house, the family seemed to be a prosperous one.

Cho and Ha-sang were ushered into a room with a warmly heated floor. An old man with a long, silvery beard covering his chest welcomed them with a gentle smile. No sooner had they taken seats than refreshments were served on a cloisonné platter, sweets and cakes exactly like those made in Korea. The old man said something in Chinese to Cho.

"The old gentleman says," Cho explained to Ha-sang, " 'Please help yourselves.' As you can see, they don't speak Korean, and they wear Chinese clothes, and live in Chinese-style houses, but they long for their homeland. For two hundred years they have retained the Korean way of cooking. In this town we can still eat food pleasing to our taste."

Cho unwrapped the bundle he was carrying, and out came a man's outercoat, a jacket and a pair of trousers, cotton socks, a horsehair headband, and so on.

"Oh, oh!" The old man stood up and gathered them to his breast with deep respect. His eyes filling with tears, he thanked Cho profusely, while Cho smiled back and nodded.

Cho exchanged a few words with the old man in Chinese. From the intonation and gestures, Ha-sang surmised Cho was saying they must leave because they had to make an early start next morning. Looking very disappointed, the old man signaled to a middle-aged man who appeared to be his son. The son in turn gestured to his wife. She disappeared into an inner room and soon emerged with a servant bearing a bundle. Her husband took the bundle, and as his father said something to him, with his head bowed, he presented it to Cho. Cho sprang to his feet, waved his hands vigorously, and shook his head, refusing adamantly to accept the gift; it was clearly not a gesture of merely being polite. Without proper leave-taking, they dashed out of the house. Outside, a slender moon was sinking.

"Did the old man ask you for a Korean scholar-gentleman's outfit?" Ha-sang asked as they walked through a narrow alley.

"No. But I once heard him say that his last wish in life was to be buried in his native dress, since he could not fulfill his fervent wish to be buried in his ancestors' soil. His ancestor, who was taken prisoner and brought here, was a scholar-gentleman. The family remembered the stories about the country they came from and handed them down from generation to generation. Save us, merciful Buddha."

After a long silence, Ha-sang spoke, his voice scarcely audible, "What an admirable family." Then he added, "Brother, you are a good person."

Ha-sang looked up. The stars, awesome in their profusion, studded the icy sky like jewels.

◆　◆　◆

As soon as they entered Peking and were quartered in the official hostelry provided by the Chinese government, Ha-sang's master, Son, and the other translators began their busy daily routine after only a day's rest. Son had been a translator since his youth, but judging from the fact that he had not yet reached the civil service third rank, his language proficiency was probably of dubious distinction, both in Chinese and Korean. However, his long experience had made him expert in handling small, miscellaneous chores, and he had become indispensable.

All the members of the tributary mission changed into their formal attire on the day of their arrival in Peking. Bearing the message from the king of Korea to the emperor of China, they proceeded to the Board of Rites. First the chief envoy prostrated himself and delivered the document to the minister, announcing, "I came with this message from the king of Korea." The minister, accepting the document, bade him raise himself. Only after that did the envoy retreat to the waiting-room. The message was then carried by a translator and presented to the Ministry of Protocol. The Korean diplomats made a round of ceremonial calls to various ministries, and, returning to their residences, awaited the summons to the imperial audience. Feelings of humiliation constantly tormented the envoys as they endured the ritual obeisance to these Chinese officials, whom they secretly despised.

The situation of the translators was quite different. Since their responsibility was to be the mission's ears and lips, regardless of their real feelings about the Chinese, their frenzied activities imparted the impression that they were in full command. Those who depended on the services of the translators often became anxious and impatient, hoping that they were performing their duties correctly, and were conveying the mission's intentions without misunderstanding.

On the Chinese side, the government had dispatched their translators to Ch'aengmun to meet the mission and escort it to Peking, and at the end of the mission's stay in Peking, to accompany it back to the border. Six Chinese translators and six assistant translators stayed in the room assigned to them outside the eastern gate of the mission's hostelry. However, the linguistic competence of the lower-level translators from both countries was dubious; their knowledge of each other's language did not seem to exceed that of a child. Moreover, many among the translators were unscrupulous individuals, especially the chief translator from Korea this year. Going between the Chinese and Koreans, he exaggerated small matters, pretending to have accomplished certain grave tasks; and, taking all the credit for himself, he succeeded in making both parties suffer over trifles.

The translator Son was not only a man of integrity and honesty but also good to his servants. He had accompanied the delegates to the Board of Rites to present the royal message, but after that he mainly stayed in the mission's residence taking care of details. While serving his master, Ha-sang made many friends among the Chinese guards stationed at the gate. The residence complex contained four houses; the first one was used by the three envoys for official meetings, the second for the chief envoy, the third for the deputy envoy, and the fourth for the recording secretary. Each house had a separate wing and corridor to accommodate servants and lower-level translators.

When each foreign mission left, the hostelry was kept empty; for the next mission's arrival, the entire household would be refurbished. This year, before the Korean mission arrived, the workmen had been dispatched, and the old window paper had been replaced with new, the walls had been freshly papered, blinds had been hung, and a storage shed had been built next to the building. Ha-sang was quartered in the hall of the house where his master was staying with the recording secretary, but from time to time he would visit his companions, the packhorse drivers, who occupied a room made with reed-mats in the cellar underneath the hall.

Since four residences were not enough to accommodate the entire mission, the Chinese had also built a separate house outside the walls, naming it the North House, and transferred there the envoys' cooks and attending translators. On the remaining property, they allowed the merchants to build their own houses with reed-mats. Those with money had their floors heated and furnished the interiors with some luxury. There were not enough rooms for the packhorse drivers, so some shared a room outside the official hostelry, and some even camped out. The horses, too, suffered. Left out in the open, their lot was no better in the midst of the splendors of the capital than it had been in the wilderness of the border country.

At journey's end, the packhorse drivers had nothing to do. In the reed-mat room, they talked, complained, and joked. Sometimes fighting broke out among them. In one such fight the combatants remained in a sitting position, since the ceiling was not high enough for grown men to move about upright. One bitterly cold day, as one of them came in from outside, he inadvertently tripped over his companion, who had been leaning against a wall. Losing his balance, he clutched at the reed-mat floor as he tried to support himself, and a splinter got stuck under his fingernail. A fierce fight broke out among these coarse men, which ended only after the prison guards dashed in and separated them, shouting, "You goddamn sons-of-bitches, if you get into another fight, you'll be flogged to death. Do you understand?"

After the guards had left, no one opened his mouth, not because of the guards' threat, but because the fight had somewhat soothed their long pent-up frustration.

The wind crept in and swept over the floor.

"I'm so cold. Why in hell does this cold never go away?"

"We can't even build fire here in the cellar."

A man in the corner, hugging his knees, started to hum:

In the flowering capital of Peking
There is many a gate,
Many a palace.
In the lordly mansion
The windows are glass,
The roofs are glass.
Light a jade lamp,
Three thousand palace ladies
In their silken quilts and pillows . . .

"Yes, go on!" Another man beat out the tune.

Woe is this wretched packhorse driver's lot.
Am I but a mole?
Am I but a grub?
In this drafty cellar
Without a light
Without a woman . . .

"To tell the truth, last night I had a whore," the singer announced proudly, even before the song was finished.

"You swine. I've been to a pleasure palace myself. So what?"

Everyone roared with laughter. A courtesan in a Peking pleasure palace was far beyond the reach of packhorse drivers. Even with fifty Chinese silver coins, they couldn't so much as look at an unregistered prostitute with a reasonably pretty face.

"I couldn't stand the itch in my groin any more, so I went out and bought myself a whore; but how those Chinese wenches disgust me! Their faces are covered with powder and their lips painted crimson. It's like the Buddhist funeral custom of putting a jewel between the lips of a corpse. It scares me to death. And their feet. Why do they bind and cripple their feet?"

"You are right. Have you seen a woman barefoot? Even a beggar woman doesn't show them. You build the Great Wall with a woman, you'll never see her barefoot. I hear they look like diseased fists. They begin binding their feet when they are babies so the feet don't grow any bigger. Their toes are all stuck under their soles and their feet look like hawks' beaks. Their soles can't touch the ground, so they can't stand up or balance themselves. They raise themselves only by holding onto walls or pillars."

"But I hear Manchu women don't bind their feet."

"So I hear."

"Anyhow, they don't please me. They neglect their womanly duties. They sit around all day putting layers of makeup on their faces. And all those things hanging from their heads—hairpieces, flowers. They pierce their earlobes and wear earrings like Catholic devils."

"And what about their husbands? Their clothes dripping with filth, they cook, wash, sew, and weave. They look like their wives' slaves."

"Idiots!"

"They deserve to be castrated."

"You'd better learn a lesson from this. Now you take good care of your own wife. You've never spent a whole year with her, have you? It's your karma to wander, because you're born under the sign of the post-station horse."

"My poor, wretched wife. Her hands and feet are worn out serving her father-in-law, who is like a tiger, her mother-in-law, who is like a rake, her bitch of a sister-in-law, who is like a fox, and her cantankerous brother-in-law. What does she get for reward? A miserable bowl of rice. And when I return, this husband of hers—"

"Look here, enough of your—"

"No, it's true. I'm a sinner."

Touched by the sincerity of his words, no one made fun of him any more.

A long silence followed, and then someone else spoke. "When you go home this time, why don't you bring her some Chinese face powder and rouge? Be good to her."

"Why, I did that already," he answered, "but the fool went out and sold them to an apothecary to buy her father-in-law a new fur hood and her mother-in-law a new coverlet."

"A filial daughter-in-law, indeed!"

"A true woman of Korea!"

"Yes, our women are the best in the world."

They all became solemn, sunk in longing for their homes and wives, now that months had elapsed since they had left.

Embarrassed by these frank exchanges from the corner of the room, Ha-sang crossed the room stealthily and went outside. The wind whipped his cheeks, and he turned his back to avoid it. As he turned around once again, he noticed a house with its reed-mat walls flapping in the wind and two horses grazing upon the outer layers of the reeds. No one seemed to be inside the house, and before his very eyes, the house began to crumble. He shouted and ran toward the horses, but they kept grazing and did not move until he made a big fuss beside them. A guard came running from outside the gate, and, upon seeing the house reduced to ruin, was wide-eyed with disbelief.

"Look! The horses ate them. They must have been hungry," Ha-sang shouted in Korean, making a chewing gesture and rubbing his stomach.

Standing absentmindedly, the guard shook his head.

"I understand these horses are to be well supplied with soybeans and fodder every day. What has happened to them? You didn't feed them enough, so they were hungry," Ha-sang protested, using his hands and body to convey his points.

The Chinese guard, unable to comprehend, returned to the station and came back with an interpreter.

"What did the horses do?" the interpreter asked Ha-sang in a strange accent.

Ha-sang explained hastily what had happened. "You'd better give them enough to eat," he added with a menacing stare.

"We have done nothing wrong. We feed them plenty."

"I haven't seen them get any soybeans. Give them some from now on."

"We give them soybeans every day," the interpreter insisted.

"Very well, sir. I shall spread the word that in the official hostelry, the horses feed on houses. The news will surely reach the emperor."

Silent for a while, the interpreter went back to his station and did not return. Five days later, the daily allowance given to the mission by the Chinese government included enough soybeans for the horses.

After the presentation of the message to the throne, the Chinese government delivered provisions for the mission every fifth day. This year, the mission had arrived in Peking on December 26th. Since Chinese government offices closed on odd-numbered days, the envoy was unable to present the document until the 28th; therefore, the arrival of provision was delayed for a day. The allowance, which included staple food and raw materials for side dishes, firewood, oil, and feed for the horses, was generous. The chief and deputy envoys received enough food for lavish banquets every night, and for the other thirty members of the mission and their thirty attendants amounts were given commensurate with rank. Since Chinese units of measure were twice those of Korea, the amounts were indeed staggering. However, taking advantage of the differential, the mission's officials responsible for the distribution appropriated the extra half for their personal gain. Even the allowance for the servants and horses did not escape their greed, and the Chinese merchants, eager to deal with these officials, flocked around the gate.

Corruption on the Chinese side was also rampant, since the officials were susceptible to bribes from the merchants. By law, both public officials and private citizens were carefully watched within the walls, and the opening and closing of the gate was performed with strict adherence to the proper procedure. Each day about three in the afternoon, the translators locked and sealed the gate, returning at daybreak the next morning to open it again. Each day the guards announced to the envoys the opening and closing of the gate. Their shouts to the Chinese merchants to leave the premises at day's end disturbed everyone; nevertheless numerous merchants continued to move freely through the gate with their goods and carts. The foreign diplomats, accompanied by their servants, openly went sightseeing in Peking—although it was forbidden by law except by special permission—thanks to their generous bribes to the guards.

Ha-sang had heard that though the Chinese were slack about checking provisions for members of the mission, they carefully watched the allowance for the horses. With this information in mind, he took his chance and threatened the guard on the night he found horses grazing on the reed-mats. What he had heard must have been correct, because it had not happened again. The horse manure heaped within the walls was another matter. It was sold as fertilizer after each mission's departure as part of the Chinese ambassador's legitimate income.

Among the humblest of the party and a first-timer, Ha-sang was still especially careful not to draw attention to himself until he could accomplish his personal mission. Even after that, he knew he must remain extremely alert. He got along well with his companions, joining in their boisterous outbursts so as not to cause suspicion. While behaving like any other packhorse driver, he wanted to find out from them either the location of the South Catholic Church within the Hsuan-wu Gate, which he had heard was not too far from the hostelry, or the church outside the Tung-an Gate. Unfamiliar with both the language and the streets of Peking, he was quite aware of the difficulties that awaited him, and to make things worse, he would be conspicuous in Korean servant's garb. He fully expected to attract contemptuous gazes from the Chinese. With a companion, the going would be easier, but he could not risk being found out.

In the meantime, the New Year's holiday had begun. As they had heard, the Chinese celebrated with exuberant gusto. Firecrackers exploded incessantly outside the walls. Ha-sang's companions took turns going out in groups, and when they returned, they were full of stories about the strange sights and customs they had seen.

"In this country, everything closes until the fifteenth of the month, so all the shops in the Glass Factory Market are closed, but,

I tell you, the Elephant House and the Tiger Park are more crowded than usual."

"You stupid fellow. You talk as though day and night you do nothing but roam around places like that."

"Of course! Every time I come here I go see them. I like ferocious animals."

"That's right. You went to see your own brothers."

"You don't know how gentle and noble a creature a tiger is. He's handsome too, not like you, you demon-chasing mask dancer."

"You think I haven't seen one myself? A tiger, the noble creature as you said, fed on a piece of meat thrown at him, and the children thought he was a plaything, throwing stones at him and teasing him."

"But did you see him bat an eye at the children's mischief? Even though he is caged, he is still the king of the mountain. But compared to tigers, elephants are a disgrace. He's a mountainous creature, but he does his little tricks when a tiny elephant trainer whirls his whip around him. He can lift a timber as big as the post of a mansion, and he can stand on one foot, which is as big as a pillar."

"You're a disgrace yourself. I went to Mansu [Wan-shou] Temple and prayed and made offerings to Buddha. I bought some charms, too. In the coming year, I'm going to be a worthy man."

"To tell you the truth, there is too much to see in Peking. We call them Manchu barbarians, but they're kindly, too. Remember Kŏbuk, the one we left on the road because he became sick with chest congestion, and couldn't move? We were so afraid he might freeze to death?"

"Oh yes. I hear he came back."

"The neighbors took care of him, though they couldn't even communicate with each other. They gave him a warm bed and fed him gruel and clear pork soup. Chest congestion becomes worse in cold weather."

"How kind of them!"

Someone sneezed, and here and there a chorus of sneezes rose as though caught from one another.

"Damn! Why is it still so cold? It's nearing 'Spring Onset.' "

"My guts feel as cold as ice."

"That's why the saying goes, 'In January and February, huge

earthen crocks crack, and the chilly wind of the flowering season makes middle-aged men catch cold.' "

"Well, I know one that goes like this: 'A widower catches a draft of easterly wind around his neck.' A man is meant to sleep with his wife in the same coverlet."

"I'll be glad to be your wife." A hairy man slithered toward him and wrapped his arms around the man's neck.

"Have you ever seen a wife with a bearded face, you creepy, disgusting fellow?"

All burst into wild laughter.

"Shh . . . Let's be quiet. It's nearing midnight. We mustn't disturb our master the recording secretary's sleep," someone warned.

"He is a good gentleman. I was told that the noise we make keeps him awake at night, but feeling sorry for our lot, he doesn't want to complain."

"Indeed. But I feel for the poor souls in the cellar of the deputy envoy's house. He orders them to be quiet, so they can't have any fun talking like us here. He is a difficult master, so no one is allowed to talk, but all night long they annoy him by repeating, 'Oh, so cold; oh, it's so cold!' "

"I wonder if he ever feels sorry for them."

"He may not feel human emotion."

"But have you seen the Buddhist monk he brought with him?"

"Yeah."

"He's quite a man, that's for sure. Within the wall, he goes about as a monk, but once outside, he's a man about town. As soon as he arrived here, he closed his monk business and went all over Peking enjoying the sights."

"He's a disgrace to the master."

"I wonder how much he bribed the guards. He slips through the gate under their very noses."

Some sneezed and some let out dry coughs.

"Hell! I should have learned witchcraft."

"Do you think just anyone can learn black magic?"

"I could use a magician's trick right now."

"Why all of a sudden talk about witchcraft in the middle of the night? Come to the point."

"Look. It goes like this. If I were a magician, I'd just strike my hands together and breathe out. Then all of a sudden this cellar would be transformed into a luxurious mansion with warm rooms, and we would roast our backs on the hot floor, just like we do at home."

"That sounds so good."

"When we were thoroughly warmed, once again I'd strike my hands. Then would come a table with rice packed solid in a bowl, our kind of rice mixed with barley, and beside the rice, a delicious, thick beanpaste soup, and a big serving of pickled cabbage at the height of its flavor."

"Is that all? You said it's a lordly mansion."

"Aren't you happy with that? What else do you want?"

"But we must have some women."

"Let's bring in my wife. I'll call my wife, waving my hands like this." Closing his eyes, he rambled on, "She's wearing an apron and on the chignon on her head with a red ribbon tied around it, I see a threaded needle stuck into it."

"This fellow, who does he think he is kidding? When you go back to your house, you don't need magic; you'll be bored to death seeing such a sight. Just be good to her before she starts nagging."

"If she nagged, I'd just make her disappear right then and there, or I'd come back here again."

"Then what's the use? You're right where you began. What a dull fellow you are! Damn this cold."

Everyone gathered his own filthy coverlet around himself and laughed embarrassedly.

"Let's get some sleep. Our dreams work magic for us," whispered someone.

"This goddamned cold keeps me from sleeping."

The talk continued for awhile longer. One described a performance in which a magician had waved a piece of cloth in front of the spectators to show nothing was in it, then he wrapped it into a roll, and when he opened it again, out poured dozens of precious stones. Another magician swallowed a piece of cord a few inches long, then he pulled it out from his mouth endlessly. Still another swallowed a jujube fruit, clapped his hands and smoothed his throat, and a flame rose out of his mouth. Yet another man had seen a magician put a little girl into a wooden crate, and begin sawing. The box was unmistakably halved, but the girl came out of it smiling. All had mysterious tales to tell.

Although they talked about strange happenings, no one mentioned anything about Catholic churches. Ha-sang resolved in his mind that he must get beyond the wall somehow and find the church by himself.

The fierce midwinter cold had diminished somewhat. As more servants went through the gate, the incidents of misconduct among them increased. Not a few of them were characters of dubious moral principles; thick-skinned and brazen, completely without a sense of honor, they were frowned upon by the citizens of Peking. They had lost face, and their comings and goings had to be strictly checked at the gate.

In the meantime, one morning as he was feeding the horses, Ha-sang noticed a young scholar-gentleman standing beside him.

"Whose servant are you?" he asked Ha-sang.

"My master is the translator, Son."

"I must borrow you today."

"What, sir?"

"I mean you shall accompany me on a sightseeing tour of Peking. You seem like someone I can use. I've had others, but one is too talkative, and the other a real blabbermouth."

Ha-sang stood there blinking.

"I'll inform your master myself. My name is Yi Si-myŏng. I'm the envoy's good-for-nothing nephew."

Ha-sang was still wordless.

"What is your name?"

"I am called Chu Ŭi-jong, sir."

"All right, Ŭi-jong. We'll see a novel sight today. You may already have heard about the Catholic Temple. We will have come to Peking in vain if we return home without ever having seen it. That's where I want to go with you."

Ha-sang's heart stopped beating. He wondered if the man knew his true identity.

"Yes sir. But is it all right to go there?"

"No one can know about it. That's why I asked you to accompany me instead of my own servants."

At about three in the afternoon, they proceeded outside. The guards at the gate let them pass with meaningful but good-natured smiles. Since the incident of the horses, Ha-sang had become a good friend of theirs. Rakish and fearless though he might have appeared, it was obvious to Ha-sang that Yi was hesitant about going to the Catholic church. However, he knew exactly where it was located. Yi, already familiar with the streets, never once faltered. He headed for a soaring structure whose inscription, Cheng-yang Gate, made Ha-sang's heart beat with a loud clamor, for that name had been indelibly marked in his memory as the one that would signal the church was near.

Very soon, a strangely magnificent building began to rise before them. Its unusual tiled roof, together with its great height soaring aloft without the support of cross-beams, made it unmistakably recognizable. It was, indeed, the great church he had heard so much about. Tears filled Ha-sang's eyes as he found himself standing with Yi before its splendor, and marvelling with him at its seventy-foot height and intricate design. The building was high and narrow. The narrow front facing the street had three doors. The doors, too, were of enormous height, and the flower-shaped stained-glass windows above the center door shimmered brilliantly in the sunlight. At either end of the flat roof stood towers as tall as watch towers. Above the three doors as well as above the highest section of the tripartite façade were gables bordered with sculpture and crowned with six crosses rising into the light.

"Oh, the cross of Jesus Christ, who died to save man from his sins, the symbol of pain endured and victory won in his name, the cross which in Korea, good, truth-loving Christians were never once able to carry openly, the cross whose mere shadow was cause enough for cruel persecution." Overwhelmed with the intensity of his own sentiment, Ha-sang felt his cheeks streak with tears, which he hastened to wipe away with his sleeves. He found himself clenching his fists and trembling as his determination grew stronger that he would someday make it possible for the holy cross to soar proudly toward the Korean sky.

Yi, his horsehair hat in danger of falling from his head as he looked up at the church, finally turned to Ha-sang and said, "Look! How magnificent! It seems to pierce the sky. It's not only majestic, but delicate and exquisite in its details. And look at the towers and those gables up there, how they add nobility to the structure!"

"It seems like it, sir, but my neck hurts just looking at them, and my eyes are blinded . . ." responded Ha-sang, still blinking, his words disappearing in a mumble.

"Yŏnam, Pak Chi-wŏn's pen name, in his *Jehol Diary*, which is an account of what he learned in his travels in China, described this church, making only a passing remark about its exterior, tall and extraordinary, but he did not grudge his admiration in describing the furniture, paintings, and sculpture of the interior.[1] From his description, I can well imagine what it's like inside, how wondrous and exquisite it must be. Imagine! We came all the way here and can't see the inside." Yi clucked his tongue in frustration.

"Why don't you go in, then?"

"I wish I could, but we are forbidden to enter."

"The man you called Yŏnam, you said he was inside?"

"When do you think he was here? But it's no use. It's idle of me to mention Yŏnam or his *Diary* to you. You're an ignorant, illiterate servant." After embarrassed laughter, he continued, "The situation's changed since then. Here, too, they've begun to persecute Catholics. Look, all these doors are locked. To tell you the truth, we'd better not even stand here like this any longer." Yi turned around, looked up longingly at the church once again, and moved away.

As they left the church, Ha-sang was convinced that what he had heard in Korea was true: Chinese Catholics were also persecuted.

The date of the mission's departure for Korea was fast approaching, and Ha-sang was growing increasingly anxious. One day he stood before his master, Son.

"May I go to town and see some sights?" he asked with an idiotic smile, rubbing his hands together.

"Of course. You must see those magic shows. Go and see the elephants and camels, too. You'll regret it if you have nothing to tell your friends when you return. Don't forget the Glass Factory Market." Son was happy to grant Ha-sang permission.

Cho Sin-ch'ŏl, familiar with the streets of Peking, accompanied him as a guide. Cho took Ha-sang to the Horticultural Garden, the Garden of Exotic Birds, and the magic shows, which were his fellow packhorse drivers' favorite places to visit, but none interested Ha-sang. Usually quiet and soft-spoken, Cho became excited when he brought Ha-sang to Liulichang, the Glass Factory Market.

1. Pak Chi-wŏn (1737–1805) was a Sirhak scholar and man of letters. He was a member of the Winter Solstice Mission in 1780.

"As you saw," he began the explanation, "the palaces and Buddhist temples here have tiles and bricks of different colors which are as brilliant as glass. They are manufactured in a government factory called the Glass Factory. But not everyone is permitted to go in there. When they receive orders, the workers bring with them enough food to last a few months, and once they enter the factory, they can't come out until they finish the orders. The marketplace on the south side of the factory just outside the Chŏngyang [Chengyang] Gate is called Liulichang. Once you get there you'll find out that the entire length is, without exaggeration, two miles, so it's divided into the East Market and West Market. They have goods from all over the world, anything under the sun: food, dishes, clothes, all kinds of treasures, trinkets, calligraphy scrolls, paintings, books, stationery, just about anything."

From the facile way he managed to pronounce the names of all those fancy articles, which most ignorant servants could hardly even imitate, it seemed to Ha-sang that Cho must have acted as a guide to members of the mission in the past.

"I would like to buy some brushes and inkstones for my scholarly neighbor," Ha-sang said casually.

"Then we must go to this place called Myŏngsŏng-dang. They carry all sorts of goods of the highest quality; papers, brushes, inkstones, all fit for an emperor. I've seen people buy such things."

The shop did indeed have many precious objects, but contrary to what Ha-sang had expected, the prices were reasonable, since they were local products. For Tasan, he bought some White Palace paper, Green Palace paper, inksticks of Misty Purple Jade, and ivory brushes.

"Is that all you're buying? Why don't you buy some more? You can sell them at a profit when you go back to Seoul."

"He gave me only money enough to buy these."

"Since you're here, you might as well buy some Chinese face powder and rouge for your mother or sister, or your wife."

"I have no one to whom I can give such things."

No woman he knew wore makeup, his mother, his sister, even Mistress Teresa or Maria.

"You are not married yet?"

"No."

"You don't even have a girl?"

"No."

"Then all the more reason to use the opportunity to make a little fund for your wedding. I'll loan you some money. Buy whatever you fancy. These are not illegal articles and don't take too much space, and in Seoul they'll sell like hotcakes." Cho must have thought that Ha-sang remained unmarried because of his poverty.

Ha-sang did not answer. The dizzy array of articles displayed in the stores had no relevance for him. As they traversed the market, his eyes sought only a tobacco shop, because he remembered that the secret messenger, Yi Yŏ-jin, sent by the Korean Catholics in 1811 to present a petition to the bishop of Peking asking for a clergyman to come to Korea, had been aided by a tobacco shop owner; through him Yi had finally succeeded in meeting the bishop.

Tobacco production in China had been taught by European missionaries, and among those engaged in the trade were many Catholic converts. Remembering the advice that it was safe to assume that houses without images of idols pasted on the doors probably belonged to Catholics, Ha-sang carefully observed each tobacco shop they passed. Almost all the shops had red paper talismans with charms written in gilt or black on their doors. He saw a number of tobacco shops, but all of their doors had the same strange pictures of idols. Finally he came upon one without them. He felt his heart lift.

Next afternoon, in his filthy, Korean servant's outfit, Ha-sang went alone to the shop, where the owner welcomed him quietly. There was no one in the shop, and taking advantage of the moment, Ha-sang produced a piece of paper from his jacket and placed it in front of his host. In the center of the paper was the sign of the cross. The shop owner cast his eyes upon it, and stared at Ha-sang, who drew a small cross upon his chest. The man quickly took Ha-sang's hands and led him into another small room where heaps of tobacco leaves were stacked against a wall. Ha-sang gestured for a brush and paper, and on it he wrote in Chinese: "I am pleased to meet a fellow Catholic."

Once again, the owner's eyes widened with disbelief, seeing before him a servant who could write a message with a masterful calligraphic hand. Unlike other Chinese merchants, who were mostly illiterate, the owner appeared to have some education, and he kept nodding his head joyfully. At that moment, these total strangers suddenly became dear friends, united by the bond of their faith. A customer entered, putting an end to their written communication, but Ha-sang had managed to impart his real name, his identity, and his mission. His new friend promised that if Ha-sang would come again the next day around sunset, he would take him to the Catholic church.

Next day, Ha-sang left the mission's hostelry about three in the afternoon, but it was the time for the gate to be closed, so the guards stopped him. Looking at Ha-sang's meaningful smile, they let him pass with a knowing leer, as if they were saying that they knew his intentions. That night, he had dinner in the shopowner's back room. The dumplings he was served were delicious, but Ha-sang had no thought for food. They waited for dusk and then left the shop, which was just outside of Hsuan-wu Gate; the church was within the gate. It was near the end of the month, and the moon had not yet risen, protecting them from being seen. In the gloom, the church appeared even taller and more magnificent. Wang, the tobacconist, pushed open a door in the wall that encircled the church. The door had been left unlocked; Wang must have informed someone that they were coming.

Inside the wall was a large property with several big houses. No light came from them; they seemed congealed in darkness. There was, however, a lone, lighted house, and Wang led Ha-sang there. The house had neither eaves nor a gate, but light flickered from the long, narrow windows. They climbed up the short, stone stairway against the wall and found a massive door with a horseshoe-shaped knob. Wang knocked lightly. A dog barked within, and the door was opened in a flood of light. A Manchu man with a queue welcomed Wang. The dog, large and of a strange breed, stopped barking and wagged its tail. Inside, the room had a wooden floor, but the style of architecture was foreign to Ha-sang. There were wooden doors on either side. From the beamless, plastered ceiling were suspended two curious-looking lamps on slender chains, their flames capped with potbellied glass tubes.

The Manchu man led them to one of the wooden doors and knocked gently. Foreign-sounding words came from within, and their guide pushed open the door. In the large, brightly lit room, a bareheaded European man in Chinese dress sat facing a desk. He stood up and came toward them, motioning them to sit down, and he himself sat down. Instead, Wang knelt in front of him. Following Wang's example, Ha-sang knelt beside him. The foreigner stood up and drew the sign of the cross over their heads. After the blessing, everyone took a seat. The European was as tall as Ha-sang, with a large nose and deep-set blue eyes. His complexion was clear and white, and his luxuriant beard and sideburns were the color of chestnuts.

On the paper Wang had brought with him, he wrote: "The Korean fellow Catholic, Paul Ha-sang Chŏng." With a tender smile, the foreigner nodded toward Ha-sang. Then, Wang wrote again: "The acting bishop of Peking," and showed it to Ha-sang.

Ha-sang stood up and made a deep bow, concluding their preliminary introduction. He then took over the brush and paper and began to write: "As the Catholic leaders of Peking must already know, in Korea, the Catholic church was born unaided by any missionary effort, which can only be attributed to a miracle." Ha-sang went on to describe the predicament of the Korean Catholics: "After the martyrdom of the Chinese Father, Chou Wen-mu, we have been without a leader and are unable to follow Christian teachings. We suffer both from extreme poverty and cruel persecution." He explained that his mission to Peking was intended to make known the longing of the suffering Korean Christians to be blessed with the presence of a priest. While moving his brush, Ha-sang had to pause a few times to wipe his tears, which were dropping onto the paper and making the ink run. Tears also filled the eyes of the other two men as they watched him.

The alien clergyman's face clouded with pain. He was a Lazarist, Father José Ribeiro, representing Bishop Joachim de Souza Saraiva, who had been appointed to succeed de Gouvéa as the bishop of Peking, but had so far been unable to enter Peking because of Emperor Chia-ch'ing's extremely hostile policy toward Catholicism. At the same time, the French Revolution had shaken the Roman Catholic Church, which was no longer able to send missionaries abroad. Now, confronting this pure youth pleading for a clergyman to come to his country, Father Ribeiro, his own fate precarious, agonized over his inability to grant an answer to Ha-sang's entreaty. Although proficient in Chinese writing, he could not pick up the brush. Instead, grasping the youth's hands, his face darkened with sorrow and tears glistening in his eyes, he could only look at Ha-sang and promise him that he would do whatever was in his power.

Even though he was greatly disappointed by Father Ribeiro's

response, Ha-sang was filled with an ineffable sense of comfort because he was at last able to partake of the sacraments—confession, confirmation, and baptism. Until he left Peking, he visited the church often and attended mass. His determination to work for his sacred calling strengthened each time he was touched through the service by the grace of God; he felt his soul gaining new courage and his life being transformed.

On February 4, the mission left Peking. Ha-sang received many gifts from Father Ribeiro: Bibles, prayer books, books of catechism, rosaries, sacred paintings, and crucifixes. Summoning up all his resourcefulness, Ha-sang hid the sacred objects in his belongings. He was on his way back home a completely changed man.

The weather was now milder, so the return passage was much easier. Since there was no need for strict inspections, the mood of the mission was also relaxed. Everyone felt carefree, as if on an excursion. However, the Chinese imperial gifts to the Korean court were much more numerous than the Korean gifts to Peking, and twice as many horses were required to carry them back. The Chinese wagons had carried the goods as far as the border, but from Ŭiju they had to be loaded on the horses. Ha-sang managed to escape the scrutiny of the inspection, but in the confusion he was assigned a horse that he knew would cause him trouble later on; because of his youth, however, he refrained from complaining to the elders. Even before they reached P'yŏngyang, the horse injured its leg. Ha-sang was left behind and arrived in Seoul a day later than the rest of the party. As he was approaching Hongjewŏn in Seoul, holding the reins of his limping horse, his steps weary, a man appeared before him out of nowhere.

"Welcome back," said the man.

"Ah, Uncle Pae!" cried Ha-sang, happy to see him. "I'm sorry to be late. My horse sprained its leg."

"No. Oh, no. It's good that you are late or you would have been one of them. It's all our Lord's will," Pae said, putting his arms around Ha-sang.

"What are you talking about?"

"Paul, a disaster struck. Last night, Master Peter Cho and Mistress Teresa were taken away."

"Mistress Teresa?"

Ha-sang collapsed in his tracks on the road.

Chapter Nine

♦ ♦ ♦

Embrace

Teresa Kwŏn was the youngest daughter of Kwŏn Il-sin, Francesco Xavier, who was one of the first Catholics in Korea. Her mother had died when she was only six years old. A renowned Sirhak scholar and a devout Christian, her father had been banished to Cheju Island in 1791. However, Francesco was a filial son. When his mother became critically ill at the age of eighty, there was no other choice left for him but to recant his faith so that he could return home to look after her. Ironically, weakened by torture, he died on the journey home. Thus Teresa was left an orphan in the care of her uncle, Ch'ŏl-sin, who reared her with generosity and compassion. Those in the clan who survived the persecution were closely knit and helped each other.

When Teresa was seventeen, the Persecution of 1801 took her uncle, who eventually died in prison, leaving the Kwŏn clan devastated. Teresa left her hometown for Seoul, taking with her one of her nephews. Since early childhood she had been a virtuous girl; the repeated misfortunes in her life had turned her into a woman with a gentle and humble disposition.

Because of her beauty, she attracted many suitors, but discarding all temporal comforts, she offered her love only to the Lord. After her baptism by Father Chou Wen-mu, her determination grew even stronger. However, those around her urged her to marry before passing the marriageable age; they warned her against bringing another disaster upon herself by remaining unmarried. Finally she gave in and married Cho Suk, whose baptismal name was Peter, on the condition that, following the example of the Virgin Mary and Joseph, they remain a celibate couple. At first, the groom could not believe what the bride proposed, but they overcame the human frailty of the flesh again and again and succeeded for fifteen years in maintaining a celibate married life. (Examples of this practice can occasionally be found in the annals of the Catholic church.) Ha-sang had come to know this holy couple through his teacher, Cho Tong-sŏm, Justino, who introduced him to Cho Suk, his close relative, and Teresa had become as dear to him as if she were his own sister.

While waiting anxiously for Ha-sang's return from Peking, Cho Suk was captured when a liturgical calendar was found on his person. This condemning evidence belonged to a man who was preparing to become a Catholic under Cho Suk's guidance, but the authorities had been informed that it belonged to Cho Suk. Cho, without protesting, confessed that the book indeed was his. He was immediately taken to the police. Teresa followed him to the prison, declaring that she, too, was a Christian. They were joined by Barbara Ko, whose husband had been banished to Musan with Justino, and had studied Catholicism under him. When her husband died there, Barbara buried him in his ancestral burial ground, and came to Seoul to live with Cho Suk and Teresa, helping them with household chores. Only a day's delay saved Ha-sang from the same fate, an accidental delay caused by his crippled horse on the weary journey back from Ŭiju to Seoul.

The three prisoners appeared to be infinitely happy. In prison, unafraid, unashamed, no longer with anything to hide, they followed their faith with beatitude and devotion, waiting only for the moment of their ultimate glory, martyrdom. The prison officials showed no mercy for the women, torturing them throughout the interrogations. But the three gladly submitted to the pain, believing that their suffering would enable them to experience the supreme happiness of becoming one with Jesus Christ.

Having succeeded in bribing the prison guards, Ha-sang was able to visit the couple. He was overwhelmed by the filth and stagnant air of the tiny prison room. Realizing the tenacity of life that could survive these conditions, as well as the hunger and thirst, Ha-sang felt a sharp pain boring into his heart anew.

The government policy toward Catholics had changed drastically since the Persecution of 1801. In Seoul, the authorities had become

lax in rounding up Christians, believing that they had already succeeded in eliminating their leaders and those with personal wealth.
However, the Queen Dowager Kim's Edict of 1801 remained in
effect until the Treaty of Amity was concluded with the French
government in 1886. In the outlying districts, Christians suffered
persecution intermittently at the hands of corrupt local officials, or
as the result of personal grudges against them, or by those who
informed against them for material gain. There was no widespread
policy of persecution throughout the nation, and rarely had death
sentences been carried out even when district governors submitted
their decisions to the central government. The Cho Suk case, therefore, was a tragic exception in Seoul, where Catholics were in general more free to pursue their faith.

The punishment had also changed. Whereas the process of sen-
tencing following interrogation and torture had once been swift,
sending the culprits quickly into exile or to their execution, now
prisoners died a lingering death in their cells under conditions beyond human endurance. Cho and Teresa had already been in this
cesspool of a prison for more than a year and a half. Since none of
the three prisoners would betray the names of their brethren even
under the most cruel torture, further escalation of the incident had
been contained. Without knowing the intentions of the authorities,
Teresa prayed ceaselessly for the day when she would attain her
martyrdom.

Unable to see Cho and Teresa freely, Ha-sang waited in agony.
For this reason, since the day he had learned from Matteo Hong,
the proprietor of the inn at the bamboo grove, that Maria's father,
Kwŏn Ho-sin, was being held in the prison at Kongju, he had been
unable to take Maria to visit her father.

Matteo Hong, in the meantime, sold his inn and moved to the
hamlet where his aunt Agatha lived, not far from Kongju. It had only
thirty or so houses, but there were some tile-roofed houses scattered
among the well-padded, thatched ones which seemed to be refurbished annually. Agatha was two years younger than her nephew.
Matteo's mother, the eldest of her siblings, had given birth to him
when she was sixteen; at about the same time, her own mother, at
forty-five, gave birth to her youngest sister, Agatha. Since her
mother was too old to produce milk, Matteo's mother nursed both
babies, so that the aunt shared her sister's milk with her nephew.

For this reason, Matteo and Agatha's relationship had always been unusually close; even in religious matters, they were equally devout.

The uncle, Thomas So, who had narrowly survived the persecution, supervised the tenant farms of a wealthy landowner. Both master and tenants liked Thomas, who was compassionate to the farmers and gave no cause for the master to think him insolent; the master trusted his honesty and diligence and the farmers depended on him. In the winter, unlike those who congregated in the servants' quarters wasting away their idle time in bawdy talk and gambling, he wove straw sacks and ropes, and, handy with his chisel, made boxes for tobacco, wooden trays, and basins. In the inner room, the neighborhood women gathered, bringing with them their winter sewing, or showing off their skills in wicker-making. While their hands were dexterously engaged, they exchanged stories and witticisms. Even petty soldiers sometimes wandered into their house and joined in their merry-making. In spite of their childlessness, their home was always filled with cheerful hubbub.

Matteo Hong bought a small house in the village with a bit of land. He came to be known as Agatha's brother from Seoul, who, after squandering away his considerable fortune, had come back a reformed man to be near his "sister" and her husband in his hometown. Matteo and his wife were a handsome couple—the husband tall and clean-shaven and the wife composed and comely. They had but one blemish—their only son. Looking at the son's unbecomingly huge frame and vacant yet ferocious expression, the villagers wondered and felt sorry for his parents. The "son" was really the servant boy Pŏm, who had worked for Matteo in the inn. Matteo was now known as Mr. Hŏ and Pŏm as To-sŏng.

"Who would want to leave anything to an only son like him? No wonder he is broke," said the villagers. But as the busy rice-transplanting season arrived, opinion changed. "Talk about a crippled son being filial; look at Mr. Hŏ's son, To-sŏng. From morning to night, he never lets his eyes wander. He does all the heavy work with never a complaint. Wait and see. The half-wit will soon earn back all the money his father has lost."

"You are so right. The old sayings are never wrong."

Everyone envied Hŏ for his half-wit son. Among these simple villagers, Hŏ acquired a reputation as a worldly man with experiences beyond their narrow confines, a daring man who thought nothing of squandering away his fortune. Soon they began to regard him as one of their own.

Though healthy in appearance, Hŏ's wife had long suffered from a stomach ailment. Her dim-witted son looked after her with devotion, but a woman's hands were needed in such a situation. Since no bride could be found for their son, his younger sister had married before him, contrary to the conventional marriage order. It was this daughter who came one day with her husband to take care of her mother.

Judging from the appearance of the groom, they had married their daughter off before the family fortune had declined. The groom, though a bit too tall, was a scholar-gentleman with impeccable manners and appearance. When the villagers beheld the daughter's face that emerged out of the dust-covered, hooded cloak, they marvelled at its beauty—a celestial fairy had descended.

"You said Korea is big? In this wide, wide land, no one could be as beautiful as she."

"I've never seen a face like hers."

They were lost in admiration. However, the young couple's conduct amazed the good-natured villagers even more. During the month's visit allowed by her husband's family, never once did the bride enter her husband's room. No matter what it took, she said, she would stay with her mother every moment until she was completely well. The groom's wet-nurse accompanied the young couple to help the bride, but she insisted on doing everything herself, from brewing the medicinal herbs and massaging her mother's body to changing the bedding. The nurse, unable to help her mistress, spent her time darning the master's socks and taking care of his clothing, which had become shabby after the long journey.

The month's stay was fast coming to an end and, unobserved by others, the daughter often wiped away tears. Only To-sŏng, too stupid to realize time's swift passage, remained jovial, dashing between the house and the village.

Two days before the end of the visit, the bride's aunt invited them for dinner. Almost every other night they had been invited to dinner at various households, since it was their long overdue first homecoming. To get to the aunt's house, they had to cross the village. As they approached, they heard tumultuous folk music coming from the brightly lit area.

"They must be having a shaman rite," complained To-sŏng.

"We picked the wrong day," the tall groom grumbled, frowning in displeasure.

"No. On the contrary, it's better on a night like this. In the darkness and the jostling crowd, they can hardly distinguish one person from another. And no doubt all the prison guards will go to the shaman rite, and after the orgy they will be drunk and disoriented," whispered To-sŏng, suddenly assuming an air of intelligence and firmness.

"But, of all things, we will come face to face with the shaman."

"We must take advantage of it."

"Do you really think so?" The brother-in-law was not quite convinced.

In the dusk, the young man's face was visible, broad cheekbones with thick eyebrows over large, elongated eyes, and smallish lips defined by a thick black beard. It was Chŏng Ha-sang, now a proud scholar-gentleman.

Judging from its size and scale, the house where the shaman rite was being performed seemed to belong to a wealthy landowner. The women who gathered around the gate were exchanging gossip.

"This household is blessed with fifty thousand good fortunes. It's all because of their virtue in never neglecting the offering of prayers to the Mountain God, the Supreme Household God, the Seven Stars Spirit, and the Underworld Spirit, and they never forget to feed all the spirits of those who met untimely deaths. This time, the mistress of the house brought the shaman from her own home district and is having her perform the rite with no expense spared. It's been going on for a few days already, this cleansing and untying, so that no trace of uncleanliness will remain."

"The mistress is from Imsil, Chŏlla Province, I hear."

"They say there is an awfully good shaman in Imsil. No one knows where she came from, and she is still a virgin."

"Goodness! How old is she? How can a virgin perform the rite?"

"No one knows how old she is, either. But her rite is so miraculous that she is often invited to perform in other districts. You know very well if someone else did such a thing, she would surely be murdered."

"That's right. When she sings the 'Princess Piri Ballad,' they say no matter how hard they try, they can't stop the tears from covering their faces."

"Because this household always has this rite of exorcism, it is never touched by misfortune. Last year at this time they had the same rite. The following month, the young master passed the civil service examination and his first son was born, remember?"

The autumn sunset came early. The sun sank behind the mountain abruptly, like a gourd dipping into well water. From the alley came a clear, lovely voice.

"It's already time for the 'Fishermen Ballad,'" cried the women as they ran toward the sound.

Fishermen, fishermen,
Frightening fishermen;
Thirty-eight fishermen in the upper court,
Twenty-eight fishermen in the center court,
Eighteen fishermen in the lower court.
Those who died on alien soil
During the war with Japan in 1592,
Those who died of longing,
Those who died on the road;
Now thirty fishermen in the upper court,
Now the center court is the lower court.
Fishermen within the gate,
Fishermen without the gate,
Fishermen who carried the flags.

The clear voice was at once pathetic and sensuous. A slender young girl came out carrying a gourd that contained small amounts of flaked dried whiting, rice cake, soybean, and dried meat slices, all mixed with rice wine. She kneaded the morsels with her fingers and scattered them in front of the house, all the while singing:

Fishermen who ascended to heaven into the realm
Of the soul, ten thousand miles away
During the war with Japan,
Those who died of thirst and hunger,
Those who died of plague,
Those who died sitting, standing, or sleeping.

What was being sung was so incongruous with the girl's loveliness
and her tender age that the contrast made the ballad sound even
more brutal and terrifying. At that moment, whispers rose among
the women who were following the girl.

"Heavens! Look what happened. The gourd fell facing toward
the house."

"A strange happening, indeed."

Without flinching, the girl picked up the gourd, walked toward
the ritual table for the fishermen, gathered the offerings into the
gourd, and poured some wine into it. Mixing the contents with her
fingers, once again she scattered them around the alley. She resumed the song unperturbed:

> Souls who died of flogging,
> Who died from arrows,
> Who died from bullets,
> Souls who died within the gate,
> Souls who died without the gate.

The singer continued her incantation with an icy detachment. She
threw the gourd, and again it landed facing the house, but she remained unshaken.

The "Fishermen Ballad" was sung at the end of the twelve-step
rite of exorcism. The shaman gathered into a gourd the offering food
from the table that had been set outside the gate and sang while
mixing the morsels to lure and feed the inauspicious spirits. The
swarming spirits, thus entertained and appeased, would not violate
the peace of the household. Because this rite was performed to exorcise the devils from the house, in order for the rite to be successful,
the gourd had to land facing out. If the gourd landed facing the
house, it was believed to be a bad omen. For this reason, as the girl's
gourd twice landed inauspiciously, cold shivers passed through the
onlookers' spines.

At that moment, a party of travelers was crossing the alley: a tall
gentleman, a delicately built woman in a hooded cloak, a stout
young man, and a plump middle-aged woman. Butterfly, so far un-
ruffled, picked up her gourd once again, gathered into it the remaining offerings from the table, and threw the entire contents at the
travelers, all the while continuing her incantation in a smooth, unaf-
fected manner:

Those who were flogged to death,
Those who died on the road,
Those who died of thirst and hunger,
Those who died of smallpox, chicken pox, and plague,
Died of soldiers' grudge;
Fishermen, oh frightening fishermen,
Receive this rite today
And cleanse this house and courtyard.

The four passersby were covered with an unexpected shower of offerings. However, this time the gourd fell facing outward.

"Shaman bitch! I'll wring her neck. How dare you, sorceress, insult a gentleman like this? I'll drag you to the magistrate." To-sŏng was furious.

"To the magistrate, did you say? Let's go, you devils," Butterfly dared To-sŏng. "Some good will come of going to the magistrate!"

"There's something fishy about this! Twice the gourd fell facing toward the house, but as soon as the shaman threw the gourd at the travelers, it landed facing outward," a woman mused aloud.

As the argument grew louder, people came out of the house.

"We shun excrement for its filth, not out of fear. We must not keep my aunt waiting. It's best to leave, the sooner the better," Ha-sang advised.

To-sŏng followed him, panting, unable to contain his anger.

"You fishermen devils! Your father beheaded, your mother pushed to her death by a wicked man. You bitches and sons of bitches, you, too, will become wandering devils!" Running after them, Butterfly shouted and spat three times.

To-sŏng fumed with anger, but Maria gathered her cloak tightly over her eyes. The girl appeared too young to be a shaman. Maria wondered if it was her nature or the circumstances of her life that had made her language and behavior so rough in spite of her loveliness and strange air of nobility. Maria had never seen a face such as hers, incredibly beautiful and aflame with a bewitching spell, yet its expression empty, bereft of soul, dark as a void. But there was something familiar in that face. In spite of the shaman's vehement, vulgar language and behavior, Maria could not help feeling for her an emotion close to love.

Then Maria remembered the name—Cecilia; her sister was named by her great uncle after Saint Cecilia, the patron saint of musicians, because at her birth the infant's cries were like the twittering of beautiful birds. As they traveled on, Maria could hardly suppress the impulse to turn around and go back to the girl who had sung the ominous and ghastly incantation. The shaman's curse did not anger Maria; instead, she felt as if this child had been her companion for a long time.

As the darkness thickened under their feet, Ha-sang, who walked behind, protecting Maria, was beginning to feel increasingly apprehensive; he realized that where they were heading was not to the house of Maria's aunt, but to the prison.

Contrary to his appearance, To-sŏng was intelligent and decisive. As he had predicted, the prison guards were deep in drunken slumber. Unlike the Seoul prisons, which contained separate rooms for thieves, debtors, and ordinary criminals, and sleeping quarters for the guards, in addition to rooms for corpses and coffins, this provincial prison was a log hut, filthy and small, with low ceilings and two small barred windows, the only source of light. If bribed well, the guards would allow non-Christian family members to send in some food or exchange a few words with the prisoners at a tiny hole through which the prisoners' wastes were emptied. At night the guard bolted and chained the only door, and after locking it with an enormous padlock, he would often go home for the night; if a fire broke out, there would be no one to save the prisoners from burning to death.

After taking part in the five-day shaman rite, devouring food, drinking, and dancing, the guards lay snoring. To-sŏng slipped the key from the belt of a guard and opened the gate. Calming the half-dazed prisoners who had been awakened from their sleep, they began looking for Kwŏn Ho-sin. Moonless, starless, the night was black as lacquer, and as they opened the gate the stench was so overpowering that they were forced to retreat a few steps.

"Anyone who wishes to escape, do so now," To-sŏng whispered. "We are only to bring with us Mr. Kwŏn. But you must hurry. The guards are dead asleep now, but if any one of them should wake, it will be the end, I assure you."

A few prisoners tried to move, but were so weakened by long confinement that they could only stagger. Some managed to get out, supporting each other. Although it was pitch-dark, accustomed as they were to the lightless room, the prisoners moved about without confusion. A baby started to whimper. Its young mother quickly gave it her breast to stop the crying.

"Mr. Kwŏn, Mr. Kwŏn, where are you? We are here to take you home," To-sŏng asked under his breath.

No answer came: they could only hear phlegm-filled coughing.

"Is that you, Mr. Kwŏn? Hurry, hop on my back, your daughter is here too."

"My daughter? Which one? Maria? Cecilia? Or Juliette?"

"It's I, Maria, father. Our Lord granted that I see my father . . ." Maria began to sob.

"Who are you?" someone whispered, weak yet coherent. "We can't move because we are shackled. You must gag the guards and tie them. You never know when they'll wake up from their drunken sleep. It will be a disaster if the guards come to their senses."

To-sŏng went out, bound the guards as the man had suggested, and lit the lamp he had been carrying.

"Please be quiet. You are all right if you don't make any noise. From time to time the guards play games, so they are used to seeing this much light from outside." Though the prisoner's speech faltered, what he said made sense.

"As you can see," the voice continued, "Mr. Kwŏn is over there in the corner. I suppose you must be their loved ones, but I think he does not wish to leave this prison."

In the semi-darkness, the interior became dimly visible. The speaker was leaning against the wall with a few others, his ankles, like theirs, pushed into holes on a heavy wooden board, a torture device. The straw mats on the floor were rotten with the blood and pus from their torture wounds. The sight of the prisoners covered with sores was piteous, yet it provoked an involuntary sense of revulsion. Those who had just returned from the fresh round of torture lay half dead, and those who had somewhat recovered from their wounds were nursing them. The prisoners were given only a few spoonfuls of thin gruel a day, so that the hunger was harder to endure than the worst torture. To assuage the hunger pangs, they ate the lice that inhabited their clothing and chewed on the blood- and pus-soaked straw.

Maria could not find her father in the small prison room. Half-crazed, she searched for him until finally her eyes rested on an old man leaning against a wall where the light did not reach, but he

was a stranger to her; he could not be her father. He was making
something, his hands moving dexterously even in the dark.

"Father, where are you? It's Maria! I've come to take you home!"
Maria raised her voice in spite of her usually decorous manner.

"You must be a daughter of Mr. Kwŏn, an offspring of the illustrious family that prospered for many a generation. I know the story
of your misfortune. Seven or eight years ago, I hear, your family was
driven to ruin by the slave they had raised. Your beauteous mother,
and the daughters as precious as flowers, all disappeared without a
trace. But now a daughter has come back. I rejoice in your felicity.
Your father endured the severest torture without a word; the only
words he spoke were in praise of our Lord."

Maria could not bear the sorrow any longer. Throwing herself
upon the old man's knees, a heap of rags, she writhed in pain. "Father, father, oh, father!" she cried.

"Who still among the living calls me father?" the old man asked,
waving his hands, his throat choked with phlegm.

"Father, I am Maria. I am living with a group of celibate Christian
women, and each day we observe the Christian ritual. We are happy
serving our Lord, the Father of the heavens and the earth," Maria
pronounced, grasping tightly his fragile, twiglike fingers.

"Oh Lord, hear our praise!" When the tear-filled eyes were
opened, even in the dim light, it was clear that the old man was
blind.

Pain seizing her anew, Maria muffled her sobs.

"What happened to your mother?" he asked after a long pause.

"That demon, Sŭng Nak-chong, caused her to fall from the cliff."

"She died, then," he continued. "Maria, remember what Saint
Vincent de Paul said: 'No one can fathom divine Providence before
it is revealed.' "

"But, mother, to fight off the demon's advance—"

"The Lord's grace protected her chastity." Kwŏn spoke serenely.

"But if it were not for this Satan, our family would not have met
this fate!" Maria continued to sob.

Until that fateful, nightmarish evening, just as her mother's
beauty had been peerless, so had her father been handsome and
lordly, a vigorous man in his prime. Aware of the suffering and pain
that had caused him to age beyond recognition within a mere seven
years, Maria felt her heart torn to pieces.

"We cannot linger any longer, Mr. Kwǒn. Please let me carry you," To-sǒng whispered, turning his back to him.

"No. I'm stronger. Let me—" Ha-sang insisted.

"I thank all of you. But this is where I want to remain. There is no other place I wish to go, nor am able to go," Kwǒn said, remaining motionless.

"Mr. Kwǒn—"

"Men doubt and err, and God judges."

"Mr. Kwǒn!"

"These words sustain my strength. I would follow what our Lord teaches me; I, an ignorant and undeserving servant."

"Mr. Kwǒn. Please, you can talk later, but now let me carry you," urged Ha-sang.

"We Koreans are all sinners, so our Lord has not allowed the great day to arrive. Until that day comes, we bear testimony to our faith and endure our sufferings." After a few faint coughs, Kwǒn continued. "You young people don't realize how ardently we pray for the grace of our Lord. There are many Christians who are steadfast in their faith even after repeated persecution, severe punishment, hunger, and their families' disintegration. But there are also those who are weak in their faith and are ready to apostatize at the slightest sign of persecution. And above all, we are blessed. In Heaven there are countless martyrs, and on earth are those who bear witness to Him. Look at these good people in this tragic prison. Before long, this place will burst forth with the flowers of their martyrdom and sainthood, and they will be a catalyst for the great awakening."

"Mr. Kwǒn. We have no more time. Please let us go," Ha-sang urged him once again.

"He will never leave here. He is our leader, the comfort and support of all of us here," the man in shackles said firmly. "It will be better if you go back."

"Yes, he is right. You must go back right now. I have no more wishes in this world, now that I have embraced my daughter here on this earth, whom I hoped only to see in paradise." As he spoke, Kwǒn's voice was filled with joy.

"I cannot leave here," he went on haltingly. "Though his family name is unknown, the noblest of men, my intercessor, died in this prison. He was an emaciated old man. As you may already know,

they are letting the prisoners die slow, lingering deaths; therefore
food is always a problem. Here in this prison, because each is responsible for his own meal, the prisoners make straw rope, shoes,
caps, and so on, and have the guards exchange them for food. Some
have their families send in food. But those without either skill or
relatives must depend on the kindness of the villagers. The old man,
André, when he found out that the villagers were too poor even to
feed their own children, was so tormented that he stopped eating.
He could not endure others' suffering for his sake. Since then, I
have chosen him to be my intercessor."

"Mr. Kwŏn, we really don't have a moment longer," To-sŏng
said impatiently.

"You said your name is Paul? Paul and Maria, I will not leave
this place. The Lord's grace enabled me to learn the skill of making
straw shoes. Though I am blind, my hands can make sturdier shoes
than any made by men with eyes to see. This unworthy skill helps
those without any resources to survive the hunger and thirst, for
however short a time that might be."

"And," the man in shackles added, "he gives us courage and
comfort. When our faith weakens, he gives us new strength; like a
father, he takes care of us." He paused, then begged feebly, "Please
don't take him away from us."

Here and there sobbing was heard. All the people who had ini-
tially tried to escape, now changing their minds, returned. On that
night, except for the one who was lying in the corner, there were
only Christians in the prison.

"If you want to help me, before you go you must leave the prison
just as it was before, put the key back on the guard's belt and lock
the gate from outside. You must not leave any trace of your having
been here, or we will face more horrible torture." Kwŏn went on,
"Before long, we shall meet each other in Heaven and enjoy everlasting happiness together, although I believe that paradise is actually right here in this prison."

"Yes, indeed. Listening to Mr. Kwŏn's words, and watching him,
we never doubt that this is our paradise," the man in the shackles
agreed with all sincerity. "Maria, dear, do you know who that man
over there is?" he asked. "As you can see, he can't speak; he can't
even turn around."

"Is he dead?" asked Maria.

"Death is grace. That man doesn't deserve death. He is the most heinous criminal. That is the man you called Satan."

"Sŭng Nak-chong!" Maria screamed.

"Yes. That demon sent many a Christian to his suffering and death. After that, he became a thief. He dared to steal the tributary rice that was on the way to the court. He even had a ship ready on the beach. But our Lord had no more mercy. The villain managed to take over the wagon loaded with the rice, but it fell from the cliff, killing most of his accomplices and severely injuring others. Sŭng survived, but his head injury left him paralyzed, unable to move or speak. He is like a vegetable. He is only able to swallow when someone feeds him, and he has no control of his bowels or bladder. Who wants to look after such a man? Since the day he came here, Mr. Kwŏn has been taking care of him so that he can hang onto life."

All fell silent, tears streaming down their cheeks.

The first rooster of the dawn crowed from somewhere. Maria, Hasang, and To-sŏng embraced Kwŏn, the last embrace of those who would never meet again in this world. After leaving the prison, they locked the gate from the outside.

As Kwŏn had said, the church had been outwardly annihilated, and the faithful driven away from their homes and forced to live like beggars; nonetheless, countless Christians had achieved their martyrdom, and on earth there remained men like Kwŏn Ho-sin bearing witness to their faith and fulfilling the Christian responsibility of loving their neighbors. Ha-sang felt the blood surging through his young body as he once again firmly resolved that he must find a priest as soon as possible to lead the Korean Christians, and to work toward the reconstruction of the fallen church no matter what difficulties awaited him.

The restoration of the church depended upon close contact with the Peking diocese and on its assistance. However, the previous year Ha-sang had been unable to go to Peking with the Winter Solstice Mission. The old master, the translator, Son, had asked him to go, but he felt he could not leave with Teresa and Cho Suk still in the prison. Now he made up his mind that he must go to Peking this year, entrusting their fate in the Lord's hands. If it were the will of Providence, they would someday meet in Heaven, if not on earth, free from corporal torment and able to enjoy everlasting happiness.

Ha-sang could not leave Kongju without seeing his uncle, Tasan.

While Ha-sang went to Kangjin to visit his uncle, Maria stayed with Matteo's wife, who had now become as close to her as her own mother. For some reason it was always autumn when he traveled to Kangjin, and once again he was happy to observe the farms ready for a good harvest. The air was sweet with the fragrance of ripening nutmeg and opening tea flowers. Reflecting the rays of the setting sun, the silvery reeds swayed in the perfumed air.

Hong-nim was the first to recognize her cousin. Without even greeting Ha-sang, she ran toward the thatched cottage. Spotting him, the disciples, too, rushed down the slope of Mount Mandŏk. About a dozen of them were helping Tasan take care of the tea bushes. A lover of tea, Tasan had transformed the mountain into a veritable tea-mountain by painstakingly planting new bushes from seed and carefully transplanting and pruning the indigenous groves.

"Is it you, Ha-sang?" Tasan's face was gaunt as he came down the hill to greet Ha-sang, shaking the dirt from his hands. Neither the cool, clear autumn breeze, nor the brilliant sun could force color back into the face of this man, who had spent his days in hard work and confinement. Only last spring he had completed his monumental work, *Admonition on Governing the People*, and before the beginning of autumn, *On the National Rites*. The completion of his major works and the cultivation of his beloved tea bushes filled him with contentment, and the sudden visit by his nephew brought unexpected pleasure to a man who seldom betrayed emotion.

P'yo-nyŏ, who had treated Ha-sang with excessive deference even when he had come in the guise of a base servant, now could not even bring herself to look him in the eye, let alone greet him. She bent her middle-aged body in respect for the scholar-gentleman he had become. Hong-nim, now a blooming, well-groomed maiden unlike the other village girls, stood under the tree steadily watching her cousin. Her features were her father's; her eyes, too, unmistakably like his.

Old man P'yo, upon hearing of Ha-sang's visit, came to greet him, bearing a black snapper of an astonishing size, newly harvested soybeans, young, tender cabbage, freshly laid eggs, and a hen which he himself had slaughtered.

After the late lunch, to which all the disciples were invited, the uncle and nephew sat facing the window overlooking the garden pond. The disciples thoughtfully removed themselves so that the two could enjoy an intimate visit with each other and catch up with the news.

"So, do you go to Majae once in a while?"

"Yes. Everyone from the first uncle's family down is very well. The fourth aunt especially is in good health, and Hag-yŏn and Hag-yu, my cousins, are studying very diligently, never wasting a moment of their time."

"You look more mature than ever. What have you been doing all this time?"

"The year before last, I went to Peking as I had planned." Speaking quietly, Ha-sang took a small package wrapped in colored paper out of his sleeve and shyly presented it to his uncle.

"What is this?" asked Tasan.

"Paper, and some inksticks and brushes."

"Oh, this is White Palace paper and this, Green Palace paper; and these, Misty Purple Jade inksticks and ivory brushes!" Tasan was overcome, unwrapping the package.

"Yes. I bought them in Myŏngsŏng-dang at the Glass Factory Market."

Tears ran down Tasan's cheeks. Because of the late king's patronage, he had once enjoyed abundant supply of these precious implements of the highest quality, coveted and valued by scholars and men of letters. How arrogant and impertinent he had been! Longing for his departed king, Tasan took a long time to dry his tears.

The silence lengthened, as Ha-sang, too, was sunk in remembrance. In the meantime, a commotion rose from outside.

"Come out and receive the king's message."

The two looked at each other, puzzled.

"There is a message from the court for the former high state councillor, the exile Chŏng Yag-yong. Please come out and accept it."

In that seaside land of banishment, it was hard to know where all those people had come from, who gathered around staring curiously at the house.

Tasan changed into a freshly prepared, long formal outercoat with a blue sash tightly wound around his chest, and put on a wide-brimmed horsehair hat. He came out into the yard and stood in front of a small table covered with a red cloth that stood on a carpet. It had been placed facing north, the direction of the throne. The governor of Kangjin, in his full formal attire, stood next to the royal emis-

sary from Seoul, and some of the district officials lined up at attention on either side. The eighteen disciples, their expressions frozen,
knelt with their heads on the ground.

Tasan knelt on the carpet, facing north, and prostrated himself
four times. Breaking the utter silence, the emissary unfurled the
scroll, and raising his voice, read out: "The exile, the former State
Councillor Chŏng Yag-yong, is hereby freed on August 2, 1818."

"The Boundless Grace of Your Majesty!" the disciples shouted
in unison, and let loose their unabashed wailing of gratitude.

◆   ◆   ◆

The setting sun lingered on the surface of the slow-moving,
marshy, dark-green river, making it shimmer like scarlet silk brocade embroidered in gold and silver thread. Yŏyudang, Tasan's residence in Majae, whose name means "hall of tranquillity," was situated on a hill overlooking the river. On the opposite side, the golden
sand outlined the bank, and beyond was an open field. Since coming
home, Tasan often let his gaze wander toward a small, sparsely
forested knoll beyond the field, where Yak-chong had been buried,
wondering about the condition of the grave of a heretic, uncared for
and claimed by no one. But now, he trusted that Ha-sang, a grown
man and a filial son, was taking good care of his father's grave. In
the past Tasan had not allowed this thought to come completely to
consciousness, nor had he let it pain him. In the deep crevices of
his unconscious, his feeling for his brother taunted him, like envy,
pain, and shame. The hill was covered with ordinary rocks, nothing
anyone would consider curiously or interestingly formed; reflecting
the setting sun, however, they became things of beauty.

"My lord, it's becoming chilly. I shall close this window, lest you
catch cold," came the voice of the old servant Sŏk's son, the younger
Sŏk.

He appeared noiselessly and knelt on the stone step in front of
Tasan's room. Some wisteria leaves clinging to his shoulders were
reminders that the vines creeping over the barn and wreathing its
roof were now almost bare.

"No, don't. You always keep the floor so warm that the wind from
the river feels refreshing," Tasan said softly. "I am more worried
about that boy, Chang. You must tell him not to go places where he
can hurt himself."

Chang was Sŏk's grandson. His master's freedom had been slow in coming, and the younger Sŏk, the child Tasan had left behind, had become a young man; it was he who had commuted to Kyuldong, a distance of two hundred and fifty miles, bringing news of Majae. While in exile, Tasan had always looked forward to the arrival of this servant with letters from home. But too often the letters had plunged him more deeply into melancholy, and his departure had left him with an emptiness and sorrow even more painful to bear. In such moments he would appease his pain by composing poems entitled, "Sending off the Servant from Home." That pigtailed youth had married a slave girl and their son, Chang, was now a nimble thirteen-year-old who helped his father cut firewood in the mountains, sometimes even going alone.

That day, Chang must have gone to cut some wood while his father went to the marketplace in town to buy some dried whiting or salted fish for the mistress. Tasan was worried that Chang was not with his father.

With misty eyes, the younger Sŏk looked for a long time at his master's pale face and then disappeared as noiselessly as he had entered. He had been a vigorous young man in his prime when he had commuted from Majae to Kyuldong and wept for his master's misfortune, but now he was bald except for a spot at the back of his head. Even that thin remaining hair was turning as white as his thick beard, while his master's topknot was still plump, though his hair and the characteristic "three brows" were as white as frost, so that an air of almost sacred otherworldliness emanated from him.

Tasan's room was very well tended by the three generations of his servants, the old man Sŏk, his son, and now Chang. Even with the windows open, the room was delightfully warm. On an unassuming stationery chest was a large, white porcelain dish filled with Chinese quinces and pomegranates, their subtle fragrance enveloping the room. Fruit trees of many varieties thrived in Majae; apricots and peaches ripened in the summer, and grapes, pears, chestnuts, Chinese quinces, and pomegranates in the fall. Although the house had always felt deserted and its occupants had led a cheerless and discreet existence while the master was in exile, Hag-yŏn, the eldest son, as the head of the family in his father's absence, had never neglected his responsibilities in managing the household affairs. The younger Sŏk, too, ever faithful to his master's wishes, looked after the fruit trees, covering the quince trees with straw for the winter, and burying the roots of the pomegranates. Now he was busy readying the trees for the winter cold.

"You have a guest from Kyuldong," the younger Sŏk announced. A middle-aged scholar stood beside him in the inner courtyard.

"With season's greeting, I respectfully inquire after your health," the scholar saluted, prostrating himself. Then he raised himself ceremoniously.

His face flushed with joy, Tasan ran into the yard in his stocking feet and grabbed the scholar's hands.

"Hurry, let us go inside. You must be very tired from the long journey." Tasan lovingly led him inside.

The scholar was none other than Yun Chong-sim from Kangjin. Sŏk, straining his bent back, took a large package from the guest's shoulders and placed it on the floor.

After the servant had left, Chong-sim explained, "I brought you some nutmeg cakes and tea, and some citrons which I am afraid are not yet fully ripe. The tea is from Monk Ch'oŭi; he brought it himself with his letter to you. I went to considerable trouble to get this assignment this year, because everyone wanted to have the honor of visiting you."

After their teacher had been pardoned through the memorial presented to the king on his behalf by Yi T'ae-sun in 1818, Tasan's disciples formed the Tea Believers Guild to strengthen friendship and promote mutual understanding among its members, and at the same time to preserve respect and love for their teacher. Among his disciples were the sons and relatives of distinguished Catholics who had perished under the persecution. However, a puzzling question still remained as to why Tasan had neglected his own brother's family and Ha-sang's education, while he so compassionately looked after and educated the offspring of heretics.

The Contents of the Tea Believers Guild is still preserved in the hands of Yun Chae-ch'an, a descendant of Chong-sim, dated the last day of August 1818. It includes the names, pen names, and dates of birth of Tasan's eighteen disciples, followed by the agreement. The first part of this document was believed to have been written by some of the disciples and the second part by Tasan himself. In the agreement, which is assumed to be the codification of Tasan's instruction, it was decided that the society would meet twice a year, in the spring and fall, to strengthen their friendship and to send Tasan some tea, bolts of cotton, and nutmeg. Special emphasis was also placed on the care of the Eastern Cottage—the thatched roof was to be refurbished before the arrival of the winter solstice. In the second half of the document, the names of Tasan's most trusted disciples were frequently mentioned. On these ink-smudged pages Tasan exhorted them to cooperate with the townspeople and to be friendly with Hyejang's disciples, making it clear to them that in human nature there was no difference between Buddhists and those who followed Confucian teaching. Now six years had elapsed, and they still upheld the agreement.

"I suppose everyone in your family is well?" Tasan asked Chong-sim.

"Yes. My father enjoys longevity."

"My congratulations."

"Thank you." A man of few words as usual, Chong-sim steadily looked at Tasan, his eyes filled with affection and respect.

"Why is it so big, especially this year? You must have had a bad time on the road with it," Tasan asked, glancing at the package.

"No, not at all. I had a sturdy servant to carry it. This year we had a very good harvest."

Suppressing their mutual love for each other, intimate and tender, the teacher and the disciple remained serene, exchanging only a few words punctuated by awkward silences.

After a long pause, Tasan asked matter-of-factly, "How are Hong-nim and her mother?"

His eyes downcast, Chong-sim remained silent. "The mother and daughter left town," he answered finally.

Tasan flinched, supporting himself with one hand on the floor. His lips imperceptibly trembled, but he uttered no words.

"And the old man, P'yo, died last summer," Chong-sim went on.

"He lived a long life," Tasan mused.

"And his sister, the innkeeper woman, died before him."

"Both were good people. They will be rewarded in the here-after."

Only these two had been generous and kind to Tasan. These humble people, themselves despised by others, had nevertheless taught him many lessons and helped him in his time of trial. Thinking of them, he could not suppress the tears that filled his eyes.

"With her father gone, it must have been hard for P'yo-nyŏ to go on living alone. Poor things. I hope they are in the care of a good man," Tasan sighed.

Betraying his usual calm, Chong-sim rushed to correct him in a fluster. "Oh, no. She did not remarry."

"Then why did they leave Kyuldong?" Tasan asked, somewhat agitated.

"As you know, my aunt is from Imsil. Do you remember a lady guest who came to pay her respects when my uncle's household had the funeral? She is my aunt's sister-in-law. Since they have no son but only a daughter, the parents adopted the son-in-law. They are a wealthy family, and they wanted the wedding to be a big affair. As the wedding day approached, they needed a helping hand. Remembering Hong-nim's mother, who had helped at the time of the funeral, the lady sent for her in a hurry. Though at first Hong-nim's mother respectfully declined the offer, she finally had no heart to refuse the anxious entreaty."

"I understand now."

"Even after you left, Hong-nim's mother kept your cottage impeccably in order, and she was always very kind to us."

"Poor things!"

The Confucian precept of the time stressed strict separation of the sexes, so that the relationship between husband and wife was a hierarchical one, subordinating the wife to her husband. Although she had borne Tasan a daughter, P'yo-nyŏ, young enough to be his own daughter, had served him with fear and respect, his eminence overwhelming this country-bred, lowly woman. Some exiles, succumbing to the temptation of the flesh, lived with local women and fathered their offspring. Although the government did not interfere with the exiles' personal affairs, after their pardons they were strictly forbidden to return home with these women and the children born during the banishment. Therefore the women were left behind, abandoned from the day their men became free. Tasan, however, had not lived with P'yo-nyŏ because he lusted after her; the relationship had been consummated spontaneously as a result of their constant proximity.

Tasan pioneered the idea of equality in a society hierarchically stratified by law as well as in practice, proclaiming, "There is only Heaven above and people on earth," and "Heaven does not ask

whether one is a scholar-official or a commoner." He asserted that
all were equal in the eyes of God, and here his theory corresponded
to basic Christian teachings. Above all, he recognized the individual's innate worth as inviolable, a fundamental premise of demo-
cratic ideology. Such thinking was unprecedented among the Neo-
Confucian scholars of the day, and Tasan's views can be attributed
to his extensive reading in Catholic doctrine. Tasan denounced government hiring and promotion policies that discriminated on
grounds of birth, and partisan and regional factionalism. He strongly
recommended instead equal opportunity to enter public office regardless of social station or circumstance of birth, so that sons of
secondary wives, of lower-class families, and of *chungin* families
would have access to public office equally with legitimate sons and
sons from noble families. He further argued that government positions should be awarded regardless of political alignment, instead
of favoring those from a select few lineages who had held a political
monopoly for many years. At the same time, in his book, *Village
Field Law*, he stressed the need for land reform, including more
just methods of land distribution: the government should guarantee
land and income according to labor, which would entitle those who
farm to ownership of the land. By recognizing the rights of the sons
of secondary wives, Tasan also acknowledged the legality and rights
of secondary wives. For an enlightened man like Tasan, it appeared
contradictory that instead of denouncing a system that allowed men
to have secondary wives, he tacitly encouraged it by recognizing
the rights of their issue.

P'yo-nyŏ had not even been Tasan's secondary wife. She was
only a short episode in his life, and Hong-nim, their daughter, an
unexpected outcome of that union. Unlike other exiles, however,
Tasan had been kind to them. It is recorded in *The Contents* that
he had come to own some land during his banishment, though no
one can explain how his ownership of land had been possible. The
document mentions that his disciples' savings had all gone into
the expenses of Tasan's homecoming and that the property Tasan
owned would become part of the holdings of the guild, which could
be interpreted to mean that Tasan wished the land to be kept by his
disciples for the hapless mother and daughter.

On the day Tasan left her, P'yo-nyŏ set a breakfast table laden
with his favorite dishes. Unwilling to rob them of their precious last

few moments together, those who wanted to offer congratulations and to bid Tasan their reluctant farewells waited in the reed field beside the path leading to his cottage. P'yo-nyŏ, as usual, did not betray any emotion upon her face, but Hong-nim occasionally stole a glance at her mother. On the table that morning was a long-necked white porcelain wine bottle, though Tasan never touched wine with his breakfast. With unaccustomed hands, Hong-nim filled the cup three times with the wine brewed from newly harvested rice. His heart no longer able to contain his feelings, he left the last cup untouched and grabbed his daughter's soft, warm hands, noting upon her fingernails the half-moon shaped stain of crimson balsam-dye, a memento of the now-faded summer.

After removing the breakfast table, as she did every day, P'yo-nyŏ carefully and serenely dressed Tasan and quietly opened the door. She stepped down to the yard, arranged Tasan's shoes on the terrace stone, and arose. Only her firmly entwined fingers as she stood clasping her hands tightly together betrayed her sorrow.

Those who had come to see Tasan off followed him. As he headed for the governor's residence to bid him farewell, the townspeople came out of their houses to watch him pass by astride the horse the governor had sent. Riding through the reed fields sparkling in the morning sun, again and again Tasan looked back at P'yo-nyŏ. The sight of her suddenly narrowed shoulders and of Hong-nim hanging desperately onto her mother did not escape him. A memory of the day he had begun his long exile eighteen years ago stirred him once again. His wife had stood holding their youngest in the fierce wind, not daring to come near the husband who was on his way to a place from which he might never return. Held by convention and proto-col, her face covered with a hooded cloak, she had remained on the road that ran beside the banks of the Han River. Now what was enabling P'yo-nyŏ, a woman free from the restraints of protocol, to maintain her self-control? While his wife had borne a separation that was painful to them both, P'yo-nyŏ was sending her man back home from exile; while his wife had shared the pain with her depart-ing husband, P'yo-nyŏ had to endure hers alone.

"The cottage must be empty now that they are gone," Tasan ob-served to Chong-sim, coming out of his reverie.

"They tell me that Hong-nim and her mother will not return. Although nobody lives there, the cottage is kept spotlessly clean."

"I see." Tasan closed his eyes.

Behind his eyelids appeared autumn scenes of Kyuldong. It was the time of the blossoming of the tea flowers. Their elegant petals fluttered in the wind, perfuming the air, their tender loveliness as fresh in his mind now as it had been then. The citron trees, too, spread their strong fragrance, many yellow incense-lamps set among their lustrous leaves. Then came memories of the early summer days of utter joy when Hyejang and Ch'oŭi, the two men enlightened in Buddhism and Confucian philosophy, and lovers of tea, had picked the new tea-leaves at the moment of their freshest delicacy. Tasan thought of his pond, the mineral-water spring, and the rock beside it, on which he had carved "The Rock of Chŏng" for posterity; he thought of the reed field that burst into silvery splendor in the autumn sun, of P'yo, who had brought him fresh red snapper that he himself had caught, of the old innkeeper woman, illiterate but wise in the lore of nature, and of the faces of each of his disciples. Tasan sighed with longing, his yearning for the land of his banishment transcending the darkness and desolation of this place fraught with the omnipresent smell of death.

"Could this feeling be a delusion, or is it an act of Providence?" wondered Tasan.

A careful cough came from outside the paper sliding door, beyond which darkness had already settled.

"Who is it?"

"It is I, your servant. Mistress wants me to bring your dinner table."

The door slid open from the center, and the imposing figure of the younger Sŏk entered with a large table, followed by his fragile daughter carrying a smaller one.

"I must set these slaves free." The thought, which he entertained every time he watched this family of servants working for him, again occurred to Tasan.

The dinner was a feast for a back-country household: salted and fermented fish of different varieties, marinated and broiled chicken, dried whiting broiled with an abundance of spices, freshwater fish, clear radish soup, and flavorful stuffed, pickled cabbage. However, Tasan could not take more than a few bites; he ate just enough so that Chong-sim would not feel uncomfortable.

It was six years since Tasan had come home. Upon his return, he wrote eulogies to be inscribed on the tombstones of his long-dead daughter-in-law and his friends. The following years, he completed some of his major works, including *Toward a New Jurisprudence*. These were followed by his *Autobiography*, written in anticipation of his sixtieth birthday, with a bibliography of his works totalling almost five hundred entries.

However, unaccountably, Tasan had been exercising strict self-denial. His wife, sons, and daughter-in-law had spared no effort to nurse him back to health, but they were puzzled that he took only small amounts of food of modest quality, and sometimes fasted.

"He ruined his health during his banishment," his wife lamented, and asked Hag-yŏn, well versed in the arts of medicine, to prescribe restorative medicine for his father.

Tasan, who had been angered by his son's becoming a physician, an occupation unsuitable for a high-born man, threw the brews away.

Chong-sim left after a three-day stay, and Ha-sang arrived at Majae the day after, regretting that their meeting had been prevented by a mere day's span. Ha-sang, now ruddy-faced and as ever the dependable, faithful nephew, came in after first paying his respects to his aunt in her inner room. He knelt in front of Tasan.

"Chong-sim brought some nutmeg cakes this year, as usual," said Tasan, offering some to his nephew. "And how is the daughter of Mr. Kwŏn?" he asked, inquiring after Maria. He remembered that his nephew had described her plight in detail during his last visit, and since then, compassionate thoughts of her had often surfaced in his mind.

"She is a grown woman now. She still keeps herself busy copying the holy writings. Lately she has become so adept with the brush that she now works on religious paintings as well."

"She must be a young lady of many endowments."

"Above all, she is a woman with a beautiful heart. She now spends her days taking care of orphans and children who have been abandoned to the streets. It's too much work for her, though, because she is not very healthy."

"Do you mean she is rearing them?"

"Yes. I hear that in Europe many churches and monasteries take in unfortunate children and rear them."

"You must mean philanthropic work."

"Yes."

"It's all very good, but she must be careful."

"The Christian sisters, the palace lady Teresa, and the two widows, Barbara and Suzanne, are excellent seamstresses, and they also peddle various household goods for women. When they go out, they hide religious writings among their wares and ask their customers to join the church as they hand them these books. The neighbors are impressed by their sewing and laundry skills, and as their reputation grows they are flooded with orders. They tell people that the orphans and the abandoned children are their own children returning to them after staying with relatives."

"It sounds reasonable enough, but it still worries me. I daresay having many outsiders visiting them would attract attention."

"They are safe, because Maria and Teresa have a separate room well hidden in the storage shed; the entrance is blocked by firewood, so even from inside it appears to be only a storage shed for wood."

"Hm . . ." breathed Tasan, his mind strangely agitated. "And how about you; how do you spend your days?"

"As I have told you, I have a mission to fulfill, that of bringing a priest into Korea and rebuilding our fallen church. Now the persecution is easing, and the number of Christians is increasing."

Although he was only thirty, during the past ten years Ha-sang had come to be recognized as a powerful leader in the church because of his practical mind, faith, and scholarship.

"I am going to Peking with the Winter Solstice Mission again this year," he continued.

"I wonder why you keep going back to Peking, suffering so much difficulty. How many times have you gone?"

"This is my sixth journey. Because there, too, Christians are persecuted, they are having a great deal of difficulty trying to send us a clergyman. But in January of 1817, two Chinese priests from Nanking were sent to Korea. One had to return before reaching his destination. The other reached Ch'aengmun, but no one from Korea knew about his coming. He was unable to get in touch with any Koreans, and he became ill during his long wait. I think he finally died."

"Tell me, what will you do in Peking, and whom will you see?"

"I will go to see Father Ribeiro, to ask him to send a priest to Korea. He is the acting bishop. The bishop of Peking still remains in Macao, unable to enter China because of the persecution."

"I've heard the journey to Peking entails many hardships, and even worse, you tell me you join the mission disguised as a servant."

"Yes. It has been very difficult, indeed, but from this year it will be much easier."

"Why so?"

"I now have a good friend who will help me. It does not mean the journey will be less difficult, but it will give me great pleasure to go with him." After a few moments of silence, Ha-sang continued, "His name is Yu Chin-gil, a civil service translator ranked above the third degree. Almost every year he goes to Peking with the mission. He is from a *chungin* family who have been translators for generations. In his official capacity, he can travel to Peking without hardship, and there is no language barrier for him. Koreans can communicate with the Chinese by writing, but it's far better to be able to speak the language."

"I'm sure of it, but how did you come to know him?"

"It's all our Lord's will."

Ha-sang began the story of Yu Chin-gil, who would remain his lifelong comrade. Since members of Yu Chin-gil's family traveled to China almost every winter, he grew up among unusual foreign objects and books which were rarely found in the homes of a nation determined to close its doors to the outside world. Though they were *chungin*, the family was prosperous and well-educated. Some high-born scholar-officials looked down on them as mere translators, but they were men of good taste and cultivation, and possessed of a broader perspective.

Translators were hereditary technical specialists in the capital who must undergo rigorous training. Since childhood, Yu Chin-gil had studied language and had become a holder of the civil service third rank in his youth. At the time of their meeting, he was thirty, three years older than Ha-sang, and had already acquired a reputation as a genius. From his childhood, he had loved learning, devoting his entire energies to his studies in a privileged environment, and he was soon held in high esteem. Although he suffered occasional discrimination by high-born officials, he enjoyed a position that allowed him to frequent the court, meeting powerful and distinguished men. He often assisted the king himself in dealing with the Chinese delegates and emissaries from their suzerains.

But Yu Chin-gil remained unfulfilled, his soul aspiring after something beyond. If worldly pleasures were his object in life, he had enough wealth for that; he coveted neither material things nor higher position, which in any case was closed to him because of the strict social stratification that permitted no such mobility. For him, they held no meaning, because he had witnessed in numerous court incidents the ugliness and emptiness of men's unbridled ambition. His aspirations lay elsewhere, in his search for answers to his questions about the beginning and end of the universe, and of human beings. For ten years he had read innumerable books, beginning with Buddhist literature and extending beyond, until his research assumed such proportions that people called him a walking encyclopedia. But his efforts had not yielded him any clues to the answers he sought about the fundamental principles guiding the universe, leaving his soul in turmoil and his body sick. At the time of the Persecution of 1801, Yu Chin-gil had been too young, and since those around him had no interest in Catholicism, he knew nothing about the new religion. As he grew older, however, he became aware that many eminent scholars and the virtuous men of the time had been executed because of their faith, and that they had met their martyrdom with extraordinary joy and grandeur. Those stories aroused hope that he might find in this new religion the answers in his quest for truth. He began to seek out Catholics and books on Catholicism, but he knew neither a Christian nor a place to obtain the banned books. Meanwhile, his interest in the religion only grew stronger.

One day when Yu Chin-gil returned home from the court, he found the household in disarray.

"I was asked to repair the furniture," the steward volunteered apologetically.

After changing from his official attire into everyday clothes, Chin-gil went into the inner courtyard and out of boredom watched the carpenters' nimble hands engaged in the tasks of straightening loose joints and hinges, and reattaching misplaced decorative inlays. Suddenly the paper lining on the inside of one of the chests caught his attention. In prosperous households, chests were usually lined with paper instead of silk, because silk attracted moths. As he stared at the strange words on the lining—"awakening soul," "living soul," "immortal soul"—he was intrigued.

"Can you remove the lining from the chest?" Chin-gil asked one of the carpenters.

"If I wet it, I could, sir."

"Very well, then. Would you please remove it carefully so as not to ruin the paper?"

A while later, the carpenter handed him the pieces of paper, as good as new. After drying and fitting them together, he was astounded. It was a part of *True Principles of Catholicism*. Shrouded in unclear and indecipherable meanings, the writing shed no light, so that his longing for answers only intensified. He was determined to meet Catholics. To his amazement, he had no need to go far—among his servants were a few Catholics, who led him to some of the important Catholics in the capital. He received verbal instructions and books from them and immersed himself in reading, giving up sleep and food. He began to see the light; Catholicism, now clear and bright, suddenly accessible, filled his heart with faith and joy. His question was answered, and he was at peace.

Before long, Yu Chin-gil came to know Ha-sang, who impressed him not only with his personal integrity and depth of faith but also with his passionate involvement in the church and his spirit that "loved his neighbors as himself." Chin-gil had heard the story of a group of brave men who, during the outbreak of cholera in 1821, had risked their own lives to nurse the sick and work at the dreaded task of disposing of the corpses. Their leader was Chŏng Ha-sang. Ha-sang, for his part, was grateful for the appearance of a man like Chin-gil, the very person the church needed. His position as a translator with easy access to the Chinese court would facilitate their mission.

"It cannot be but the will of our Lord. I can't imagine what better help we could get; it's like having forces of a thousand strong coming to our aid." Ha-sang's face was flushed as he finished relating the story of Chin-gil to Tasan.

"Hm . . . Did you say the pages from *True Principles of Catholicism* were pasted inside the chest?" Deep in thought, Tasan's words lingered inside his mouth.

It intrigued Tasan to realize that just as the introduction of Catholicism into Korea had been accomplished not by missionary effort but by those eminent scholars who, disillusioned with the obsolete scholarship of the day, sought to solve the ills of their society, the thirst of an individual for truth had led him to the encounter with God.

"It can never be an accident; it is surely Providence," Ha-sang repeated.

"Well . . ."

"Although he has become a Christian, he has not yet been baptized. This year when we go to Peking, he will be baptized by the acting bishop. I'll accompany him as his servant. Now I don't have to worry about the traveling expenses, nor do I have to burden my fellow Christians."

"That is fortunate," said Tasan, no longer the same uncle who had admonished his pigtailed nephew in 1811.

"Master, my lord," the hoarse voice of the servant came from outside.

"What is it?"

"Shall I cut down the dead persimmon tree by the barn?"

"Do as you wish."

"I am very sorry we let it die."

"It's quite all right."

Noticing Sŏk did not move, Tasan opened the paper window. The day was as balmy as springtime.

"We have a beautiful day for so late in autumn. Shall we go outside?" Tasan asked his nephew.

"Yes."

The servant stood with his head bowed.

"Don't mind it. Nothing lives forever," Tasan said, smiling softly, and then added, "This year the persimmons have had a bad season. Last year, the branches were heavy with fruit."

"I understand that they bear in alternate years."

"Well. I wonder if last year's bumper crop exhausted the tree," Tasan said light-heartedly.

Only then did the servant, nodding imperceptibly, disappear toward the barn. Tasan did not even glance at him. He was no longer the same man who had once advocated "economic enrichment" through healthy agricultural production, exhorting people to plant fruit trees and to cultivate medicinal herbs, and warning them not to waste anything when feeding domestic animals. There was no trace in him of his once rigorous adherence to the stern principles that had so characterized his life. He truly believed that everything must have an end. With serene acceptance, he wanted to enjoy the short, warm sunshine of the late autumn days, just as he had written a few days earlier in a poem:

> I would rather wistfully watch the sunbeams flow,
> Or tighten the loosened strings of the lute that lies idle,
> Or change the worn cover of my oft-turned book,
> Or listen to the joyful noise of wild geese
> Skimming over the water.
> Observe the passing clouds cast
> Their shadows on the pines.
> It suffices that I have enough to eat in my remaining days.
> What need is there for more?

"I must leave before dark," announced Ha-sang, who had been gazing upon the river shimmering in the sun.

He walked toward the inner room to take leave of his aunt. Ha-sang did not emerge for a long time, for his aunt asked him to stay for dinner. This aunt who had tormented him in his childhood, he never forgot to bring her small but unusual gifts from Peking. Neither did he neglect to present his cousins' wives with Chinese face powder or some other small gift.

"Your bride-to-be, whoever she may be, will be a lucky woman. You will be a good provider." She never missed the chance to urge him to marry.

"I am already married to the church," he declared, smiling sheepishly and repeating the words he had long ago proclaimed to everyone.

Ha-sang rejoined his uncle in the yard outside the study.

"I shall not be able to see you again this year. I am leaving for Peking at the end of this month and will return next spring in the early part of March. I will pay my respects to you then. I pray you remain in good health and in peace." Ha-sang knelt down and bowed.

Disguised as a servant of Yu Chin-gil, Ha-sang once again began the journey to Peking. By now he had become used to the harsh weather and the icy roads, though the going was just as perilous, tedious, and cold as the first time. Ha-sang was once again with Cho Sin-ch'ŏl, who turned out to be the same age as himself. The bond of hardship forged during the repeated trips had made these two men as close as blood brothers, and they even argued in playful persistence about which of the two should assume the role of elder brother. The longer Ha-sang knew Sin-ch'ŏl, the deeper his respect had grown for his friend's soft-spoken manner, honesty, and integrity, rare exceptions among the rough servants who accompanied the mission.

Once in Peking, even though Yu Chin-gil was very busy with his duties as a translator, Ha-sang managed to bring him to the South Catholic Church. The acting bishop, Father Ribeiro, welcomed them, having been informed of their coming. One bitterly cold, starry night in December 1824, Yu Chin-gil was baptized inside the magnificent edifice, taking the Christian name of Augustine.

Ha-sang returned to Seoul in March of the following year. Before he visited Majae to pay his respects to Tasan, he went directly to see Cho Sin-ch'ŏl. He brought the puzzled Sin-ch'ŏl to Yu Chin-gil's mansion. There, Ha-sang and Chin-gil announced to Sin-ch'ŏl that they were both Christians and asked him to join them. Sin-ch'ŏl was so perturbed by the proposal that he reacted vehemently in an effort to refuse it. Beside himself with fright, trying to flee, Cho opened the closet door instead of the door to the outside. Later these three would often joke good-humoredly about that incident among themselves.

Cho Sin-ch'ŏl had lost his mother very young and had been sent to a Buddhist temple where he had been reared in extremely harsh circumstances. Upon reaching adulthood, he had left the temple for the secular world. After many years of hardship doing odd jobs, before he was twenty he had become a servant accompanying the mission. Now he was married and owned a small house. Sin-ch'ŏl was absolutely unwilling to risk this small security in his life for the heretic religion. But he had come to respect Ha-sang's character through many years of friendship, and now Yu Chin-gil's position, his wealth, and above all his gentle persuasion calmed Sin-ch'ŏl's shock. Ha-sang visited Sin-ch'ŏl almost every day until he was finally able to persuade his friend to accept the church and become a Christian. Sin-ch'ŏl was baptized with the name of Charles. From that moment until the day they met their martyrdom, the three pursued together their mission of restoring the Korean church. Together these three were canonized by Pope John Paul II in 1984.

Chapter Ten

◆ ◆ ◆

Encounter

Two ritual tables for the household gods stood in the main hall of the house, the smaller one set with a white porcelain wine cup filled with unrefined wine and a couple of dried whitings as the only offerings, the larger one still bare. On a straw mat in front of the table, the shaman Man-nyŏn sat with Butterfly, luminous in her white costume. She prayed, rubbing her hands together, as two slave women carried in a large earthen steamer filled with rice cake generously garnished with red beans from which the steam rose like smoke. The women placed it on the empty table. After they left, Man-nyŏn picked up a carving knife from under the table, plunged it into the steaming cake, and drew the character for the number ten.[1] In that instant, Butterfly felt a sudden vertigo. She watched the cross on the rice cake float toward the post and remain stuck on the main beam. Meanwhile, the knife on the rice cake flew toward her, hitting her right hand with its handle. Instinctively, she covered her injury, but the shaking hand, slipping out of its protection, moved toward her bosom, and as if manipulated by some unknown force, made the sign of the cross. Everything Butterfly saw was illusory, and she was unaware of her own strange behavior. Overcome by dizziness, she lost consciousness even before the prayer came to an end.

When Butterfly finally regained her senses three hours later, it was almost nine in the evening. Fortunately, the governor had been away attending the banquet given in honor of his new post, but

1. The Chinese character for the number ten resembles a cross.

Man-nyŏn was extremely embarrassed by the incident. She did not dare to face the mistress of the house, because for a shaman to fall unconscious during the rite was certainly an inauspicious sign. Had she seen the strange movements of her daughter during her prayer, she would no doubt have fainted, too, but her eyes had been closed during the supplication. The rite on that day had therefore ended in vain, but Man-nyŏn was determined to find ways to appease the myriad spirits who had been angered by the incident. Calm and strong-willed though she was, Man-nyŏn was perturbed. However, looking at her daughter's inert face, astonishingly childlike for a girl of seventeen, and watching her painful breathing, the thought never occurred to her to admonish Butterfly; it was only pity that filled her heart. The mistress, too, instead of being offended by the incident, knelt beside Butterfly to wipe away the beads of sweat that had formed on the girl's forehead.

Despite the government ban against shamans as priestesses of obscene cults, there was a growing interest in them even among the royal women, who clandestinely sought shamans and diviners. The newly arrived governor, a man of impeccable character who had passed the civil service examination as a mere boy, opposed the performing of shaman rituals. The mistress, too, the wife of a literati-bureaucrat, shunned their superstitious dealings, but she gave in to the persuasions of the staff and servant-women who had long been accustomed to the shaman rites being regularly performed in the governor's household. They had seen their former governor, a man with an overly stern sense of propriety, crippled after falling on perfectly level ground, forcing him to leave the district, and his successor, an uncompromising follower of Confucian ethics, lose his son, whom he had left behind in Seoul. They advised the mistress: "Because this mansion is so old, you have to offer prayers to the Supreme Household God, the Ground God, and so on, and appease the demons swarming in the latrines and in the stumps of brooms. If you don't do anything, all the wretched bachelor ghosts, the ghosts of unmarried maidens, of those who starved to death or were flogged to death, or those who drowned, will crowd around your house. Just imagine how many were flogged to death in your house, this place where criminals were kept!"

Thus, the inspired Man-nyŏn had been summoned in the governor's absence, and this was why, in spite of the fact that shamans must not be seen frequenting an official household, she had come to perform her rite in this place.

Butterfly had seen phantasmagoria during her spirit-sickness. In a secluded and well-tended room sat a middle-aged gentleman and an exceedingly beautiful woman. Three young girls with long plaits and red ribbons tied in the shape of a swallow at the end, all looking alike, sat facing their parents. Fragrance seemed to emanate from the tiny plaits that ringed their ears, and met at the back of their heads. Behind the girls, looking proudly at them, a woman of about forty knelt.

"Let us now offer our morning prayers," the man said, picking up a book.

The middle-aged woman, sliding forward, handed a book to each girl. In unison, they flipped the pages. The man began to read: "O Jesus, through the immaculate heart of Mary, I offer thee my prayers, works, joys, and sufferings of this day, for all the intentions of thy sacred heart, in union with the holy sacrifice of the Mass throughout the world, in reparation for my sins and for the special intentions of the League of the Sacred Heart."

The wife and the daughters responded to him. During the long recitation of the morning prayers, no one showed any sign of boredom, and the girls appeared happy, proud of being able to read the prayer, which was written in the vernacular Korean alphabet; the middle one shone especially with intelligence.

As if it were a part of the daily routine, Butterfly, without stumbling over a word, recited the prayer with those in her fantasy, a scene and a prayer she had never known in real life; the only difference was that she had no prayer book. Finally the long prayer came to an end, but Butterfly went on all by herself: "Our Father who art in heaven, hallowed be thy name . . . Amen." Momentarily, putting the middle finger and fourth finger of right hand together, she made the sign of the cross across her breast.

"She must be coming to herself," the mistress said, looking at Butterfly's fluttering lips.

"Butterfly, Butterfly, can you recognize your mother? Your mother is right here with you." Bursting into sobs, Man-nyŏn embraced her daughter in a frenzy.

"Calm yourself. She seems to have a pain in her chest. Look, her hands are plucking at her chest," the mistress lightly chided Man-nyŏn.

"Yes, ma'am. How stupid of me."

Only then did Man-nyŏn remember to untie the sashes of her daughter's blouse and skirt, which were bound tightly around her chest. As Butterfly's radiant breasts were exposed, the two women closed their eyes as though blinded by their loveliness. Butterfly once again drew the sign of the cross over her bare bosom, and opened her eyes. Her still-dazed eyes first reflected her mother's face, and then the shadow of fear clouded them.

After the incident, Butterfly plunged often into depression.

At seventeen she was considered past her prime, and no request for her hand in marriage had been forwarded from other shaman districts, because everyone took it for granted that she would marry the son of Man-nyŏn's husband and his concubine. This woman, also a shaman's daughter, was kept by Man-nyŏn's husband in a separate household. Since the territorial right of a shaman was handed down through the male line, Man-nyŏn belonged to her husband's district, and had no choice but to perform her rites there to the accompaniment of her husband's flute. Although she considered the situation humiliating, such was the fate of being a woman in a shaman household.

The son of the concubine, Pong-ch'ul, was now seventeen years old. When Butterfly had first appeared she was just the size of Pong-ch'ul, so her age was determined to be the same as his, and the day of her appearance was marked as her birthday. Butterfly was known as Man-nyŏn's daughter; therefore, the union of these two would technically be considered incest. In many cases, among the hereditary shamans—unlike the charismatic shamans, who often developed an aversion to sex after experiencing spirit-possession—sexual mores were not strictly observed. But Man-nyŏn, unusually righteous, did not welcome their union. What she feared more was that it would also expose to her daughter the fact that she was not Man-nyŏn's daughter by birth—a fact known to everyone except Butterfly. Thus, the marriage had been put off. However, knowing that the truth must be told someday and that the concubine would become Butterfly's mother-in-law and the boy her husband, Man-nyŏn taught her unmarried daughter everything she knew. The other shamans tolerated Butterfly, a virgin shaman, even as she performed rites in their districts. Man-nyŏn, a barren woman, believed from the depths of her heart that this was the only way to keep her daughter near her, for Butterfly was to her a gift no less precious than if she had been her own flesh and blood, and Man-nyŏn loved her more than her own life.

When Butterfly was thirteen, soon after she had overheard someone call her Pong-ch'ul's bride, she had begun to lose her cheerful disposition. The proud, cool bearing, a demeanor carefully cultivated in her by her mother's devotion and love and heightened by her own beauty and intelligence, gradually took on a melancholy, even savage air.

"Pong-ch'ul's bride? Then who am I? Aren't we brother and sister, though we have different mothers?" she would muse. "Am I really my mother's daughter?" The doubt and pain would visit her at indiscriminate times. She had no recollection beyond the earliest memory of being fed millet gruel by the maid while being held in her mother's bosom. "Why can't I remember anything before that?" she wondered to herself.

One day Butterfly asked her mother, "Mother, did I suckle your breasts when I was a tiny baby?"

"Why, all babies grow up on mother's milk."

"But I once heard the aunt who lives in the house by the paulownia tree say, 'The shaman has breasts as firm as those of a virgin because she has never suckled an infant.' "

"So! That wicked woman has nothing else to do but to talk about someone else's tits!"

Her mother's vehement reaction surprised Butterfly; she had never seen her become so angry. Butterfly's bewilderment grew deeper.

"Mother, why am I so stupid? I don't remember even a tiny bit what happened to me when I was a baby."

"What a foolish child! Who says anyone can remember anything about the time when she was but a suckling babe?"

Though Man-nyŏn responded light-heartedly, the split-second fluster that appeared on her face did not escape Butterfly's sharp perception. More and more, Butterfly's mind became darkened with confusion. Her attitude toward her mother, too, changed. Unaccountably, she would one moment be extremely sweet and filial, and another, suddenly icy and indifferent.

"The child acquired without the pangs of childbirth, who is not your own flesh and blood, is nothing but a tiger cub," said the innkeeper woman, who knew everything, clicking her tongue with a meaningful shaking of the head.

One spring day when the azaleas were in full bloom, Butterfly had a rare holiday. Lured by the beauty of which she had been unaware while she was preoccupied with the rites, and with a sudden sense of freedom, she walked along the stream lined with willow trees cascading their lime-green threads over the soft pinks of the azaleas. Her eyes, bedazzled by the flowers, suddenly caught sight of a couple walking toward her: it was Pong-ch'ul and his girl. Although people depended on shamans for their spiritual well-being, and regarded them as the protectors against calamities, they nonetheless held them in contempt. The strict protocol of male-female relationships, too, did not apply to shamans; it needed only to be observed by ordinary people, while shamans' dallying was openly tolerated by the people of the district, who considered the matter none of their business. Thus, this couple's walking together in broad daylight would have caused no head-turning.

The two young people, confronting the sudden appearance of Butterfly, were too embarrassed to look her straight in the eye. "It's you, Butterfly," Pong-ch'ul muttered in a voice barely audible as she was about to pass them by, completely ignoring their presence.

Without a word, Butterfly moved on, but not until her chilling stare had fastened on the pinkish azalea stain on the girl's blouse.

Butterfly felt a palpitation in her heart, not from jealousy or the shame of being wronged, not even from loss of self-esteem. Anger alone reverberated in her like the shout of an incensed adult rebuking an insolent child: "How impertinent! A base man, the son of a drum-man, and only to become a male shaman himself!" All the while, she was laughing at herself contemptuously. "Then, who am I? I know shamans marry each other; a shaman must marry a drum-man. If Pong-ch'ul is the son of a male shaman, I am the daughter of a shaman myself. Aren't we well-matched, like a pair of chopsticks or a pair of straw sandals?"

However, Butterfly never considered herself as inhabiting the same ground as Pong-ch'ul, nor for that matter did she feel a bond with other shamans. Her technique inspired people to experience the divine presence, and the reputation for her miraculous power was widely known, but she had not experienced the ecstasy of spirit-possession, nor the awesomeness of receiving her god into her body. She worshipped a pantheon of shaman gods, more than three hundred, but she had never once encountered any of them. Butterfly began to question the existence of these gods with whom she had never had spiritual union. At times she would ask, "Is something lacking in me that I am unable to meet with the gods? Is it because I have no shaman blood in me?"

Her mother, too, had once questioned her own inability to experience the possession-sickness of charismatic shamans; however, she had never doubted the existence of all those gods she served. Man-nyŏn's doubts concerned only the reflection that her performances were not religious, but merely ceremonies of song and dance, nothing but showy theatrics. Whereas Man-nyŏn had questioned her ability as a shaman, her daughter doubted the very existence of such gods.

"Who am I?" The question persisted in her, even while she performed her rites.

As Butterfly outwardly became increasingly calm and self-possessed, her skill reached such abstruse depths as to bring tears even to her mother's eyes. When she abruptly changed her slow, floating, waltz-like dance movements to brisk, pouncing, frenzied steps, all the spectators, even the master of the house, were swept into the vortex of mystical excitement. Unaware of the warring demons in her daughter's mind, Man-nyŏn took Butterfly everywhere.

However, since the mishap at the governor's mansion, Butterfly had been indisposed and unable to accompany her mother. Early October was a busy time for Man-nyŏn, for after the harvest every household ensured its good fortune by having thanksgiving rites performed with offerings of newly harvested grains, vegetables, and fruit. One day, after one such rite, Man-nyŏn entered the room where her daughter lay ill, crumpled to her knees, and sat beside the sick girl amid an outpouring of sighs.

Butterfly turned around and smiled faintly. "Mother, there is an oak leaf in your hair . . ."

"My poor, poor daughter!" Man-nyŏn cried at her daughter's words, embracing her fiercely and bursting into sobs.

After removing the leaf, Butterfly tenderly stroked her mother's hair, while Man-nyŏn sobbed in her arms. Butterfly was vaguely aware what had caused her mother to weep with such intensity.

The rumor had been spreading among the gossipy womenfolk of the district that Pong-ch'ul's girl was with child by him. On her way home that day from her rite, Man-nyŏn met a woman who told her what she had already suspected: that the pregnancy had been confirmed by Pong-ch'ul's mother herself. "It's just as well. The girl is nothing but a witch," the woman added in an attempt to comfort Man-nyŏn.

The despair caused Man-nyŏn to stay bedridden for a few days. Her turbid eyes suddenly became cold with murderous hatred and she would mumble to herself, "What curse aroused the underworld demons to cause the mother and the son to haunt us like enemies?" Watching her mother, Butterfly remained serenely free of jealousy or rage; it was rather a sense of release that filled her.

"I am above a base man like Pong-ch'ul," she declared with an icy smile flickering on her lips.

However, Butterfly often sat as vacuously as her mother, not because she was overcome by anger at seeing her intended take a concubine even before they were married, nor because of sorrow at having been scorned. At such moments, on her expressionless face, her eyes alone would flame with longing, for her soul remained unfulfilled. With all her being, she was in search of something beyond, something fundamental. She could not erase from her mind the phantom scene she had seen in her delirium at the governor's mansion; the character ten, the floating cross that Man-nyŏn had drawn in the rice cake, and the knife in the middle of the cross which had been thrown with such powerful force. Remembering it sent a chill down her spine. The fantasy that had followed, and the prayers or incantations—which she could not distinguish—had all disappeared from her consciousness. Only the strange, indecipherable phrases "our Father who art in heaven" and "Amen" remained with her. "Father in heaven" could refer to the spirits she invoked in her incantation, who were said to inhabit Heaven, but what did the word "Amen" mean? She began to believe that if she could only decipher this mysterious word, she would know the secret surrounding her birth. She grew increasingly pensive and spoke less and less. She became completely preoccupied with the effort

to unravel its meaning, and the word "Amen" never left her consciousness.

In this manner two years elapsed, and Pong-ch'ul had another
son. Then a rumor began to circulate in the district that Butterfly
had lost her mind. The neighborhood women exchanged whispers.

"I saw it with my own eyes. She sat there as if her soul had left
her, mumbling something and she tore at her bosom."

"I understand it perfectly. No wonder her heart is broken: the
bitch who stole her husband just had another son."

True to what the women said, Butterfly could often be found
mumbling the word "Amen" and making the sign of the cross, all
involuntarily. Even when she was performing, she would see the
cross floating between the posts, and in the midst of the smoothly
recited incantations, the word "Amen" would suddenly pop out of
her mouth, muddling the incantation and confusing her listeners.

One day, the wealthiest family of the district had a rite performed
to the household gods. If the shaman's supplication succeeded in
moving the spirits, the sacred bamboo pole would vibrate with mys-
tic potency, signaling their presence, and the rite then reaching
its climax would transform the worldly place where it was being
performed into a sacred realm. That day the rite had failed to arouse
the gods to descend. Even after the sequences invoking the Guardian God and the God of Fertility and Longevity had been concluded, the sacred bamboo pole remained still. The rite was well
into the sequence dedicated to the Ground Spirit, but still the pole
did not stir. The atmosphere became tense with a strange anticipation; the spectators looked at each other and shook their heads in
bewilderment. The face of the head of the household flushed crimson, then grew pale.

The incident soon became known throughout the entire district.
People wondered if Butterfly's rites were no longer as efficacious
as they had been. The bewitching child-shaman had become a peerless beauty elevated by her nobility and gracefulness; she had been
transformed into a creature whose elegance was incongruous with
her environment. In spite of her strange behavior, on the occasions
when she did complete her rites successfully, her impenetrable
grace and nobility only added sheen to her aura as a shaman. At
such times it was clear that she had lost none of her power.

Again it was the season of azaleas. Man-nyŏn was busy with the preparation for the Flower-Welcoming Rite, a celebration shamans offered not for their clients, but in order to pray to their gods for professional success. These rites took place twice annually, the Flower-Welcoming Rite in the spring and the Foliage-Welcoming Rite in the fall. Magnanimous on a grand scale, Man-nyŏn invited shamans from the neighboring districts and staged a celebration so sumptuous and merry that even the eldest daughters-in-law of the head families were emboldened to join the dancing. On a balmy spring day, with the stirring shaman music urging the crowd into the shoulder dance, and the skillful balladeers and lavish display of offerings enticing them, Man-nyŏn's yard was full of jostling spectators.

For this occasion, Butterfly wore a scarlet vest and a red cap. Holding in her right hand a fully-opened fan and in her left the bells, she sang the "Flower Song" with consummate artistry.

> Like a sage of old,
> Leaning against the stone column of a house
> Built on good deeds,
> I behold the whole world around me.
> In the dusk of the sunset
> I cannot calm the disquiet I feel in my heart.
> In the layers of the mountains
> Scenes of the four seasons unfold.
> Flowers and evergreens
> Idle away the year unseen.
> Today, now that my love has returned,
> Beautiful, too, are the flowers.

Butterfly's lips, usually grave, quivered in an imperceptible smile, which imparted such a chilling sensation that, instead of being swept into the dancing with her song, the audience merely stood frozen, oblivious of themselves. Looking at her, some just rubbed their palms together. Butterfly no longer appeared to be a priestess offering supplications and paeans to the spirits, but had become their very incarnation.

The rite consisted of nineteen steps performed over three days, seven steps more than the usual twelve, the main emphasis on those dedicated to the Mountain God, the Ground Spirit, and the ancestor spirits. It was on the second day that the strange occurrence took place. Butterfly continued with the songs and dances she had begun the day before. Since the southern shaman rites began and ended with songs, for two days she had sung in a clear voice without a trace of fatigue. It was during one of the most important sequences, the one offered to the ancestor spirits. Attired in a deep pink skirt and a lime-green jacket bordered with crimson, holding the fan and shaking the bell, Butterfly performed a slow, stately dance, then she entered the inner room and emerged from it with the boxes of the ancestors' souls, which contained their clothing. She opened the boxes, took out the clothes, and draping them over her arms, began dancing again. She put the clothes on and continued to dance, the faded clothing moving grotesquely in the bright sunlight. At this point, the rite called for the shaman to improvise a death scene: the audience would gather around her and, rubbing their hands together frantically, pray to the accompaniment of throbbing drums. With the beat of the drum, the shaman would slowly rise and resume her dance. Accordingly, Butterfly fell, descending like a butterfly folding its wings and floating to the ground. The spectators flocked around her and began to pray. The drum reverberated with deep pulsations. Butterfly did not move. The prayer became even more fervent, and the drums beat in frenzied crescendo, and still she did not rise. Stretched on the ground in her many-hued outfit, her pale face turned skyward, she was a bouquet of spring flowers, a rapturous splendor. Tension like a whirlwind swept the festive ground, and after the singular stillness cleared, there rose a chorus of whispers: "Butterfly is dead!"

But she was not dead. Under the red sash of her jacket, a slight flutter could be discerned. She remained thus for three days and three nights of opaque, milky mistiness. Then the mist lifted, and on a night of blue-grey clarity, shooting stars traversed the sky like green sparks from a fire, the largest among them breaking into a sprinkling of blue powder across the sky. Dreaming in ecstasy, Butterfly called, "The shooting stars! The shooting stars! Catch them for me!" Frightened by her own voice, she woke from her sleep.

"Was it a dream?" she asked herself.

The shooting stars did not disappear from her vision upon waking. She was quite sure that she had seen those shooting stars somewhere, sometime before.

She remained in bed for even longer than when she had been stricken in the governor's mansion. There was no fever or throbbing infection; only languor and weakness prevented her from leaving her bed. Staring at the ceiling, she was impatiently searching for something, wondering if the shooting stars, like the word "Amen," might hold the secret of her birth. As she chased after the dream stars, which bedazzled the sky like green sparks from fire in the woods, they gathered together as would beads of mercury, forming one single, huge, luminous star, and disappeared beyond her grasp forever.

Looking at her daughter, Man-nyŏn felt a lacerating pain in her heart. Without knowing the affliction of her spirit, Man-nyŏn attributed Butterfly's frequent fits of fainting and illness to the pangs of a woman scorned. Thinking thus, she only pitied her daughter more. "I must take her away from that bitch and that son-of-a-bitch, so that she doesn't have to look at them. Somehow I must soothe her heart," Man-nyŏn resolved.

Soon after the news of the birth of Pong-ch'ul's second son had reached them, Man-nyŏn decided to take Butterfly to the capital for a sightseeing excursion. They left Imsil before the leaves had lost their tender spring color, the servant boy at the inn carrying their travel load. Like well-bred women, they hired a sedan chair and horses, and Man-nyŏn had long hooded cloaks made for the occasion, even though base shamans like themselves usually went about their way without covering their faces.

Mindful of Butterfly's weakness, they traveled slowly, and by the time they crossed the river on the ferryboat, the weather had become so warm as to make them perspire. They spent the night in a lodging on the outskirts of the city. The next day, as they proceeded to Seoul, they were amazed, never having seen a road so wide as the one leading to the gate of the capital. The road was thronged with a crowd of people whom they had not seen the day before. Pressed by the crowd on all sides, the hooded mother and daughter were unable to move.

"Butterfly, are you all right?" Anxiously, Man-nyŏn put her arm around her daughter's thin shoulders. Butterfly silently nodded, for she had no other choice in this milling crowd.

"What's happening?" came a man's rough voice from behind them.

"A big spectacle," a craggy voice joined in, and the speaker punctuated his statement by spitting.

"What do you think you're doing, spitting all over?" came another angry shout.

"Hush, why make trouble—"

Pushed by the crowd, the servant boy staggered behind Man-nyŏn. As she turned around to give him a helping hand, pulling him by the sleeve, her desperate eye caught sight of two splendid sedan chairs adorned with tassels of five colors. A gentleman stood with a troubled look in front of the sedan chairs, which were flanked by slave women and menservants carrying wicker trunks.

"Heavens! A bridal party!" whispered Man-nyŏn.

Finally pulling himself together, her servant boy, an uncouth country bumpkin, asked a man in his thick southern dialect, "Excuse me. What's happening?"

"Did you ask me what's happening? We came to watch the Catholic devils go to their paradise in Heaven," a man with a white kerchief tied around his topknot said incredulously.

"Catholic devils? What's that?"

"Catholic devils are Catholic devils, you idiot. See, the ones who do this." The man crossed his chest with his right hand.

"That's weird, isn't it?"

"That's for sure. Weird, indeed."

Everyone around him burst into laughter. Disturbed by their shouting match, Butterfly stared at them icily, but in that instant, her heart stopped beating, for she saw the movement of the man crossing his chest, and remembered the cross and the character ten she had seen in her delirium during the rite in the governor's mansion. Since then her right hand continuously formed the sign without her willing it, and when she became lucid, this frightened her. Now this man was making exactly the same gesture. Like a spirit-possessed bamboo pole, Butterfly began to shake uncontrollably.

"Darling, come to your senses. Butterfly!" Man-nyŏn held her tightly, half weeping.

"I'm all right. I'm all right." Slipping out of her mother's embrace, she continued to shiver.

"Be patient a bit longer," Man-nyŏn said, drawing her daughter closer once again.

Suddenly, a shout arose: "Here they come, here they come!"

The crowd became agitated with excitement. The servant boy craned his neck in the direction of their pointing fingers.

"Who are they?" he asked again.

"Be quiet, you stray moron, don't bother me," said a man angrily.

"It's the officer and prison guards leading the Catholic devils," offered another.

"What are they going to do to them?"

"What do you think they are going to do? All of them will have their heads chopped off—like this." The man made a sawing motion at his throat.

"Heavens!" The boy's eyes were wide with fright.

"You're in luck today. We haven't seen this for a long time. Moreover, all the Catholics today are women, and they say among them is the world's most beautiful woman. That's why there are so many people."

"Hush. Be quiet," cried angry voices from all around them. But the man added, "If you believe in the Catholic god, you'll be dead, too. They put to death all Catholic zealots, because they are baser than animals; they don't serve their king, nor are they filial to their parents."

A strange procession approached. First came petty soldiers with long, red-tasseled spears, pushing the crowd back and shouting at the top of their voices, "Get away! Move away!"

Next came a bearded and whiskered gentleman on horseback. He wore a hat with large beaded strings tied under his chin and wooden shoes, and carried a sword at his waist and a whip in his hand.

Overpowered by the dignity of the gentleman, the clamorous crowd was held back for a while, casting fearful glances at him. Taking advantage of the clearing, the servant boy pushed his mistress and her daughter forward through the crowd. "Here, you'll have a better view. This is a rare treat, they say," he urged.

"Why are you stepping all over me? Stop pushing me!" someone shrieked.

Immediately behind them, the sedan chairs, pushed and shoved by the increasingly maddened crowd, were in danger of falling apart even though desperately defended by the servants; already the five-colored tassels had been torn away.

The scholar-gentleman was at his wit's end. "There is no other way. The bride has to come out; the sedan chairs are going to be pulled apart," he advised.

The carriers opened the door, bending gently with reverence. The maid who stood close by hurriedly took off her hooded cloak, and rushed to cover the face of the bride. "You must come out, ma'am," she said in a southern accent that betrayed her genteel origins, and facing the other sedan chair, she added, "And you, too, must come out."

A young girl emerged from the sedan chair, a tawny, smooth-skinned maiden of about sixteen, whose elongated, deep-set eyes were full of fear. All at once, the crowd's gaze was focused upon them.

Then a shout was heard. "Look, look! It's true; it's not a rumor! How beautiful she is!"

The crowd's attention was now instantly riveted in the other direction.

Following the bearded gentleman on horseback and the petty soldiers came two squeaking, rattling oxcarts carrying the prisoners to their execution. Four prisoners were on each wagon, all bound with crimson ropes. Teresa and Maria were in the first wagon with Barbara and Martha. Their white outfits were now blotched with blood and dust, and their hair, left uncombed for many days, swung with the movement of the wagon, accentuating their emaciated, prison-worn, tortured faces.

Teresa, the former palace lady, stood erect, disclaiming the stooped posture that characterized all the palace ladies whose lives were spent lowering themselves in the presence of royalty. She looked up somewhere higher and farther, a mystical smile floating around her lips, her face no longer of this world. The pale faces of Barbara and Martha, too, were full of peace and beatitude. In a time when widows were discouraged from remarrying, with no hope for the future and only pain and loneliness accompanying their lives, these two childless widows trembled in anticipation of the ultimate joy and glory of the holy feast. Their only regret was in leaving the orphans behind with no one to look after them.

"Please take care of our children and look after all the orphans in the world!" From the wagon that moved them toward their death, the women addressed their entreaties to the clamoring crowd who were shouting their jeering denouncements and abuses, and occasionally some words of sympathy.

To their plea, the crowd turned up their noses. "Are you crazy?

You tell us to feed orphans when we have nothing to give our own brood? Why don't you renounce your damned Catholic bigotry and raise them yourselves?"

A stone flew across the wagon.

Maria was beyond seeing and hearing. Her head slightly downcast, her cruelly bound body sat gracefully. She was trying serenely to listen to something within. Her luxuriant blue-black hair, unlike that of her companions, glistened like a blackbird's wet feathers, her slender neck laboriously supporting the almost burdensome weight of her head. Nothing—not the oppressive heat, the rough ride in the wagon, or the blood-splattered dress betokening the severe torture—could mar her beauty. Her crescent-moon eyebrows, like the stroke of a master calligrapher, the nose perfectly sculpted, the softly folded lips, all were exact replicas of her mother's features. Her alabaster face, framed by the wooden cage, was like a masterpiece portrait by a supreme artist. The crowd held its breath as the wagon passed by.

The soldiers were unable to restrain the milling crowd, which now grew even more chaotic, following the wagons to watch this beauty's decapitation.

"You stupid people. Be quiet, I tell you! Be quiet!" Brandishing their spears, the soldiers pushed the crowd back. Watching them, Teresa spoke with a faint smile.

"Leave them alone. It's their nature not to miss cattle being slaughtered. How can you stop them now that women are being murdered?"

She began to recite the Lord's Prayer: "Our Father who art in heaven—"

Straightening their bound bodies, the rest of the eight women joined with her: "Hallowed be thy name; thy kingdom come; thy will be done on earth as it is in heaven . . ."

Looking at them, Butterfly began shaking violently.

"Darling. Butterfly. Be patient a bit longer. Hold on just a little longer. We'll be able to move as soon as this crowd is gone." Perturbed, Man-nyŏn could only hold her daughter closely. But Butterfly pushed at her mother's arms with her elbows, and from her lips came strange words: "Give us this day our daily bread; and forgive us our trespasses as we forgive those who trespass against us; and lead us not into temptation, but deliver us from evil. Amen." Her words flowed smoothly, serenely, ending as she made the sign of the cross upon her breast.

"Butterfly, what are you doing? Come to your senses, wake up!"

Butterfly was totally oblivious of her mother, who was now half-crazed with fear.

"Amen." Butterfly drew the sign of the cross once again and stood vacantly.

In the next instant, a powerful flash pierced through her.

"Yes! It's my mother! It's my sister!" Butterfly cried out. The crowd's eyes turned toward her. Butterfly could see nothing now. She dashed blindly into the middle of the street, thrusting through the thick crowd with awesome strength. Thrown back by her pronouncement, they shrank from her path. The wagons had already passed them, making their way clangorously ahead. Waving both hands wildly in the air, Butterfly followed the wagon, pushing, shoving, and held onto the bars, dangling on the back of the wagon.

"Mother! Sister! It's me, Cecilia, daughter of Kwŏn Ho-sin! Maria, oh my sister!" she shouted, crying and laughing.

Her head bent, Maria heard a voice she had never forgotten. With a stab, she lifted her eyes and saw Cecilia running after the wagon, holding onto the bars.

"Sister, oh my sister, sister!" Butterfly repeated as if trying to make up for the years of yearning for long-lost love.

Maria squirmed toward Cecilia, threw her bound body forward and pressed her face against the bars. Her emotion too powerful for words, the tears poured down her face.

Cecilia caressed her sister's face through the bars. "Yes, it's you, it's really you, my sister!"

The memory of many years ago, when she was six, came back afresh for the first time. Now she could recall the countenance she had engraved on her heart, her mother's image. She had no doubt now that the face she held belonged to her sister, the exact copy of that beautiful image. Cecilia's face, aglow with joy, and the face she was holding in her hands, were two halves of a gourd.

The soldiers, immobilized by the confusion at the sudden, unexpected turn of events, now came to their senses, rushed toward Cecilia, and roughly tore her off the wagon. Another soldier struck her with his spear, while she desperately hung onto the bars.

"Who the hell is this blockhead of a girl? Get away, get away!"

"At this rate we'll never get to the place of execution before sunset. You, woman, get away from here!" A soldier kicked her in the stomach. "You crazy bitch! The executioner will die of waiting, and his sword will rust!" He snatched her violently from the cage and threw her to the ground.

"Don't hurt her! She's only a weak woman," Maria shrieked.

"Catholic bitch, who do you think you are, ordering me around?" the soldier, glaring, shouted back at her.

Reaching between the bars to strike Maria, his hand got caught, hurting him, and he became enraged. "You crazy bitch!" he screamed at Cecilia. "Unless you want to die too, get away from her!"

Cecilia held onto the soldier's legs, desperately beseeching, "Please, honorable soldier, sir, let me die. I, too, believe in the Catholic God. I am a Catholic. My name is Cecilia."

At that moment, wading out of the milling crowd, Man-nyŏn caught up to Butterfly. Sweating profusely, her eyes bloodshot, her hair flying wildly about her, the hooded cloak long since lost, and her outfit all in disarray, she grabbed her daughter. "How did this happen? What a disaster! We must leave here at once now that the street is cleared," she cried.

She turned to the soldiers, and rubbing her hands together and bowing, begged, "Look here, honorable masters, she is only a country maiden fresh from Imsil. She is as innocent as a village hen."

The soldiers scrutinized her sharply.

"You are a bad omen. Take this mad wench away from here and don't bother us any more!" one of them growled, and pushed Cecilia roughly toward her.

But Cecilia was adamant. "It's true! I have looked for this sister of mine all my life! Please take me along with her!"

"No, please! Don't let her come in here!" Maria shouted from within the cage.

"Butterfly, are you out of your mind? Hurry, come with your mother! Let us go to the governor's house at once!" Man-nyŏn was shrieking at the top of her lungs.

The crowd again became agitated.

"I wonder what this means? They look like twin sisters."

"See how beautiful they are!"

"Look! The girl jumped into the cage!"

"How light-bodied she is!"

Alighting on the wagon, Cecilia held onto the bars and pulled herself erect, her heart and body on fire. Scintillating and burning with fire-flowers, she was untouchable, a tower of flame.

◆   ◆   ◆

The world was clothed in a purifying green. All the trees—chestnuts, gingkos, zelkovas, persimmons, magnolias—strained to emit their verdant essence. Borne by the wind, a fragrance of overwhelming sweetness from the chestnut flowers filled the air.

Tasan looked around him. Before him, white hydrangea flowers opened like a torn piece of cloud. Wisteria trees suspended their lavender flower-clusters, and the peonies were at their peak. His gaze rested on the barley field, undulating like a green sea in the early summer wind. During his eighteen years of banishment, awake or asleep, he had longed to be in Majae in this enchanting season. His native land boasted no soaring mountain ranges, sweeping plains, or magnificent pine forests, but the rippling river with its whitewashed sands was always clear, and the hills were cushioned with grass. Except for the gingkos in front of Yŏyudang, no grand, ancient trees adorned the place, but in early summer the trees sprouted their young leaves like jets of green water, and flowers fought with each other in their haste to open. Tasan loved the genteel, unostentatious coziness of the place, among whose inhabitants were very few with surnames other than Chŏng; thus it had always been for Tasan his clan village, a place deeply rooted in his heart.

Yet, in the midst of his beloved hometown and in his favorite season, Tasan was deep in contemplation. Now that he had come home, he could see that this house he had longed for in his banishment was really nothing but a faded structure, certainly no grander than the thatched cottage of his Kyuldong exile. In this house, only his aged wife's lament, and his sons, in fear of their father although they were themselves at the threshold of old age, awaited him. During his exile, he had had dear friends and disciples who loved and respected him, and a woman who had attended him with the utmost devotion. Although humble, his house had always been meticulously looked after, and it had provided him with an atmosphere conducive to his writing. Tasan mentally shook his head, but he could not suppress the emptiness he felt. It was as if he had been betrayed. He would have preferred his house to be more serene and better ordered, as befitted the home of a gentleman-scholar; his wife more graceful in her appearance and nobler in her deportment, as befitted the mistress of a grand family; and their sons more dignified without being pompous, as befitted the scions of a celebrated clan. Dissatisfied though he was with them, he understood well that their lives, spent in seclusion as the family of banished "criminals," accounted for their shortcomings. As for Tasan himself, he conferred upon himself the pen name, Yŏyudang, meaning "one who dwells in the hall of tranquillity," to remind himself that his fate was to live in uneasy seclusion.

Realizing that what he had been dreaming of day and night during his exile—his family, his hometown—had been nothing but an illusion, a bitter smile played on Tasan's face. Now at seventy-two, which from ancient times had been deemed the Age of Rarity, he continued to toil, writing, editing, and revising his earlier works. Although he had vowed to put an end to writing when he reached sixty, suffering from deteriorating vision and the pain of arthritis, he could not give up his brush. He was becoming easily tired, and Tasan well knew it signaled the decline of his life-force. In the tranquillity of his retired life, whenever he felt weary, he would go into the yard and sit on a rock under the gingko trees to gaze upon the river. In the spring the river was full, and in summer the leaves on the trees along the river made the water glisten with lovely green. These moments of repose gave some semblance of vitality to his now-failing health.

Abandoning himself to the mellifluous wind, Tasan let his eyes roam afar. The wind that traveled across the river, sweeping over the aspen trees and barley fields, blew against his face. Then, suddenly, the wind changed its course, blowing from the opposite direction, turning the leaves over and making them glisten like fine silver filigree. Tasan remembered the story recorded in A Descriptive History of the Three Kingdoms, of two sages, Kwan'gi and Tosŏng, who lived during the Silla dynasty [668–918], secluded from the world on Mount P'o. Kwan'gi lived in the southern valley of the mountain, Tosŏng in the northern cave, about two-and-a-half miles apart. They were close friends, often visited each other, and always knew when one was coming to see the other. When the trees swayed toward the south in the northern wind, Tosŏng in the northern cave would say to himself: "The wind blows in the direction of the south.

It means that I must go and see my friend in the southern valley." In the same manner, when the trees leaned toward the north in the southerly wind, Kwan'gi would visit Tosŏng in his northern cave. Thus the two friends knew when to visit each other according to the direction of the wind. Tasan wondered, "Were they immortals, transcending man's affairs and in harmony with nature? How I envy their timelessness!" His eyes tried to find the wind's direction, but this balmy early summer breeze was without a destination. Now the wind, pregnant with leafy fragrance, blew confusedly in both directions across the river, the site of his brother Yak-chong's grave. He wondered if his brother's soul, freed long ago from the prison of his flesh, was trying to visit him. In the land he had longed for, even amidst the mellow season he so loved, Tasan was mournful.

The wind that had quieted for a moment began to stir again, causing the branches of the weeping willows on the river bank to sway like a woman's long, dishevelled hair. He watched the rise and fall of the wind as though witnessing the mystery of nature for the first time.

Suddenly Tasan remembered the words Maria was said to have uttered when she was asked the standard question the authorities used when they interrogated Christians—"Have you seen your Lord?" She replied, "In a small village, they have never seen the king. Does this mean that he does not exist? When I behold everything in the universe, I cannot but believe in the existence of a supreme king, the Father on the highest, the Creator of all."

"Freakish woman! How dare you talk back! Flog her harder!" the enraged officials shouted at her.

Maria suffered the severe punishment; then, undaunted, she went on calmly but firmly, "No one has ever seen the wind. But look at those branches. Don't you see they are shaking? Just as clearly as I see the wind causing them to sway, so do I believe in the existence of our Lord, whom I have never seen." Then she lost consciousness.

Tasan was told that just as it was now, so it had been in the early summer then. In the prison courtyard a lone zelkova tree stood trembling in the wind, tinting the place green as the leaves fluttered. It was related to him that her amazing wisdom, the permanence of her faith, the strength of spirit that enabled her to withstand the cruelest torture deeply touched even the hardened officials accustomed to punishing criminals.

That was 1825, exactly nine years ago, the year Ha-sang had paid a long-overdue visit to Tasan. His nephew had appeared listless, and his eyes were clouded.

His family, which now included grandchildren, out of respect for his wishes spoke very little and behaved in front of Tasan with a careful quietude. None of them dared to express opinions regarding his personal affairs or news of the outside world as freely as could Ha-sang. So Tasan always looked forward to the visit of his nephew. With age, Ha-sang had grown more prudent and considerate. His bold decisiveness combined with a capacity for clear judgment had made him the mainstay of his fellow Christians and the leader of the Korean church, which had been slowly rebuilding its strength.

As ever glad to see Ha-sang, Tasan led him to the bamboo bench under the gingko tree and sat facing his nephew.

"You don't look well. Aren't you feeling well?" Tasan inquired with concern.

Expressionless, Ha-sang remained silent for a while, but, becoming conscious of his uncle's probing, puzzled gaze, he answered with a slight fluster, "Oh, no. Nothing is wrong."

Sensing something must have happened to Ha-sang, Tasan added, "In the summer heat it is easy to get indigestion. You must take care of yourself." His words were tinged with love and concern for his nephew.

His eyes downcast, Ha-sang remained silent, as if he had been admonished. Tasan looked intently at his sturdy and imposing nephew, who sat respectfully with his hands placed on his knees, his posture just as tall and solid as when he stood. His long, bushy eyebrows and prominent nose exuded dignity. The muscular expanse of his shoulders, his bronze complexion, the large, rough hands that had known hard work, his whole being bespoke his character and chronicled his life.

"A manly man, indeed!" thought Tasan admiringly. However, he could not erase from his mind the first time he had seen his nephew, many years ago when Ha-sang had come to see him, a bright, fresh youth in servant's guise, illiterate at almost twenty, yet unembittered by the persecution he suffered as the son of a beheaded heretic, and by the hardships of poverty that had plagued his young life.

Indeed, the beauty of his nephew's character, his steadfast faith and dedication to his mission, provoked only admiration in Tasan. Trying to determine his age, remembering that Ha-sang had said that he was sixteen when he had visited him in Kyuldong in 1811 and it was 1825 now, Tasan guessed that he must be thirty. He gazed with emotion-filled eyes at his nephew, who sat silently facing him with an uncharacteristic gloom on his face. Tasan had seen him with such an expression only once before, in the year following his pardon in 1818. It had been a hot summer day. Just as now, they had sat facing each other on the same bamboo bench under the same gingko tree. Ha-sang had been just as silent and his expression just as melancholy. Only when he was about to leave after a day's stay did he mention the fact that the celibate couple, Cho Suk and Teresa Kwŏn, had been executed. Now looking at the same expression on his nephew's face, Tasan felt a premonition and broke the silence.

"What happened?" he pressed.

Ha-sang did not answer, but soon Tasan was struck with a sight he had never expected to see—his indomitable nephew weeping. Watching the broad shoulders shaking, he could only stroke his own beard. What was causing this man to weep, who since his childhood had had the strength to endure and overcome loneliness, poverty, and persecution? Whatever the pain that was tormenting his nephew, to leave him alone would be the only charitable thing Tasan could do now. A bird swept by the gingko tree, leaving a trail of lovely twittering, then followed by stillness. The scene was as stark as if the sun had bleached everything around them. Time stood still, until at last Ha-sang wiped his tears away with his fists and lifted his face toward his uncle. As if cleansed by his tears, his expression had returned to its usual serenity. "If you don't mind, please tell your uncle what has happened," Tasan was finally able to say.

After a moment's hesitation, Ha-sang told him about Maria's martyrdom, and that of the other Christian women with whom she had lived. This news greatly perturbed Tasan. Ironically, repeated persecution had unwittingly become the vehicle for the spread of Catholicism. People no longer viewed Christians as creatures baser than animals who served no king, were filial to no parents, and who severed the ethical bonds of human relationships, and shared both wealth and women with each other. Many now had come to believe that among the Ten Commandments, the fifth taught men to be filial and to respect hierarchical relationships, and two others stressed a severe code of behavior for men and women. People also noticed that even the lowliest among men, confessing their faith, openly loved and helped others in need. Although most failed to grasp the religion in its entirety, they no longer unconditionally condemned Catholics as enemies of society, as had been decreed by the government.

"It is indeed regrettable that such things still go on in the capital," said Tasan, letting out a long sigh.

"And people's attitudes haven't changed much, either. They shouted obscenities as the women were carried away like caged animals in the wagons, and some even cast stones at them." Ha-sang's voice trembled.

"That's mob behavior. People in a mob are swept away by the excitement, regardless of how they feel in the depths of their hearts."

"Why is that so? What is wrong with our holy religion? What are our crimes? We are strong in faith, ardent in hope, sincere in love. Are these criminal offenses? Is it a sin to believe in Almighty God, Creator of the universe, One omnipotent and omniscient, infinitely compassionate and boundlessly righteous? Is it wrong to love one another, regardless of station, as brothers and sisters, all children of God? Why? Is it because this is an alien religion? Then why do Koreans value everything else from abroad and yet deny this?"

Tasan had never seen Ha-sang, usually calm and discreet, in such violent agitation; he was trembling with anger and mortification.

"Sooner or later the time will surely come when misunderstanding will be cleared away and barbarity will cease. Until that time comes, we must endure. The Edict of the Queen Dowager Kim is still in effect, don't you see? That's why we must be very careful, as I have said before," Tasan said gently. His sudden outburst having released his pent-up emotion, Ha-sang was silent once again. After a long pause, he spoke again listlessly. "We have been careful."

"But something must have gone wrong."

"It's all because of the orphans."

"That's why the children must be well-disciplined," Tasan sighed.

"They watched them very carefully. But the children were still very young and unaware of their circumstances. It happened when they were playing in the yard, thoughtlessly calling each other by their Christian names." Ha-sang went on, "His name was Peter. A customer heard the other children calling him by that name, and the next day the police raided the house. Not realizing what the children had done, they did not have a chance to prevent the disaster." Ha-sang seemed still unable to resign himself to what had happened.

Neither man touched the fresh fruit punch brought in from the inner room, or the peaches just picked from the backyard. Knowing the tragedy had been caused by the use of Christian names, Tasan did not condemn his nephew's repeated mention of these forbidden names, as he had done many years ago in the land of banishment when Ha-sang had first come to see him. And now if their conversation was no different from a clandestine exchange between secret agents, Tasan was unaware of its implications. A heavy silence settled once again. The shadow of the gingko tree reached the bamboo bench, playing a dizzying pattern on it, and then stretched toward the east.

With his head bowed, Ha-sang finally spoke. "The reunion of the two sisters was truly touching. They looked like twins, both of them so beautiful that from the spectators came a ceaseless sigh of admiration."

"How tragic—the meeting only hastening their farewell!"

Ha-sang jumped at his uncle's words.

"A parting? Not at all! Together, hand in hand, they ascended to eternal paradise in Heaven; they would never let go each other's hand."

"Then you mean to say that the younger one, too, was beheaded?"

"Yes. She proclaimed loudly that she was Cecilia, and a Christian. They had been separated when she was only six, so she must have had no chance to offer prayers or read the Bible. But I was amazed at her intelligence when she recited the Lord's Prayer and the Hail Mary without missing a word."

"How pitiful!"

"Yes. But they were the victors. Yes, it's true. In prison, they tried to get the officials to understand the principles of Catholicism. Although these tenets were explained by mere womenfolk, the officials could not dispute their logic and rationality. These women really understood the true meaning of Catholicism, and the teachings of our Lord."

"It seems that the Korean vernacular has been a great help to them," Tasan murmured as if to himself.

Those with classical learning, including Tasan, looked down on *hang'ul*, an indigenous writing system designed to express the language of everyday speech. Upper-class men continued to prefer the difficult Chinese writing system, in which they had been arduously schooled, over the Korean alphabet, in order to retain their monopoly on learning. But the Korean alphabet, created in 1446, had slowly become a powerful vehicle for spreading knowledge among the lower classes and among women, who previously had been denied access to learning. Catholic writings translated into the Korean alphabet had helped the otherwise unschooled to understand in depth the principles of Catholicism.

Tasan was deeply impressed. "In the near future, there will be some changes in the way people express themselves in writing," he thought. Suddenly the image of his brother, Yak-chong, surfaced in his mind. Tasan cried out in his heart, "My brother was a man of foresight!" In the early days of the Korean Catholic church, many leaders had engaged themselves in the task of translating Catholic writings into Korean, and Chŏng Yak-chong had written *A Summary of Catholic Teachings*, the first book of tenets in the Korean alphabet, hoping this would make the church accessible to everyone. Tasan had not written a single book in the Korean alphabet; nonetheless, he could not deny its scientific merit and logic, and he understood the reason why, after having been ignored and snubbed as a vulgar script, it had finally come to be accepted as the official script. These Catholic writings designed to spread the message as simply and widely as possible had played an important role.

After a long meditation, Ha-sang spoke again. "Only a few days ago was I finally able to obtain permission to visit the execution site and claim the bodies abandoned in the sand. After little more than a month, the bodies were completely without flesh, only bones, white and clean . . ." He could not go on. Once again Tasan could only look at his nephew, who was now openly sobbing.

Composing himself quickly, Ha-sang continued, "Everyone had the privilege of becoming a martyr. No one was left behind." His voice was now clear, and he went on, "As I told you, I followed the procession all the way, and among the crowd I saw Hong-nim . . ." He could not finish, because at that moment he caught a glimpse of his cousin, Hag-yŏn.

Bearing their mother's family traits, the brothers were not well-built. Possessed of considerable learning and well-versed in the arts of medicine, Hag-yŏn, if asked, would offer a diagnosis and prescription by feeling the patient's pulse. A man of integrity and upright conduct, he was a true gentleman. However, the sons did not measure up to the father's expectation of them. Tasan still harbored a hope that his sons would excel and bring luster to the reputation of the family; in the recesses of his mind still lingered a worldly ambition he should have abandoned when he was condemned to banishment. Tasan himself had an immense knowledge of medicine and had published a medical text, entitled *A Comprehensive Treatise on Smallpox*, but he approached the art of medicine only as a scholarly pursuit, not as an occupation. He disliked seeing his son dispensing medical advice by feeling the pulses of country women. "A scholar-gentleman becoming a medical practitioner!" he admonished his son in anger. Such an attitude contradicted his support of equality among men—even he was vulnerable to human frailty. Aware of their father's disappointment, the sons were always timid before him.

"The news came that the Yun household has just had a son," Hag-yŏn announced to his father quietly, kneeling ceremoniously before him.

"Yun household" meant the very daughter, his favorite, to whom Tasan had written a poem in his exile, "Remembering a Young Daughter." In an upper-class family, a married daughter was addressed only by her husband's family name, never by her own name; thus, because Tasan's daughter had been married into the Yun family, her own family members addressed her as "Yun household." During Tasan's exile, a match had fortunately been found for her, a daughter of a banished heretic. She had been married amid tears of longing for her father, and the memory of the painful wedding day still lingered in her heart. Only after he had returned home did Tasan meet his son-in-law for the first time and reconcile himself with the daughter he had left behind at the age of four, suddenly become a woman with two daughters of her own. After bearing three daughters, she had now finally delivered a son for her husband, who was an only heir.

"Good for her! I'm so proud of her! How extraordinary!" Tasan did not hide his joy, and repeated the same words over and over again; he was no different from any other country grandfather enjoying the news of his long-awaited grandson's arrival.

Looking at his father, Hag-yŏn was released from tension and noticed Ha-sang for the first time. "Ha-sang, is that you? I haven't seen you for a long time," he said softly.

"How are you?" Ha-sang rejoined just as quietly.

Ha-sang was aware that Hag-yŏn disliked him, believing that Catholicism had been the cause of the family's tragedy. Hag-yŏn wondered why his cousin, a Catholic to the core, a believer in the cursed religion, came so frequently to pay his respects to his father. He felt dejected when he saw how pleased his father was to see Ha-sang.

After bowing respectfully to his father, Hag-yŏn cast a sidelong glance at Ha-sang, who shared more of his father's features than he did himself, and left.

Alone with Tasan now, Ha-sang resumed the conversation. "I saw Hong-nim in the crowd along with her mother. She is grown now, and lovely."

Eyes wide open, Tasan stared at Ha-sang without a word, as if he had lost the capacity for speech.

"I might have been wrong," Ha-sang added, flustering, "It is not likely that they would be in Seoul, and even if they were, they would not possibly have been among such a crowd."

Although Ha-sang tried to leave the matter in an ambiguous light, the thought occurred to Tasan that his nephew could have been right after all. He remembered what Chong-sim had said when he came last year to pay his respects to Tasan with the gifts from Kyul-dong—"My aunt's sister-in-law came to the funeral of my cousin, and saw Hong-nim's mother bustling about. The lady asked her to come help with the wedding of her only daughter, her pride and joy."

Tasan could reconstruct the sequence of events that might have brought them among the mob of people who had come to watch the Catholic women being led away to their execution. The bride might have been married into a capital household, and that might have been the day of her entrance into her husband's house. The party nearing the gate to the capital would then have been forced to confront the appalling procession. Tasan wanted to say, "The mother and daughter must have been the members of a bridal entourage," but he decided to remain silent. His thoughts returned to Yun household, and he wondered whether he could be so openly pleased if word should reach him that Hong-nim, his illegitimate daughter, had had a son. His heart torn with confusion, he bowed his head.

Tasan's speculation was correct. Separated from her father in 1818 at the age of eleven, Hong-nim was a maiden of eighteen, which was considered past the marriageable age. She possessed a luminous, though tawny complexion, and her eyes were a bit too elongated to be called beautiful; nonetheless, people regarded her as handsome. As Tasan suspected, Hong-nim and P'yo-nyŏ had accompanied the bridal party to Seoul, and near the gate they had witnessed the spectacle. Though they had accompanied the bride to the capital, they soon had to leave her since they were not servants. In a short time Hong-nim had become a close friend of the bride, Kung-nim, now the second daughter-in-law of a Kim family in the capital. Thus, on their way to the house of the bride's new in-laws, they had confronted the inauspicious procession that had forced the bride to dismount from her sedan chair. Kung-nim's uncle, who had escorted the party, feared this to be an ill omen, and the dark shadow between his brows had lingered for a long time.

The disturbance Kung-nim felt, however, was greater. When she slipped out of the sedan chair, the scene before her eyes seemed too theatrical to be real, but a strange chill ran down her spine when she overheard the repeated exchange of the names, Maria and Cecilia. She had heard them somewhere; they were familiar names, forgotten names washed away by the current of time. Searching deep into her memory, she tried to recall the ones who had borne them. Although memory, so near yet so far, eluded her grasp, she could not keep herself from trembling violently.

After the procession had moved away like a windstorm, Kung-nim returned to her sedan chair, which had been stripped of its festive adornments. At that instant, a memory came back in a flash, still intact: a prosperous-looking matron was playing with a child, asking it, "How old are you?"

"Four," the child answered.

"What is your name?"

"Kug-a, and they also call me Juliette."

"Kug-a and Juliette? What strange names! All right, let's call you Kung-nim from now on. It's a good name." The compassionate lady clapped her hands in joy.

Since that day, she had been addressed as Kung-nim, changing the ideogram *a*, an elegant Chinese character, to *nim*, a vernacular and more popular and countrified word. Her memory did not go back further than that time.

Now she remembered that she had added something more, without being asked.

"I have two sisters," she said, "the elder is Maria and the second one is Cecilia."

"What kind of names are those? What weird names, indeed!" The lady merely laughed off the child's remark.

The child had kept her own names as well as those of her sisters hidden deep in her heart. But she had failed to connect the names she had locked away in her memory to the reality that had exploded in front of her very eyes. Only after she had returned to her sedan chair, in a strange turmoil, did everything become clear.

"Yes! They were my sisters! I was called Juliette as well as Kug-a." She tried to stand up in her sedan chair, but once again she collapsed in her seat.

She realized that she was not free to follow her impulse. She could not betray her adoptive mother's love, and the care and devotion with which she had been reared. Her mother cherished her like a jewel in her palm, and showered her with luxuries, but even with all the wealth in the world, her mother always appeared lonely; Kung-nim could not hurt this generous woman. Somewhere in this world must be her natural mother, but this mother was the only one she knew. Sitting straight, Kung-nim calmed her agitation. In her mind once again surfaced the images of her two sisters; she recalled Maria's nobility and grace, and Cecilia's passionate beauty being flung at the cage like the mad flight of a gorgeous butterfly. Painfully, Juliette gathered the images and locked them deep into her heart, dabbing at her beautifully painted bridal face with the silk handkerchief hidden in her sleeve, so that her tears would not mar her makeup.

That was nine years ago, and it was now 1834. Without sending word to Tasan as to their whereabouts, Hong-nim and her mother had disappeared.

That evening, Tasan had too much to drink—a rare indulgence, for he had been exercising extreme self-discipline since his homecoming. Soon after the evening meal, he fell asleep. When he awoke, moonlight flooded his room. Overcome by the weight of remembrance, Tasan went out and sat in the moon-drenched garden. The full moon rode in the sky and was mirrored in the river, but even the wine cup filled with moonshadow could not comfort him in his desolation. Those whose eyes had once glistened with the same moonbeams were no longer there; he was all alone. He felt more keenly than ever the loneliness of having survived the death of his dear ones. Unconsciously, words swirled in his mouth: "O Lord, have mercy on us." Totally unaware of what he was doing, he made the sign of the cross upon his chest. He felt his heart reduced to absolute humility. Into that meekness flowed the moonlight, and in the early summer breeze, his desolation was gradually soothed away. Memory pursuing him like a bitter woe or longing, Tasan returned to his room and lit a candle. On his writing table, upon which was a newly bound book, he began grinding the inkstick. In a sweep, he wrote the title on the book: *The Posthumous Works of Manch'ŏn*. Then he sank deep in reverie, thinking of the way he had acquired the materials for this project, and of his late brother-in-law.

Manch'ŏn was the pen name of Tasan's brother-in-law, Yi Sŭnghun (1736–1801), Korea's first Catholic. He had been baptized in 1784 by a French missionary, Father Louis de Grammont, in Peking, where he had accompanied his father on the Korean mission to the Chinese court. His Catholic name was Peter, which Father de Grammont gave him so that he might become the rock upon which the Korean church would stand. He had been beheaded as a heretic in 1801.

In the early summer of 1827, two years after Ha-sang had told him of Maria's death, Tasan received a personally carried letter from one of his friends. After his sixtieth birthday, although Tasan had continued to isolate himself and had severed all ties with his acquaintances, he still corresponded with some of his literati-official friends. The letter referred to the fact that there had been a motion in the court to restore Tasan to his former position, but the idea had met with opposition from Tasan's former adversaries, who almost succeeded in sending him back to prison, reviving the old enmity at a time when there was a new surge of Catholic persecution in the country. Troubled and agitated by the letter, he had been secluded in his room with the windows shut, mindlessly turning the pages of a book he had been reading, when he heard someone outside the room trying to make his presence known.

"Who is it?"

"The aunt at the Yŏmsoch'ŏng Bridge has come to see you," the voice of his younger son, Hag-yu, had answered.

Tasan threw the book away and stood up abruptly. She was the widow of Yi Sŭng-hun and his own elder sister.

"At her advanced age, how did she manage to come all the way here?" Wondering, he hurried toward his wife's inner wing, where he had not been a frequent visitor lately.

Sitting decorously there in the honored seat, the old lady was engaged in an intimate talk with Tasan's wife about things she had kept in her heart for a long time. Seeing Tasan enter the room, she tried to rise, but he motioned her to stay seated, and deeply bowed before her.

"That is absurd at your honorable age, my dear sir," she protested, shocked at his uncommon courtesy and returning his kowtow with one of her own.

"I should have been the one to visit your home to pay my respects. I deeply regret that you should have been forced to travel such a distance to come here."

"Not at all. I wished to visit the house of my birth once more before I die." Tears glistened in her eyes, sunk deep in a valley of wrinkles.

"You seem to be well, for which I am grateful."

"My life should have ended in 1801," she asserted, her voice trembling.

Tasan did not dare to look into his sister's face, but said to her, "Please stay here and rest as long as you wish. The cherries are ripe now, and I hope to have the pleasure of dining with you tonight at the same table. Until then . . ."

The lady stopped him as he stood to leave.

"To tell you the truth, although I wished to come home once more before I die, there is also something I wanted to give to you, my dear sir." She motioned to a woman who had accompanied her, who placed a package wrapped in black cloth in front of Tasan.

"What is this?" he asked, puzzled.

"It's all written in Chinese. I, a mere woman, have no way of knowing, but they are my late husband's manuscripts. I have been hiding them for a long time, hoping to preserve his writings."

The old lady unwrapped the package herself, and out came a bundle of faded and soiled documents.

"These are from your brother-in-law's document chest," she said. "We used to have many more collected works, and a considerable number of framed calligraphs and hanging scrolls as well. But we lost all of them in that horrible storm. It took a lot out of me to save even these ..." Unable to finish, she turned her head away, her bony shoulders trembling, and her toothless mouth quivering.

"My dear sir," she continued at last, "I know you are in trouble yourself, but have pity on your wretched sister, and keep these writings of my late husband for later generations, I beseech you."

Her own sons' fate then precarious, she had only her brother to rely upon for the preservation of her late husband's work. Tasan was deeply moved.

Among Manch'ŏn's manuscripts were miscellaneous collections of farmers' songs, and some poetry and essay collections, all written in a graceful, erudite style. Reading them, Tasan was seized with an ineffable emotion. In private life these brothers-in-law had both been young elites from the oppressed Southerner faction. Reaching public office via a long, arduous road, they had finally come to be trusted and loved by the late King Chŏngjo. Together, these young scholars, forward-looking and ambitious for reform, first sought new truth through Western learning brought back from China—which at the time was synonymous with Catholicism—and finally accepted it as a religion. As the persecution grew, both had been forced to renounce the religion by submitting written statements; Yi Sŭng-hun wrote his ambiguous "Poem Renouncing Catholicism," and Tasan, his "Confession." However, after many attempts at apostasy had failed, Sŭng-hun had been executed along with Chŏng Yak-chong, on February 26, 1801. He had been a man in his prime, forty-five years old. He left behind a poem of farewell to his life on earth, which could not possibly have been written by an apostate:

Though the moon disappears from the sky,
It remains in the heavens;
Though the water evaporates on the surface,
It is undiminished in the pond.

Since the day of his sister's visit, Tasan had begun collecting
the writings of the Southerner scholars implicated in the heretic
learning who had fallen victim to the Persecution of 1801. He had
edited them into a book of one hundred and twelve pages divided
into fifty-six chapters. He had been groping for a title for the book
when he was inspired to name it *The Posthumous Writings of
Manch'ŏn*. Although his writings constituted a much smaller pro-
portion of the volume than those contributed by others, it was a
fitting title, reflecting Tasan's manifold emotions. Tasan repeated
in his mind: "Even the apostle Saint Paul betrayed his Lord three
times."

In the preface, Tasan had written: "Having spent thirty years as
a criminal condemned for treasonous offense, my life barely spared,
when I stepped back into the world, I saw that the sky and mountains remained unchanged, that the clouds were as white as ever,
and the sky as blue. But where have the wise men and dear friends
gone? Now, alas, my wretched life, worthless as sticks and stones,
wanders aimlessly, and I am without the will to involve myself in
the affairs of the world. I had the good fortune of acquiring a few of
the poems and essays of the venerable Manch'ŏn, which brought
me to compile and edit this book, although unworthy of such an
honor. I entitled it *The Posthumous Writings of Manch'ŏn*. The
easterly wind melts the ice and causes the leaves to sprout. Spring
rejuvenates nature through the boundless providence of the Lord-
on-High. Such is the universal truth, and only those who are enlightened and can realize the difference between The Great Ultimate
and The Boundless, can come near the will of the Lord-on-High."
He signed it Mugŭk-kwanin, the Beholder of the Boundless.

Although Tasan signed a pseudonym to the preface, it had taken
great courage and resolution to write such a statement when once
again the capital was beset by a new wave of persecution, since the
identity of the signer and the contents were obvious to everyone.
By signing as the Beholder of the Boundless, he had boldly acknowledged the Christian doctrine of resurrection, implied his

Christian faith, and attributed the troubles in his own life to Providence. Finally, Tasan had come to the encounter with his God.

Later in 1874, a French clergyman, Charles Dallet, in his book, *Histoire de L'Église de Corée*, would quote repeatedly from the *History of the Spread of the Gospel in Korea*, the authorship of which Dallet attributed to Johann Yag-yong Chŏng, Tasan. The book does not survive; however, from the fact that both Dallet, in his *Histoire*, and Bishop Marie A. N. Daveluy in his *Memoire* referred to it, one can reasonably assume that it was indeed written by Tasan. Dallet explained that the book may have been destroyed by a fire that occurred in the mission house, or it might have decomposed while hidden buried underground. Among the voluminous writings that have survived there is no evidence that Tasan was a Christian; he was known only as the foremost Confucian scholar of the time. However, in his early book, *Lecture on the Doctrine of the Mean*, one can glimpse the influence of Matteo Ricci. At the time, many considered him "outwardly Confucian and inwardly heretic," or as one who "serves Confucius and follows Western learning." Others thought him to be in line with Matteo Ricci's approach, which represented Christianity as a system of wisdom and ethics compatible with Confucianism. However, Tasan never confused the two systems of thought. Instead, fully acknowledging their incompatibility, he believed in the possibility of their coexistence on equal ground. There was no need, in his mind, to choose one over the other. This conviction enabled him, as Dallet mentioned in his *Histoire*, to spend his last years as a devout Christian practicing self-denial like a desert ascetic, never taking off the metal belt he had fashioned for himself, while at the same time remaining a consummate Confucian, holding steadfast to that tradition.

As for Ha-sang, he had been unable to visit Tasan for many years. After nine journeys to Peking and long, arduous effort, he finally persuaded the Vatican to grant Korea, this small kingdom tucked away in a corner of the Far East, independence from China and to establish a new diocese in a nation that had miraculously accepted Christianity not through proselytizing but on its own. Pope Gregory XVI declared in 1831 the establishment of the Korean diocese and appointed Monsignor Bruguière as its vicar apostolic, thus recognizing the sovereignty of Korea. This was a diplomatic victory as well as a religious one. While Bishop Bruguière was on his long journey to Korea from Siam, a Chinese priest by the name of Father Pacificus Liu Fang-chi, who had studied in Milan, wished to come to Korea and work for the church until the new bishop arrived. Ha-sang left to meet him at the border, at the same place and in the same secret circumstances, as was done in the case of the martyred Father Chou Wen-mu. Since his appearance was no different from that of any other Korean, Father Liu arrived in Seoul safely. He stayed in Ha-sang's house under the most devout care of his mother, Cecilia, and his sister, Elizabeth. For all these reasons, Ha-sang had been unable to visit Tasan for a long time.

Now that he had come, Ha-sang became deeply concerned about Tasan, who was almost unrecognizably emaciated, as if the sufferings of his life had suddenly taken hold of him, reducing him in flesh and wasting his body away. Looking at his uncle, Ha-sang was conscious of something in him beyond sorrow, a new revelation.

After reporting to Tasan the joyous news of the establishment of the new Korean diocese and the arrival of the clergyman, Ha-sang said hesitantly, "Now that we have a priest, we can receive the holy sacraments." His voice was grave.

Tasan intuited what Ha-sang meant.

"Now the priest can perform the Sacrament of Extreme Unction," he mused.

"There are many Christians who live a long time after receiving that sacrament," Ha-sang comforted his uncle.

Tasan was silent for a long time.

"Can I meet the priest? I wish to make a confession of my life, and with my soul so cleansed, I desire to leave this world," he asked finally.

Suppressing a sob, Ha-sang left his uncle and returned to Seoul. Three days later, accompanied by the priest, he came back to Majae; Yu Chin-gil and Cho Sin-ch'ŏl also came with him. Their mission accomplished, all three had been freed of the necessity of going to Peking.

Tasan appeared even weaker than he had been only a few days earlier. He sat facing the white cloth-covered table set with a sacramental cup and plate, and a crucifix between two candles. By the time the priest put on his surplice, draped his maroon stole around his neck, and lighted the candles, Tasan appeared too weak to go through with the procedure to the end. However, as the priest finally drew the sign of the cross, sprinkling holy water around the room and over the heads of those present, and intoned: "Peace be unto this house," Tasan gradually regained strength and serenity. Though he could not understand Father Liu's Latin, he felt his heart tremble with a powerful emotion. The Sacrament of Extreme Unction, bestowing grace and strength to meet the bodily and spiritual struggle of death, continued in solemn devotion. Finally, the priest motioned the other three in the room to leave so that he and Tasan could continue the confession.

Although Tasan was a great Chinese scholar, he could not speak the language; he could communicate with the Chinese clergyman only in writing. As soon as they were alone, Tasan picked up his brush with a trembling hand. He was about to confess the sins of his life. No one knows the contents of the writing; it was kept only with the Lord. The priest wrote: "Look upon the Cross of Calvary, and like a martyr bear the pain of death with joy." Touched by these words, basking in the Lord's infinite benevolence, Tasan let tears flow down his cheeks in thanksgiving and comfort. The heavy burden of his sins slipped away from him; his apostasy, his life-long torment of guilt, too, he let go. As a Confucian scholar, he had sinned against Confucianism, too, by renouncing its Five Canons. Absolved thus from all his sins, he felt the completeness of his redemption. After the sacrament, his solemn and stern expression changed to one of brightness. Everyone assumed that Tasan was improving. He even enjoyed playing with his great-grandson.

In the middle of February 1836, the ice began to melt in the river, and a hint of spring was in the air. This year, since the fifteenth of the month, the Chŏng household had been receiving relatives, disciples, and friends from all over the country in preparation for the celebration of Tasan's wedding anniversary, which would take place on the twenty-second. At a time when a man's life expectancy was only fifty years, it was an occasion for great rejoicing for a man and wife to have shared each other's lives for sixty years. For this rare occasion the two celebrants would wear on their heads, now snow-white, the formal cap of an official for the husband, and a bejeweled head-dress for the wife; they would sit in front of the banquet table, looking altogether like a bride and a groom. Tasan was looking forward to this festive occasion. Most of the Chŏng males, beginning with his own father, had been widowers; only

Tasan and his wife would have the good fortune of soon being able to celebrate their sixtieth wedding anniversary. It was an event of great felicitation for the entire clan; however, it was most important for Tasan, for it would be an acknowledgment of his deep feeling for his wife. He wanted to pay tribute to the spouse who, having borne him six sons and three daughters, all except three of whom had met untimely deaths, had then endured interminable suffering, first with her husband, and then by herself during the eighteen years of separation spent in loneliness and fear.

But six days before the celebration, Tasan's condition took a turn for the worse, plunging him into a near-critical condition. On the nineteenth, to the relief of those around him, he had a short remission. Nevertheless, Tasan was aware of the imminence of his death. Calling everyone to his bedside, he stated his last wishes. Among them were instructions for his funeral. He forbade the employment of an official geomancer for the selection of his burial site, insisting that his body be buried in a simple Confucian rite on the hill behind his house, Yŏyudang. This could be taken to mean that, as a Christian, he dismissed as mere superstition the theory of geomancy, a traditional method of selecting propitious sites by divination, yet as a Confucian scholar, followed its convention.

Tasan fumbled for the creased hand of his wife, who sat at his bedside. As he grasped it, a faint smile surfaced on his emaciated face. Though they had not been generous to each other in their married life, he had been a thoughtful husband who remembered to send her from his land of banishment fabric for a skirt on which he had drawn paintings. He sat up with assistance and asked for paper and a brush. With an unsteady hand, he composed a piece of poetry:

"A Poem in Commemoration of the Sixtieth Wedding Anniversary." (Written three days before the occasion)

Sixty windy years have gone by
In the blink of an eye.
Let the peach blossoms come forth
For spring is the color of new marriages.
We grow old, suffering many a separation
In death or in living apart.
But sorrow is short,
Happiness long,

All in the grace of our king.[2]
Now on this eve,
Our voices join in tenderness.
Once parted,
We are together again.
Let us hand down this completion,
Like two halves of a gourd,
To our descendants.

Finishing the poem, Tasan let the brush slip from his hand and lay down, peace and thanksgiving illuminating his wan face.

Three days later, on the very day of the celebration, as he lay prone in his bed, Tasan drew his last breath. At the moment of his death, a wind of great magnitude swept the ground, so that the yellow sand eclipsed the sun. One of his disciples from Seoul reported that the night before Tasan's death he had dreamt that a great cross-beam had fallen.

On April first, as he had instructed, Tasan's body was buried on the hill behind Yŏyudang. When the earth was thrown and the grave was sealed, a rainbow appeared as if sprung from the grave. As it arced skyward beyond the river, everyone shouted, "Ah! It is heading toward Paealli, where his brother is buried."

No one doubted that the end of the rainbow would come to rest on the grave of his brother. Tasan's soul, oppressed all his life by the awareness of his brother who had chosen the path of martyrdom, was thus finally released from the torments of his conscience. Borne by the rainbow, more magnificent than the wind of the ancient sages, Tasan's soul leaped toward Yak-chong's grave. He was on his way, crossing the river to meet his brother.

Among the clan members, and among Tasan's descendants, the story of the rainbow is still repeated.

The Persecution of 1839 ensued three years after Tasan's death, even as the memory of the rainbow was still fresh in the minds of Majae villagers.

In the meantime, Ha-sang continued to lead a busy life. His missions to Peking resulted in the arrival of the Chinese priest Liu Fang-chi in 1834, and in providing the church of Korea with its first

2. The ideogram for king here is also used for Lord.

European priest, Father Pierre-Philibert Maubant, in 1836. The year after, Father Jacques Honoré Chastan arrived, and Bishop Lament Joseph Marius Imbert the following year. Thanks to Kim Cho-sun, the father-in-law of King Sunjo, who was a member of the Party of Expediency and influenced the court in favor of Catholicism, the Korean diocese enjoyed a period of relative peace. With the help of the three missionaries sent from the Paris Foreign Mission Society, and with the dedication of faithful members like Ha-sang, Catholicism steadily gained strength until by 1839 there were about nine thousand Catholics, an increase of three thousand.

However, Andong Kim's power gradually declined as the P'ung-yang Cho clan, the current in-law family, began to dominate the court. Aligning himself with the newly powerful Cho clan, the Prime Minister of the Right, Yi Chi-yŏn, known for his hatred of Catholics, spearheaded an extreme anti-Christian policy. On March 5, 1839, he submitted to the throne his "Policy of Catholic Persecution and Eradication," and once more the nation was engulfed in a storm of persecution. Again Catholics became pawns of a court power struggle, just as the Dowager Queen's personal grudges had precipitated the Persecution of 1801. As a result, the three French priests, as well as countless Korean Christians, met their martyrdom.

In the same year, on June 1, Ha-sang and his family were arrested. To Yi Chi-yŏn, his persecutor, he presented his "Letter to the Prime Minister," which he had already prepared. Containing thirty-four hundred characters, this document in three parts explained the Catholic tenets, defended the faith, and pleaded for freedom of religion. The first part was Ha-sang's attempt to prove the existence of God from the Confucian perspective, and to explain its practical ethical system by citing the Ten Commandments. The second part was his defense of the Catholic faith, emphasizing it as a system not incompatible with the Confucian teachings. At the end of this part, however, he attached an addendum in which he argued the irrationality of the practice of enshrining tablets for the worship of ancestors. In the third part, demonstrating that Catholicism was not outside the tradition of Neo-Confucianism but actually an improvement of its social ethics, he pleaded for religious freedom. Written in a flowing style, it was a remarkably erudite document, which quoted extensively from the Confucian classics and was embellished with historical allusions making evident the depth of his learning. It is not known when Ha-sang actually wrote this letter, but he must have prepared it in anticipation of his eventual capture and subsequent martyrdom.

The persecutor, Yi Chi-yŏn, scanned the document and shouted angrily, "This is written in the *yŏmun* style. No heretic could command such a style. No doubt it was written by Chŏng Yag-yong, the uncle of the traitor, during his lifetime."

Yŏmun, a rigidly structured style of belles lettres, was rigorously studied by the students of the National Confucian Academy in preparation for the Higher Level Examination. Though illiterate until he was twenty, Ha-sang had eventually acquired enough learning to be able to command this style. Yet as Yi Chi-yŏn intuited, there was no way of knowing whether this heart-wrenching document had been composed under Tasan's direction. Yi Chi-yŏn's hatred grew.

Bound by the ceremonial scarlet cord signifying that he was a state criminal, Ha-sang was brought to the court. His topknot was undone, and his untamed hair fell over his face, but his features remained peaceful, and his six-foot frame was, as always, carried with dignity. Sitting among the prosecutors, Yi Chi-yŏn cast a glance at Ha-sang from his high position, and was seized with a nameless thrill. Like lightning, a scene flashed in his mind. "It's him!" he thought. "He is that powerful youth of twenty years ago, his clothes pulled down by the rough hands of the inspecting officers, his exposed naked body undaunted, that insolent fellow, that outrageous one, who was said to have crossed the hazardous road to Peking a dozen times. He is that very man!"

Before his eyes rose afresh the scene he had witnessed amid the howling winds of the northern wilderness. Shaking with unfathomable anger, Yi Chi-yŏn was the first one to interrogate Ha-sang.

"I ask you, Chŏng Ha-sang, having survived the Persecution of 1801, how dare you present this vile document out of your vengeful hatred for the country? Your crimes do not allow you to live. How dare you lay your own traps, defying the ethical principles, violating the laws of the nation?" His voice trembled as he cried out.

In contrast, Ha-sang's defense was orderly and presented with equanimity.

"I hereby speak out. This humble servant pursued the teachings of the Lord not to gain worldly fame and wealth, but only through the longing to enter the heavenly paradise. Granted, I violated the law of the nation; however, I wish to deny your accusation that I did so out of treasonous intent. I make this clear."

Yi Chi-yŏn's voice grew louder as he answered Ha-sang's dauntless pronouncement.

"You betrayed the laws of the nation of your own free will, which is the same as disobeying the command of Heaven! One who defies the Mandate of Heaven is surely a traitor!"

Ha-sang remained calm and resolute.

"I committed this unpardonable crime of my own free will. I have nothing else to say. I humbly beg for your good judgment. Punish me according to the law."

In a rare departure from the usual protocol, the interrogation that followed was conducted by the chief prosecutor, Yi Chi-yŏn, who lost his composure, and became more agitated than the one he was cross-examining.

In a vehement outburst, he shouted at the guards, "Club the criminal. Harder! Harder!"

The vilest tortures were then repeatedly inflicted on Ha-sang: arm-bending, sawing of the legs, pricking the flesh with a sharp bamboo stick. Finally, the death sentence was imposed. Ha-sang was beheaded in the Small West Gate on August 15, at about four in the afternoon, the day after Bishop Imbert, Father Maubant, and Father Chastan had been martyred. Ha-sang was joined by his life-long friends, Yu Chin-gil and Cho Sin-ch'ŏl. He was forty-four.

That night, in his guest quarters, where the harvest moon shone through the paper window, Yi Chi-yŏn exchanged a drinking cup with the commanding general. He was drunk with the wine celebrated for its flavor, which had been brewed from freshly harvested rice, and he felt a burden slip away from him, now that the heretic toward whom he had felt such a murderous hatred had been executed. The evil religion was at last uprooted. After his guest left, Yi Chi-yŏn fell into a deep slumber.

In his dream, a robust giant of a man stood before him. Picking up a whip, he struck the giant. In an instant, fresh blood flowed from the wounds. He trembled with an exquisite pleasure. Adding more force to his arm, he struck again; from the wounds, now growing larger, gushed more blood. He repeated the whipping in a frenzy, the pleasure and pain slicing through him; he suffered more intensely than the one who endured the beating. As if oblivious to the pain, a hint of a smile played around the youth's mouth. Exhausted, Yi Chi-yŏn threw away the whip. As he let his gaze drop to his own body, he could not withhold the scream that escaped him: he, too, was naked and covered with wounds as numerous as those he had just inflicted on the young man. He was bathed in his own blood.

Yi Chi-yŏn was awakened by his own screams. The nightmare was exactly the same as the one he had had twenty years ago in the tent pitched near the northern border. He began to shiver. Outside, the moon flooded the night. On the paper window, the shadows of the trees trembled, swaying in the soft breeze. Against the quivering shadows appeared the luminous face of the youth, the same as that of the heretic who had borne to the end the most ruthless tortures. With a gentle smile upon his lips, he looked at Yi with eyes filled with compassion.

"You, wicked man!" Without realizing it, Yi raised himself up. His body began to ache as if he really had been thrashed. A strange oppression came upon him, and he acknowledged the powerful sensation of complete defeat.

Less than a month later, on October 21, Yi Chi-yŏn was removed from the position of Prime Minister of the Right, a casualty of yet another factional conflict. He had become a useless fixture, now that the Cho clan's power was assumed in the court. The following year, on October 14, he was exiled to the north. He died in banishment a year later.

In 1925, Paul Ha-sang Chŏng was beatified, and in 1984, on May 6, he was canonized by Pope John Paul II. While the names of the oppressors defile the pages of history, that of this saint is repeated in the prayers of Christians as their intercessor. And today, as Korean Christians, their numbers multiplied, invoke the name of Saint Paul Ha-sang, many also remember his uncle, Johann Yag-yong Chŏng—Tasan—who succumbed to the temptation of apostasy a number of times, but who nevertheless arouses in them the reverence accorded to sainthood for his sufferings and for the enlightenment he achieved in his life.

Compositor: Maryland Composition
Text: 10/13 Caledonia
Display: Caledonia
Printer: Maple-Vail Book Mfg. Group
Binder: Maple-Vail Book Mfg. Group